THE ENEMY GODS

The Enemy Gods

Oliver La Farge

Introduction by Everett A. Gillis

A Zia Book

UNIVERSITY OF NEW MEXICO PRESS
Albuquerque

INTRODUCTION

Although Oliver La Farge was not a native of the Southwest, his name is closely woven into the regional fabric through his lifelong preoccupation with the southwestern Indian tribes. On his very first visit, as a fledgling anthropologist, to Harvard University's Arizona "digs," he immediately fell in love with the fierce raw grandeur, the sheer size, the far-reaching vistas of the southwestern landscape, and felt his blood pulse to the Navajo tribal rhythms that were to constitute the center of his fictional delineation of Indian life and custom.

Born in 1901 of long-established New England stock, La Farge spent his boyhood on the family estate on Narrangansett Bay, Rhode Island, and his formative years at Groton School. The Groton experience, the harsh impersonal regime of boarding school discipline, was traumatic, as he declares in his autobiography, *Raw Material;* he took refuge in daydreaming and fantasy, thereby strengthening certain innate romantic tendencies he later felt to be detrimental to the quality of his earliest Indian tales.

Harvard, where he matriculated in 1920, gave him, in contrast, a sense of freedom and well-being. His major in anthropology laid the foundations for a compatible profession, and his presidency of the university literary journal, the *Harvard Advocate,* allowed him to dream of a possible literary career.

On his graduation, La Farge secured a position at Tulane University as assistant to Frans Blom, its chief archaeologist, under whose tutelage he gained valuable practical experience at excavation sites in Guatemala and southern Mexico. His relative freedom at Tulane also gave La Farge time to complete his first long fictional work, a novel set against the Indian background that was to become his stock in trade for several years. *Laughing Boy,* published in 1929, the story of a young Navajo couple caught in the mounting pressures of the modern Indian world, brought him immediate recognition—it won the Pulitzer Prize for fiction for the year—and provided him with enough financial security to break away from academic life and launch out on his own as a free-lance writer.

Laughing Boy was followed during the next two decades by two other Indian novels—*Sparks Fly Upward* (1931), capitalizing upon his archaeological experiences in Central America, and *The Enemy Gods* (1937)—and by a collection of short stories, *All the Young Men* (1935), published earlier in *Saturday Evening Post, Cosmopolitan,* and other popular magazines. The same period saw the publication, in addition, of several books of general and scientific interest geared specifically to La Farge's ethnological interests, including *Tribes and Temples* (1928), in collaboration with his former colleague Frans Blom; *An Alphabet of the Navajo Language* (1940); and *The Changing Indian,* a collection of essays on the modern Indian issued under La Farge's general editorship in 1942.

The tone of social protest in *The Changing Indian,* to which La Farge also contributed as a writer, suggests a concern already manifested in his fiction for the plight of the American Indians as wards of the federal government. As president of the Association on Indian Affairs intermittently from 1933 on, and later as field representative of the federal Indian Service, he immersed himself in the enormous task of helping to alleviate the basic inequities of Indian life that resulted from the administration of the national Indian reservation system by a monolithic federal bureaucracy. Engaging in varied educative projects, he also badgered the Congress with persistent appeals for legislation favorable to the Indian tribes.

As a result of his continuing publication of Indian-oriented books, La Farge woke sometime in the late thirties to find himself in danger of becoming stereotyped as a writer of popular Indian fiction. He grew increasingly aware that perhaps his integrity as an artist had been impaired by the romantic escapism that had conditioned both his choice and treatment of subject matter. The chief outcome of this artistic stocktaking was a firm determination to write thenceforth only out of that which he had come to know through firsthand observation, and thus to make his peace as best he might with his artistic conscience.

The first result of this spiritual wrestling was the novel *The Copper Pot* (1942), the setting of which, the French Quarter of New Orleans, La Farge knew well. It depicted the struggles of a young New Englander—much like La Farge himself in his particular artistic dilemma—to develop his own independent painting style. La Farge also began publishing new kinds of short stories, collected later in two volumes: *A Pause in the Desert* (1957) and *The Door in the Wall* (posthumous, 1965). The first drew principally on his memories of growing up on Narrangansett Bay and his student days at Groton; the second tapped an entirely new vein for La Farge, in some respects one as specialized as his Indian fiction, but growing out of his own experiences: the life of the working anthropologist involved in field excavation or in the humdrum routines of university life.

La Farge's own account of his search for a means of renewing his integrity as a writer is his autobiography *Raw Material* (1945), in which he sets down with dispassionate candor not only a description of his artistic clarification but the larger process of his maturation from the provincialism of his New England upbringing toward a wider knowledge and appreciation of America. Begun on a Guggenheim fellowship in 1941, *Raw Material* was finished just prior to Pearl Harbor; the final touches were added after La Farge had entered military service as head of the historical section of the

Air-Transport Service Command. After the war, in 1946, La Farge settled permanently in Santa Fe, New Mexico, where he lived until his death in 1963.

La Farge's complete absorption in the life of his adopted city and region is reflected in his writings of these years, typical of which are *Behind the Mountain* (1956), a group of biographical sketches about the growing up of his wife Consuelo Baca de La Farge as a girl on the Baca ancestral estate near Santa Fe; *Cochise of Arizona* (1953), a fictionalized biography of the great Chiricahua Apache chief; *The Mother Ditch* (1954), a description of irrigation farming in the region and of much southwestern history and geography as well; and *Santa Fe: The Autobiography of a Southwestern Town* (with Arthur N. Morgan, 1959), a casual handbook devoted to Santa Fe's colorful past and present. His particular interest in Santa Fe found further expression in a weekly column he wrote for the Santa Fe *New Mexican,* in which he offered informal, chatty comments on all aspects of Santa Fe, often using as his mouthpiece a genial, crotchety gentleman referred to only as The Man with the Calabash Pipe—the name also given a representative selection of the columns issued in 1966, after La Farge's death. In the picture that emerges from *The Man with the Calabash Pipe* of a learned man, eminently human, witty, blessed with a sort of Bohemian *joie de vivre,* there is probably much of Oliver La Farge himself.

La Farge's ultimate reputation as a writer will probably rest upon his two major Indian novels, *Laughing Boy* and *The Enemy Gods,* written eight years apart in the first flush of his literary success and revealing much the same basic theme: the efforts of modern Indian youth caught in the turmoil of a changing society to find its own place in that society. In some respects these two works are very much alike. Both, for example, exhibit a relatively simple plot structure, in which character rather than action dominates; both involve a clash of Indian and American cultures, to which the protagonists must adjust; and both are marked by a uniform excellence of fictional art: narrative, description, characterization, and a command of graphic, at times essentially poetic, language. But the first is flawed, in La Farge's own opinion at least, by a puerile romanticism that weakens it as art; indeed, La Farge once described the book as an effort on his part to escape into the past—back to the Navajo Age of Innocence, somewhere around 1915, when Navajo tribal unity had been only slightly tainted by the white man's materialistic values. *The Enemy Gods,* on the other hand, confronts the later, contemporary reality of the Navajo nation in full decline, reflected in the rapid falling away of its traditional customs and the gradual erosion of the authority of the elders and the ancient gods.

In further contrast to *Laughing Boy,* once categorized by a reviewer because of its simple plot and delicate style as a prose idyll, *The Enemy Gods* is a powerfully constructed novel, rich in scenic detail and representing in its central thrust an attack upon a major social problem of the American scene. Its hero is, additionally, a much more complex personality than his counterpart in *Laughing Boy.* After ten years of training in the American mission school, Myron Begay has learned to think like a white man, having absorbed all the attitudes and arrogance of the average Anglo-American toward the blanket Indian. At bottom, however, his mind is sound—practical, philosophical, tolerant. Myron is ready to acknowledge his own as well as others' weaknesses; he is capable of sublimating private needs into a larger recognition of the problems threatening the Navajos as a people.

The drama of personal development recorded in *The Enemy Gods* also has greater depth than that exhibited in *Laughing Boy.* In the earlier work, Slim Girl's attempt to escape from the limbo world of being neither white nor Indian, caused by her walking of the White Man's Road, into the Indian world through her marriage to Laughing Boy and her relearning of the arts and crafts of a Navajo woman, is simple and direct. But Myron faces not only the thorny problems of practical rehabilitation within the narrow confines of the reservation after his many years at the American school, but a deeper and more crucial problem—loss of religious faith—which must also be resolved before he can feel at home once more among his native surroundings. The thorough indoctrination into Christianity he has received at the mission school has for him transformed his native gods into enemy gods, and their ceremonial rites into superstitious nonsense. If he is to assume once more his birthright as a Navajo, he must propitiate the Navajo gods through suffering and a formal rejection of Christian faith; then only will they smile upon him again.

As opposed also to *Laughing Boy*, in which the love of the two major characters is the chief structural motif, the theme of love in *The Enemy Gods* is only one of numerous minor strands within the larger thematic framework. Myron and Juniper, moreover, are older and more mature than Laughing Boy and Slim Girl—especially Juniper, whose regard for Myron is tempered by the experience of an earlier unhappy marriage, and who is consequently wary of giving herself once more to one as uncertain of himself as Myron. It is only when Myron does arrive at a final acceptance of his destiny as a Navajo that she agrees to consider sharing that destiny as his wife.

Finally, *The Enemy Gods* reveals a greater social vision than that found in *Laughing Boy,* being concerned not simply, as in the earlier work, with one character's painful readjustment to a lost native inheritance, but with the survival of the Navajo nation itself. Myron, with his white man's arrogance, once thought to bring salvation to his tribesmen as a Christian Indian preacher, and even when he is forced by circumstances to return suddenly and permanently to reservation life, he still retains something of his former vision of himself as savior, though now in the lesser roles of counselor and teacher. And he is willing, as part of his self-abnegation, to wait until his fellows call upon him out of their own volition and accept him as one of themselves, rather than attempting to force upon them the wisdom he feels he has gained within the white man's world. It is only by such means, through his earning of this right by traveling the Indian Road in true humility once again, that he can hope to be worthy of the task he sees as his life's work.

The special insight regarding the Navajo people that evolves from Myron's long ordeal of reimmersion into Navajo society is both simple and profound, as all such visionary concepts are: the Navajos in the future must continue to cling to whatever still remains of their ancient culture that is valuable and acceptable to their special temperament, rejecting fully only that which has become outmoded in a changing world, yet at the same time borrowing from the white man's culture whatever may be found to be of benefit. Myron is perhaps reflecting La Farge's personal solution to this problem as a trained professional ethnologist when he says to Juniper in the closing pages of the novel: "Our world is changed. . . . Just following the old Navajo way won't save us, and we can't walk in the white man's trail. We have to give up a lot of little ideas, that we have held because they were the best we knew. If we want to save ourselves, we have to learn to use the white man's knowledge, his weapons, his machines—and—still be Navajos." Such is the wisdom Myron will one day share with his tribesmen when in the course of time they come to know and trust him.

Everett A. Gillis
Texas Tech University
Lubbock, Texas

FOREWORD

ALL the characters and incidents in this book are fictitious. If by chance any resemblance occurs to a living person, such resemblance is purely accidental, and entirely unintentional on the author's part.

Writers of fiction about the Navajo and other tribes have freely plundered the works of ethnologists, without acknowledgement. I myself must plead guilty to this offence in the past.

In this novel I have used and misused material gathered by Doctor Gladys Reichard, Doctor M. E. Opler, Mary Austin, Natalie Curtis, and others. Above all I have depended upon the great works of Doctor Washington Matthews, including especially his magnificent translations of Navajo poetry. These I have taken the liberty of occasionally altering, on the basis of the texts which he also published. Scientists place an enormous wealth of exciting material at the disposal of the imaginative writer, for which he must remain permanently indebted.

OLIVER LA FARGE

NEW YORK, 1937

THE ENEMY GODS

PROLOGUE

PROLOGUE

ALL things touching their people flowed through the minds of the War Gods in their high place. Child of the Waters turned to his elder brother, Slayer of Enemy Gods.

'We have sat too long, listening to the music of the chants,' he said. 'Our children still pray, but they are being broken, the Enemy Gods are back among the Navajos. Elder brother, I think it is time you loosed an arrow.'

The older War God considered.

'True, we have been dreaming with the chants, but against whom shall I take aim? Do We go slaying poor mortals? Or will you draw your knife against your Brother, your Father, your own Self?'

It is said that they are the War Gods, two persons who speak together, beautiful young men, their long hair falling like dark rain over their shoulders, their bodies perfect. Sunbeams stand around their heads, lightning rustles in the arrows of Nayeinezgani's quiver, it plays around the edges of Tobadzischini's stone knife. They are twins, it is said; they were born of two mothers who are one, of two fathers who are one father. They are the gods of war, and yet they are the protectors of their people.

When people here on earth wish to pray to them, two men take their names, and put on masks which have no features, but pictures of ideas painted on them. When they tell of these divine ones talking together at the end of the Rainbow Trail, when they paint the symbols on the masks, they are only pointing towards things beyond the reach of mortal minds.

Slayer of Enemy Gods said: 'Let us look closely at our people. We must consider the whole and the different parts, until we contain it all. Let us pay attention, not only to the Navajos but beyond them, to the sources of all that afflicts them.'

They rose and stood together up there at the end of the Rainbow Trail, above the sky, two youths of unbearable beauty, two divine warriors. For a brief hour, for the human span of sixteen years, they watched.

PART ONE

CHAPTER ONE

THE enrolling clerk at Tsaili Boarding School mopped his brow with his sleeve. It was very hot in early September; the room, overcrowded with children, was stifling.

'All right, next,' he said.

Bido Tso, the policeman, shoved forward another frightened little boy. His hand on the child's shoulder was firm, not rough, and he spoke to him kindly in Navajo. The clerk looked at the boy. Thin and big-eyed, the kind that gets T.B. and dies on you. His long hair was utterly untidy, he wore a torn cotton shirt, very dirty calico leggings, and moccasins which were coming to pieces.

'What's his name?' the clerk asked wearily.

'Ashin Tso-n Bigé. It's his fadder's name. He's dead.'

'His father's called Ushin Tsone Begay?'

'No, dat's dis one. He's his son. It's his fadder's name, his son.'

The policeman meant that the boy was called Ashin Tso-n's Son, but the clerk was too harassed, and spoke no Navajo.

'Hell,' he said. 'He's Begay, hunh?'

The policeman gave up. 'Yes.'

'Begay. What'll we call him, Miss Sparks?'

The first-grade teacher looked at the poor little rat. 'Call him Myron,' she said. 'It kinda suits him.'

'Myron Begay, then.' The clerk stared again. 'Age — humm — six. First grade. Your name is Myron, see? Where's he from?'

'Beykashi-ha-Bik'é.'

'Oh Lord! What's that near?'

'Joneses store.'

'Home address, Joneses Trading Post. All right, next.'

The policeman told the boy, 'They will call you Mylon, you understand, grandchild? When they say that, "Mylon," you come.'

The child stared without speaking, hardly comprehending. He was pushed on. The policeman was used to this, he had become toughened to it. Big Salt's Son. That man had been a leader, a person of distinction. Well, that's how the whites are. He brought up a little girl, who was crying.

Events had been bewildering since the boy found himself in the crowded truck jouncing over the ungraded road. The bewilderment increased progressively in rate. He never did get the next period of time straight in memory; it remained blurred, intentionally obliterated later, a matter for casual joking when one was an older boy, a shock never really forgotten. Under a variety of hands, along with other children some of whom wept, some struggled, some were stolid, he passed through swift and astounding treatments. There were white voices and faces and the white language, bursts of laughter and grunts of effort. The Field Matron and Boys' Matron in uniforms, the Disciplinarian — an Indian face, but strange, not Navajo — others. He was held, his hair cut, shorn, like a sheep, he was stripped, scrubbed, deloused, passed from person to person, examined swiftly and none too thoroughly by a rough-handed doctor, clothed again, and at length turned loose in the sunshine through another door.

For a brief space he wandered blindly, trying to recover his scattered integrity. Casual personal contact revolts the Indian, handling is offensive, even a stepchild has recognized personality, a right to his dignity. It seemed as if there were nothing left of himself to gather up. His crop-head felt uncovered, naked. His clean blue work-shirt, too large for him and turned up at the cuffs, and very old, clean blue overalls were not entirely strange as a costume, but the shoes confounded his walking. Heavy, ill-fitting, hard leather boxes, high-laced, prison-made at Leavenworth, and of none too good quality, shipped in thousands by an erratically thrifty government to weight down feet accustomed to the soft lightness of moccasins. Unconsciously the boy walked with an awkward, unnecessary lift of the weights which would characterize his gait for some years to come.

Another boy of his own age wandered ahead of him, across the dusty square between the old and bleak brick buildings, identically shaven and uniformed save that his overalls were new and too long. The chance resemblance of a Navajo word, and the sour humour of the clerk, had named this boy Jack Tease. He moved like a sleepwalker, until, standing between two buildings on the far side of the square, he could see through the hard frame of their corners the mass of Black Mesa, far but recognizable. The deep afternoon shadows lay on its slopes, and against the sky rose the high point of Tlichisenili, not far from his home. He stopped and stared.

It looked infinitely distant, almost another world. He could see Tlichisenili, and in his mind could equally well see the long, brownish valley behind it, dotted with piñón and cedar, the sheep, the yellow cut-banks of the arroyo, his mother's hogahn. He took another step, and stumbled in the boxlike shoes.

A bigger boy came past, his face blank and guarded. He paused beside the beginner to whisper quickly in the forbidden Navajo language, 'Don't try to run off, little brother. They watch. They will punish you.' He hurried on. A moment later Jack heard him call something in English to another, older student.

The child simply stood there, looking, with shattered dignity, anger, loneliness, and grief coming out of his eyes in slow tears. One woke from a nightmare, and there were one's parents and brothers asleep close by, a faint glow still over the fire, warmth and familiarity of dimly seen things at night and known, definite smells. His sacred hair, worn as Spider

Woman taught them, was gone. He knew from the stories his father told at night that one could hardly be a Navajo without it; it was the sign of the essence, a declaration. His head was naked. He stood staring at the great mesa which made almost the whole western horizon, remembering the men holding his mother, his father facing a rifle. She cried out and fought, but just as terrible was the way he stood helpless, and the look on his face. The older children got away, but Jack's legs were too short. Then the truck, fearful in itself, the dazed and frightened newcomers, and incomplete words of cheer that older children gave them — 'You'll get used to it — you'll get home next summer' — and the confusion and manhandling at the school. He fought his tears. They were rough with mother. Out of the welter of feelings hatred slowly came to the top.

Myron Begay stood in a corner of the academic building. The walls gave him some sense of shelter while he took stock. This was not as hard for him as it was for Jack Tease; Ashin Tso-n died when he was three; now his mother had another husband and two small children to hold her interest. Without intentional cruelty, his stepfather was hard and exacting. He knew what it was to be struck, to eat leavings, to get the rough end of things. When there was a ceremony or any kind of gathering, he was the one left to herd sheep. He knew he was unloved; his last doubt of it went when his mother agreed to her husband's suggestion that he be sent to school. He was lazy, the man said, he played games when he was supposed to be herding, he forgot about things and dropped things and got into trouble. Let Washington feed and clothe him. So, almost alone of that year's entering class, he was not snatched but brought by his parents to the truck. The things which followed were dreadful enough, but life at home had been meagre and lonely. Perhaps one could get accustomed to this, as the big boys said.

He came out of his corner and was immediately conscious of his shoes. He walked for some distance, head lowered, studying his feet. Then he sat down and examined the laces. These things were tied on to stay, they would be hard to sleep in. The criss-crossing through the little holes was ingenious. He felt of the different leather parts, the hard, square toes, and the stitching. By and by that subject was exhausted. He ran his hand over his head. The nape of his neck felt cold.

He looked around at the brick buildings, not seeing them as shabby and ill repaired, but monumentally strong, the impregnable power of the white man. The corner of one had given a sense of shelter, but now their bleakness afflicted him. The enclosed square was hard-packed dirt, entirely bare. Some other children wandered or stood about it, showing him how odd he, too, must look. The girls were crop-headed, too, and ill-at-ease in uniforms as drab as the boys'. The new children did not speak to each other, they wanted only to be let alone.

He drifted again, around the corner of the building to a space between two others. Various wooden objects, a pile of tin cans, some refuse, gave variety to the scene. Actually, he was between the kitchen and the commissary. His eye lit on a big barrel on trestles. It was bigger than the one his stepfather used for hauling water, and it had a nose. A faint pulse of interest woke in him. He approached the thing cautiously. The nose was ridiculous, a spidery, wooden contraption, but it did look like a nose. It was comical. He became really interested. There were no eyes and mouth, but still one could see a face there, and rather a pleasant one. Hesitantly he touched the barrel. It certainly was big. He touched the very end of the downward-projecting part of the nose. It was wet. There was a spot of something brownish on his finger. He stared, then tasted. It was sweet, it was very good. His eyes widened as he contemplated the existence of so huge a barrel full, not of water, but of something more delicious than the sugar in the bottom of a coffee-cup. He put his finger more forcefully against the spigot, rubbed hard, and secured another sweet taste. With the relaxing of consternation, his interior awoke to hunger.

Now the thing yielded no more. He tried other parts of the nose. There was a sort of handle, crossways at the top. It gave a little when he tried it. The concept of anything that could be opened by turning a stick was unknown to him. He pushed at this idly.

A voice roared from the window opposite him, someone came running. With a convulsive jerk he turned the spigot full on, releasing a thick column of molasses. Terror smote him and he ran, his mouth already wide open. Within a few yards the shoes tripped him, throwing him flat with a breath-destroying thump. Hands caught and jerked him up roughly, he was dimly aware of two men and a woman, and the incomprehensible English words threatening destruction. He took terrified refuge in sound, his voice rising thin and high, then bursting out in a full wail, his face all mouth, his eyes wrinkled tight shut. He was shaken, the voices pounded at him, he shrank himself away and downward, wincing in advance from the expected blows.

Another voice spoke calmly and his captors' tone changed. There was colloquy. He allowed himself a quick glimpse of a third man, dressed in dark clothes, then returned industriously to a wailing part instinctive policy, part the genuine expression of terror. The twisting grip on his collar relaxed, a gentler but firm hand took his arm. The new voice spoke kindly to him in bad Navajo, of which he fully understood only the last word — *shinali*, 'grandchild,' a friendly manner of address. He felt safe. His outcry relaxed to whimpering, and jerky sobs which he could not have stopped had he wished.

'Come with me, grandchild,' the man said.

Myron tagged along, his hand held loosely, his sobs slowly dying away. They went past the commissary to another, smaller house with grass in front of it and a fence. The man called for someone, then sat down on the step and wiped the child's face. A middle-aged Navajo, short-haired and dressed entirely like a white man, came from behind the house. The two men talked together for a few minutes, then the Indian squatted and spoke to the child.

'Don't be frightened any more, it is all right. There are many new things here; you should look and learn about them before you do anything.'

The boy said, 'I didn't know. It just came out of the nose.'

'You will have to learn, so be careful and watch the others. That way you will be all right, I think. This man has told them you did not know. They will not punish you, he says. He is the Black Coat here; he is your friend. He is a good man and will help you.

'Now listen carefully. Tomorrow they will divide the children, those who belong to the Dragging Robes and those who belong to the Black Coat. The Dragging Robes are no good. You must say you want the Black Coat, do you understand?'

'Yes.'

'What are you to do?'

'I say I want the Black Coat.'

'That is right. Now come along with me, it is time for the bell.' The Indian rose.

The missionary said, in his bad, amiable Navajo, 'All right, grandchild.'

The boy stared, then went with the interpreter. In the midst of unreason and fearful happenings he had found authority with kindness. He was sorry to leave it, and he would surely ask for Black Coat, though he seemed to have heard his elders speak hardly of the Jesus people.

He jumped in fear when a great bell burst into motion.

The interpreter said: 'Don't be afraid. That means it's time to eat. Soon you will learn all the times when the bell rings. You will be all right here. Just go in that door.'

The child hung back, reluctant. In there was where he had been manhandled. Other children were entering; a detail of older boys and girls shepherded the beginners.

'Go on in, little brother. It's all right. They'll give you supper.' The interpreter pushed him gently.

Slowly he went forward, entering confusion again. The older children would not speak to them, save the few assigned to guiding them and temporarily permitted to use Navajo. The Matron and Disciplinarian got them into line mainly by shoving. The Disciplinarian was a semi-educated Seneca, willing to be kind, but impatient and deeply contemptuous of these children of 'blanket Indians.'

The formation of lines and military march into the dining-room were not very successful. No one expected they would be. Later the children would move with routine perfection, but now the staff was exhausted by the little ones and still dreading the next few days' mess. The newcomers faced the strangeness of a huge hall in which a hundred and seventy sat down to eat, and the novelty of tables, chairs, knives, forks and spoons. They were too miserable and too shy for food, only a few even fiddled with the coffee.

After supper there was a bare, ill-lit room with scuffed and splintered floor and a few backless, wooden benches, the common room, where in winter overcoats and sweaters were hung. Older children played outside while the Disciplinarian and Boys' Matron set to undressing the dozen little boys and putting them to bed. Toothbrushing was not attempted at this time; the rushing water and the dark, wet, semi-subterranean lavatory terrified some of the children as it was.

In the dormitory were seventy-five beds for a total of ninety boys. The iron frames, in need of paint and with springs sagging, stood in rank on rank, twelve inches apart. On a rail at the foot of each, its occupant hung his clothes. Two enormous stoves, empty now, loomed in the room for winter heating, the floor around them and from them to the door was smudged black with coal dust and ashes. From time to time a few new beds or new mattresses were secured to replace the most completely ruined, the rest continued in service like lame soldiers.

Myron stared with deep depression at this great, homeless cavern and the unending iron frames and dark, army blankets. Limply he climbed into his assigned place beside Jack Tease. The two of them lay still for a long time, as did the others. Then the older children came to bed in disciplined quietness and the lamps were blown out. There was a slight, hushed movement in the dormitory. The boldest of the newcomers slipped to the ground and rolled up in their blankets under their beds, finding some sense of protection there. Here and there a child cried in the privacy of darkness. An older boy whispered a hasty word of comfort in Navajo, his eye cocked toward the Disciplinarian's door. Slowly the place became silent.

CHAPTER TWO

MRS. BUTLER looked up anxiously when her husband came in. He had his puzzled expression on, that meant he was tired. 'My education goes to my head,' he used to say. She was humourless and revered a D.D., but she knew what he meant; he had doubts, thoughts which did him no good.

'How did the class go?'

'All right. The usual number fell asleep, of course. Only the boys; Father Joseph and I agreed to excuse the girls until this clears up.'

She looked at him questioningly, with a suspicion of alarm.

'Five new cases among the girls, today,' he said. 'But the boys aren't touched yet, we must keep them isolated.'

'That was wise of you. I'm glad Father Joseph co-operated.'

'I'd have done it with my class anyhow, but one can count on him.'

She let it pass, eyes on her knitting. It hadn't happened, so she wouldn't raise an issue. She wished he wouldn't think so dangerously; if the Catholics held their full Thursday evening class, and he dismissed the girls from his, the Board would have been right down on him. Once he had been full of revolt, constantly bringing discipline upon his head, but time had taught him discretion.

Five and eight — thirteen. 'Thirteen cases,' she said. 'It's an epidemic. Have the Sisters offered to nurse?'

'They will, I guess.'

'I must, too. It'll run through all the girls' side. No measles for two years, only the older ones are immune.'

'Thank you, my dear. This fills the hospital, they'll be

putting up screens in the dormitory next.' He sighed, running his hands over his face, probing at the edge of an old irritation.

Frustrated convictions came back recurrently to harass a man who had learned to acquiesce.. Those septic beds in which disease upon disease had been housed without change of mattress, temporary screens in the cavernous dormitory, moving out and out until they enclosed half the room, the matrons, Minnie and himself, Father Joseph and the two nuns fetching, carrying, toiling — hard to hold Rome at arm's length after those passages. A decent hospital dear Lord these low-priced doctors culls of the profession but I like Migham casual casual underpaid I wish — I wish — send them home no souls if the bodies are destroyed...

Watchful, his wife said, 'The boys seem to be going to escape it, don't they?'

'The Lord be praised, they do. We won't be sure for another week, but it looks as if the doctor caught it in time.'

Watching his tired frown, her mind scouted in time with her knitting for a cheerful subject. She wished his calling didn't bar smoking, it had done her father so much good. She had a letter from their daughter at Arizona State — worry there, though, the new short skirts, flappers — thought hovered briefly over an old desire, if Allan could have a University post. He's a scholar. She put it aside. Chitchat of the few converts — John the interpreter — no newspapers till Friday — what had been recently pleasing? Her needles hesitated a moment.

'How did Myron do this evening?'

Her husband smiled. 'Went to sleep just before the end of instruction, but I think he really is receiving the Word.'

'He's gained weight this winter, too.'

'He was a miserable little rat when he came, wasn't he? Neglected at home, you know. Unusual for Navajos, but it happens.' Mr. Butler chuckled. '"His fadder dead, his step-fadder don' like him. He's kinda maverick, you oughta corral him."' That's what John said after he turned the molasses on.

John's very direct sometimes. If we can give him love and kindness, surely that's the true road to Christ.'

His wife nodded. 'Will he go home this summer?'

'He'd be allowed, of course. But it would only mean he'd be overworked again. The school's drab in summer, but I think he'd be willing to stay.'

She considered a moment. 'We can do a lot to make it pleasant. He's easier, too, than some of them.'

'Yes. I count on you so, you know.'

It was sweetly said, and a warmth of response rose in her.

Mr. Butler, his face slightly relaxed, half smiling, picked up the Bible for their evening reading.

2

The heavy pressure of the epidemic lasted eight weeks, ending with only two girls dead and one, tuberculous, shipped home, since illness had so advanced her chronic ailment that she was obviously hopeless. Just before time for the Principal to send word to parents to come and get their children, Mr. Butler picked up the threads of normal life, with his wife entirely free to take care of his home once more. In the late afternoon he wandered towards the dormitory, feeling lassitude now that the strain was lifted.

The building formed a square U; its two wings enclosing a narrow strip of hard-pounded earth on which the boys played. The girls, strictly segregated, used an area to the south of their wing, on the other side. He stood still, thumbs in belt, contemplative. The brick mass oppressed him with its known content of dormitories, scuffed pseudo-common rooms, kitchen, dining-hall — those stoves, and the lavatories — he shook his head to clear it. The boys paid him the tribute of not noticing him. Uniformed and shorn alike, half were in his congregation, half in Father Joseph's, divided as they entered, even to the Black Coat, odd to the Dragging Robe. As like as peas — what difference which way they go? They backslide in the end. Why not? 1919 — twenty years on the reservation, eight right here. I've seen — anyhow — well — over a hundred die in the school. Ought to keep a tally. Five adult converts here. The Padre and the Sisters — Joseph and his sistren — have six, I think. Not counting rice Christians — beans, coffee and old clothes. Some count them, though they shouldn't. The Boards like a showing.

The children played quietly, tired after a day spent half in study, half in labour about the school plant. Vocational training — engineering — go stoke the boiler. He looked for Myron among the all but identical brown creatures. Heaven knows they work at home, sheep, chores, harvest, irregular food, but it seems different. A missionary's not supposed to praise Indian home life. Plenty the matter with it. Oh well. There he is.

'Oh Myron!' he called.

The child stood still. The others paused in their aimless games.

'Will you come here a moment?'

Myron came readily, until at close range the Indian school habit conquered and he stopped, head lowered so that his eyes, fixed on the man's hands and waist, were entirely hidden. The missionary used to try and make them look up, but it was an endless struggle, and when it succeeded caused pain. With time and kindliness one could conquer it, here and there. Perhaps this one soon —— After many years one becomes entirely accustomed, and still from time to time one sees.

'I want to talk to you a minute, Myron. I want to find out what you want to do this summer.'

The little figure gave no sign.

'Do you want to go home?'

'I dunno.'

'Would you like to stay here?'

'I dunno.'

'If you want to stay here, you can come to my house right along and eat there.' He made a conscious effort not to urge. This child is more than hopeful. I can rid him of fear.

'All right.'

'I don't want you to do it for me. You must do what you want best. The summer is yours. If you want me to, I'll tell Mr. Linsdale to let you stay; if you want to go home, that's all right.'

The crop-head was raised a fraction of an inch. 'You tell Mist' Linsdel, pleass.'

'That's fine!'

Myron Begay turned and walked slowly back to the others. He would not have to go home and work for that man. School was hard, but his stepfather was worse than the Disciplinarian. Mr. Bucla liked him, really liked him. Mr. Bucla and Miss Winters are nice. Mr. Bucla owns the Jesus Trail. He saw the long-haired, blond Jesus, a white *yei* who liked little boys whose fathers had died; like his uncle, only a *yei*, a holy one. Mrs. Bucla would give him cookies. Who wants to be a Navajo?

He found himself facing Jack Tease's back. His bedfellow stood motionless, hands in pockets, hunched together. Myron felt fine, he wanted action. He gave Jack a violent shove between the shoulders. His friend merely walked off, did not even turn his head.

Jack wanted to be let alone. He wanted to be by himself, solitude was a priceless and unobtainable thing, like water when you can't have it.

The Disciplinarian had come up to him just a few minutes ago, face not unkind, saying 'Hey, fella!' He had looked Jack over and told him, as if it were funny, 'Mr. Linsdale says you ain't goin home this summer. He thinks you'd take to runnin on all fours again if you did.'

Not go home. From just around the corner of the building one could see Tlichisenili standing up, red in the morning sun. He wanted to be alone. Nowhere, at no time, could one be out of sight, nowhere cry, nowhere be free to think, until at last in the darkness one could pull into his own side of the cot and by the exercise of intense stillness be alone.

CHAPTER THREE

A BOUT fifty youngsters would stay at the school that
year. The parents of some lived too hopelessly far
away to come and get them, of others, particularly
younger children, the school did not know where
their hogahns were, or through carelessness failed to notify
their people, who in turn did not know that their children
could be reclaimed. A few, like Jack Tease, were kept because
from their own character or that of their intractable parents
it was clear that the chance of recapturing them would be slim.
Some, mainly older children thoroughly institutionalized,
their native language half forgotten, adjusted to the barrack
routine, chose to stay. They were the school's successes; the
ones who went home reverted to Navajoism, paganism, de-
feating the dominant purpose of breaking family and tribal
bonds.

For the greater number life re-awoke with the end of term
a fortnight off. There were high spirits and scuffling, and the
Disciplinarian was kept on the job. At night he found it
worth while to parade his whip, to awe the dormitory into
quiet. There was a mild revival of the game of 'teasing Tease,'
which had worn out in midwinter. Soon the wagons and the
saddle ponies would come, the long-haired fathers and the
mothers in their brilliant skirts. Then one's own tongue and
kind, the campfire smell, the pots of mutton and the round
loaves of bread, the hard ground to sleep on, no adequate roof,
lice, risk of trachoma and impetigo, laughter and freedom and
love.

Myron was happy to be staying. In a world which since

his all-but-forgotten father's death had been sudden and un-
reliable, Mr. Butler emerged as security. Home was trouble,
jealousy and contempt. The missionary had spoken to him
again. He was going to stay a Christian, he was going to be
something of his own. He was happy enough to sing, too
young to find it incongruous that one of the Anaji songs came
to his throat for humming when he knew so many hymns.
All music delighted him, his singing had been the one thing
that interested his stepfather.

Jack sat hunched on the schoolhouse steps. Myron stopped
humming.

'You been cryin again.'

'Maybe I have.'

'Why you wanta go home? We can have a good time here.'

Jack looked at him. He could have answered in Navajo,
not in English. 'I dunno. Lemme alone.'

'All right.'

Myron wandered off. As he turned the corner, his voice
unconsciously rose to audibility — *Hé-yé-yan-a* . . .

Jack caught it, it pulled at his vitals. He rose, walking
blindly. His youngest uncle going out at dawn to catch a
horse, from far across the valley a voice sounding faintly as
one began to awake, *Hé-yé-yan-a, Shidzedé lan do idashilan,
Hé-yé-yan-a* . . . The children stirring, the crackle of the fire,
its flame still strong in the half-light, the smell of coffee and
smoke, his mother moving about. *Hé-yé-yan-a.*

He stood still. He was by the corner of the hospital, where
the ground fell away into the dry wash. Ahead of him he
could see the wide sweep of desert, then the great wall of
Black Mesa and the peak he knew so well; far away, tremendous distances for a little boy, far enough to be rather blue at
noontide. The space between was a whole unknown world to
traverse. He looked around. No one was in sight. He slid
into the arroyo.

He was out of bounds now, but it could appear to be only
play. He occupied himself picking up brightly coloured

stones, moving quietly, listening intently. No one had noticed. He worked his way along the dry river-bed to the bend. Then he ran. His leaping heart stopped him finally. Breathless and with his face burning hot, he crawled into shade and partial hiding under a cut-bank, lying close against the sand. He could not make himself wait there long, only until his lungs came under control, then he set out, plodding, and a little farther along climbed up the west bank with infinite precaution.

Behind a quarter of a mile of scattering greasewood and chamisa the red-brick buildings stared at him. He crouched, frightened by their malignant dominance. He crawled a way, then walked bent over till a rise of ground cut off even the slate rooftops and long chimneys. The sun hovered just above the edge of Black Mesa, which was turning to a deep blue and rising higher, closer, in the evening sky. Tlichisenili reached out to him. Steady, determined, he walked, no taller than the bushes, a tiny figure of seriousness on the face of the desert.

The valley-blanketing shadow reached out over him with coolness, making his cotton shirt and pants turn thin. The mesa was blue-black with gold above it, Tlichisenili a silhouetted finger. Desert-bred, he knew how far he had to go. Step by step, hundreds upon hundreds upon hundreds of steps, each one tiny, so infinitesimal a gain. He was thinking my mother, *sha-mah, sha-mah*. Step after step, steadily. Evening star came out in the dusk. Solitude was a great boon if it would be not too long intervening between himself and home. 'Teasing Tease.' No more of the rotten, alien fun on his name, the son of Teez Nantai. After dusk came ground-dark, when the bushes turned to mysteries and one could fall in a hole, but the western sky was still clear, with only the biggest stars pale in it. From high, the black line of the mesa became a low, distant edge of the horizon; his landmark dwindled with it. Dark follows hard on dusk, the hostile night full of magical dangers. A jackrabbit leaping up almost under his feet startled him painfully. I'm going home, *sha-mah, sha-mah*.

He was hungry. Looking back from a rise of ground, he could see no lighted window. He had come far.

Away to the left a fire gleamed, a ground-star, growing and dwindling. Over there they sat in warmth before the brush enclosure of their summer hogahn, the mutton pot, the dogs, the long-haired, quiet man and his calm-faced wife, children, sheepskins to lie on, kindness for any traveller. He stopped, lonely and on the verge of tears. It might not be safe. Questioned, they might tell. I intend to get home. They'll know how to keep me safe. He went on. Sitting at his father's saddlebow, going to the highest part of the mesa-rim where the wild cattle are, and his father, smiling and amused and patient, teaching him the Tset Dilth songs as they went. But now I'm big enough to manage my own horse. He owned a pony and four ewes, given him by his parents as part of his education. Last year his wool and lambs were sold separately, and with some of the money he bought a bag of candy as big as a hat.

He fell into a hollow and scratched his hands. The air was colder in the rounded depression. It was night now, the western guiding marks were gone, the stars showed too many, confusing. He remembered old tales of warriors and hunters, and the crippled twins who sought their father. He scooped a sandy bed for himself under an arching bush and curled up, cold, hungry, and exhausted. A coyote's voice quavered through the night. The world is so big.

Thirst and bitter cold woke him when the east began to lighten. The instant his eyes opened he remembered. He was stiff and shaking. As he had done so often at home, he ran furiously a few score yards and back again, arousing his blood.

The light in the east was increasing. He tried to remember his father's prayer, Dawn Boy, Little Chief. He thought of Dawn Boy as about his own age, his hair not fully grown coming loose in stray locks from the knot behind, but very well dressed — green velveteen shirt, red leggings, many silver buttons on his moccasins. A boy *yei*. He was coming now; after him Sun Bearer would warm the day. Dawn Boy, Little Chief — I don't know all the words yet, but my father knows them. He's saying them right now, at home. Help me get home. Beautiful before me, beautiful behind me, beautiful above me, beautiful below me, in beauty I walk. I haven't any pollen; Mr. Bucla took it away from me. My father is giving you pollen. I want to find water soon and something to eat.

It was too cold, standing still. He trudged on westward, swinging his arms for warmth from time to time. Dawn spread through all the sky above him, he could see the peak, not visibly nearer than when he was at school. The Disciplinarian took the little bag of pollen from him and when he asked for it, referred him to Mr. Bucla. Mr. Bucla said he could have it when he went home. And they weren't going to let him go home. That's how white men are.

Now he was in sunlight when he crossed high ground, and the shadow in the dips was not too chilly. He felt tired and creaky in the joints. Step by step, eighteen inches and eighteen inches away from the school, a stride and a stride nearer that far-off place. He found a long depression with a small wash in the middle of it, running east and west, and followed that. A couple of juniper bushes to his right showed that he was beginning to approach higher ground, a friendly sign. He spotted a group of small, low-clustered leaves — that was food. He knelt and dug for the little, potato-like roots. A horse's feet sounded behind and on his left. Looking up, he saw the policeman riding towards him, and after him the red face of Mr. Shovely, the farmer. He stayed motionless, feeling the world rock and turn grey, wanting to be sick but unable for lack of matter.

The policeman, riding up beside him, said, 'It's too bad, grandchild, you have to come back.'

Only his eyes could move. Looking down at him, the big man saw the tightness of the mouth — not going to cry.

Terrified, and not going to cry. He reached down, caught the boy by the waist, and lifted him to his saddle. The farmer arrived then, full of profanity and threats. Jack kept his head down, limp, and made no answer. As they neared the school, the policeman said to him, 'Cover your tracks, boy. Next time cover your tracks.'

He was handed over to the Disciplinarian just before noon, stolid in the certain expectation of a flogging, but the Seneca and the Boys' Matron led him to the Sewing Room.

The great bell rang for dinner, the children fell into military line in front of the dormitories. All of them knew that Jack had run off, a few had seen him brought back. There was a movement among them as he came in sight dragged by the Disciplinarian and the giggling Matron. His face showed taut and haggard above the absurdity of girls' clothes. While the Principal watched, smiling, he was shoved into place, the Matron's jibing tongue distributing among the boys prime material for teasing Tease. He was to wear those clothes until term ended.

CHAPTER FOUR

THE Principal walked over to the employees' club with Mrs. McConnell, the second-grade teacher.

'That girl's dress idea is a good one,' he said. 'That'll keep him from being a hero.'

'Yeh. Who thought it up?'

'The mission school at Twin Peaks. They been doing it for a couple o' years.'

'It ought to be a cure. They're sure stubborn. It don't matter how much trouble you take. No gratitude. At that, these Navajos are better than some o' the northern tribes. Were you ever at Fort Hall?'

'Yeah. These Injuns are a lot better.'

After a few strides in silence, Mrs. McConnell changed to business she had much in mind.

'Say, Mr. Linsdale, I sure hope you'll help get Mr. McConnell here as mechanic. He wants to be back in the Service, and he'd be useful. It'd be a lot nicer for me too. I'll sure appreciate it if you'll ask for him.'

Linsdale nodded wearily. 'Yes. You told me his qualifications.'

They climbed the rickety porch of the club and sat on the one bench there.

'That's right. And remember, he's right good at police work. There ain't any Injuns can bluff him.'

'That's useful.'

'He settled old Waitin Bull at Rocky Boy, you know. He handled him real firm.'

'Yeah. I'll do what I can.'

His wife came onto the porch just then, other employees were drifting up. When the bell rang they herded in together.

Over-roast mutton, coffee or tea, canned milk, canned peas, potatoes, canned pears, bread and butter. Mr. Linsdale ate steadily without any functioning of the taste-buds. While he ate he thought. This McConnell business was a problem. The man had been fired at Rocky Boy. He knew old Waiting Bull, an intelligent old leader. McConnell had beat him up. Hadn't ought to have done that. But Mrs. McConnell would intrigue and make trouble and work her friends in the Washington Office until he came. Talk it over with my wife, stall along and avoid trouble. Someone was due to be made Superintendent of the school, the post had been empty all winter, and he with great satisfaction signing his letters 'Acting Superintendent.' He had a chance. Twenty-four hundred a year. If only I could have qualified to stay in the public schools I'd be getting better than that right now. Hoped to go through this year without a runaway. Why can't they settle down, we do our best for 'em. They all go back to the blanket anyways. That girl's dress idea is good; harsh punishments only make 'em more hateful and they get to be heroes. Don't like to be harsh. Well, only one runaway and that caught; measles epidemic kept from spreading to the boys. Thanks to Doc Migham, he ain't generally so on the job. Tease is a bad proposition dunno if we can break him. Hates us. Myron Begay volunteered to stay good man Butler unusual for so small a child promising every way. Mention it in annual report counterbalance Tease acting superintendent unusual good record for school year twenty-four hundred a car new overcoat take Sarah to Californy on annual leave never can tell what Washington will do when is the Supervisor coming through twenty-four hundred yours truly Thomas Linsdale, Superintendent canned pears again...

CHAPTER FIVE

THE hogahn was an irregular semicircle of juniper boughs laid against poles, with a roof of the same construction. One end led into a piñón tree which added to the shade and sense of enclosure; under the tree the loom was set up, a little farther out from the door was the ash circle of the fireplace, a black coffee-pot and a Dutch oven standing by it. Roan Horse lay in the deepest shade of the structure, flat on his back, knees drawn up and crossed, showing an awkward view of moccasins, plaid calico leggings, the torso in foreshortened perspective, and the head half propped up on a sheepskin, strong-boned, hawk-nosed, rather handsome, with a displeased mouth. One hand lay idle across his chest, the other, raised above the face, held a brown cigarette.

He looked out beyond his feet, past the baby asleep and the child playing, to the woman seated at the loom. Here his displeasure centered. Attractive still, long eyes, oval face, breasts and waist well preserved, she was about to cease to be young. Her hands moved deftly with fork and batten; lifting the shed, she put the weft-strand through with a decisive motion. A good weaver, although erratic, a brilliant weaver when she chose to be. She didn't like to work long, herding sheep bored her. Shortly he was going to have to go back to the flock so that she could be free to weave, and if he objected she would point out that they needed the good money promised for that blanket, and that it had been his idea to send the boy to school, she would hold him with the threat of her sharp, reminding tongue. He felt angry, abused. The fact that she was quite capable of turning him out, that he owned but little property in his own right, and finding a new husband would be no problem to her, did not add to his pleasure. I never should have sent the boy away, he thought, his mind moving from irritation to irritation, the extra herding loaded on him because he got rid of that constant shadow and namesake of a greater man. I'll go when I finish this smoke. The boy could have come back for the summer. Conscience remembered harshness. Got to move them across the wash, and then back this evening. The slow movement of the flock like a white, thick substance pouring, guiding them this way and that, persuading and urging the leaders. Well, there are harder kinds of work.

Roan's Wife saw movement out of the tail of her eye, and turned her head to look where the trail came into the miniature canyon. A man and woman on horseback, easy to recognize, her eldest brother and sister. That looked like family business, she felt uneasy.

'Here come my elders,' she said.

Her husband grunted. He didn't like their coming either. He didn't like to have the clan's strength forced on his attention. He was a Honagaani from further west, married into a stronghold of Lokhadine, Reed People. She was getting tired of the man; hearing his grunt of distaste, she minded less her relatives' approach, although brother and sister coming together meant business of some kind, probably disapprovals.

The horses trotted soft-footed in the dry sand. As they two drew rein, Roan's Wife said, 'Come in,' with a fair show of warmth. Her husband rose to his feet.

They dismounted, Shooting Singer saying, 'It's pleasanter out here,' and made themselves comfortable in the shade of the scrubby tree.

'Where to?' Roan Horse asked.

'Just here.'

'From your houses?'

'Yes. To see each other. It's a long time now.'

Deer Woman, the elder sister, said, 'You are hot in this little canyon.'

Roan's Wife said, 'Yes, but it keeps the wind out.'

Her husband asked, 'How is the rain, your way?'

'Good enough. A he-rain yesterday. And here?'

'Good. You can see how the grass is sprouting.' He told his wife, 'Give them food.'

Shooting Singer said, 'But the whole country seems dryer than when I was little, fewer reeds, more gullies. It's drying up, I think.'

Fifteen years older than the last of his sisters, more uncle than brother, he was reaching an age for casting back. Roan Horse considered him now, as they carried on the leisurely courtesy of unimportant talk — the old-fashioned silver loop earrings, the rugged, square face, the headband of heavy material almost like a turban, conservative, already one of his clan's leaders. The younger man felt restless. He was tired of the Reed People. Something was up.

His wife was putting food on the fire. This would be about the boy. One can't help what Washington orders. Her brother slightly resembled her first husband; one had been always thinking of the Salt Clan, the other of the Reed. Roan Horse was saying that the corn was poor this year. He'd been careless, so had she. Hoeing corn, drudgery. She glanced at him. Handsome, a great man for fun, not useful. Almost as dull in the long run as Ashin Tso-n had been. I've had bad luck. I want a husband near my age, but a solid man. Not my fault, after the older one. Anyone could choose wrongly.

Roan Horse thought, if it's about the boy, I'd best get out of here.

'I have to watch the sheep,' he said, moving to the far side of the fire.

Shooting Singer told him, 'A man is never free.'

He knew from that that they didn't need him. 'I'll be in at sundown.'

They ate a moderate amount, without haste — stew left over from their host's meal, bread and coffee. When that was done and cleared away, and the brother had a cigarette started, there was a little pause while they turned themselves to seriousness.

'We came here for more than just to eat your mutton, little sister,' he said.

'I thought that.'

'We've been thinking about our nephew, at the school over there.'

'Washington has kept him, they say.'

Deer Woman asked, 'Is that what they told you?'

'Yes.'

There was an instant's hesitation before the brother said, 'We have just heard something else.'

'What did you hear?'

'Slender Hair's Son came back from there. He said that your son stayed because he wanted to. He asked to stay; he was taking the Jesus Trail, he said. This I heard last night. I talked to the boy carefully. He knows my nephew. He knows what he is talking about, I think.'

The young woman's mind raced. Implications and accusations plain to see. This was the first she knew of why the boy wasn't home. Instinct said throw it on Roan Horse. They were watching her; not directly, obviously, but watching.

'That is true,' she said.

Navajo etiquette forbids staring in a person's eye. A speaker looks down, watches his hands. This was useful for a moment. Her face was smooth, but her long, attractive eyes were calculating until she was sure of her going.

'That is true, I say. I have been ashamed. For that I said Washington kept him.' She hesitated, then said, as if it were dragged out of her, 'Someone did not want me to go get him, and my son is not always happy here, I think.'

Shooting Singer looked pleased. His sister was talking true

at last, one could draw closer to her. They had opposed this marriage, what she had just admitted was a lot.

'You must go get him now.'

'Perhaps he will not come.'

'No child really wants to stay in that place, I think. If he knows that everything is all right here, he will come.'

'How then?'

'If anyone does not want him here, if anyone is harsh to him, say that here is Reed country, Reed and Salt. The boy's clan and his father's clan stand together here. If an outside person hurts one of our people, he hurts us all. He will need to go away. He might encounter troubles.'

Her relief at her brother's words was real. This would put Roan Horse right in her hand. She studied the ground for a few seconds, then said, 'I'll go tomorrow.'

'Good, then.'

Deer Woman spoke, and Roan's Wife listened anxiously, for her sister could be hard to satisfy.

'We want you to do well, to be happy,' she said. 'When you do the right thing, we are altogether ready to help you. It is for you to see to it that our nephew, our child, has what a child deserves. While we three are together, no one else is an excuse for anything.'

'Good.' She felt the warning in the words.

They turned then to lighter talk of her other children and general matters, and rode away in the mid-afternoon. She went back to her weaving. She would tell him when he came home. He wouldn't like it. He didn't want to lose her, so he'd agree. The journey was a nuisance, but the boy was getting old enough to be useful. A nice boy, really. And if the right man came along, a solid man, here was a real step towards marrying him with her family's support. She wove rapidly, feeling that life was hopeful, that in time one might get rid of all the burrs.

2

She left her wagon at the trading post and walked into the school grounds, a young woman nervous and unsure of herself, but showing to the world a calm face. She had been to the Agency once or twice in her life and seen the school there, but still she felt uneasy on Washington's ground. So many buildings. Her free stride took her rapidly down the main roadway, while from above the shawl pulled across her face she glanced left and right, wondering. She couldn't bring herself to go to one of those doors and enquire. If only she knew someone. Most government people spoke no Navajo, they shouted at one and showed amusement, contemptuous when they were not cross. She left the central road, following a path aimlessly. He was her son, and she had left him here, these endless walls and windows, this drab strength. She felt guilty. But it was the man's idea. I won't do it again, I'll stand by him, and by and by I'll find a better man, the right man.

A girl, almost full grown, came around the building. Roan's Wife turned towards her. The girl stopped and waited.

'Eh, little sister,' the woman said.

'Eh, elder sister.' The answer was awkward, stiff. She stared sidelong, her manner a mixture of shyness and superiority.

'Do you know where Ashin Tso-n Bigé is?'

'Big Salt's Son?' the girl repeated. 'I don't know who that would be, that name.'

'A little boy, seven his winters. He is staying here this summer.'

'There are several here.' The girl studied the silver necklace with its turquoise and silver pendant. This was the blanket Indian, she was turning her back on all this. Ignorant. 'There's one from Tlichisenili, is that the one?' The colours of the shawl were handsome, the dress was gay, pleasing. Full skirts, unsanitary, savage.

'No, from Beykashi-ha-Bik'é.'

The girl thought. 'Oh yes, I think I know. Myron Begay'.

'Mylon Bigé? His father was never called Mylon.'

'They don't mean it like that, elder sister. It's just a name. They don't understand Navajo. But that's the one.'

'Where can I find him? I'm his mother.'

From the whole span of childhood the girl had known too well what the unlettered mother's thoughts and feelings were, what they would be when she met her converted son. One's own mother in the early intimacies, and later when the change occurred, the mind's clear picture deeply loved, and despised by determination, pulled up raw sympathy, too many remembered pains to clash with the will to superiority. The girl turned sullen.

'Over there, that little house under the tree, I think.'

She made a botched job of indicating it, for she refused to point with a push of her lips, Navajo style, and the outstretched finger seemed suddenly awkward, ill bred, before the older woman. The girl felt clumsy, then spiteful.

'It is the Black Coat's house. You son is walking on the Jesus Trail, he is one of the best of them all, they say.'

The woman's expression went blank. Hers was not a strong or great face, only a rather pretty, Indian one, but she, too, could put on the unreachable dignity of her people. The blow struck, but half turned back upon the striker. She arranged her shawl with a quick, decisive jerk.

'I shall go there.'

The girl stood looking after her till she had gone a score of paces, then turned away.

A wire fence around the one-storey house enclosed a yard in which grass struggled sparsely. The cottonwood tree made the place shady. It was better kept up, more homelike, than the government buildings. On the porch two small boys played cat's cradle. They looked up as she drew near and frankly stared. She stopped at the gate, unsure of its mechanism, unsure of trespassing upon the Black Coat's ground. She had to look twice before she recognized her son. She knew all school-children were clipped and uniformed like that, she had expected it, but the reality was different. She felt jolted. She was shocked by what she and her husband had done, for that moment she understood her elders and was one with them. This is my child, this is mine, Navajo, the child playing in the hogahn, working and making trouble and set aside, the baby eclipsed by other babies, forgotten in the active boy. Early and recent a complex of feelings pictures prides the tang of regret not new but newly sharp that shorn figure and the veiled face staring without love Navajos Reed People my son.

She said, almost timidly, 'My child.'

He rose slowly and came towards her, feet dragging, eyes not on her face but on the silver pendant gleaming dully against the deep green bodice. Not afraid, but taking time to adjust. Had the man come, he would have frankly stayed back in triumphant enmity, but here was a stronger more complex turbulence unanalyzed in a small boy. He did not imagine that he hated his mother, but behind silent tears in the hogahn, weary back and legs and feet bringing in the sheep at night to a household returned from pleasure, the shocks and terrors of school, his stepfather's hostilities, this figure stood acquiescent. He stopped a pace from the gate, still watching the heavy ornament. So much desired might still be had if she had really changed. He lowered his head, schoolboy style, his eyes on the green band that went around near the bottom of the dull red skirt.

The metal gate, like a miniature bedspring, stood between them, unlocked, transparent, tangible. She half raised her hand to it, but could see no way to work it. The sense of having been cumulatively wrong bore hard upon her. If she could pick him up, mother him, straighten all this out. Roan Horse was nothing. Reed People.

'*Hallah hotsan!*' she said, as warmly and gaily as she could.

He answered in a low voice, '*Eh, sha-mah.*'

He would not tell her to come in. Jack was staring at him

from the steps, he knew; Jack would think him crazy. This was Mr. Bucla's ground, the enclosure of stability in a shifting, unreasonable world. He slowly summoned manners.

'Where from, mother?'

'From our house, of course.'

'Today?'

'No. That truck you came on was fast. The wagon takes two days.'

'You came alone?'

'Yes. Your uncle wanted to come, but there is a Shooting Chant at Ha'anoichí, he had to be there.'

She put her hand on the gate, as though resting it. 'He wants you to come there in the wagon with me.'

Save for a little talk with Jack this summer, Navajo had been distant from his ears. His mother's words recalled things as sharply as a sudden smell of mutton and piñón smoke. His uncle's memory was altogether good. To go to the Chant — he had always been the one to herd sheep when those were being held. He had a vague idea of a gathering, much food, and mysteries. He trusted his uncle. He gazed through the wire at her skirt, at her red moccasins, and the white buckskin wrapping above them.

'Your uncle and your aunt and I are sorry you have stayed here so long. We want you home for the summer. My husband, too, he is sorry.'

Steady pressure of her hand failed to move the gate.

That man — Mr. Bucla urged the homegoing children not to betray their new religion. I am a Christian. That man. All his mother's failure stemmed from him, his handsome, angry face clouded the whole foreground of Navajo life.

'I promised to stay here. They will not let me go now.'

Jack Tease had come slowly to the fence, and stood to one side, watching eagerly. Here was a mother like his mother, a little younger, not quite so nice, lacking that unfailing look, but a mother. Myron was holding her off. What was wrong with him?

'But then nobody came for you,' she said. 'Now I am here, perhaps they will let you go like the others.'

'No, I think.'

The gate remained unyielding. He surely knew how to open it, but he had not offered —— She felt his resistance. A sharp, angry impatience quickened in her. Here she was ready to do all she should at last, and it was important. Her brother and sister, clan support, if she should find a better man. He must come home, I must bring him home. Her expression changed slightly.

'Still I think you can come,' she said. 'Let us ask the man, whoever he is. Your uncle will be glad to see you. There will be many people at Ha'anoichí.'

He did not see her face change, but caught tones of familiar irritation in her voice. His confidence closed. Something moved on the road, caught by the edges of his eyes. Mr. Bucla was coming. He felt relieved.

'Here is the man,' he said.

She saw no black coat, but a tall, elderly, spare man with a kind face, who wore shirtsleeves, and a small felt hat pushed back on his head. As he reached the gate, he greeted her in barely comprehensible Navajo, correct in form.

'Hallah, grandmother.'

They touched hands as she answered, 'Grandfather.'

He asked the boys, 'Somebody's mother?'

Jack said, 'Myron's.'

'Your mother, Myron?'

'Yess.'

'Ask her in. My goodness!'

Myron hung his head and dug with his toe. Mr. Butler tripped the latch, swung the gate wide and said in Navajo, 'Enter, grandmother.'

So his mother was in Mr. Bucla's yard. The boy stared at her, her diffident manner, she or Roan Horse powerless in this place.

'Tell him I want to take you home, my child.'

Myron looked down again, silent.

'Tell him.'

'What is your mother saying, Myron?'

He knew how Jack was staring. He felt mixed up. 'She wants to take me home.' His voice was muffled.

'Do you want to go?'

My uncle and the Chant, Beykashi-ha-Bik'é, firelight, Roan Horse.

'I dunno.'

'You are free to do as you like. If you want to go, I'll have Mr. Linsdale give you permission right away.'

He had thought Mr. Bucla would settle it for him, but he had to choose, with his protection, his mother, his friend, all watching, the unlike, strong interests converging upon him.

She asked: 'What does he say? Tell him we'll bring you back when school starts. Tell him you want to come.'

She urged him with her voice, he felt the push of it, and he was afraid of her. He had adjusted to this, here where she had no power; she wanted him back there. Roan Horse, the quick, harsh word and blow, fatigue, the lonely place in the crowded hogahn.

'I don' wanta go,' he said.

The missionary asked, 'Are you sure?'

He caught the pleasure in the man's voice and his heart responded.

'Yessir. I'm sure.'

'You must tell her then.'

He would like to have told an easy lie, but Jack was listening.

'I am staying here. I will not come with you. I'm going on the Jesus Trail. I'm going to be just like a white man.'

'He told you to say that! He is bad, that man!'

Myron took a step backward. She turned anger upon the missionary, a flow of words against which his little Navajo was helpless. Both boys withdrew to the porch steps. Roan's Wife checked herself in mid-course, for shame. She was beaten, that was that. She pulled her shawl up, turned, and went out the gate which had been left open, her face composed to calm, her mind seething. Mr. Butler went into the house.

While they waited for him, Jack said: 'Why did you do that? I know about your stepfather, but if I could go away from here, I'd go with anyone.'

Myron answered in English. 'I don' wanta go. I'm goin to be a Christian. I ain't goin to be no blanket Inyan, I'm goin to be civilized.'

Civilized was a newly learned word, a bright one which called up shiny concepts; as he said it he felt a new assurance of something to be, importance and reality for a waif to acquire on the white man's road.

CHAPTER SIX

THE trader at Tsaili was staging a horse-race and chicken-pull on the flat beyond his store; a modest investment of flour, mutton, and cash to break the August monotony, liven trade, and increase goodwill. The tribesmen came drifting in during the preceding day, until by dusk the flat was sprinkled with little fires and parked wagons, and hobbled horses dotted the surrounding country. Older children were allowed to visit during the afternoon, which they did, some eagerly, some with awkwardness, but pulled by the open generosity of mutton pots and flat, round loaves of bread. The summer diet at the school was more generous than when the place was full, but even so, hunger was fairly constant. The big bell pulled them back at six for supper, and many went to bed delightfully gorged. One girl developed cramps from an excess of watermelon. A little current of excitement ran through them all. It was extra hard to turn in when darkness had only just started, and the windows still showed a purple colour after lights-out.

Jack had a bed to himself now, into which he climbed in unusually contented frame of mind. He'd been too young to be let wander that day, but Mr. Butler had arranged for him to go unsupervised tomorrow — on honour — and told him it would be a test. If he behaved himself, this along with other signs of grace might mean he'd go home next year. He didn't wholly trust Mr. Butler, his bag of pollen was still in custody, but the summer had shown that the man was kind.

Through the open windows came the sharp drumbeats that make one's blood vibrate in pulse with them. A few beats, a pause, a few in different tempo, someone warming up while the people drifted together to celebrate the mere fact of a gathering. Now the drummer got going steadily, the penetrating, quick sounds reaching clearly from beyond the trading post into the darkened room, then the leader's voice rose, high and sharp and true, and the massed singers followed. There was a stir in the dormitory, heads raised on elbows, here and there a hand marked the time. One older boy slapped softly on his mattress, the children snickered, then fell into a moment's alarmed silence.

Lying with one ear pressed against the pillow, Myron heard the beats and felt them through the springs, through the length of his body, thrilling the whole course of his vitals. The bright pattern of the high obligatos against the choral mass, the rushing attacks, the crescendos and swinging middle passages enraptured him. Anaji songs are gay, their words often ridiculous, but the effect on him was disturbing, an ache for something unknown, a hopeless restlessness, a sadness which he would not have given up for any consideration, and a keen excitement. Only once had he been taken to a dance, but once was enough to recall now vividly the blanketed couples circling slowly in the firelight, the swaying crowd of singers, the elders sitting about by small fires or in the dark while children played, listened, dozed, the dimly seen surrounding wagons, and the men slouched comfortably on horseback.

He raised his head, nodding it in rhythm. A boy two beds from his was whistling softly through his teeth, the dormitory was very much alive.

A turning doorknob warned of the Matron's approach. The Disciplinarian was on leave. She entered a room of utter quiet. Not a child moved. All in their places. How on earth they slept with that yowling going on was beyond her. She doubted she'd be able to sleep. Indians have no nerves, anyhow. She yawned and went out.

One of the oldest boys stole from his cot. With very few,

slight sounds he slipped into pants and shirt, and took his
shoes in his hand. Another followed. Each in turn blocked
a window a moment with his body and was gone. The rest
quaked as they watched, then listened tensely, hearts pounding. No sound, no watchman's voice. They had done it.
Envy and fear and a vicarious release filled all but the most
completely de-Navajoized.

When he relaxed from the excitement of watching them slip
out, Myron's feelings swung into an entirely new course.
They were doing a wicked thing, risking unimaginable punishment. He had recently learned the word *backslide*. To be born
an Indian and live and die and worship like one was bad
enough; to learn better and backslide was infinitely worse.
Mr. Bucla had been very emphatic on the subject. Now he
knew just what it meant, the motion of the boys as they went
over the window sills was so visibly backsliding. That was
what the Indians wanted to make people do. Another phrase,
understood vaguely as *he then sermons*. The songs and dancing
out there were a *then sermon*. One ought not to like it. The
cheerful tune sounded suddenly mocking. The figure of Roan
Horse, of his mother. He buried his head under the pillow.

2

The two boys had got back safely, the school's calm was
unruffled. After lunch the children were marched out to the
trading post. Some of the government employees were there
already, the others came as outriders with their charges. An
attempt was made to keep the children bunched, apart from
the other Indians, but it was not diligently carried out. Some
attached themselves to Navajo friends, a few hovered close to
the matrons, Mr. and Mrs. Butler, and the two nuns. The
greater part drifted through the crowd, secret to themselves,
suspended between two worlds in neither of which they quite
belonged.

There were perhaps two hundred Navajos, noisy enough in

their way, but much less individually intrusive than the government employees. Those people, more especially the women, seemed to feel it necessary to reiterate their superiority to what they had come to see. They were diligently loud in pointing out anything that struck them as comical or cute, they had innumerable jokes with one another. The Indians ignored them, the trader and his assistants responded politely when spoken to.

After a time Myron left the missionary's shadow for a place where he could see better, then he began to drift. He was enjoying himself. The flash of racing horses, the general movement, crowd, colour, called to his virile Navajo sensuousness. Pleasure in the show did not conflict with a smug attitude towards blanket Indians, kept forward in his mind by the omnipresent whites. Mr. Bucla had a horse, almost never used. Perhaps Mr. Bucla would let him ride it, and Jack, too. Then Jack might not feel so badly. He wanted his friend to come over to his side.

In the latter part of the afternoon there was a long delay — some business of finding a horse to run against a particularly famous sorrel. In the pause, Myron found that he was hungry and dry. If he had a dime, he could get pop from the trader, but he had nothing. Maybe he could find an older boy with money, or someone with fruit or pop to spare. He worked away from the main crowd, passing around the group of wagons. A woman's horse started to buck suddenly, in the middle of a group of people mounted and afoot. There was shouting and laughter, scurrying, and the woman sitting tight and grinning, her wide skirts sailing all over the place, until the animal was quieted. Myron was delighted. Following this show had taken him past a heavy screen of chamisa, and now he found himself watching, from about five yards' distance, four people who sat around a very red, juicy watermelon. At the sight of the fruit he felt overwhelmingly hot, dusty, and parched through every fibre of his body. There were a big, ancient man, a middle-aged man and woman, and a schoolboy, Homer Gatewood, who was a couple of years older than Myron. The old man was remarkable enough to keep him staring for some time. Big, big-boned, a big, square face in which chin and cheekbones were strongly blocked out, a craggy nose and wide mouth. Modern conservative Navajos wore headbands, velveteen shirts, calico leggings cut rather like pajama trousers, but this man followed a far older mode. The skullcap of buckskin with a tuft of feathers at the top and another at the back was a warrior's ornament of the days of independence. He wore a fringed, buckskin shirt, dyed red, and his leggings were stuck into red buckskin gaiters with silver buttons running from ankle to knee. He seemed to the boy as incongruous, and carried the same indefinable authority as a heavily bearded man in grey beaver hat and frock coat would have to a white youngster of a respectful turn of mind.

Homer, looking up, called, 'Come on. Have some.'

His mother smiled at Myron. 'Come and sit, my child. It's a hot day.'

He came shyly, settling himself beside, and a little behind the other boy. The woman gave him a big chunk of melon. It was ripe, cool, and juicy.

'Is this another child whose parents couldn't come?' she asked.

'These are my people,' Homer explained to him. 'They couldn't come before, now they are here. I'm going back with them.' His face glowed. Then he said to them, 'This one is staying here because he wants to, I think.'

They barely glanced towards him, but Myron caught the sense of their surprise. He felt uncomfortable and lonely. These were nice people, a real mother and father, kind, dependable. If my uncle had come for me. He reversed himself quickly: I'm going to be civilized, different; something stronger than anything the Navajos have.

'In a month I'll have to be back here, too,' Homer said. 'They promised Mr. Linsdale. I wish I could stay away.'

The old man spat out a mouthful of seeds and set down the rind of his piece.

'No, my grandson. You want this schooling, even if it is hard. There are many tribes of Long-Haired People, of Earth People, many strong warriors, but this one tribe, the *Bellacana*, conquered them all. Why? Because he knows more, I think. By paper and by wires he talks to his friends in the distance, he leaves his words behind him when he goes away. He makes things we cannot make. He is here, he is all around us, we cannot get rid of him. Therefore we must learn his secrets that we, Navajos, may continue. Long ago we asked for these schools. We want them. It is not pleasant for you, but you need it, I think.'

He bit into a fresh piece of melon, swallowed and spat out more seeds.

'Now you, grandchild,' he looked towards Myron, 'I think you are making a mistake, too. If you learn all the white man's way and forget the Navajo, if that happens to our young men, then we die, we are destroyed, as surely as if by warfare. The man who will serve his people in the years to come, the man who will strengthen them, is the man who can learn all of the one without losing the other. That is what we are hoping for, we who used to be warriors and leaders, and who still wear the old-fashioned clothes.'

Homer's father said, 'I think the race is going to start, let us go over.'

They went back into the crowd, and presently Myron left them.

The singing started again shortly after dark. Myron lay, hearing the relentless drum, puzzling. One could think of the old man as absurd, but he carried an authority which stood up against all the visible authorities of Washington. His actual helplessness before the white machine did not count. His belief in schools, his reasonable point of view, surprised the boy. Destroyed as surely as by warfare. Destroy what? He then sermons, backsliders, ignorant blanket Indians, mother, fatigue struggling home at night with the sheep ignorant dirty — catch-phrase and imitative prejudice — Mr. Bucla a Navajo is cobweb-nothing to blow away civilized is strong those old people old talk all finished. Mr. Bucla owned a Board, a magical Board, something to do with Christianity, overhearing him tell his wife — tell my Board, they'll see that Washington... The ultimate power who wants to be ignorant old-fashioned helpless wear a necktie be respected civilized is strong.

PART TWO

CHAPTER ONE

WHEN his secretary answered the bell, Commissioner Hartmann said, 'Tell Mr. Dilwater to come here.'

She nodded and went out.

'Anyhow,' he said, continuing a broken conversation, 'he's a Democrat, and a speech proves nothing. He isn't on the committee.'

The Congressman said, 'Well — he can get some committee members to stir things up. McCune ——'

'Sure. McCune's laying for me. You leave him to me, don't worry about it; I can handle him any time. Come in, Dilwater. Congressman, this is Mr. Dilwater, Director of Education — Congressman Newell of South Dakota.'

'I'm surely glad to make your acquaintance, Mr. Dilwater.' The Congressman had a firm handshake, a clear, direct, and friendly eye.

'Glad to meet you, sir. We've been hearing of you ——' The Director's words, said with an effect of earnestness and slight diffidence, went well in the ears of a new member.

'Mr. Newell has some interesting suggestions about the schooling,' Hartmann told him. 'I want you to hear them.'

Dilwater sank into one of the heavy leather armchairs and looked attentive. 'You're the man on the spot,' he said. 'I haven't been in your section for nearly four years. We need fresh viewpoints.'

The Commissioner said, 'Go ahead, Congressman. Give us the whole of it.'

Newell nodded. 'It's very simple, gentlemen. As you

surely know, the Women's Clubs have been concerning themselves with Indian affairs recently.' He looked at the Commissioner, who nodded sourly. 'A fine civic influence, the
Women's Clubs; I'm glad to see them enter this neglected
sphere. Well, sir, the district secretary has written to me —
a motion of their committee — concerning the Newmarket
School.'

Dilwater looked worried and said nothing. Hartmann was
expressionless; as yet, he had not really sized up this Congressman.

'Here's a copy of it.' Newell tossed a paper across the Commissioner's desk. 'They say they don't approve of sending
little tykes six and seven years old away to a non-reservation
boarding school. They want the boarding schools reserved
for older children only, the younger ones trained at home —
day schools or something. That'll summarize a three-page
letter for you. Personally, I think the point is well taken; any
humane man cannot help but be disturbed by the picture of
those babies so far from home.'

Both the Indian Office men saw in his words the germ of
a speech for the record on the floor of the House, and possible
difficulties in committee. Hartmann said, 'What about it,
Mr. Dilwater?' He had confidence in his man.

The Director of Education's forehead wrinkled with an
effect of deep thought. 'Well, sir, I wish you could help us
get it done. O' course, children in the non-reservation schools
stay away from home. They're less likely to go back to the
blanket, that's a fact. We might have some opposition from
the Mission Boards if we kept *all* the young ones home.
O' course, day schools are out o' the question. You just can't
keep Indians in a day school. They won't stay.'

'I'm not sure of that, if you'll pardon me,' Newell said.
'Red Hill's in my district, and those Indians are asking for
more schooling.'

'They do, sir. They do that. But when they get it they
kick about it and won't co-operate. That's a fact. We know.

Now, to put all one age-group, say, at Newmarket, and all another at Red Hill would cost money. You know the President's economy policy.'

Hartmann glanced distastefully at the chopped-up oddments he had to use for memoranda. Economy. Newell nodded and faintly smiled.

Dilwater continued: 'Well, sir, we'd have to transport a lot of equipment from each place to the other, and get a lot new altogether. Little children can't do much in industrial training; if we concentrated them in one school, we'd have to hire more help for the laundry and farms and so on. It would be right expensive. And yet we'd like to do it, that's a fact.'

'By expensive you mean what?'

'Well, it's hard to say offhand. I'd need a week to get you figures. Extra employees and equipment and transfers of goods and staff ——' The vision of changes danced before the Director, files and orders and complaints and a whole system disrupted. 'Well, sir, it could not be done under half a million, I guess, but o' course that's only a guess. I wouldn't say for sure till I looked into it. It might be more.'

Newell recognized an obstructionist when he saw one, but he was unsure of the answer. The Mission Boards carried a lot of weight, and with the President pinching pennies while the nation cheered... He didn't like to push the Commissioner, an old war-horse, wise as a fox, who'd promised to handle McCune.

'How about it, Mr. Commissioner?' he said.

'I think we can work something out. Let us study on it and report to you later, will you? I see your position.'

'When will I hear from you?'

'In a day or two, perhaps sooner.'

'I'll surely appreciate it.' The Congressman rose. He liked those Sioux on the Red Hill Reservation, he wanted to help them. He felt that he was being put off. I'll see what they do produce. He looked at Dilwater. That man's an old pillow. 'I won't take any more of your time. Good day, gentlemen.'

When he was gone, Hartmann grunted. Another Indian-lover in Congress — but they'd get him over that.

'About the Mission Boards,' he said, 'they're acting up, too.'

'How?'

'Here's a joint letter from three of 'em.' He named the denominations — 'About the improper conditions in the town of Newmarket. I was going to see you about it anyhow. Pool-halls, liquor, prostitution, immature young people exposed, etc., etc., etc., *and* they say the Girls' Matron is "gravely to be suspected of commercial relations with some of the worst elements in the city." What's the matter with that place, Dilwater?'

'Nothing's the matter with it, Mr. Commissioner. We just built a new auditorium there, they've got a college-grade football team and the Chamber of Commerce advertises 'em. If we can get extry beds enough on the annual estimate so's we can fill the dormitories as well as the sleeping porches, we'll have an enrollment of six hundred. And we've got a dandy printing class there, with all the latest appliances. You've seen some of their jobs, sir.'

'Yep.' The Commissioner considered. 'Nothing ever suits the Missions and the Women's Clubs are hard to beat. There's three yearners' associations now, and you know they licked the Lennisfall bill. That — what's it? — National Indian Welfare Association — they're yelling about day schools, too. Newell may be new, but he's strong. He's an old hand locally, and he might be next national committeeman from his state. He's got a big pull of some kind with Motley on Appropriations, and Jenkins on Senate Appropriations, too. If he doesn't wind up Senator, he'll go on House Appropriations himself. Indian Affairs is his only committee now, and it's our chance to train him. Lemme see.'

He took out and lit a cigar, and leant back in his swivel chair, then came forward abruptly.

'First off, you transfer that matron. Send her to Toadlena or some such place in the middle of a reservation, and never mind how much anybody squawks. Somewhere where these churches don't have missions, see? Then — lessee — tomorrow — Thursday noon you bring me a program picking out four non-reservation schools, including Newmarket, where the experiment of only taking older children will be tried, and stating what reservation schools will send 'em every child twelve years old, and receive all youngsters instead, see?'

'But ——'

'We can do it. It won't last. I'll get an additional twenty thousand for it, and I'll get it on the regular budget where it'll stick.'

'That's hardly ——'

'We won't get more. Deficiency Appropriation's been passed already. That's got to do, see?'

'Yes, sir.' Dilwater hesitated, then asked with a different tone of interest, 'About investigating the vice?'

'I'll take care of the vice.' The Commissioner picked up a thick file of papers.

'All right.'

The Director of Education walked out. A whole system to be upset, new files started, trouble and confusion. But no one could buck Hartmann, and it might have been worse.

Just before five the Commissioner took up the phone. 'Get me Congressman Newell — Newell — at the new House Building.' It annoyed him that his memorandum was written on a pad made of old mimeographed sheets cut to size and stapled together. Economy! The country was never richer. 'Is Congressman Newell there? May I speak to him? This is the Commissioner of Indian Affairs.' God knew the Indian Service was starved for cash. Indian-lovers can be useful if you know how to handle them. 'Congressman? Hello, Hartmann speaking. We've been making some plans. I've been in touch with the Mission Boards ... Yes, I think we can pacify them ... If you can help us get another ten thousand for law enforcement... Yes, that's what they want, and Mr. Newell, we need it. If we can get that on the regular appropriation for 1926, too. Can you help us... That's mighty fine. Now about the schools; we can start your idea as an experiment at four centers, see? We'd like to put it across. If the experiment works, we can justify increased appropriations to spread it... Yes... Well, about twenty thousand dollars the first year. If we could count upon that for several years... Will you take it up with him?... That's very good of you. We want to see your idea succeed, Congressman; we believe in it. The Committee on Appropriations is so... That's splendid... Thursday afternoon, the whole schedule, with costs... Not at all, we're for it, sir. That's what we're here for: to help the Indians... All right, sir. Goodbye.'

2

Mrs. Boyle was a magnificent cook and her husband, like many lean, nervous men, demanded lavish meals. The four missionaries moved back into the parlour sated and quiescent. Boyle urged Butler into the morris chair; it had vaguely the character of the place of honour, and as ordained minister and senior missionary, his guest presided in theory if not in fact. ' McCarty and Snyder took the sofa, their host the cushioned rocker, his high knees and upright posture making him seem always about to move, restless, unrelaxed.

Butler, looking around the room, felt old, completed thoughts about these men projected behind his vision and the main occupations of his mind like under-lighted lantern slides. The move from the dining alcove had broken the thread of talk. One heard Mrs. Boyle and the servant, a young convert who was not deft, clearing the table. The single cluster of lights overhead flickered occasionally when the engine in the garage wavered. Bleak, he thought, compared to oil lamps. The room needed a fireplace.

McCarty said, 'These lights are a wonderful improvement, Lucius.'

Boyle smiled deprecatingly. 'It's a great convenience, particularly when I have to work at night.' There was a faint undertone of defence in his manner. 'I was hooked on to the Agency plant you know, but they shut down at nine. When I found that by thrift and care this could be managed, I decided it would pay dividends in my labours, and of course the convenience is great. I won't deny that comfort and work went hand in hand.'

Boyle had a gift for tending to his comfort. It was like the rich supply of fresh vegetables at dinner, harvested from the truck garden he irrigated so freely. Butler never had been able to get straight just how his colleague had established a right to precious water from the Indians' ditch. He pushed the thought aside.

McCarty was making some very reasonable comments on the inversion of turning government light plants off at night. The operating room in the hospital. He spoke correct and fluent English with only the faintest Navajo accent.

As he had done before, Butler tried to put back on this man the trimmings of his forebears. Wide shoulders, big chest, tapering to slender hips, the slight bay window invisible as he sat — one could imagine the buckskin shirt, or the more recent velveteen, and silver on the dark wrists. Circular earrings — long hair sweeping back over the ears to a queue — the features were there to be framed, cheekbones, and nose and jaw, but the mouth would not fit, nor the sleekness which was not so much in the face as a quality hovering over it. The difference between a dog and a wolf. He was ashamed of the comparison even while it amused him.

Snyder cleared his throat. 'Returning to business, the school here is shipping some children to us.'

Boyle nodded. 'Yes. We can all be thankful our charges pass into your hands, Paul. There will also be some Episcopalians.'

Snyder said, with a faint smile, 'There is no one of that denomination at Yellow Earth; ourselves, the Mennonites, and the Catholics.'

'I'll provide you a list of our own and the Episcopalians. They'd ought to join our communion there.' Boyle's smooth manner allowed no smile. 'Of course, we shouldn't try to proselytize, but just accept them in trust for our co-workers. If we assure Reverend Hilton —— '

Snyder said, 'Of course. Is Reverend Hilton High or Low Church?'

It always irritated Butler slightly to hear people using Reverend with last name only, like Mister.

'Low.'

'That's good. Some of the High Churchmen might favour the Roman mission. I guess,' Snyder smiled again, 'I guess likely some of these will end by joining us.'

Some of their hostility towards Rome lapped over into their feelings towards Episcopalians. It pleased them that a school where that church was dominant should become feeder to one where they were strong.

McCarty said, 'This new arrangement doesn't do us any harm, but it's a queer idea. The children who go off the reservations young are the ones who progress farthest from heathen ways. I'm proud of being a Navajo, but I long for the day when my people will turn to the light.'

Boyle said, 'I guess it won't last long. It's that Welfare Association stirring things up, and the Women's Clubs. You know how they carry on about Indian art and that stuff.'

'We can't tell,' Butler said. 'The business of removing little children far from home can be made to sound badly in Congress. This may be permanent — if so, the Boards will have to get together and arrange a new distribution. Don't forget, Paul,' he looked directly to Snyder, 'if Episcopalian children come to us at Yellow Earth, ours will go into Episcopalian hands at Mushkaha. They're trying this experiment in four districts. We don't know what it portends. A grasping attitude might lead to a most un-Christian interdenominational war.'

Snyder nodded. 'That's good sense. How would it be to offer the Episcopalians use of our facilities if they want to send a visitor?'

'I'll recommend it to the Board. By the way, I have one boy I specially want you to look out for, a most promising little chap called Myron Begay. He's twelve now, so he goes to you.'

'Myron Begay? I'll remember.'

'His father, who was a leader of the Salt Clan, died when he was little.'

'Who was he?' McCarty asked.

'I'm not sure of the name. He lived near Jones's store.'

'Oh — Ashin Tso-n. Yes, he was a man of power. And the mother's family, Reed Clan, you know, are very strong in that district. One of them is a medicine man and a powerful enemy of progress.'

'That's right. The mother remarried, you know, and neglected this boy. Now it seems she's changed husbands again and moved away. He has found his comfort and security in our church, and I have great hopes for him. I think he might follow in your footsteps, Jerome. Perhaps we can arrange to have him spend a vacation with you.'

'I'd be delighted.'

'He has a good mind, his command of English is excellent.'

'His Navajo?' McCarty asked.

'Rather weak. That's something you could do for him, overcome his reluctance to use the tongue.'

'I was the same way once, until I saw how it could be used in my calling.'

'That's right. He's musical too, and he's shaping up to be an athlete. I surrender him to you reluctantly, Paul.'

'I'll try to do as much for him as I know you would, Allan.'

'I'm sure you will.' Butler hesitated, framing his thoughts. 'His emotional feeling against the Navajo language is a symptom of a general attitude. He is headed now merely to turn his back on his people, whereas I think he is a boy who ought to develop loyalty to the tribe.' He saw Snyder's doubtful look. 'We estimate forty thousand Navajos. That's a nation. Its problem can't be solved just by teaching gifted individuals to melt into the white world.'

McCarty said, 'You're exactly right,' with emphasis.

A general discussion arose over his thesis. Boyle and Snyder held with the established policy of completely dissolving the tribes, but the native missionary among them was living evidence of the other possibility, and forty thousand souls... The argument ran between them and McCarty. Butler stopped following it, thinking of the boy, whom he loved, and then of his daughter, who had become so distressingly modern.

'Wake up, Allan,' Boyle said good-naturedly. 'We need a Doctor of Divinity here.'

Via discussion of special attitudes towards Indians, and the particular question of letting them have even the least acquaintance with liquor, they had worked around to the Methodists' adoption of grapejuice for communion, the double pressure of national prohibition and the Indian liquor laws. Thence they had moved to the theological problem. Butler leant forward, half smiling, a man assured of himself in a matter of scholarship. The Hebrew *yayin* and *tirôsh*, the Greek οἶνος, but in the establishment of the Supper He said 'Fruit of the Vine.' Compare so many passages, Hosea, Song of Songs, Acts: Two: Twenty-three, specifically indicating fermentation... They listened with real respect as he expounded these matters. In the Gospels — Matthew: Twenty-six: Twenty-nine — the Hebrew *géphen*... But more important than the physical nature of that which is consumed...

CHAPTER TWO

TSAILI had been a shabby little spot in the desert compared to Yellow Earth, but its faults had their advantages. There was no electric light plant there, no dairy herd, no farm, and so there had been ever so much less work to do. Of course the crops and cattle made the allowance of eleven cents per child per day for food go a lot farther, you weren't so hungry, but you got tired of feeling tired. Myron liked potatoes, he didn't mind the greens, and he certainly appreciated the extra meat from the yearly butchering of a dozen or so steers and an occasional old cow. Milk, which they said was so important, still tasted unpleasant; it had nauseated him at first. How did white people get to like it so? The food was better, there were more and better things to study, one felt more adult at a school where there weren't any babies, but the Apaches were irritating, there was too much fighting, and the constant, unrelenting grind ran day after day from early morning until one sank into bed at night, chores, classes, work with a gesture at instruction, study. A boy could try to think, to take stock, but his mind seemed deadened. On Sunday there was the half somnolence of two services and the Sunday School. You had to keep awake at that, Mr. Snyder was a lot sharper than Mr. Butler. Myron wished he could see Mr. Butler soon. He'd gone up to stay with him the first summer, but he'd been too much of a kid then to get the good of it. Things his protector told him were confusing. You can't be both a Navajo and civilized; if you want to go forward you must cross over to the white man's side.

That was the way Mr. Snyder saw it. He didn't really like Mr. Snyder so much, but he guessed he made sense.

Now he was fifteen and beginning to become solid. This fall he'd discovered football. Jack had gone right after it; that and fighting the Apaches seemed to come natural to him. Myron wouldn't join those fights. Mr. Snyder called them relics of barbarism, and the boy who was going to be really civilized outgrew his tribe. On account of Jack, and because good football players got light work around the school, and because he was tired of being set apart, slightly despised by his fellows, he'd gone out for it this fall. A new world opened for him, a completeness of active joy that he hadn't known existed. Naturally intense, quick on his feet, a fighter, he got a place as substitute halfback, although he was still short on weight.

The Superintendent believed in a team that could make a showing against white high schools. Chores were lightened, the drag of tiredness relaxed, he found even a little spare time. There was only one drawback to being an athlete; having proven he wasn't a weakling, he found that Navajos and Apaches alike thought his refusal to join in the constant tribal fights all the stranger. Acceptance still evaded him.

He was thinking about this as he wandered across the sandy campus in the long, slack Sunday afternoon, avoiding with an appearance of aimlessness the groups that idled here and there. Even Jack had little to say to him nowadays. He put it to himself that he was Navajo no longer. He was smarter than these other Indians who hung on to old ways. The argument wasn't entirely satisfactory, for others did as well in their studies as he, and almost all of them assumed the same attitude of contempt for native culture. He wasn't following definite arguments, any more than he had formulated a thought, I am lonely, he merely compensated a sense of lack with an assumption of superiority.

Now in the idleness of Sunday he felt as if things had been piling up inside him for a long time with increasing pressure, he wanted to do something. As he passed a group of girls, so constantly seen and so completely segregated, he was aware of them, or rather, because of them uncomfortably aware of the automatic meandering of his legs, the slouch of his back, how his arms led down to his pocketed hands, the very hair on his head. Another disturbance, unclear but recently intensifying. Some of the oldest children sneaked out at night, and if the watchman caught them they got plenty — whipping, labour, the jail-closets. Mr. Snyder said it was a sign of backwardness, one must conquer the natural immorality of wild Indians. Resenting the girls, he kicked a stone and sent it flying.

He was becoming a good drop-kicker. Unless he put on a lot more weight he'd need to be a top-notch kicker and passer to get to be a first-string back. Myron Begay the triple-threat man. It was swell being in a school with a football team. Mr. Snyder believed in athletics, so did Mr. Butler. Jesus was an active man, he pulled a burro out of a mudhole, and you know how burros are. In stature and favour with God and man. That would be Jack if only he wasn't so hostile. He felt a sort of longing when he thought of his friend, his firm face with its regular features, and the way he looked going down the field under a punt, the way his jaw set when he got ready to tackle. Jack had a bag of pollen, he took a pinch secretly and made a Navajo prayer every time they went to church. No one else was like that. Myron had prayed and prayed, but still he knew that blasphemy or no blasphemy he'd never tell on him. If he could convert Jack — it might be done with Mr. Butler, but Mr. Snyder wasn't the right man. Jack and he had kind of separated this last year, even with the football.

A boy at the corner of the academic building shouted '*E-yah! Chishi! Chishi!*' and followed the cry with a shrill, coyote-like bark, '*Ou-ou-ou!*'

He disappeared, running towards the football field. The scattered grouping of boys broke up as first some, then more and more moved and began to run after him. The girls, keeping carefully apart, followed slowly.

Myron's feet took him along as if they were weighted. He would have nothing to do with it, but he had to go and see. That old war, so desperately bloody between two closely related fighting tribes — first cousins — was ended sixty years and more ago. This kind of thing was backsliding. When he was near the field he stopped. Boys coming in by ones and twos struggled around a central, flailing mass that looked like two teams at the end of a line buck. Outnumbered at Yellow Earth, the Navajos needed all their champions. The Disciplinarian was an Apache, he thought the fights were funny, and argued that they were good for the boys, good for football, particularly when his side was out in force as it was today. The Navajos were in for another licking. That was like a Chishi, just as they raided and murdered in Canyon de Chelly when the men were gone, but we caught them at Wide Reeds and wiped out the war-party. Mr. Snyder would stop it if he knew about it. He stepped forward again. More boys jumped in, generally with a yell and the same wild, barking sound. Mr. Snyder or Mr. Vail would stop it . . . but you can't be a tale-bearer.

Jack came by on the run. He stopped short and swung around, snarling in Navajo, 'What's the matter with you?' Then he spat out in English, 'Halfback!' and dove into the fight.

Two girls to his left looked towards him and giggled. He heard them whisper. I ain't Navajo, I'm civilized. He felt unhappy and excited, the muscles of his stomach were pulled tight, his heart pounded. One Apache grabbed Jack from behind and another punched him in the face. Myron's mouth opened of itself. '*Ou-ou-ou.*' He was leaping, weightless on flying feet, then dove in the hardest tackle he'd ever made and heard his man groan as the breath was knocked out of him. He was up with a leap to help Jack with the other Apache. This was like football, but far beyond it;

in all the rush, the giving and receiving of pain, he knew he was utterly happy. He was in the middle of a heaving pile when the Disciplinarian and a squad of teachers broke up the riot.

He got to his feet and looked around, getting his bearings, remembering himself. He had a bruised eye, cut lip, and skinned knee. Here was Jack. They started off arm in arm. Mr. Snyder's going to be mad at me, he thought. Plenty mad. Perry Hanson, the big first-string halfback, caught up with them and threw an arm across his shoulder.

'Well, you sure woke up,' he said.

Myron grunted, then grinned. 'Aw, dere's too many of dem Chishi, we've all got to join in.'

Jack squeezed his arm. 'Attaboy.'

2

An unseasonable, heavy snowfall that began to melt and then froze, put a one-day stop to football practice. Mr. Trimble told the squad to chase themselves around, get some exercise, and be careful not to catch cold. The final game with the Papagos was only two weeks off. Jack and Myron walked together towards the pine woods north of the school grounds, talking in Navajo sprinkled with English words.

'If it would really snow, we could have an Apache-fight,' Myron said.

'Yes.' Jack kicked at the crust. Myron had improved a lot. 'This stuff's no good. You couldn't make a snowball with it.'

Just beyond the grounds stood an Apache wickeyup like a very neat haystack. As they passed the door an old woman came out. Myron greeted her heartily in the Apache form, '*Njoh shichiné.*' She answered, '*Njoh,*' studying them. They showed gaiety repressed. Her eyes were keen.

'*Yotahenné,*' she said, 'Navajos.'

'*Aoh, Yotahenné.*'

The boys laughed. She menaced them with her fist, then asked them in. They told her they might visit her another time.

The ground-covering was more like real snow under the trees, spotted with ice-encased pine needles, marked here and there with tracks. Jack became more alert, studying the sign.

'A coyote here,' he said.

They followed the prints aimlessly to a little stream.

'I didn't know this was here,' Myron remarked.

'Yes. I came this way sometimes last summer.'

'It runs in summer?'

'Yes.'

'How black it looks under the ice!'

Perennial woodland streams were unfamiliar to the two Navajos. They listened to its gurgling, studied the crinkly formation of the thin ice.

'Do you think any animal could cross on that?' Myron asked.

'I don't know. It's very thin.'

'When I was a child, in winter the water froze in the barrel, sometimes as thick as my thumb.'

'That's nothing. My mother sent me to the wash one time to fill a water basket. When I got back to the hogahn, it was frozen across the top so that we had to punch it with a stick before it would pour.'

Stooping, Myron pushed the ice gently with his finger. It gave flexibly and made a faint squeaking.

'What's the smallest thing that will break this?' he asked.

'I don't know.'

'Let's try. We'll start with the very smallest thing.'

'All right.' Jack dropped a pine needle. 'Like that? That won't do it.'

Neither would a scrub-oak leaf or a small twig, but a good piece of frozen snow made a hole through which the water came soggily. Myron whittled two pencil-sized sticks.

'Here, these are spears,' he said. 'We'll see who can make the most holes.'

It was ridiculous, trying to get force into such light missiles, they almost threw their arms off. They shouted. It became necessary to make rules and keep score. Jack slipped, fell, and his hand went into the stream.

'*Chindi!*' he swore. 'Well, that's a big hole — ten points.'

'It's a foul, you lose ten.'

They wrangled and compromised. The game began to pall. Jack noticed a sizeable, flat rock which their scuffling feet had uncovered. Grinning, he stepped back and stooped. As Myron made his next throw he tossed it, so that rock and twig landed in the stream together, at the same time, shouting, 'Good shot! Ten points for you!'

Myron, well splashed, jumped back and shoved his friend. Grunting and twisting, each of them tried his best to get the other into the water. Neither of them really wanted to do it, but neither would give in, so in the end they rolled to the brink together. They were tired of this, too, their necks and shoes were full of snow, and they were none too warmly dressed. They lay watching each other, weary, panting, uncomfortable, then without saying anything let go and got up.

'*Eh!*' said Jack. 'I'm wet.'

'So am I.'

'Have you any matches?'

'No.'

'Let's go back to that Chishi woman's and warm up.'

'All right. Let's hurry, it's getting late.' Myron always bothered about things like being tardy.

As they back-tracked themselves, he said, 'Let's get them, those Chishi, to show us how you make fire with sticks. Then we can have a fire any time.'

'Yes, let's. I saw my grandfather do it once, but I forget.'

The first evening bell rang through the woods, sounding unexpectedly faint with distance. It was dusk.

'Golly!' Myron said. 'We'd better hurry.'

'We can find out about the fire-sticks another time.'

They broke into a steady trot.

'Yes. They'll be useful.'

Side by side, swinging steadily at the durable, Indian run, they passed through the woods and across the school grounds, by a last, mad scramble managing to arrive, half combed and none too well washed, in time for supper.

No talking in the dining-room, save when one asked for something to be passed. The scrape and bang of spoons on tin plates, of tin cups set down, filled the room with the sound of some kind of utterly erratic machinery; the technique was to eat as rapidly as possible, before the bread and extra potatoes were all gone. Myron wasted no time, he was good and hungry. Beef tonight, that was fine. With the taste and solid feel of food in his mouth, chewing busily and reaching for another slice of oleomargarine-spread bread, contentment surged through him. Everything had changed since he stopped being a sissy about the fighting. If they learnt about fire-making, they could pretend to camp in the woods Sundays. By and by they could let a few other boys in — Perry — he reached again, spearing the last potato. He wondered if he'd get into the big game this year. Perhaps if they need a goal kicked. He imagined the scene vividly. As he stacked his plates and carried them out, he held the football in his hands, pointing down, and thinking so took the preparatory step, remembering just in time that this was tinware, not pigskin.

Two pieces of meat with their gravy caked about them stood in a dish on the kitchen table. He got both with one quick swipe, crammed one into his mouth, wrapped the other swiftly in his handkerchief. As he hastened out of the building to darkness that would hide his chewing, he was dancingly happy. He'd slip the second piece to Jack, he decided. He could eat it himself, but he'd rather share.

CHAPTER THREE

BRADFORD Y LEÓN was a big, solid blond, showing his Spanish blood only in his smooth voice and a suavity of manner.

'If it hadn't been for the oil scandal we'd be all right,' he said. 'We had a reasonable Secretary of the Interior in those days, a cattleman himself.'

'But surely,' Pritchard said, 'there are legal means. If these Indians are squatters on the Public Domain, why —— '

He was sent out by a Kansas City bank, and after the long ride from Albuquerque into the mountains had entered a section of a wildness he had thought to exist only in cheap fiction. These three men attracted and alarmed him. They were wild, too, and strong, and their frankness was amazing. He was used to doing things prettily under a cloak of reasons and phrases.

Strang, the leader, said, 'Not a chance. In the first place, the Republicans are running this state, and they wouldn't let me mend a busted bridle if they could help it. But that ain't all, because maybe then Jack and Dick might swing it and I'd trust 'em to deal me in. It's the Indian-lovers we got to beat out.'

'The — ?'

'Those associations, specially that Indian Welfare outfit.'

'How do they come in? If it's Public Domain.'

'Look here.' From his roll-top desk Strang picked a pamphlet the cover of which showed the figure of an Indian in a war bonnet sandwiched between headings of bold type. 'I'm a politician, so I study my enemies. I get their bulletins.'

He smiled. 'It's that kind o' thing Jack and Dick don't think of; that's why this county goes Democratic right along.'

Bradford y León smiled, Dick Beardsley nodded and spat into the unlighted stove.

'That's a sign, see? Same as Apaches makin smoke signals in the old days. It's all in there, about how there's nine thousand Navajos on the Public Domain east o' the reservation line, and it's the traditional Navajo homeland, and Roosevelt added it to the reservation but Taft took it back. You bet he took it back. We had Senators who amounted to a damn in those days. Well, they're warmin up, you see.'

'But this Association, has it any real power?'

Beardsley said gloomily, 'They licked the Lennisfall bill. Not only that, but they went ahead and got the Land Readjustment Act passed and gave a lot of irrigated land to those Pueblos who didn't need it.'

'And that was the end of Lennisfall,' Bradford y León said.

'Yeah,' Beardsley said, 'that cut him right out. He was a good Congressman too.' He sighed. 'I wanted to go ahead and renominate him, but it couldn't be done. Not just because his bill might have been a little bit greedy, *entiende*, but his failure sure bounced back on some of his supporters.'

'Like ropin an old cow,' Strang explained; 'it charged right up the rope at him. That started things. We've always had Indian associations, a good thing too. Somebody's got to stand up for them poor fellers. But when all the artists and yearners in Santa Fé and New York and California joined in on account o' their love for the Pueblo Indians, and then cleaned up the way they did, things sure changed. They just about want to give the West back to the red man.'

The banker looked surprised.

Beardsley nodded and said with his usual gloom, 'They sure ride the Commissioner. Hartmann's a good man, and a competent one, but he just can't seem to please 'em. And they got some o' those radical Senators lined up. That's why it's no use us goin to him for help. They're after him and the Secretary all the time to set that whole big area aside for the Navajos — about the half o' four counties.'

Strang grimaced towards his friends. 'And O'Donnell's right in with 'em. That's the Republican Party for you, sends an Indian-lover to the Senate.'

'We never guessed it, Tom,' Bradford y León said. 'We just thought he was liberal. He sure has the Mexican vote tied up.'

'Yeah, he's a liberal. Sure. He's tellin all the rancheros that us big stockmen are crowdin 'em out. Hell, suppose we do take up the range, we hire 'em to herd for us, don't we?'

Beardsley rolled and lit a cigarette. 'He may be all o' that, Tom, but he's a good politico and he knows how to get re-elected. If I could show him where Jack and me could put Ciervo County in the Republican corral just once, he'd give us what we want. Only you won't play.'

'M-maybe,' Strang's voice was a parody of doubt. 'And maybe you'd find out he meant what he said all along. I don't trust him, he might be sincere. Anyhow that's a desperate remedy. You take a Mexican you've been trainin all his life to put an X under the star and tell him to put it under the eagle, and you corrupt his moral fibre. First thing you know he'll be votin a split ticket.'

Pritchard set the tips of his fingers together. 'Just what is your proposition, gentlemen? The bank wants assurance that you won't default further on your interest payments. Then there's the question of a loan for your winter feed again.'

'It works like this. We been buyin feed because our winter range is over-grazed, but that half-Navajo country in Andalusia and De Soto counties is in pretty good shape. Besides the Indians, there's just one big outfit in the southern part and a few little owners — fifty and a hundred head o' sheep — usin the Public Domain. But the Indians are located on a lot o' the water, and you can't use the range until they've been pushed off o' some of it. Is that clear?'

Pritchard nodded. 'Certainly.'

'Well, we aim to move a few thousand head in there this winter. It'll be Jack's, because he's got relatives over that way.'

Bradford y León nodded. 'Two sheriffs and so on.'

'We'll have to spend a little money, here and there. Anyhow, we figure to crowd the Indians some. And it's likely they'll get impatient and run off some stock and maybe do some fighting. All those people out that way, their daddies and granddaddies were Navajo fighters, and they ain't forgotten the bad old days. So we'll get an authentic popular clamour to have the maraudin Indians put back on their reservation where they belong.'

Pritchard nodded without speaking. There was a similar technique in industrial troubles, but these men were so frank.

Bradford y León said, 'At the same time, with the help of my relatives there, we'll buy out some of them. Some Indians can't resist a cash offer, some with little bunches will let them go for cash and a job as herder. With one thing and another we'll get control of the water, and then we can hold the range.'

'It'll take two-three years before we can put the bulk of our stock there,' Strang said. 'Meantime, you got to help us. Otherwise, you'll wind up ownin about fifty thousand head o' sheep and cattle.'

Pritchard raised his hand deprecatingly. 'Lord forbid.' He took out, cut, and lit a cigar, making an exact performance of it to gain time. Kansas City had looked like the far west to him when he moved out there. How did one judge these men? He liked them; ruthless but straight. This was another age, the 1880's of finance and the frontier, a generation and more from service clubs, business ethics, and the new suavity. His decision hinged on the men, and he had a romantic urge to look them in the eye and say, 'We'll back you, pardners.'

'If you'll pardon me, gentlemen,' he said, 'there's one

question I want to ask. Please don't take offence. I have to be able to satisfy my directors.'

Strang said, 'Shoot.'

'We-ell — I gather that you gentlemen are political enemies.'

'Sure.'

'Yet — you see — your plan, which involves political repercussions, calls for close co-operation between you — it calls for good faith. Isn't there possibly a conflict — a paradox?' He spoke carefully, feeling his way. There was a revolver lying on Strang's desk. This was the frontier. 'I must be frank, please don't take it personally. As I understand it, Mr. Beardsley and Mr. Bradford here would like to break Mr. Strang's hold on the county.'

The two Republicans nodded. Strang said, 'They sure would.'

'Well, Mr. Bradford is to move onto this new range and consolidate himself there. You, Mr. Strang, are our biggest debtor. I — ah —— ' He broke down.

'You mean would Jack double-cross me?'

'Oh, of course, not that, no, but —— '

'It's a reasonable question,' Bradford y León said. 'You answer it, Dick. You're the oldest.'

Beardsley rolled and lit a cigarette. 'This country up here used to be wild. When Tom and me and Jack's daddy, old John T. Bradford, came in here, there weren't any other white men, nor hardly a wagon road you could recognize, and the Apaches down south of us, and the Navajos, were still kind of on the loose. There were some other old-timers came in, some of 'em left again, some died one way or another, some are still here. But the three of us, we kind of organized the place.' He spoke with accents of deep gloom, but through it ran a deep love of the times and the place he told about. 'Santa Fé didn't rightly know this place existed till we took to drummin and raisin smoke signals.

'Well, sir, we got roads and schools and bridges, we

founded the towns, we developed the country and started a real cattle business and later sheep. We tied the Mexicans to wheelbarrows till they learnt to walk on their hind legs — no offence, Jack.'

Bradford y León smiled. 'It's true enough, Mr. Pritchard. My own grandparents refused to eat off a table for a long time after my father married my mother. *Payosos que fueranos.*'

'Old John T. and me, we were Republicans, and Tom here, he was born a Democrat, so that's the way we lined up, and o' recent years he's kinda got the drop on us. It shifts about, accordin to who's quickest with the mavericks. For over forty years we been borrowin from each other, and helpin each other against outlaws and Indians and blizzards and the fool ideas that come out of the legislature and so on. We play our politics. Jack and me are keepin cool with Coolidge, and I guess Tom's freezin to death with Davis, but when it comes to the real, deep interests o' Ciervo County and the cattle business it depends on, we stand together.'

He threw his cigarette butt into the stove.

'We aim to make money, we aim to take care of ourselves, sure. And we're strongest when we stand together. But there's more than that to it. A lot more. I don't know if a city man like you can get it, but it's there all right.'

Pritchard nodded.

Strang said, 'That's right.'

Bradford y León said, 'That's what I was brought up to.'

It was a good risk. These men knew what they wanted to do, and were able to do it. The banker felt a breath of the frontier, a sense of participating in something from bygone days. He wanted to answer them in kind, direct and manly. He opened his mouth, searching for the strong words.

'Gentlemen, I think I can say my bank will decide to back you,' he said, feeling thin and bloodless as the habitual, cautious phrases came out.

CHAPTER FOUR

BUCKSKIN MAN rode wth his head lowered, staring at the trail. Today and yesterday the little boy he held on the saddle in front of him had been lively and demanding in the mornings, but in the afternoons became tired, dozed from time to time, and drew on his four-year-old reserves of stolidity. He led a poor little procession, his wife and daughter riding on inadequate, thin ponies, a burro loaded high with household goods. He himself was thin, and shabby in old blue trousers, a checked shirt of thin flannel, an ordinary cotton handkerchief around his hair. His wife was called Singing Beads, but she wore no jewelry.

The horses plodded westward, and the sun, swinging part way down the sky, was still warm; soon the autumn cold would begin to sharpen. His son stirred restlessly, readjusting himself. Buckskin Man felt the weight of the child's head hard against his ribs, the pressure was intensely personal and significant. Now he could think to the somnolent plod of unshod hooves on dry earth and rock. They would be there well before dark. He rode in search of help, but he dreaded the meeting with his relatives. *My fault is not a reason for letting go, but for holding on harder. I know I am still a man; very well, then, let me prove it.*

The ground sloped away steeply to a round valley, its western side already in shadow. Scattered evergreen trees were dark balls against the brownish land. Still in sunlight were the green masses of two summer hogahns, and the brightly coloured piles of harvested corn in front of them.

He called over his shoulder, 'Here it is!' and told his son, 'just a little longer now.'

When he looked back he had seen his wife's face. During these past days she had made no comment, she was waiting. He had not tried to explain himself, it was up to him to make them all strong again. That is what will count with her, he decided. I can do it, I shall not carry my head low. By the signs of the trail, several people had recently come this way. Horses and a couple of wagons stood in front of Shooting Singer's hogahn. He had hoped to find his cousins alone. It doesn't matter, a few people or the whole tribe; I am not going to carry my head low.

Following Warriors sat with her daughter, husking corn. She looked several times at the group as the ponies picked their way delicately down the trail, and it was not until they were in the flat of the encircled valley that she recognized them.

'Go tell your father my cousin and his family from Tsé Zhin are here.'

She stripped a couple more ears while she watched. It was some years since she'd seen Buckskin Man, she hardly knew the wife. A little boy, and the girl was half grown. How poor they looked. People out east, in the Diné T'ha were generally hard up, Buckskin Man had made a poor match for reasons of his own; but now she sensed some disaster.

He halted his pony a couple of yards from her, looking down at the comfortable, middle-aged woman in a wine-red bodice, sitting in the wide circle of her blue skirt, an ear of yellow corn in her hand, the corn piled all about her, red, blue, white, yellow, squashes and orange pumpkins. His wife and daughter rode up beside him, the pack burro immediately moved upon the pile of plenty. Singing Beads pulled the animal back with an angry jerk of the lead rope.

Following Warriors said *'Hallahani!'* in welcome and surprise.

Buckskin Man smiled slightly. 'Eh, cousin. You have a pretty place.'

'Yes. Where from?'

'From Tsé Zhin.'

'Where to?'

'Just here.'

Shooting Singer came out of the hogahn. 'Get down, get down,' he said. 'How long on the road?'

'Four days.'

Buckskin Man touched Following Warriors' hand, then turned to her husband. The two men were fond of each other, since the old times when Shooting Singer, half grown, let a neighbour's little boy tag along after him. Their hands remained together while they studied each other's face. Whatever the older man saw, he remained smiling, saying twice, 'This is good.'

He turned to his wife. 'Let us have supper early.' Then to his visitor, 'Come in. We've been talking things over.'

Singing Beads and her little girl stayed to help their hostess and her daughter. The two men, stooping, went through the low door of the hogahn. There were three others inside. Buckskin Man guarded himself while he settled on a sheepskin, letting his eyes adjust to the dimness, making out just who was there.

The building was an irregular square with thick walls of juniper boughs, the inner ones sere, the outer layer, laid on this summer, still green and fragrant. The smoke-hole in the middle of the roof let in a moderate shaft of light, the fire below was all but extinct. A man laughed, exclaimed, and reached towards Buckskin Man with outstretched hand. He recognized Big Nose and responded. Shooting Singer made himself comfortable, and broke the quiet with a humorous remark. Idle talk sprang up, drifting to other subjects when they felt that the newcomer was reluctant to answer questions about crops and sheep. There was a man unknown to him, and one he believed to be Tall Man — yes, that must be he.

Tall Man's father, Steven Trumbull, from whom he got his English name, was white, and he had been well educated, going through the highest government schools, and yet in the end he had come back entirely to his mother's people. At home with whites, he was able to compete in their world, and had captured the trucking business between his district and the railroad, running a line of trucks with Indian drivers. He was not entirely popular with those traders and officials who thought Indians should stay in their place. A member of the powerful Big Water Clan through his mother, he had made himself a leader, and was now one of the most effective delegates to the still new Tribal Council which the government had set up. To many Navajos, particularly younger ones, he represented the achievement of being fully Indian while understanding and mastering the white power. Buckskin Man thought he was a good person to meet in this crisis.

The women came in, bringing water and firewood.

Shooting Singer said: 'We'll eat soon, I hope. It is good to have you here, younger brother.'

'It is good to be here. But — we are sorry for what made us leave. There is trouble out there, in the Diné T'ha. It caught up with me, and so we came here.'

Everyone was listening, knowing that he was ready to explain himself.

Shooting Singer said: 'Good. You came at a good time. We are here, talking about things to be done. This man here is a delegate, this one,' he indicated Big Nose, 'is an alternate. And that one next you, he comes from Tlichisenili. He is a leader among his people up there.'

'What is happening?' Trumbull asked.

'You know we are outside the reservation there. It is Navajo country, but Washington drew a line farther west. For a long time the Mexicans who live there have run their sheep on the range. It was all right. There was a little trouble now and then, but we knew each other. Then since the time when wool was up to thirty cents, some Bellacana with big flocks and cattle have been moving through, going from their winter to their summer range and back. They pushed us. We pushed back, we got along, but there were too many animals for the grass and we lost many sheep.

'All the time it's been getting more crowded, and the country seems to be drying up. We had a small flock, and no room to make it larger, but at least we had that, and a spring of water and a place where corn would grow. Nobody is rich out there, but we got along. Then last winter new people came with thousands of sheep, all belonging to someone who lives to the south, they say. They were marked so.' He drew a crude BL on the ground.

'People who used to be friendly became hostile at that time. The police kept bothering us. There was trouble over water-holes, and a lot of talk about Indians stealing horses and stock. They said we had moved into country which was not ours, and soldiers ought to come and move us back.'

His wife spoke from where she knelt, working the dough for tortillas. 'They said that! Since long before there were any Bellacana, my people lived there. Why else do they call it Diné T'ha? It is our first home, the oldest of all.'

Buckskin Man continued: 'Some people did steal a horse or two, I think. Perhaps some butchered a steer or a sheep, to eat or because they were angry. Anyhow, a good many Navajos have been locked up this past year. One time when the judges let two men go, a lot of those people, cowboys, came after them and wanted to kill them right where they lived. They wanted real fighting to start. We got word to the Agency, and some Government men came and put an end to it.

'It's been going that way ever since. And if they can't drive out a man who is holding a watering place, they try to make him sell. That way they came after us.'

He paused and changed his position. There was his wife, turning a tortilla in the pan, and his daughter cutting some meat. They were listening, he wished he could read their minds.

'In the end I gave it to them. I did it, in this way. We had gone up to gather piñón nuts, and I came back to move the sheep. A Mexican came along whom I knew, and he had whiskey. He gave me a drink and pretty soon we drank it all. I rode into town with him to get more. You know how it is.'

One of the men grunted.

'Then they put me in jail. When I was sober but still sick, they took me to the judge. He said I had to pay money. I told him I had none. He said I had sheep. I said no, they were my wife's sheep. That made no difference to him. They took me out there, they rounded up the sheep and drove them in, and said yes, there were just enough.'

'Seventy-five head of *my* sheep,' his wife said.

Trumbull made a mental calculation and said 'Hell!' in English.

'They gave me a paper, and they kept me waiting around that place until the next morning. Then they let me go.'

'Have you the paper still?' Trumbull asked.

'Yes, here it is.'

The delegate studied it, holding it close to the fire while they all watched him.

'It says you paid two hundred and fifty dollars, for doing all sorts of things. Let me keep it. Perhaps the Superintendent can do something about it.'

The man from Tlichisenili said, 'Then what happened?'

'I went home. My wife was still in camp up in the hills, I knew she would be wondering about me. The gate to my cornfield was open — I have a fence around it. Someone had opened the gate. My two horses were in there, and the burro, and some other Navajo horses, and two with Mexican brands. The field was ruined, just as we were ready to harvest. I looked at those brands, I knew them. Those horses had come two hours' ride, all the way from the town, to walk into my cornfield. Horses don't stray like that right to where a gate is open, without any help at all.

'It seemed to me that very soon some men would come back to find them. It has happened before; they would be surprised and they would say I had stolen them. I thought it was best to get right out of there. So I saddled and packed and went straight to where my wife was, then we came along, to see how we are going to live.'

He stared into the fire. 'Any man will drink sometimes. You all have done it, I think. But I did it with my enemies. So my wife lost her sheep, the corn is gone, and we are here.'

Everyone waited for Shooting Singer to speak first. He took several slow puffs on his cigarette, staring at the ground between his drawn-up knees.

'We here, what can we do for the people out there? Nothing, I think. If we fight, in the end the soldiers will come. Perhaps you councilmen can do something, if the Washington Chief will listen to you. But now, we must help my younger brother here.'

Big Nose spoke angrily. 'We can talk at the council next summer. My grandfather there,' he nodded towards Trumbull, 'can help vote on something. The delegates and alternates from over that way can talk, but will the white men from Washington listen? No, I think. That's how they are. They fought us and beat us, so we obey them. They draw lines on the earth that we can't see, and tell us not to cross them. They find out ways to show that we are doing wrong when all we are doing is sitting still.'

Trumbull, who had heard Big Nose many times, interrupted. 'My grandfather,' he indicated Shooting Singer, 'is right, I think. The first thing is what can we do for this man. He has three horses, a burro, no sheep, no jewelry.'

'His relatives are all around here,' Shooting Singer said. 'They won't go hungry. But nowadays there is very little farming land.'

'My sister has a few sheep belonging to me,' Buckskin Man said. 'About twenty, I think. They came to her last spring.' He avoided a direct reference to his mother's death.

'I'll go see her tomorrow. But you can't live off a little bunch like that unless you can keep all the young ewes for several years, building it up. How is the grass here? Is there room?'

'Not on the summer range,' Big Nose said. 'There is no room there.'

'Can I get work for money? Does any trader near here need a man to chop wood and haul things?'

Trumbull said, 'I think not. Do you know anything about motors?'

'Only to ride off the road when I see one coming. Is there any farming land?'

Following Warriors swung the big pot full of mutton and squash out from the fire. Piles of tortillas and two coffee-pots flanked it. Everyone changed positions. The pleasant dominance of food broke the talk. Buckskin Man felt the satisfaction of seeing his two children cramming themselves, and knowing that for a little while, at least, they were secure.

The man from Tlichisenili had said almost nothing. Now, while he chewed with steady thoroughness, he frowned in thought. His name was Cottonwood Leader. He was a strongly made Navajo of middle age, with a square-cut face, not at all clever-looking, and a definite, strong jaw and stubborn set of mouth. A thin black moustache gave him a sad look. With his second cup of coffee he came to a conclusion. He washed a chunk of tortillas down with a loud sup, then looked hard at Buckskin Man.

'You're a farmer, grandfather?' he asked.

'Yes. I can really farm.'

'Perhaps I can do something for you. I like to run cattle, I don't mind sheep, but I do get tired of hoeing corn. Up back of Tlichisenili we have a big cornfield. We keep working at it, the four of us up there, because my wife doesn't want to let it go; but I'm busy with the stock, I need my son to help me ride herd, and my daughter for the sheep. It's good summer range up there; when the snow flies, we move down below. You can bring your sheep, and if you'll really farm it, really work it, we can share what you raise. When the children marry, though, if they stay home it is theirs, you understand?'

Big Nose said: 'It's good land, yellow. There is a seep at one end, an industrious man could store the water and then spread it over the field from time to time. But it's big.'

'How big?'

Cottonwood Leader considered. 'From this hogahn, more than halfway to where you came down onto the flat.'

A very big field. Buckskin Man looked at his hard hands. Twenty head of sheep. He glanced towards his wife, meeting her eyes briefly.

'All right, my friend. I'll farm it for you.'

'We'll be moving down in about ten days. Come up before then and look at it.'

Cottonwood Leader rolled himself a cigarette, then tossed the makings over. He drew a twig with a red end from the fire, puffed, and leant back.

'There's another thing about the white men,' he said. 'They took my son to school — eight years ago now. He was at Tsaili, and they wouldn't let him come home till three summers ago. Then they moved him down to Tlinj Tletsoi. How can I get him back from there? If I had him, I might not need any help.'

'My daughter has been going to school,' Buckskin Man said, 'but not any more. We're through with those ways. We want to be left alone, that's all. I don't want her going around with an American name. She has her true name, and the one that people call her; then they gave her another that I can't ever remember.'

'Et'el Harding,' his wife said.

The girl looked down and smiled slightly.

He stated with slow emphasis, 'Let my son speak no English.'

'You're right,' Big Nose said. 'Keep away from all their things, I say.'

Shooting Singer moved his hand emphatically. 'We need the schools, I think. We need to know what they know, so that they can't take advantage of us any longer. We must be as wise as they are; we can do that and still be Navajos, I think. Look at my brother over there; we didn't pick him for delegate because he had a white father. It was because he took pains to learn their ways and their secret weapons, and still he is ours, a Navajo. That is the best, I think.'

Trumbull agreed. 'That's true, I think. If this man understood English, if he knew about their rules and their tricks, they would not have been able to take his sheep. Lots of times you can trap the white man in his own rules, if you know about them.'

Big Nose answered: 'That boy is learning all our friend here says, all you spoke of. He came home twice, but now he is out of reach. What kind of Navajo will he be when we get him back? Like the others, you have to bring him up all over again, if he doesn't come dying of the coughing sickness.'

'My son is staying Navajo,' Cottonwood Leader said. 'I gave him his medicine bag before he left Tsaili; he takes pollen each time they make him go to their medicine lodge.'

The medicine man sighed. 'I have a nephew who has not been home in ten years. He is hardly a Navajo now, I fear. How can we bring them home?'

'That's our ignorance again,' Trumbull answered. 'Washington has rules about sending them home, only we don't know how to make them follow their own rules.'

He was watching Cottonwood Leader, knowing his limited, yet direct mind and the firmness with which he held to a view once he had taken it in. He swung a big group of Indians up there on top of the mesa, and if they once took up Big Nose's policy of hostility, he, Trumbull, might cease to be delegate.

Cottonwood Leader said, 'What do we do then?' He liked action and definition.

They all looked to the delegate.

'We'll do what we can in the council, of course.'

'Yes, if they'll let you talk about it,' Big Nose interrupted. 'You know how they are sometimes.'

'That's true. But there's something else. Last week I talked with a white woman. She is hired by some white people who want to help the Indians, she goes around finding out things.' He could have translated Indian Welfare Association, but decided not to take the time. 'She is a friend for us, I think. I tell you, she and her people are willing to help us. She goes to Washington, she talks with Washington Chief and with their councilmen there, she says. Those people saved a lot of land for the Pueblos, they say.'

'Who will believe a Bellacana will help us?' the alternate remarked.

Shooting Singer answered, 'We all know white men we like and trust.'

Cottonwood Leader said, 'True. Fat Man at Ozei, for instance, and Red Face at the Agency.'

'It won't hurt us to try, I think,' Trumbull said. 'This woman and I talked a long time. She is good, I think. Now I shall write her a letter, and you two, each of you, write to her.'

'Why don't you write them for us?' Cottonwood Leader asked.

'Perhaps she might think I made them all up. Each of you get someone to do it for you. I'll write out her name for you to have copied. Say that you want your son, your nephew, to go to school, but you want them to know their families, too. Then bring them to me, and I'll send them along. That way we can try out that woman and see what she is for.'

Shooting Singer's hand fell forward in hearty agreement. 'You say well. Let us do it.' Turning, he smiled at Buckskin's Daughter. 'You have been to school, granddaughter?'

She answered with a shy 'Yes.'

He smiled more broadly. 'You will write my letter for me.'

The girl looked at her hands in her lap, confused and pleased. The older people glanced towards her kindly.

Following Warriors said: 'Yes, let the women go to school, I say. They need to know what it's all about. You men ——— ' She stared at Trumbull. 'You vote on things in the council, then you have to come home and explain — if you can. Like all that talk about sheep last year. Whose sheep? Of any ten, nine belong to us women. We need to go ahead with you, I think. You men stand out in front, you talk and you decide things, but suppose you decided something that *all* the women think is wrong ——— '

She laughed, and the others joined her.

The medicine man considered her words. 'Good. It is good. Let her go to school, too, let her go on learning. She is one who should. Mine is too old now.'

He glanced towards his thirteen-year-old girl, seeing in her a young woman all but ripe for marriage.

Singing Beads said slowly, 'The men and the women must go ahead together, just as they share each other's mistakes together.' Her eyes rested briefly on her husband's face. 'As long as the women stand behind the men when they are trying to do better, in the end we shall be all right, I think.' She looked around the hogahn as if to see if anyone disagreed with her, met her husband's eyes again for a moment, and then stared into the fire.

Buckskin Man's face relaxed for the first time that evening. For the moment he forgot how tired he was, and he noticed the comfort of the sheepskins on which he sprawled. There was a big cornfield to be farmed, there was much hard work to do, and he was the man to do it.

CHAPTER FIVE

WITH the softness of springlike touches on all his skin, Myron raked slowly at the gravel road. The rake had become infinitely heavy, manipulated by equally heavy arms. His eyes, staring at the roadbed, reported red and grey crushed stone over yellow clay to an unreceptive mind. He was thinking hard, figuring ——

A girl's laughter jerked his thoughts awry. One was always seeing and hearing them, always remote from them. There were two, Apaches, walking arm in arm across the campus. One of them laughed again. He had thought it was Sally Lanman.

Now the line of thought was gone, something in which he had been utterly absorbed so that the loss of it was painful. Going to bat and not striking out — the team — football — Haskell and playing against real college elevens — telling Walter Nanta what he really thought of him — no — it was lost, completely lost. He was aware of gravel and rake and self again. Why are girls so obtrusive? He moved farther along the road. Sally was a good Christian, he watched her in Sunday School and liked the way she talked. Neat always, and in class... He had hardly exchanged a word with her, she did not really exist in his mind as a person but as the crystallization of this general disturbance of girls which coloured the emotional background of football, prominence, success.

He had finished the driveway. Resting on his rake handle, he looked over the job to make sure it would pass. By the

westering sun there was still nearly an hour till supper bell.
He walked slowly past the main row of buildings to the toolhouse.

You oughtn't to think too much about girls. Some of the
boys never forgot about them, some of them sneaked out at
night to do dirty things. Sometimes the watchman caught
them, then there was punishment. Last winter a girl got
pregnant, whispering disgrace and shame. The thing to do
was to keep a clean mind and wait to be grown up and marry.

At the toolhouse Mr. O'Brien said, 'All done?'

'Yessir.'

'An easy job, hunh? Well, I'll look at it later. Mr. Snyder
wants to see you.'

'Now?'

He had planned to go watch the team practising, solitude
and idleness lying on the warm grass, with the undemanding
occupation of the thrown ball, the bat and the moving figures.

'Yeah. He's over at the mission. Run along.'

'O.K.'

He didn't mind seeing Mr. Snyder, neither did he go
readily as he would have to Mr. Butler. There had been
some trouble about his entry into the tribal fights, but that
had blown over, and when the men from the Board visited
Yellow Earth in March, the missionary presented him as a
hopeful worker in the vineyard, and the best English-talker
in school. They had a special hour of English study together
Tuesday afternoons. It got him out of work that day, but
he hoped it wouldn't continue in football season.

Mr. Snyder met him at the door with 'Come in, Myron,
I want to talk to you.'

The boy felt that something was wrong, the tone of latent
condemnation. When he was told to sit down and make
himself comfortable, he settled stiffly onto the edge of a chair,
facing the desk. It was more difficult than when one stood,
to watch the white man's face without revealing one's eyes.

'A little healthy adventurousness is natural to boys, but

we who are responsible for you have to keep tabs on what you do, you know. I want you to talk to me frankly, Myron, and don't fear blame. That's not what I'm after.'

It was a bad, familiar type of opening, known in the school as scouting. You find out where to attack without alarming the victim, then, when you know all about it, comes the war-cry. Myron studied the front of the desk.

'Don't be afraid to talk to me about boyish fun. I sympathize heartily. I know boys — have to. After my years here, if I didn't know and like boys, I'd have gone crazy.' Snyder smiled at his own levity. 'You children have educated me.'

Myron looked at the two big, stubby hands clasped on top of the green blotter. He didn't risk a glimpse of the face just then, because this line of talk made one feel wrong inside.

'Do you understand?'

'Yessir.'

'I want you to tell me what you and Jack do on Sundays.'

Myron didn't attempt to answer.

'Come, now, tell me about it.'

'Nuttin.'

'*Nothing*,' he corrected. 'Hardly that. You don't have to have any hesitation with me, you know. Tell me about it.'

'Go in de woods.'

The painful extraction of information from an Indian, fragment by fragment, was always irritating to Snyder.

'You light fires, don't you?'

'Yessir.'

Myron couldn't imagine anything wrong in their camping, but it was a violation to tell white adults about it, and one never knew what might turn out forbidden.

'What do you do with those fires?'

'Nuttin.'

'Don't say "nuttin" to me! You're being indirect, and I don't like to see it. A manly boy answers straight out. What do you do?'

'Cook someting.'

'What do you cook?'

'Rabbits, or maybe squirrels.'

'How do you get them?'

'Trap dem.'

'Come, now, don't you — ah — swipe a little food from the commissary or the kitchen?'

'No, sir.' It was a definite answer.

'I want the truth, Myron. Don't you?'

'No, sir.'

Mr. Snyder laid that aside. 'Where do you get your matches?'

'Don't have no matches.'

'Myron! Don't lie to me like that. *Where do you get them?*'

'Don't use no matches.'

'What do you mean?'

Myron decided to get this over with. He was telling the truth, and could see nothing to fear.

'We make fire wit ——' he hesitated, unwilling to use an Indian word, not knowing the English. 'Wit ——'

'Yes?'

'You know — *kon bitsin* ——' He made a motion of rubbing and pressing.

'Fire drill?'

'Yessir.'

'Where did you boys learn that?' Snyder's voice had become entirely suave.

'Dat man — dat Apache — over dere beyond de school, he taught us.'

'Old Ishteen?'

'Yessir.'

'You've been visiting that medicine man?'

'He didn't tell us no medicine. He just showed us how to use dem, dose sticks.'

The answer was honest but not quite true. Ishteen had

told some stories, spoken of the sacred meaning of the fire-kit, but Myron had resolutely disregarded all that.

Mr. Snyder said, almost pouncing, 'So you and Jack made new fire ceremonies?'

Myron did not know what he was talking about, and neither did he.

'No, sir. We just make a fire to cook rabbits.'

'Is that all?'

'Yessir.'

'You mustn't be afraid to be frank with me. I'm trying to be your friend. Don't you make medicine of any kind with that fire drill?'

There is a frustration in telling the truth and being disbelieved, in being urged towards a false confession.

'No, sir. We cooked rabbits. We used dat drill because we didn't have no matches.'

'Didn't have *any* matches.'

'Yessir.'

Mr. Snyder drummed on the desk, looking baffled and annoyed. Since he didn't mention forbidding their expeditions, Myron concluded correctly that he's already been to the Superintendent and Mr. Vail had turned him down.

Vail had said that life at a school like this was drab enough anyhow without depriving two good boys of so healthy and natural a pastime. For the hundredth time he told Snyder to go ahead and get him fired if he could. If the missionary could only produce proof of wrongdoing and negligence, he could end a long-standing feud. Perhaps he could get rid of the Tease boy too; something doubtful about his Christianity, a visible defiance, if one could get hold of tangible proof...

'You're a Christian, Myron?'

'Yessir.'

'I've always regarded you so. How about your friend Jack?'

'He's Christian.'

If he burnt in hell forever, that was one lie he had to tell.

'Not so good a one as you, I fear.'

'He's all right.' This was dangerous ground.

'He seems a strange choice for your friend. When did you begin to be pals?' The questions were coming aimlessly.

'When we were kids at Tsaili.'

'But why Jack?'

'We slep' in de same bed.'

Snyder's attention focussed. 'This fire-making, when did it start?'

'Last fall.'

'Exactly when?'

'When it snowed dat time.'

'Oh — I think I remember. You came in late and badly mussed up.' The voice was purposeful again.

Myron made no answer. The questioning was unpleasant.

'You made a fire that day?'

'No, sir. We just kinda tought of it.'

'Why?'

'We wanted to get warm.'

'You wanted to get warm?'

'Yessir.'

'What did you do that day?'

'Broke de ice.'

Snyder leaned forward. 'Broke the ice! What do you mean?'

'In de brook. It was froze.'

'Oh,' Snyder said a little flatly. 'Was that all? Was that how you got so mussed?'

'Well, we wrastled.'

The missionary's expression changed, his voice became friendly, almost unctuous. 'Tell me about it, Myron.'

If he explained about Jack's throwing the stone, about trying to put each other in the brook, they might find something wrong in it.

'We just kinda wrastled, you know.'

'I'd think that would make you warm.'

Something unpleasant in the air, in Snyder's voice, not understood but unpleasant.

'We got a lotta snow down our necks. When we quit we were cold.'

'You had your clothes on?' the voice was silk.

'Sure. Gee, it was cold dat day.' Myron showed frank surprise.

'Have you — ah — wrastled much since then?'

'Sometimes.'

The air was sticky and full of evil. He wanted to get out of here.

'By the fire?'

Myron felt bewildered. 'Just — you know — fellers wrastle. To see who's strongest, kinda.'

'A little more now in this nice weather, eh?'

'No, we ain't got time.'

'Why not?'

'We gotta ball and two gloves. We practise.'

Snyder looked angry again. He drummed on the desk. 'We all know that boys your age have their problems. I want you to come to me frankly, without fear. I'm here to help you, not to punish you, so that you can become a fine, clean man and a Christian.' He waited, watching, and smiling spuriously.

'Yessir.'

'Have you told me everything?'

'Yessir.'

'I'm disappointed in you, Myron. I don't like indirectness. I feel that Jack is a poor influence on you. I wish you would drop your dabbling in heathenism, and stop associating with him. I'm thinking of your future.'

'Yessir.'

'Will you promise me?'

Here it was, a trap. 'I ain't doin no headenism.'

'I want you to stop going with Jack, unless you can frankly tell me what passes between you.'

'Nuttin passes. He's my friend.'

'Myron —!' The voice was sharp.

The boy felt desperate, cornered, slightly ill. 'Mr. Butler liked Jack all right. We were friends togedder at Tsaili wit him. Mr. Butler said for me to be a Navajo *and* a Christian, just like you told me to practise up on talkin Navajo.'

He knew that Snyder didn't like to be reminded of the minister, and he knew that his friend was this man's superior. He used the name in last recourse.

Snyder flushed angrily, and checked his first answer. Butler had given this boy specially into his charge, and he knew that they occasionally corresponded.

'I should be sorry to give Doctor Butler a bad report of you,' he said. 'You've turned stubborn. I counsel you to pray, and search your heart, Myron. Later I trust you'll come to me.'

Myron didn't answer.

'You may go now. It's nearly time for the bell. I'm disappointed.'

The boy went out, feeling queer. It was better outdoors. When he went to wash after the bell rang, he avoided Jack in the lavatory; he felt ashamed to speak to him, tomorrow they could talk it over. Mr. Snyder was the missionary, a Christian leader; it was wicked, but now he knew he had hated him a long time. He wished he could see Mr. Butler. Impossible to write about things like this.

CHAPTER SIX

THE Commissioner said, 'I'll send for Doctor Entwistle and we'll see what he has to say.'

While he rang, and gave the order to his secretary, Miss Pitman relaxed in the leather armchair, staring without focus at the notebook in her lap. Washington tired her, the East tired her, although it was delightful to renew one's contacts and see a play once more; above all the Indian Bureau oppressed her, the interminable hall that ran on and on and on, with the close succession of offices opening off each side, the hundreds of typewriters, the memoranda and routing slips, the vast bumbling compilation within which the desperate human needs of the people she knew so well could be lost like a handful of beans thrown into a steam-shovel. When she was among the Indians, learning their specific, visible needs, she was afflicted constantly by the knowledge of this web and the balancing complexity of Congress; when she came here, it seemed as if her head would split for trying to hold, reconcile, express the knowledge of individual Indians, places, tribes, human beings, and the machinery reaching upward to this place and the Capitol, the pressures, confusions, aims, the whole complex world into whose government they were tied.

This man was good, a reform appointment, hopeful. His presence behind the desk where Hartmann used to sit was in part an answer to the discouragement she felt so often about her Association's work. A good man, with no rough, first-hand acquaintance with Indians, or with politics or bureaucracy. She knew that with him as with Hartmann she would partly use evasions, arguments shaped to fit the man. To be able really to tell the thing one saw — her hearer would have to have sprawled in a tipi, eating broiled horseflesh and watching the impetigo-filthy grandchildren of the old chief whose shining essence radiated from where he lay on a piece of quilt, sat in the sun all day to watch the Corn Dance at San Felipe reach its terrific climax, slept on the ground, the only white person save for one stockman among half a hundred Apaches while the night echoed to the lowing thunder of the tribal herd, seen the truckloads of prostitutes coming in for the Tokala Sun Dance . . .

She stared at her notebook, feeling tired, and wondering what could be done.

The Commissioner asked, 'Have you met Entwistle?'

'No, sir. This is my first visit since you came in.'

'Of course. I want you to meet the new people. We need your help.'

She thought she liked his smile, and that he was rather afraid of the task he confronted.

A huge figure blocked the wide doorway into the Commissioner's office. Miss Pitman smothered surprise and amusement at the bulbous fatness of the man which swelled his waist to an equator, reduced the neck to a transition between shoulders and skull, and made of keen, fine features and lively eyes an island of definition in a placid sea of chins and cheeks.

'Doctor Entwistle, this is Miss Pitman, Field Secretary of the Indian Welfare Association. Miss Pitman has brought up a matter for your division.'

The Director of Education shook hands — his grasp was not flabby — then let himself down into a solid chair.

'We need your advice, the benefit of your experience,' he said. 'We're beginners here, and you've had the direct contacts. Criticize us, we need it.'

It was the old bureaucratic gambit, rephrased, she thought. Is its content different? Estimating the eyes, noting the Phi

Beta Kappa key — it certainly is a change from Dilwater, anyhow.

'Will you explain the idea, Miss Pitman?' Commissioner Trubee said. 'It's in line with our policy,' he told Entwistle. 'Miss Pitman is just in from the field, and we're going over her observations.'

'This doesn't just arise from the last trip,' she said. 'It's the question of sending children home during vacations. We've been urging for years that while they are educated, they must maintain family and tribal contacts. The Women's Clubs have been with us, too, but it's been contrary to the Bureau's policy, and of course the missions are against it.'

'I'm entirely for it,' Entwistle told her. 'I'm partly responsible for the recommendations in the Merriam Report, you know.'

Miss Pitman nodded. She had a quick, comical mental picture of this balloon-like man, motoring over reservation roads, rolling, ludicrous and keen, about the corridors and rooms.

'The denatured Indian youth is a botched job,' Entwistle said, 'a palimpsest on which both writings blur each other. But we can't do much until we elevate our personnel, you know. We hope to get all the educational positions reclassified, with stiffer requirements and increased pay, as soon as we can persuade the Bureau of the Budget. Tell me, what does this business of keeping children at school in the summers amount to?'

'It's variable. You know, with all your rules and regulations, the Indian Service is astoundingly haphazard. Lack of provision for notifying parents or providing transportation, the personal bias of a superintendent, some outside pressure, or plain laziness, may keep one or many children away from home. It's disorganized, it's not explicit, but it amounts to an established policy affecting — well — perhaps twenty per cent in the non-reservation schools.'

'Will transportation involve heavy costs?' Trubee asked.

'It's late in the session for getting more money, and we'll have our troubles over the reclassifications Entwistle spoke of as it is. We don't want to risk those, you know.'

'It won't cost very much. In many cases you simply need to emphasize your policy, and make sure that school superintendents communicate with reservation superintendents, and make them, the reservation men, responsible for co-operation. Here's a case in point ——' She took some sheets of paper from her brief case. 'Here's a call by Navajos in the interior of the Northern Jurisdiction for return of children from Yellow Earth. Yellow Earth runs trucks to Gallup, and children living near there are met, so they go home. If Mr. Ensharp were required to send a truck to get his Northern Jurisdiction children, the excuse for keeping them would be removed.' She detailed the work and costs involved.

'What do you think, Entwistle?'

'This is just what we want. We can do it on our regular educational budget, and Miss Pitman gives us the kind of specific case in point we need for answering merely obstructive objections. You know,' he turned to the Field Secretary, 'a bureaucracy like this has a genius for blocking change by a sort of cotton-wool resistance.'

'I know well. I'll leave these letters with you, Mr. Commissioner. I wish you'd notice the three Navajo ones, on the top there. Do you know Steven Trumbull?'

'No, is he a Navajo?'

'Yes, one of the best of their councilmen. Will you attend the meeting this summer?'

'I'm looking forward to it.'

'I hope you'll give them greater freedom than they've had heretofore, to discuss what they want. They're reasonable people. You'll meet him there. I've met Shooting Singer, too, whose X is on one of the accompanying letters. He's a medicine man and an older leader — what the schoolboys call an unspeaking English Indian. When men like him and educated mixed-bloods like Trumbull unite in desiring education, and wanting it to serve the tribe as a whole, you've got something valuable that should be encouraged.'

The Commissioner nodded. 'These are dated 1928.'

'I took the matter up last fall with Hartmann, but got nowhere. Here it's April twentieth — can something be done in time for this summer?'

'I think so. Entwistle, if you and Cumbermore will work out an order and the proper procedures ——'

'All right, sir.'

Cumbermore was a good man, but long service had ingrained delay in his system. Miss Pitman said, 'May I sit with you while you work it out?'

'Please do,' Entwistle urged.

A buzzer sounded on the big desk. The Commissioner looked at the clock. 'I've some Congressmen waiting, about the Choctaw trust allotments. If you'll go with Entwistle now, I'll see you again about three-thirty.'

'That's fine. I want to talk to you about that Choctaw business, too.'

She went out with the educator. A thing like this would have to pass over at least six desks for initialling before it reached the Commissioner again. She decided that if it was to go through before next winter, she'd have to carry it around from desk to desk herself. What a to-do over one small reform, and the great things untouched, land being stolen by the millions of acres, that Navajo boundary business in New Mexico, the Osage scandals, sickness, poverty and despair... Building a house out of pebbles, one by one, but after eight years, looking back, one could see the gains.

Entwistle found a memorandum on his desk, and turned to her smiling. 'We've got our new food appropriation, you'll be glad to hear. Thirty-six cents per child per day; not as much as we would have liked, but at least it's as good as the army gets.'

Miss Pitman nodded. With this administration, perhaps one could really get something done.

CHAPTER SEVEN

As THEY sat in the truck, the hard board floor pounded upwards at them with each successive bump. It made fatiguing riding, but the four children — Myron Begay, Jack Tease, Carson Sanders, and Janice Peshlakai — didn't mind it much. Late in the day, with the sun crowding hot upon them and the dust swirling, they made themselves as lax as possible and were quiet, watching the country pass by.

Myron had forgotten how dried up it was, how desert. Yellow Earth had the pines behind it and perennial streams from the mountains; it was a fair cattle country of sparse but constant grass. The smaller mountains the truck was skirting now were green way up, they said. This was the dry time of year, till the he-rains began in *Ya'ish Jashtsoh. Ya'ish Jashtsoh* — he counted by moving his fingers slightly — July. The Navajo month-name surprised him, he hadn't known he knew it.

This whole business was surprising, upside down. Washington ordered them to go home, the Commissioner's circular posted on the bulletin board with big words one could hardly make out. They wanted the children to know their families — 'tribal life... cultural heritage.' Was Washington backsliding?

And his uncle had written a letter. When Mr. Vail told him, it had sounded grotesquely unreasonable till the wavering cross and 'Shooting Singer, his Mark' at the foot of the smudged, pencilled page explained the thing. So Na'atoi Hatatli was Shooting Singer. *Hatatli* — singer — well, all right. It meant the prayers and offerings and sand-pictures and all those things. Whoever wrote that letter was plenty ignorant. I'll write to Mr. Vail by and by, he'll like it. This is a desert all right. What does a sheep eat? The tiniest hidden green, unpromising leaves of shrubs, the minutest cover of the earth, the sheep moving and searching in the hot noon while a tired child watches and dozes... no more of her or that man, one good thing about this. My uncle. The letter said, 'His mother shis married some man. And gone some place we doent know wehr is she.' A good thing, changing life, taking a shadow off the thought of his home-land. If he wants to write any more letters, I'll do them for him, real good — real well.

Mr. Snyder correcting his English. Mr. Snyder thought this going home was awful, but Mr. Vail was glad. I like Mr. Vail. Mr. Snyder wants to get him fired, but he can't do it, is Washington backsliding, new Commissioner, I won't see Mr. Snyder for three months with my uncle not that man. Ride down to Tsaili Mr. Butler and get straightened out.

Carson and Janice got out at Ja'abani. Myron watched the meeting with primitive-looking parents, the shy communication, and the changing things in the boy's and girl's faces. A man with untidy hair, dressed in faded work-shirt and torn overalls, another wearing a battered, dirty hat, one mother's threadbare shawl, moccasins. Carson's parents were poor. My turn next. Uncle became unknown, strangeness, the truck jolted onward, steady engine and wheels moving without thought or feeling irresistibly to an unknown life.

Jack pointed with his lips. 'Jil Tlijini.' The tiredness went out of his dust-streaked face and his eyes danced.

The prow of Black Mesa's fifty-mile encircling mass rose along the southwestern quarter of the horizon, moving slowly to its old, rightful place as the sunset rim of the known world. Myron remembered.

'I wonder if they have my horse,' Jack said. 'If they

didn't round him up this spring, he may have drifted anywhere. Well, I'll get him, if I have to walk clear to the
Mokis. I'm going to learn to rope from him this summer,
like a cowboy.'

Jack always knew what he wanted, he wasn't bothered
about anything. He made up his mind long ago and he
stayed right with it. That medicine bag. Jack was strong.
Now he was here, they'd never get him back to school.

Major familiar formations moved to encircle them, unexpectedly returning into a life that had been clearly marked
off, threatening the simple division of the world into futile
Indians and all-powerful whites. Out of the depths of the
reservation his uncle and Cottonwood Leader had sent letters,
compelling an event within the white man's precincts at
Yellow Earth. If his uncle hadn't written, the mission would
have sent him to stay with Mr. McCarty, the Navajo missionary, far south of here. The helpless could speak and overrule.
Mr. Vail and Mr. Snyder politely snarling at one another;
each had said 'The new Commissioner,' but in entirely different tones. Perhaps the white man didn't know his own mind.
You try to understand the whole world and it mixes you up.
Jack just knows what he wants.

The stone building, with its tin roof, warehouse, corral,
nestled under the four cottonwoods against the green-striped,
dull red bluff. Scrawny horses dozing at the hitching-rail,
two wagons, Indians sitting against the wall. His interior
drew back, not fear, not embarrassment: imminence of unknown factors about to enter and change his life, his being.
There his uncle and aunt rose and came a few steps towards
the truck, then stood waiting. He got out after Jack.

His feet moved slowly as he took himself towards them.
Jack far outstripped him, he saw his friend and his father and
mother examine each other with half smiles, then the hands
touching, speech, and flashing happiness. His own relatives
waited with pleasant gravity. Indians, they just looked like
Indians, like old Ishteen. His aunt's skirt was wrinkled and

sun-faded. How much older she'd grown! Shooting Singer
wore an old, green shirt with the tails hanging free. The
jewelry, the hair, the faces, made the real quality of their
appearance, but he wasn't ready for that yet.

His uncle said, 'Nephew,' and she, 'My child.'

The boy was accustomed, had braced himself, to white
adults' intrusive greetings and immediate curiosity. He relaxed before his relatives' undemanding easiness. 'Ten snows-
returning,' his uncle was saying, the familiar voice, the man
in no way changed. His past being as a little boy extended
mood and attitude into his present. Ten years. His aunt
brought out from under her shawl a paper bag of stick candy,
the green-and-white ones he had always preferred. She
laughed as she said, 'Have you stopped liking these?' her
lightness and a shade of almost shyness removing any resent-
ment in a big boy at recall of a child's tastes. He was hungry,
candy is a rare thing always. It had always been like this
and they had not forgotten. Still protected within himself,
he took a stick with a brief 'Good.' They also chose sticks.
Sort of — well — backward, grownups sucking candy. Indian, of course.

Shooting Singer said, 'Let us go along, or we'll be driving
in the night. Do you want to buy anything here?'

'No.'

The question had been put as to an adult, without con-
descension. He climbed into the wagon. Ahead lay the
hogahn, more long-haired people, strangenesses to meet. He
guarded himself before the unknown, but it might be all right.

2

It centred in waking; consciousness came differently. First
there was the fact of being, the emergence from obliviousness
before his own identity had collected itself and separated him
from the universe. Then custom and identity came together,
and drowsy habit was confused by a sense of clarity and

sweetness, a deep well-being which it was hard to analyze. He would have begun to gather himself for the many persons of the dormitory and the rush to the showers, but now he felt the soft, snug blanket against his cheek with no intervening cotton, and the hardness beneath him. The facts of sheep-skins, camp, his cousin's voice saying something in Navajo and his aunt replying, rushed at him together and his thoughts cohered. He opened his eyes, staring lazily at a bush near his head, hardly visible in the darkness, and knowing just what the red fire looked like behind him. He didn't have to jump up in a hurry, and when he did start, there were only his shoes to put on. His mouth tasted sweet. It was cold still, the air on his face was better than water.

He'd been astonished when everyone moved his bedding outside the first night, he'd slept badly, and been astonished again at the hour of arising. Now it all made sense, and he was pleased at his own contentment as he lay there, feeling that he had mastered a part of outdoor life.

He rose, put on his cold shoes, and ran a brisk circle to get his blood going, then seated himself on the edge of the camp circle. Shooting Singer made his dawn-prayer and scattered pollen. That was all right, that was part of all this newness, he'd stopped inwardly protesting at the practice of Navajo religion around him, by a process as unconscious as getting used to sitting on the ground.

Now was a precious time, while the east grew silver and the fire still counted. There was the promise and almost the vision of ecstasy, an inaudible music which one never gave up hope of hearing, which would all go as soon as it was merely day. Shooting Singer's low voice and the ritual gestures of his hand belonged with it. At the end, he would smile at Myron. The boy might not believe in the form, but he could share the goodwill. Myron responded, and they sat together, waiting for coffee, companionable. His uncle gave him the directness of man to man, instead of the slanting, man-under-standing-boys of white adults.

He was himself, his own age and bigness as he sat there no longer feeling strange. The distorted memories of long ago had gone from the colour of his perceptions.

He didn't notice that desert life was routine and monotonous, time flowed so quietly, with no one bringing Sunday up once a week, Monday with its special routines, followed by Tuesday, making the days click as they went by, ticking out the hours. If ten identical days passed, it was because he hadn't made any effort to make them different. His hair needed cutting, his pants were dirty, he ate enormous quantities of meat and slept blissfully. In small irregularities, casualness, and ample solitude his spirit spread out.

An Indian at sixteen is just feeling himself, beginning to have a voice in things, considering marriage, strutting, the age in ancient times of war parties to show that one is a warrior. The young bloods roundabout were backward and ignorant, but they didn't know it. You couldn't even begin to make them see what it was to be a first string, triple-threat halfback. His blue-and-orange football jersey was just a handsome shirt to them. But they could ride easily when the saddle had him all one ache, they could stay on horses that pitched him off without half trying. Sheepherding was work for women and children, but a man was expected to know about the animals upon which livelihood depended. He ought to be weather-wise, to read signs and tracks, to remember any trail he had once been over. The country roundabout was full of good companions his own age, suspicious of him, friendly, quick to ridicule, able wrestlers, fast runners, strong at rock-throwing, and interested in high-jumping when he showed them about it.

They got him on to Yellow Head's burro and the snaky little beast sent him spinning. He rose from the rock, touching his agonized behind, trying to grin and seeing them laughing and wanting to punch someone's head. Skinny Boy put a hand on his shoulder.

'Don't mind it, my friend. It happens to us all sooner or later.'

The words and Skinny Boy's friendly voice answered his lonely anger. He saw — what he already knew — that the laughter wasn't hostile, and he made up his mind again that he could and would catch up with them all.

'My backside is destroyed,' he said.

'That's all right,' Travels Around told him. 'It's what's in front that matters.'

'Well, let's do something easy for a little while.'

He taught them mumblety-peg, and saw that they laughed just as hard when the jack-knife cut Travels Around's finger, and Silversmith's Son cut his lip.

He walked along towards Skinny Boy's hogahn, idling on the way because he was just a little bit afraid, although he wouldn't admit it to anyone. The trail went through the hollow between two waves of truly orange sand that seemed in motion. Examining the smooth sides of the dunes, he noticed the fine, neat network of tiny tracks, lizards and birds and insects, over the surface. The tracks were small and perfect; how could such little beasts do anything so clever? And where were they? The place was bare of life, and yet a steady traffic had decorated it. Searching along, he found one bug toiling uphill, the six legs driving the big body in its hard, shiny shell, each leg labouring. There was slow solemnity in the steps, occasional hesitation, as if with so many legs it was hard to remember which one moved next. Its tail — or the tips of its wings under the armour, he guessed — dragged a little, making two blurred lines always perfectly parallel, with the dots on each side of them, close together, absolutely even. That was a lot of heavy work to leave so delicate a trace. You look stupid, but you must know something, he thought. Harder than Following Warriors making a blanket, and nothing to show for it in the end — the wind wipes it out, or I can. He stooped, his hand spread, then decided not to.

He picked up a stick and tickled the bug, it fell over on its back, and had a hard time getting on its feet again. He tickled it once more. It raised its shell and flew off heavily under transparent wings. He grinned after it. Yes, you certainly do know something. Only why not fly to begin with? He walked on, chewing the stick. It can't fly much, I guess, so it saves it up. Yeah, like me walking; I can ride all right, only I save up.

Beyond the orange dunes he came out on a whitish flat with scattered, scrubby bushes. The glare of reflected light made him squint; he looked up and rested his eyes on the hovering mountains to eastward. A jackrabbit crossed his trail in a hurry, then he saw a brown ball of tumbleweed rolling in the faint breeze. It moved, rested, and moved like a living thing. He remembered a story about that, about the war of the eagles against the tumbleweed and the bees. The Navajo ended it by setting the tumbleweed on fire. He wondered if it would really burn, and turned off the trail. Another puff of wind rolled it again; he sprinted, then threw himself on the tangled plant like falling on a football. Of course it crumpled under him. He set a match to some of it, and it did burn.

He went on, wishing he had a ball to practise with. Then he could show those boys something. He went through the motions of a drop-kick and looked around to make sure no one was watching. Then he repeated it. Long ago, *alkidango*, in ancient times the Navajos had a sort of football game, they said. Half soccer and half slugging. You could make up an all-Navajo team. No, long hair would be tough in a scrimmage. You just couldn't manage with long hair. But you could make up a team of schoolboys — sure — all the schools. Wingate had a good team, and half of Yellow Earth's was Navajo, and that centre at Phoenix, and boys from Albuquerque and Santa Fé. He began to walk faster, excited, imagining a champion, all-Navajo team. Those Papagos think they're good, and the Apaches — well ... He thought of Haskell and Riverside, the grown men who played colleges, and suddenly he lost his captaincy to those adults. His imagination dodged the obstacle two ways, supposing a team limited to boys under eighteen, and then dropping immediate captaincy but thinking of how even at a hundred and forty pounds a fast-dodging back, a drop-kicker and long, accurate passer, could make his place. The score tied and a deadlock and the lightweight boy who originally got the team organized trots onto the field against Southern California. A drop-kicker. Open formation, and they use the trick Harvard played with Brickley, only he throws a pass. Triple threat. Without getting details clear, he had the ball and was diving into a line plunge beside the goal posts, the white boys rearing up against the line and a hole between guard and tackle, his stiff-arm right into the face of a big, blond college boy, the astonished white man's eyes and the goal line under foot... Jim Thorpe saying...

He realized that he was almost running, and his arm was curved to snuggle the ball. He slowed down, feeling self-conscious. Silly to figure out ideas like that, kid stuff. For those moments he had been important, outstanding, and the return to actuality was a letdown.

The shelter of brush and canvas came into sight ahead of him. On the nearer side of it, in a flat area of brownish soil, the young corn grew in scattered, juicy, green clumps. Behind it rose a long bluff of heavy, dark red sand streaked here and there with almost white, acid blue-green. Above that the sky was clear and hard. He identified Skinny Boy in the field, wielding a hoe with slow, idling strokes.

The sight brought up the imminence of what he had come for, and his mind stopped roving. Skinny Boy leant on the hoe, smiling, waiting for him.

'How much do you hoe in a day?' Myron asked.

'Enough to leave some for tomorrow.' The long-hair looked around the field. It was in good shape, and weeds were few. 'A little now and a little then, and pray for rain. Did you come to help me?'

'My uncle has a field, too.'

'You'll go back to school with hard hands, perhaps.'

'Perhaps. I want to ride the bay horse again.'

'*Hallahani!* You never give up.'

'I'll stay on him yet.'

Skinny Boy grinned broadly and his eyes danced. 'Come on.'

At the hogahn, Skinny Boy's mother joked Myron over his persistence, and he answered with bravado, feeling the real approval back of it. His friend went out with rope and bridle, and soon came back leading an ordinary little pony. He picked up his saddle, discarded the saddle blanket that was with it, saying it was too worn, and threw another, a red-and-green one, over the horse.

'Hold its head,' he told Myron.

The animal shied away from the saddle, started to rear when it was cinched, then quieted. They led it away from the hogahn, out onto the flat. Myron felt the excited, scared feeling again. He was making himself go ahead, and at the same time nothing could have stopped him. Skinny Boy held the horse by nose and ear; even so it circled and was hard to mount, and started fighting as soon as Myron's weight bore on the nigh stirrup. Skinny Boy let go, and the bay went off with four stiff, jolting leaps. Myron got the time of them all right, and stayed with it, then the animal changed, a sideways motion which the rider could not analyze, and he knew he was losing his seat. He felt suddenly floppy and afraid, he knew he was going. With the next buck they parted company. Myron thought he flew for yards in the air, and knew he came down on his shoulder and back with an awful thump.

Sitting up, he saw the horse still twisting and bucking, fighting its saddle, and wondered how he could have stayed on at all. Skinny Boy was running with his rope, trying to head it off. Stiffly he rose to help him. When they caught it, it was wild, and they had to manoeuvre cautiously to get at the cinch. The instant that was loosened the horse quieted; when its back had been cleared of gear, it was just a rather nervous pony, sweating hard.

An idea struck Myron. He was always given that red-and-green saddle blanket. He took it up and examined the under side. Two enormous burrs were lodged there. He turned, holding it in front of him.

'Owl! Coyote! Chindi! By golly! You ——' Words failed him and he stood staring.

Skinny Boy was grinning at him. 'Don't be angry.'

'Angry —! This ——' he shook the blanket.

'Well, you wanted so badly to learn to sit one, and there isn't any good bucking horse hereabouts. Only just this one, and he won't buck unless you give him a reason.'

The utter simplicity with which it was said disarmed him. The joke was on him; if he wasn't careful it would be tied to him. He pushed down his anger.

'But the horse — that hurts the poor horse.'

'Oh, not much. It's only for a little while. Anyhow, it isn't much of a horse.'

Myron wanted to laugh, and at the same time he was still angry. To save his face, there was only one way to take it.

'All right. I'll stay on him next time.'

His friend laughed, and there was admiration in his delight. The bridle had got entangled with a low clump of greasewood into which it had been let fall. When Skinny Boy stooped to get it loose, Myron saw that he had one foot inside the loop of the lariat. He took two quick steps, caught the end of it, and jerked. Skinny Boy went into the bush with a thump. Then he felt all right, it was out of his system. They walked back to the hogahn, side by side, thinking of lunch.

CHAPTER EIGHT

H E PROWLED around the fires and behind the wagons, until he came to a rise of ground, where he could see it all, and be sheltered in the darkness, and think. Three days ago he rode the bay horse to a standstill, that was a landmark. He had a right to tip his hat forward and walk strutting, with his hands in the front pockets of his overalls, like the other young men down there, to talk and sing with them and pretend not to notice the girls.

The big fire was in front of him on the far side of the dancing-space, hard by it the bunch of forty-odd singing men behind the drummer. In front of them and the fire the dancers moved, paired men and girls circling and turning gravely, now clearly lighted, now vague in the darkness. Mounted men, wagons, smaller individual fires, the shapeless medicine hogahn of fresh cedar, formed a surrounding wall. The songs rose up like something visible, high and shining over the gathering. The great emptiness of the desert night was all around; where Myron stood at a little distance, he was enclosed in it. Its flavour was in the gay ceremony, for the Navajos did not drive it out, but they and their fires and their songs belonged in an endless, wild country and were one with it, having no wish for walls.

He had forgotten about the singing. At Yellow Earth he had occasionally heard the heavy, droning Apache music, less exciting than a really good hymn. He swelled with the superiority of his own people. Some of the singers were no older than he, most had never been to school and even a few of the youngest wore long hair; there was no other first-string back from a big school. He wanted to belong. He liked the taste of manhood.

Heathen ceremonies. Mr. Snyder would question him, as a boy not yet fit to ordain his life or speak to a girl. Mr. Snyder prying, violating. I'll ride to Tsaili as soon as this is over. Mr. Butler and his teachings blurred and confused with much thinking over in three years. He might say — but backsliding. Perhaps Washington is backsliding. He didn't know the songs, only a few of them, distantly remembered, recaptured. This one now — yes — *lé-on lé-on lé-on lé-on é-ya* ... He moved his shoulders in rhythm. Mr. Snyder doesn't count. A letter from the backwoods overruled him, Washington overruled him.. *E né-ya yan é-yan a.* At the edge of the firelight a girl was pulling a young man from his horse. She was small and the man held fast, until another girl came to help her and he dismounted to keep from being dragged down under the animal. Myron saw why white people laughed about it, at the same time the formula, the man letting himself be dragged slowly by his blanket, made sense. A man doesn't want to seem anxious about girls. *Lé-on lé-on lé-on lé-on é-ya.* That was Jack she got. He must have come down from Tlichisenili. Bet he doesn't go back to school. The fires made a limited area of light, but the drum reached out and filled the world, through it the Navajos and the night were joined with a single heartbeat. He moved his shoulders and shifted from foot to foot for warmth, keeping time. This was vacation, it wasn't forever. September would settle everything by ending it. You don't have to figure it all out. He walked towards the crowd.

Jack paid his girl off and went back to his horse. He peered at the man standing by his stirrup, the two of them examined each other with widening smiles before their hands touched. Jack said, '*Hallahani!*' with real pleasure.

'I hoped you might be here,' he said, 'only I wasn't sure you'd come.'

'My uncle was helping in there.' Myron jerked his head towards the medicine hogahn.

'Come on, let's get in with the others.'

'All right.' The burden of decision had been handed over. They turned together towards the chorus.

'It's cold,' Myron said.

'Have you no blanket?'

'It's back in the wagon.' He'd been ashamed to wear one.

'Take some of mine.'

Myron knew that the two of them wrapped in the one blanket, cylindrically tight about them from mouth to knee, made a perfect Navajo picture as they walked along. They moved into the close-packed group. With the third repetition he knew the song and could let out his voice, hearing himself sing the tribal mode true and clear. They swayed with the rest, arms across each other's shoulders.

Song rose in a shining spiral, out of his mouth he created, participated in creating a substance in which the thread of his own voice ran gleaming. It was a state of being, union, submission, mastery, and outlet, into which one entered, floating upwards, the drum in him and he enfolding the drum, solitary and entirely one with the others.

Jack said, 'I'm hungry, let's eat,' and then again, more insistently, 'Eh, grandfather, let's eat, I'm hungry.'

Myron heard him the second time. His mind circled down with a sort of shock. He remembered what Jack had just said, considered it.

'All right. Where?'

'My people are camped right over there, I can see their fire, it's still bright.'

'Let's go.'

They passed behind the mounted watchers, to where half a dozen widely spaced fires, some still flaming, lit up the ghostly, high-looming covers of the campers' wagons. Two men and a woman lay asleep around the shadows of the second blaze, heads and shoulders well bundled in their blankets, moccasined feet projecting. A man sat on the ground in the full light, leaning against a saddle on the wagon tongue, and a girl was tending a generous coffee-pot.

'That's my father,' Jack said. 'The girl, she lives near us. She comes from the east, the Diné T'ha.'

'The people my uncle told me about, the ones who were driven out?'

'That's right.'

'We're sort of cousins.'

'Yes. That's why her father came over this way.'

Myron was interested. This was the girl who wrote the letter. He had vaguely imagined an older girl, dressed in standard gingham. Only her bobbed hair showed her to be a scholar; for the rest she was dressed as a Navajo, dull yellow velveteen, blue-and-green skirt, rich colours in the firelight. No jewelry save two silver buttons on the bodice — poor people. About twelve years old, he judged. She glanced up, saw a stranger, and ignored them both with perfect breeding.

Cottonwood Leader began immediately to make fun of them for leaving the dance, and for the exact timing which brought them just when fresh coffee was on the boil and there was still beef in the pot. They grinned, turning their backs to the fire so that they were warmed but their eyes not blinded, answering over their shoulders. Anyone will grow hungry, Jack said, why didn't he come and sing?

'We sang so hard we got empty,' Myron said. 'When we are fed, we can sing till the day after tomorrow. We really sing, that's why we have to eat.'

'You're a schoolboy, too,' Cottonwood Leader answered. 'I can tell it. You want a bell to ring, bung, bung, then you go in and eat. I've seen it at Lokha Desjin.'

'He goes to Tlinj Tletsoi with me,' Jack told them. 'His uncle is Shooting Singer.'

The girl looked up. 'I wrote a letter about you, I think,' she said shyly.

'Yes, I saw it. That's why I'm here, I think.' He added in English, 'It was a good letter, but you don't spell very good.'

'Give me time. It was hard, you know. He talked Inyan and he said so much, dose hard words.'

The coffee boiled up, and she swung the pot off the fire.

They ate and drank, beef, tortillas, and coffee. There was only a little meat left, but they dipped their bread in the savoury juices. The man and boys talked rovingly, the girl kept rather in the background. Cottonwood Leader rolled a cigarette and passed over the makings. Jack picked up the sack and the papers.

Myron's heart beat unexpectedly fast. Preachers don't smoke, this is another form of backsliding. Jack shouldn't either, he's a schoolboy. One hated to seem a sissy before that man — the girl, what did she think? Lots of boys smoke on the sly at school — not a preacher yet — this new business of being a man ——

Jack handed over the tobacco. He took it and fumbled.

'Don't you know how?' Jack asked.

He mumbled an answer. They all laughed at him, three different timbres of laughter, and he grinned himself. It became a show, ruining half a dozen papers until Jack did it for him.

He'd meant just to roll one and not use it, but now they were all delightedly watching for the next act, so he set out to smoke. That could readily be done from observation — many Indians do not inhale. He copied his uncle, cigarette between forefinger and thumb, taking short light puffs briefly held in the mouth.

'He knows this part,' Buckskin's Daughter remarked.

Jack looked faintly surprised.

'You'd make a good one-armed man,' Cottonwood Leader said. 'I knew a man whose right arm was no good. Someone always had to make his cigarette, but he smoked it all right.'

Myron grinned and puffed. The whole business was negative, pointless; the tobacco didn't do anything to him, it was neither good nor bad, it was just dull to keep this thing burning. He had a sense of anticlimax, having felt so much about nothing at all. Why did the church keep insisting? Why did people smoke? In carelessness he breathed in as he puffed, and the stuff clawed at him. He threw the cigarette into the fire even while he was coughing and trying to smile, and they all laughed.

'Whoo! Coffee.'

A half cup of liquid soothed him.

'Come on.' He stood up. 'Let's go back.'

As Jack rose, Cottonwood Leader said, 'Come up to Tlichisenili some time and eat beef.'

'Good, I will.'

They pulled the blanket around themselves and headed back for the crowd. While Myron had sat eating, the drum and voices had been a background of excitement keeping the sense of a party alive. Now that he walked towards them, they made it necessary to hurry. His concepts of heathens, of ignorant savages, stood on the sidelines of his mind, not relinquished but withheld for now.

'It's different from school,' he said.

'It certainly is!'

'I mean, things look differently.'

'Yes.' Jack's assent was unsure, as if he didn't quite follow.

'I suppose you're not going back,' Myron said.

'Yes.' The answer was definite. 'I'm going back. My father talked to me about it.'

Shooting Singer had told him about that, but he hadn't quite believed. Not Jack. He and Buckskin's Daughter had changed their minds because of the old Indians, not the white men. Things were becoming complicated by allowances and exceptions. His uncle's ideas about school were a kind of inside out of Mr. Butler's. I must see him soon, as soon as this dance is finished.

They stepped in among the singers. Song rose in a shining spiral with the bright thread of his own voice running through it. It was part of being young and grown, packed in with the others close about him, creating a state of being which enveloped the drum, the firelight, the cold sweet night, and many young men singing together.

2

Old men will surprise you. He was saddle-weary, and tired of the parching afternoon sun, but his uncle seemed entirely at ease, riding ahead of him on the narrow trail. The three nights of the dance he'd slept only after midnight, but he'd dozed and napped through the days and Shooting Singer had been busy with the mysteries. Last night he fell asleep right after supper, and waking twice had heard his uncle still talking with their host. To lonely-living Navajos, half the pleasure of travelling is in the hapchance overnights along the road, contacts and strangers and the exchange of news, but Myron hadn't cared. Now he was drowsy again in the late afternoon, and half resentful of the expedition. Old men — old Indians, that is — can certainly surprise you.

They were going high into the Lukachukais to gather some kind of medicine. Heathen stuff. Heathen ceremonies, he then sermons — the confused kid, ignorant himself. Guess I was pretty silly. Most kids are. In bed at Tsaili and the drum going, backsliding. Juniper, piñón, and jack-pine moved in slow procession past him, falling behind, sand and red rock and clumps of grass, sage and cactus, drifted across his unfocussed eyes. He knew that the country was changing, but he wasn't paying attention to that. He had not backslid. He joined the singing, but he never went near the medicine hogahn, and he had kept well in the middle of the chorus when the girls were looking for new partners. Part of the time he'd just watched the whole thing from the outside.

The horses stepped out more briskly as the ground levelled,

changing pace where the trail was worn, irregular smooth-
ness in a rock outcrop. Piñón and pine grew thick, and big
junipers made soft masses of deep green. One passed through
tantalizing moments of shade, the balsam smell suggested a
non-existent coolness.

That girl who wrote the letter — Buckskin's Daughter —
did not take part in the dance. Chance maybe. These Indians
thought a twelve-year-old girl was ready for anything. One
who did dance — hardly twelve — unpleasant seeing the
little, inadequate thing turning with solid men. Heathen.
Perhaps Buckskin's Daughter was Christian; she ought to
be, she was educated. But she put on Navajo clothes for the
summer. Most girls do. Not really Christian.

The second day of the dance he went to sleep at noon
under a bush, then he heard girls' voices speak and laugh,
and woke to see two elderly women, and felt suddenly cheated,
angered at the start of his waking. Where he watched from
darkness one night, a couple slipped out past him. He
remembered them as he rode now, male and female figures,
faceless and silent in the dark, walking neither fast nor slow,
not touching each other, yet completely not casual, fading
into the night behind him with the songs following after.

Water and grass brought him out of his doze, the positive,
delightful sensations of rest to the eye, the smell of damp,
the presentation of coolness and security. Before them the
ground rose steeply in a great shoulder capped with larger,
straighter trees. Down the slope a brook ran in manifold
rills twining through a zone of wet earth rich with grass
and mosses, to form a rounded area at the bottom, first marshy
and stamped with water-filled hoofprints, then sandy earth
showing reddish under the haze of short grass. The living
water moved in narrow lines and waited in small pools; a
hundred yards from the foot of the slope it had disappeared,
and just beyond there the ring of greenness ended.

To Myron's relief his uncle swung from the saddle and
dropped his reins. The boy followed suit. When he came to

these little, watered pockets, he always felt that he would like to just stay there, camp and live and never lose sight again of this treasure. He had forgotten at school, with its taps and showers, what water really was. He drank and sprawled, feeling the sturdy blades of grass under his back and by his cheek. Shooting Singer was rolling a cigarette. That had been all right, that time he fooled with it, not really smoking. He consciously intended morality, Christian morality, a phrase with a ring of importance, aspiration. The girl had laughed at him — that was all right —— She wrote the letter, she shouldn't wear Indian clothes. Morality — Mr. Snyder — a sharp discomfort, an unformulated perception of the last days, the cigarette, Buckskin's Daughter, singing, through Mr. Snyder's eyes. He felt uncomfortable and drove the memory out of sight. No harm in just thinking about a girl, I've learnt morality. So has she, she's been to school a long time. Snyder has nothing to do with it, he's crazy.

His uncle said, 'This is a pretty place, but we must go higher.'

They caught their ponies. Before they mounted, the old man told him: 'Now you're with me, you have to help me in a holy thing. Until I have gathered the remedies, you must control your thoughts. Nothing that angers you, nothing bad, and forget all about those girls.'

Surprised by the last home shaft, and remembering Snyder, he showed his uncle a face of mixed emotions. The medicine man smiled.

'You are becoming a man, and voices of young women pull at your age. When it is hot and one is drowsy — why not, indeed? Women and men are for each other. It will come even harder later, when you really know about it. But there are times and other times. When a man thinks about women, he is pulled aside from what he is doing, disturbed. Do you understand? Look around you from here on; watch the trail so that you can return alone. There is beauty on all sides, see it, think about it.'

He smiled again and Myron half responded, then he swung to his saddle lightly, like a boy.

Old Indians will surprise you. Thinking dirty about women is wrong — immoral. But they understand a lot. Only you oughtn't to think about girls at all until you fall in love and think about marrying. The books — true love and purity. Galahad. Going for heathen medicine, bear medicine, but I won't touch it. An impulse to think all wrong, to oppose his uncle in his head and spoil the magic was shamed down by affection. As the horses zigzagged along the tricky, steep trail, he saw the seriousness of the old man's face. You couldn't make fun of it.

Looking to westward he got glimpses of the stupendous valley, more than two days' journey wide, between them and Black Mesa. The flat-topped mountain rose as they climbed higher, the country between opened up, canyons and mesas and flats, dull red, orange, greenish-grey, washed-out yellow, and the blocks of living shadow.

From the top of the shoulder they trotted along a slowly ascending valley, broken here and there by steep scrambles. Aspen and yellow pine closed in about them, the ground was carpeted underfoot, the quality of the air changed; in daylight under greenness the eyes relaxed as though what they saw bathed them. The good, damp smells, the freshness, awoke Myron and he felt the increased drive in his horse's going. Shooting Singer looked back and smiled, a delighted, communicative smile, as though he had played a joke ending in a pleasant surprise, and the boy responded to it. The old man loved it up here. Why not? The aspen trunks rose gleaming white and straight, feminine, and the pines were ruddy, their bark full of light. The joy of vegetation above, below, before and behind — the tag of his uncle's morning prayer fitted into his thoughts. With beauty above me I travel, with beauty below me I travel... Beauty all around me, this day may I travel.

He felt just fine. He threw his head back and lifted his

voice in the falsetto opening '*ai-ya-ai-ya ai-yan, ai-yan ai-ya*...' a song learnt two nights before. It sounded well among the trees.

Shooting Singer stopped him with a raised hand. 'Not those songs just now, my son. They go towards war. I'll teach you a prayer that suits.'

Myron's pleasure stumbled and stood still. He sat his horse, staring unhappily at his uncle.

'No,' he said, trying not to sound gruff or rude. 'No. I — I'm a Christian.'

Immediately he wished he could have eaten the words, but they were out, standing between them.

Shooting Singer said: 'I know. You must go by what makes you feel right. But you will respect what I am doing.'

Myron had expected his uncle to be angry. His kindness made him feel worse. But I ought not to learn sacred songs, prayers. I ought to feel pleased with myself. Only I don't. A moment ago they had smiled at each other, completely together, and now it was interrupted. It was silly of the old man to have taken him along on such an errand.

The highland forest continued to work its magic. Irritation slowly faded to an occasional reminding twinge. Shooting Singer stopped, reining his horse to one side of the trail, and pointing downward. Myron saw the big track, almost like a human foot but entirely inhuman. His uncle stopped him as he was about to speak.

'Don't mention a name. We are visitors in another's country.'

Pulling out the bag which hung from a string around his neck, he sprinkled a little pollen, the golden dust falling through shafts of sunlight to disappear on the moss while he whispered a brief prayer. Myron felt at once inferior, and embarrassed by his uncle's superstition.

The valley up which they rode became narrower, with glimpses of red crags showing occasionally through the trees on either side. The quiet was unlike the desert's silence.

Up here it's full of them, he thought, unaware that in his thoughts he was following the taboo against the specific, shouting word 'bear.' There was a story he had heard in the hogahn, about a child one of them carried off the year before. They searched for it five days while the medicine men prayed; on the fifth day they found it in the cave. The child had been well fed on berries, its account of itself was strange, confused, and magical. Five — the number used in ceremonies to do with those persons and with war. He'd mocked the tale in his mind, though it was recent and the men concerned were named. Now his back hairs prickled. The forest was mysterious. He felt excited, and dependent upon his uncle.

The trail went over a steep ascent, then down again into a stand of mature aspen, a magnificence of white columns between which they rode for a few yards, coming out into a small, green meadow with a brook in the middle of it. Shooting Singer dismounted near the thread of water, on a slight rise of ground that showed signs of old campfires.

'We stay here,' he said. 'While I am busy, you can gather wood — plenty of it, we'll be cold up here tonight. Dead oak is good, and the pine. Aspen is not much use.'

Hobbled and turned loose, the ponies rolled luxuriantly, then fell upon the rich grass with eager teeth; Shooting Singer walked slowly up the valley and disappeared.

Myron looked around. The trees on the east side were sunlit, but the valley itself was already in shadow and the air was sharpening. This place was as enclosed as many little canyons and pockets that he knew, but its walls were living; the mind penetrated them farther than the eye could follow. In there, far or near, could lurk those — those persons, magically powerful, wise, dangerous. One could be lonely here, yet it was full of deep peace. He walked towards a clump of scrub-oak at one edge of the big trees, glad to be busy.

He got hot tearing branches, scratched his wrists and made

a small hole in his shirt. When the pile of deadwood, including some big limbs of half-rotted pine he had laboriously dragged, was truly big, he stopped to consider. He was tired. The light had left the treetops. In the clear sky, the west was becoming brighter and less blue, while the east darkened. He saw the horses, eating and hoisting themselves forward with the curious, awkward movement of their hobbled forefeet, but no sign of his uncle. He looked hard up the valley. Nothing. He busied himself selecting the best wood to start a fire, arranging it, shredding bark. He went to the brook and washed — cold, clear water, wonderfully sweet. He poked at the woodpile, maintaining occupation. Then he saw the medicine man walking easily out from among the trees, as though he were master of all this, a figure of power in a category outside his experience.

Shooting Singer smiled as he came up. 'Well done. It's getting cool.'

He had a small package of herbs wrapped in a piece of flour-sacking, which he stuck in his saddlebags. Then he squatted, arranging the bark and little sticks.

Myron asked, 'Should we not have brought something — a gun or something — for the night up here?'

Shooting Singer paused, match in hand. 'It is not necessary. I have attended to all that.'

Myron believed him. The match scratched on a small stone, its flame showed yellow-white. From it, a redder flame slowly took hold of the bark, worked upward from shred to shred, showing definite colour and warmth in the early dusk, and then became larger, leaping, the familiarity of fire. A camp came into being, a specific place with enclosure. From their saddles, Myron took the bag of tortillas — wadded into rather a lump by the day's pounding — and a side of goat's ribs. Shooting Singer brought out the salt. The meat sizzled and spat beside raked-out coals, sending forth delicious smells. Both of them were earnestly attentive, turning the pieces, respitting them. When the ribs were ready, they ate steadily, picking the bones clean and consuming plenty of bread, until satisfaction was reached and the filled stomach demanded that one lie back and sigh.

Shooting Singer piled wood generously to make a blaze. The cold night pressed against their backs, the day had gone while they were absorbed with fire and food. They pulled their blankets around them, and the old man made a cigarette.

'I wish we could go after a deer together,' he said. 'I like it up in these mountains, and long ago there used to be good hunting here. There's none now. The deer are gone.'

'There were deer near Yellow Earth,' Myron said. 'Jack — Teez Nantai Bigé — he and I saw their sign many times, and once we saw some when we went deep in the woods. We never had a chance to go hunt them. We just trapped rabbits and — well —— ' he consciously tasted the quality of their camp, the ancient, fundamental thing. 'We pretended something like this.' He wanted to confide, to restore the sense of communication he had lost. 'We didn't know about it, I think,' he said slowly, like a man describing an object at which he was looking and which he did not clearly see. 'We didn't know about it all, but this is what we were pretending.'

Shooting Singer, lying half in firelight and half in darkness, studied the bright spark of his cigarette. His Pendleton blanket, close-wrapped, made him seem long and narrow, and the pronounced design of it was confusing in the play of light. His face was quite clear, but his long hair melted into the night and the overturned saddle supporting his head was guesswork.

'At that school, you are learning what we all need to know; you're not there to hunt deer, even if their tracks come right in front of your door. Learn it. I know a little about the Utes, the Mokis, the Mexicans, the Bellacana right around here, but if you opened me up to see what I thought about the world outside ——' he laughed. 'Did you ever see someone trying to work out cat's-cradles when he didn't know how?'

Myron felt the equality in voice and manner. It was thrilling and upsetting. In a simple, black-and-white world, the medicine man should be as much the enemy of schooling as schooling was of him. White men were certain; they cut a line with a knife. Snyder, he had power. So did Shooting Singer, a different kind of power. It went with the leaf-filtered, cold night air, the heavy sound of horses moving carried through the ground to his elbow and ear, the wilderness around them despite which they lay secure, thinking, using what men have that trees and bears have not. Washington, too, had hesitated, smudged a line into vagueness. Perhaps this was what Mr. Butler had been talking about long ago. He looked at his uncle's strong face behind the movement of hand and cigarette. Perhaps now something was going to be made clear.

Without logical connection, he asked, 'What is my true name?'

His uncle suppressed a start of astonishment. 'It is Seeing Warrior. Hold to it. Your strength is there.'

He stared at the fire, and roused himself against reluctance to open too great things, possible disapproval of a loved and respected person.

'What strength, my uncle? We Navajos are beaten, we are few, I think. These old things — well — haven't they failed us already?'

To his surprise, his uncle smiled. 'Why shouldn't you think like that?' he said. 'I have, and often. You, with your schooling, you can help me with the answer, I think. Will you smoke?'

'No, I don't smoke.'

'It is easier, sometimes, when one is talking or thinking hard. It saves twisting pieces of grass, and causes more pleasure.'

Myron grinned sheepishly, looking at his handful of grass.

Shooting Singer went on: 'White men count everything. How many Navajos do they say there are?'

'Forty thousand, I have heard.'

The old man tasted the high number. 'Many people. Pass them by you one by one — many people. Eh! And Indians, all together, how many?'

'Three hundred times a thousand and fifty thousand, about that, they say.'

'Many people. And Mexicans, how many?'

'I don't know. They are counted in with the rest, the Bellacana, I think.'

'Strange. They aren't the same. But then, after the Bellacana stopped fighting the Mexicans, they came together against us. That's it, I suppose. Can you reach the wood from where you lie?'

Myron dragged out a big log and crashed it awkwardly onto the fire, driving up a tower of sparks and all but killing the flame. His uncle rose, mocking. Briefly they concerned themselves with a matter more fundamental than anything of the mind. When the fire was healthy, Myron stood up, rearranging his blanket, and felt the night air and the emptiness beyond their little zone.

'The white men all told then, between the two seas, how many?'

'A thousand times a thousand — a hundred times all that, and then twenty times it. That is what they say.'

He doubted that his uncle could in any way grasp the number he had stated. He watched the old man's concentrated face. At length Shooting Singer sighed.

'Did you ever shake water from your hand onto a plate or a board or anything like that? Each drop stands up by itself, with lots of room around it. That's how we were, we and the Mokis, the Utes, the Supais, the Apaches, and the rest. The Mexicans, too. They were many, but they were pasturage for us. But you pour a whole barrel of water onto those drops — where are they then? That's what the Bellacana is.'

Myron felt that he could speak his mind as freely as to another boy.

'Then what is there to do save be a white man? We are taken up, lost, in — in the barrel. The rest — like my name, uncle — it's all swept away, I think.'

'Before I was born, Red Shirt conquered us. We've been a drop in the middle of the barrel ever since, and there are more of us now than there were then, many more. And we are still ourselves. One can be like a white man if he chooses, but can one *be* a white man? Think about it.'

'No, but —— '

'That's the point. Think of all the People. We are still a nation, we can still be found in the barrel. We must live with the white men, we must learn their good things, all that we can. We must change, of course. But that which stands up in us is Navajo; if we destroy it, life isn't worth living.'

Myron thought hard. 'But there are so few Indians. All the hair will be short soon, everyone will go to school.'

'That doesn't matter. It isn't numbers or long hair or living in hogahns. It's that which stands up in you, the same thing which makes one man by his voice and his eyes control many hundreds to go this way or that. Numbers can't destroy that. Life is full of pains and disappointments, yet life is worth living, so long as you have that.'

Myron stared at the fire. What makes life worth living? His simple set of answers had become inadequate. Nobody had ever talked like this. Why — the old man had asked for those numbers, not to learn them, but to make him, Myron, think about them. Seeing Warrior.

'But I'm a Christian,' he said thoughtfully.

'How do you know?'

Myron looked up, startled. 'Of course I know.'

'You've never heard anything but the Jesus talk. What you believe, you will have to settle for yourself. But you can't disbelieve something you never heard of, I think.'

'Have you heard about Jesus?'

'Of course. You know the Dragging Robe at Lukachukai, the one who knows so much about our ceremonies? We have talked long and long together. I know this — our gods do not make war on each other.'

Myron dug at a tuft of grass with one hand. Of course the Catholics — he knew what Mr. Snyder thought of them. Snyder — just thinking of him he reacted to defence of his uncle. I've got to see Mr. Butler.

'Let's not talk about this any more now, my uncle. I think I'm just a child still. I feel mixed up.'

'All right. It's getting late. Build up the fire.'

He had grown used to sleeping on the ground, but it was different here in the meadow, with only one blanket. The old Indians did it, on the warpath and hunting. He saw his uncle's feet, in the thin moccasins, projecting far beyond their wrap. Old men will surprise you.

'Uncle.'

'Yes.'

'That story, about a child that was carried off, you know; did that really happen?'

'Yes. It was only last summer, the son of Atsidi Tso over by Tsé Dotlish.'

Myron covered his head, snuggling down against the ground. The horses' stamping, carried direct to his ear, sounded as if it were on top of him, and when he looked up to make sure they were far, he saw the wide, empty night. There are too many truths in this world. Next thing, I'll go see Mr. Butler. He can help me. He hoped he could sleep, but doubted it. It was beautiful up here. Lighten our darkness, Oh Lord... the prayer eased him. After much wriggling he got the right adjustment of blanket on the side away from the fire and began to feel warm, drowsy.

CHAPTER NINE

TSAILI looked funny as he rode towards it. He remembered big, solid buildings, and saw that they were small and shabby. The whole place was remorselessly open to the sun, the campus mere desert, the very few, cherished cottonwoods not enough to relieve the eye. Where the cattle-guard barred the entrance to horses, he dismounted, and tied the animal to a clump of greasewood. His uncle had given him a good horse, a bald-faced sorrel with fine legs and a good set of neck, light, wiry, quick. He was sorry there was no grass in sight for it. It passed through his mind that he might take the horse up to that meadow and camp there for a week. That would fatten it.

He stepped across the cattle-guard, looking about him, feeling changed and grown up, and at the same time recapturing the little boy deep inside him. Tsaili. One kid, way over there. A white man he didn't know going into the commissary. He wondered if Mr. Linsdale was still around. He'd expected to see a lot of kids mooning about — but of course, the new orders from Washington, only somehow you thought of Tsaili as unchanging. No one around to see his football jersey, blue-and-orange, with the big **22** on its back, or his wide hat. He swaggered slightly as he walked. There was a little girl sitting on the matron's doorstep. No family, probably.

He was halfway to Mr. Butler's, the fence and tree and the vine over the porch. Unchanged. Now it was all going to be straightened out for him. His heart pounded as he realized how soon he was going to see his friend. Gee, I hope he's home. It would be awful to have to wait, but Mrs. Butler would give him cookies. Maybe he'd be angry that Myron had let his uncle tell him the stories, but you can't disbelieve something you've never heard of. Mr. Butler would understand. Now he had reached the gate, opening it as he always had done, and holding in check the smile of the expected welcome. Someone moved past a window. Gee, I hope he's home. Cookies and lemonade. He heard his own feet on the porch, removed his hat, knocked at the door, his smile all but breaking forth.

A stranger opened the door. All his excitement reversed itself and became heavy inside him. The man was young, medium-sized, and very blond.

'Come in,' he said cordially. 'Come right in. Are you looking for me?'

Myron stayed on the threshold, staring at his hat. 'I was lookin for Mr. Butler.'

'Doctor Butler's not here any more, I'm afraid. I'm in his place. Perhaps I can do something for you?'

'I just wanted to see him.'

'Well, come in and sit down anyway.'

This man was young and unsure of himself.

'You were one of his boys?'

The hand on his elbow was urgent. Myron entered the living-room — the same room, only the bookshelves were half bare, there were more magazines, and the curtains were different.

'Sit down. Is there anything I can do?'

He remained standing. 'Do you know where Mr. Butler's gone?'

'To Fort Wingate. A more important field, you know, the big school there.'

'Yessir.' Fort Wingate, we beat them twelve to seven. 'How could I go dere?'

The missionary wanted to do his best. He wondered if

boys would come looking for him some day, would miss him the way this boy did Butler. He wanted to make some impression, not be entirely inadequate.

'If you can get to Chinli, you can easily find a truck there going to Gallup. Then at Gallup you could get a ride out to the school.'

'Yessir. T'ank you. I guess I better get goin.'

'You're starting for Chinli now?'

'No, sir. I got to go see some folks, over on Black Mesa.'

'Well, sit down awhile. Let's get acquainted. What's your name?'

Myron felt as if the man were running hard after him, yet unable to come any nearer. He didn't see what he could do about it. He remained standing.

'Myron Begay.' He remembered the other names that this man would never know.

The young missionary got hold of his hand and pumped it.

'Glad to know you, Myron. My name's Mims, George Mims.' He let go the hand. 'I think I've heard Doctor Butler speak of you. Aren't you at Yellow Earth?'

'Yess.'

It was nice to know that his protector had spoken of him, but now he wanted to go.

'Home on vacation, eh? Being a good boy, I hope.'

'Well, I got to go. I got a long ways to ride yet.'

'All right. But come in any time. I'll be glad to see you. I've got magazines and books you might like, and we often make lemonade.'

'Yessir. Good-bye.'

'Good-bye.'

The novice watched the boy go. Would he ever learn how to make them open up? What a strange people!

2

Myron still got tired when he rode many hours, but a brief rest and change of position refreshed him. As he felt the sorrel moving willingly under him again, heading west for Tlichisenili, his spirits rose. Perhaps he could talk about all this with Jack. Perhaps — Jack's sort of one-sided. This was the first time he'd travelled alone, like a man, and now he was entering new country. He didn't know just what was so pleasant about drifting along — stopping for the noon meal at one hogahn, for the night at another, meditating on the details of the country as he was carried by on the eminence of his saddle. Rocks and trees and quirks of the landscape were different this way from when one walked or merely sat among them; partly the lack of effort on one's own part, partly the slow procession of new things offered for contemplation; the world became a show given for the rider's pleasure. Where he faced a long stretch of good going, he lifted his horse to a lope. He sang Onward, Christian Soldiers, Jerusalem the Golden, and the Wildcat Song. That was a gambling song, and gambling was wicked, but he was tired of trying to figure things out and his mind side-stepped the shadow of a problem.

Clouds gathered in the late afternoon, masking the sun. Rain was overdue; he was worried about a drenching, but glad that it was coming. At school, rain was bad weather, a nuisance, but now he knew it was life itself. That was wrong, the way they taught you. In the first grade — 'Rain, rain, go away...' Blasphemy to a desert shepherd. Although it was superstition to think that words could affect the weather.

He spent the night with a newly married couple who were camped near their sheep, in a simple brush shelter. They were young and enthusiastic towards life, companionable, and he noticed their awareness of each other. A point came in the evening, a defined moment, when he felt that he was becoming an intruder, so he rolled up at some distance from their fire where sand shaped itself to a good bed. Too hot for easy sleep, though he was tired. He heard them talking in low tones — commonplace words, tomorrow's pasturage — then arranging the bedding, and the man yawned. Then he heard more. It was quiet, very small sounds, but he heard with his nerve ends and all sleep went from him.

Not disgusting, they were married. But he felt disgusted. In himself, that was, just as the frank talk of older Indians bothered him sometimes, and the feeling that the dirtiness was in himself, and he remembered Snyder. His uncle said it was natural, a young man thinking — but it makes me want, and that's wrong. He threw off his blanket until he felt almost chilly. He was tired of all these complications; he wanted a simple world. Who will I marry? Someone who's been to school. She oughtn't to wear Indian clothes when she's been to school and knows better. He saw a living-room, rather vague, but there was a lamp, and glass in the window. Progressive, up to date. But the girl wouldn't focus, only that she had on American clothes, and that kept mixing up with a long, full skirt and an image which was an archetype of a woman reaching over a fire at night and which called up infancy and all the foundations of himself. He slept uneasily, dreaming of girls' voices at school, and that he had spoken to one — an unknown one — while they were in line before dinner, insanely. A hurricane of retribution and white faces gathered about him, great wickedness; Ruth Nalchini who had been sent home pregnant got into it. There was a lot more, and Buckskin's Daughter who had written a letter sat by a campfire with her hair long and couldn't speak any English and his mother sat by a campfire and he could never get back to the meadow where his uncle waited with the Answer, a small, shining object, in his medicine bag. Snatches of unfinished dreams in a broken night and then deep sleep from which daylight roused him all too soon.

The couple made fun of him for late sleeping, joking about

the white man's ways he learnt at school. He felt ashamed before their simplicity, and his appetite went entirely when he saw that hers was the face of the girl he spoke to in his dream. Manners carried him through, and he left after half a breakfast.

A few hours took him up the first part of the climb to the top of Black Mesa. The return to a stretch of level going was a relief, and the outlook across to the blue heap of mountains, where his uncle and he had camped, eased his spirit.

A horseman approached him along a trail coming into his at a right angle, from another route up the mesa, a young man, long-haired, riding a showy black-and-white pinto. Even at a distance he could see that the rider wore a belt of hand-wide silver placques, bracelets, and a necklace. Myron reined in where the two trails joined, and the other stirred his mount to a fast trot, coming up in style. He was about Myron's age, hard to tell exactly, because blanket Indians grow up differently, older, surer, yet gayer and more naïve than school-boys. He might be a year older. He was slender, very good-looking, and his poor, torn cotton shirt and faded jeans were unexpected under the heavy jewelry. The saddle on the showy horse was poor, too, an old Navajo tree rising to high points at pommel and cantle, the leather covering pieced out with scraps of rawhide.

'Where to?' Myron asked.

'Up on top, there.' The boy pointed with his lips.

'Where from?'

'Hasbidwe T'o.'

They were riding at a jog-trot, side by side.

'And you, where to?'

'Up there, Tlichisenili.'

'Where from?'

'Ha'anoichí.'

The long-haired boy smiled. 'We both like to travel, I think.'

His smile was thorough and gleeful. Myron answered it

as he agreed. He felt the direct, anonymous friendliness of the trail, the pleasure of being unknown and unplaced.

'That's a pretty horse you have.'

'Yes, I just got him.' The boy moved his two hands forward in the sign of a horse-race. 'That one of yours looks fast.'

'He is, pretty fast.'

'Let's race.'

'We've been going three days now. The horse is too tired, I think.'

'I've been coming right along today. There's plenty of sweat on mine. It's level here, later on we have to go slow.'

'All right. Where to?'

They reined in.

'To where those two trees stand. What will you bet?'

'I have no money.' Myron's answer came out short. He didn't want to say that he was Christian and wouldn't bet. He didn't want to seem abnormal.

'One gets it, but it goes so easily. Have you a jack-knife?'

'Yes.'

'Let's see it.'

Myron pulled it out, the boy examined it.

'It's good. I'll put these two bracelets against it.'

Myron was stumped. He wanted to stay in his character of just a Navajo, he was tired of the responsibilities of being Myron Begay, but it was weak to give in like this. Anyone can see why gambling is wrong.

'I'll give you the knife,' he said, and added boastfully, 'I can get lots of them.'

'*Ei-yei!* All right!' The boy stuck it in his pocket, his teeth flashing again. 'Well, anyhow, let's try our horses.'

'Good.'

They lined up.

'Ready? Go!'

Better handled, the pinto got off quicker, Myron quirted the sorrel, and as he felt his horse straighten out under him, his blood leapt up, he ceased to have weight. Now the two horses were abreast again. There was a sense of speed such as riding in a car had never given him, his hat fallen far behind and ignored, the wind on his body, his spirit ahead of him lifting him and his horse. The pinto gained. He poured in leather, he could feel his horse putting out everything it had, but the pinto moved clear ahead.

The two trees flashed by them and they swerved to right and left, reining in, and then trotted together, loving each other. Myron went back and got his hat. His horse was so frisky it would hardly let him make the pickup, and then wanted to bolt back after the pinto. Panting, flushed with laughing, they took up the trail again, busy at first with holding down their horses, who fought their bits whenever one moved even fractionally in the lead.

The level strip narrowed until they were travelling along a wide ledge with the valley and mountains to eastward exposed again, a patterned vastness from which they could not keep their eyes. The boy pointed out where he came from, not very far to the north of Ha'anoichí.

'So many times I've gone up in those mountains and looked over this way,' he said, 'and this mesa has always been standing up in the west. I decided to come up on top of it, to see what's up here, and to see how those mountains look to the people who live up here.'

'I've never been over this way either.'

'Look, there's rain. Pretty near where I live.'

'And some over there too — see?'

They stopped their horses and sat watching. The Luka-chukai Mountains had become fuzzy where their tops touched a grey, solid sky, the red bands of cliffs lower down showed clearly in the tempered, neutral light. Across the enormous expanse of Chinli valley rose black cones, red buttes, and mesas red or buff or yellow or striped, great dominators of their own domains but mere incidents in a low-lying country from where they looked. The flats stretched golden and brown and grey, with the varied pattern of faint green as vegetation was negligible or merely sparse. Out of the roofing clouds long, dark, diagonal columns of rain, perfectly symmetrical, reached down and obscured sections of the land.

At length the boy said, 'It's almost too much.'

Myron sighed, 'Yes.'

They roused their horses. As they toiled up the second climb, they smelled wetness, and a cooler air rolled over the edge of the mesa — rain coming. At the top, among thick-growing jack-pines and piñón, it hit them, a stamping, solid, silver downpour. They bucked it for a minute or two, then the long-hair turned his mount aside and swung to earth under the partial shelter of a thick tree. Myron joined him, and they squatted close together, feeling the bark against their wet backs, holding their reins and watching their ponies' heads turn dark with water.

'Have you tobacco?' the boy asked.

'No.'

Myron felt cold and rather miserable. One ought to have a slicker or be able to go indoors. The other began humming the song about one's lazy cousins. He nodded time faintly. The stranger sang softly, '*Shidzedé lan do idashilan,*' and Myron joined, very faintly, on the following '*Hé-yé-yan-a.*' The stranger smiled suddenly, as he raised his voice, '*Alo, alo, hanana.*' They really swung into it together. When they'd been through the song twice, they looked at each other, each well pleased with the trueness of the other's high, far-reaching voice and with his own equal adequacy. Myron started '*Lé-n, lé-on . . .*' and they had that, then the Owl Song for gambling, which he didn't know well enough to sing the first time, so the other sang it carefully at him, marking time with his hand, then Myron started the Magpie Song, and so they continued. The pinto brought them back to earth, jerking his reins free.

Myron said, 'The rain has stopped.'

They rose.

'It was a good rain, perhaps we'll see a rainbow.' The boy from Hasbidwe T'o tugged at his own wrist. 'Here, my friend, take this.' He held out a bracelet.

The schoolboy despised bracelets, but he was so pleased that he could hardly manage a polite 'Good,' then, recovering himself, picked up the other's word, 'Good, my friend.'

'Let's go. It's late and I'm hungry.'

They swung cheerfully into wet saddles. As Myron felt the soaking, cold leather he grunted. The older boy made a wry face.

'When we get off, we'll look as if it had been raining upside down.'

They loped in the freshness, following the well-defined trail towards Tlichisenili's rocky landmark and singing as the spirit moved them. The demands of thought had vanished. There were the trees with water shining on the clustered needles, the changed colours of wet sand and grass and shrubs, the quality of the air, motion, and the voices in time together. Myron felt affection and gratitude to the traveller he had met, he wanted to stand well with him, simple feelings without any annoyance of reasoning; his mind was totally in the moment.

A gradual rise of rocky ground slowed them to a fox-trot. Beyond the crest, it broke away in a line of cliffs to a long valley about a mile wide with an arroyo down the middle of it. They could see three hogahns, one standing by a large cornfield, and sheep pens. The cliffs of the farther side were grey, an irregular line like a retaining wall holding back the higher level, and here and there the sand had spilled over it in yellowish, wide fans. The place looked rich. Young grass of the summer rains hazed it over, the hogahns were well built, just now the planted cornfield's rich soil gleamed like dull metal from flood-water not yet soaked in, the thick clumps of corn were sturdy and fresh, each standing well apart from its neighbours. Even in the unlikely corners the plants grew well, and one could see beans and melon vines.

Myron said: 'This is where I'm heading, I think. This is what they told me to look for.'

'You have relatives here?'

'Some friends. Do you know Teez Nantai?'

'No, but his mutton should be good, I think.'

'He'll probably have beef.'

'What are we waiting for?'

They went down a sand slope, the horses breaking into a run at the bottom.

3

He went out with Jack to move a bunch of cattle; hard work and hard riding in broken country thick with small trees. You had to set your teeth and harden your stomach to let your horse keep going all out down steep places and through scrub that pounded your face and hands, though by and by you got more used to it and the fun was real. Half-wild animals, long-horned, dun, yellow, reddish, and some of them marked with black, rangy and keen and quick, were hard to herd. They were at it from early morning till close to noon, and when they had the bunch where it ought to be, boys and horses alike were good and tired. The sorrel had stood up well, as quick and fast as Jack's boasted pony, and Myron was pleased to find himself equal in riding, even if he had not fully mastered the lariat.

They started back towards the valley at a walk. Riding ahead, Jack sat sideways in the saddle, one leg cocked around the horn, idly swinging the rope's end he had used for a quirt.

'That was a queer person for you to be travelling with, that Singing Gambler,' he said, smiling.

'He was all right. He's never been to school, that's all.'

'The two of you made good singing. We liked listening to you.' He looked mockingly at Myron. 'Gambling songs. I didn't know you had it in you.'

Myron felt pleased and flustered. 'They're pretty,' he apologized. 'They're just songs, they don't say anything special, anything wrong.'

'Why not sing them? Of course they're good.'

Myron couldn't leave it alone. 'Of course gambling is wrong. A boy like that oughtn't to be always betting. Maybe he'll get over it. But I don't think it's wrong to sing those songs, so long as you remember...'

Jack recognized the frowning forehead. 'You think too hard. If he wants to bet, he can worry about that, he and the people who bet with him, I think. You don't have to agree with him. You know the songs are all right, so do I. You know what you think is right — do it and stop worrying.'

'But how do you know?'

'I know, that's all.'

'M-m — well. But how can you tell...' Myron didn't quite know what he wanted to ask. Jack's decisive face defeated his thoughts.

'You're always asking yourself hard questions. You're never happy until you've found something you can't figure out, I think. Why don't you just let it alone?'

Myron said, 'No, I don't want to be mixed up. I just...'

He gave up. It made him feel lonely. Jack couldn't understand, he didn't need to. Jack just knew. When you tried to talk about these things, pretty soon Jack grew impatient; he felt his friend's assurance, envying it.

Jack grinned affectionately. 'Come on, stir up your red pet there, I'm getting hungry.' He swung straight in his saddle and they pushed the horses to a trot.

They came out on the rim of the valley just above the hogahn at the east end of the big cornfield. They could see three people seated around the fire in front of it, and the little flock of sheep grazing and idling between the hogahn and the crude fence.

'Buckskin Man,' Jack said. 'We're just in time for lunch.'

They welcomed the boys cordially, remembering Myron

from when they were at the dance together. Myron was vaguely surprised that they were as gay and trivial as anyone else. Knowing their story and how they had affected Jack and himself, he thought of them in connection with high purpose, and somehow expected their wrongs to be visible about them. He expected a fixed, heroic pose. The man's face and hands showed constant, drudging work — that was a big field to farm. They were poor, but well fed; Singing Beads was scolding Jack for not having brought them a beef, and Jack answered with equal nonsense, as though these were the most ordinary people in the world. The girl was pretty, Myron realized. In Navajo costume she looked more mature than a schoolgirl. Ethel Harding — Buckskin's Daughter, *Abinah Bitsí*. She was quiet, sitting between her parents, speaking little but laughing with the others.

Jack and Buckskin Man lit cigarettes; Myron refused, saying that as far as he was concerned smoking was more trouble than it was worth. The girl rose and walked off towards the sheep, the two dogs trotting towards her as she approached. They watched her move the flock up to the afternoon's grazing. Soon their host said that he had to go to work on his water ditch, and Singing Beads moved to her weaving. The boys rode off for home.

'They're working, all of them,' Jack said. 'That girl, she's with those sheep all day. It will be hard for them when she goes back to school before harvest, but she's going, they say.'

'Where will she go?'

'Lokha Desjin, I think. That's nearest. They ought to have schools right around near home, so children can help. It's lucky I have brothers.'

Jack meditated as he rode, then said, 'When someone marries that girl, he'll be lucky.'

'She's just a little girl,' Myron answered. 'She's too young.'

'Oh, not now. I'm not like the old people, marrying off children. But when she's ready.'

Myron didn't answer. He was thinking about the letters she had written; in the back of his mind hovered that mixed vision of a house with furniture and a woman by a camp-fire.

With a tone of explanation and some shyness, Jack said, 'You're related.'

Myron grunted. He understood what his friend was conveying. 'Not really,' he said. 'It's my uncle's wife who's related to her.'

Jack looked at him, and his face clouded.

'Well, we're a sort of cousin, I suppose. I hope she marries someone I like.'

It was worth it for the change in Jack's face, but he felt disturbed, and to cover up began singing.

4

Leaving Tlichisenili, he swung off the trail home, over a ridge and down into another valley. Searching it, he saw the small flock on the far side, and trotted towards it, remaining watchful until he was sure that Ethel, not her mother, was herding. The two dogs came at him furiously, but when she recognized him she called them back, hurling a stick at one.

It surely didn't seem right for a schoolgirl, the dusty, faded, full skirt, the moccasins, the disordered, dusty hair. He knew what sheepherding was like, in memory it had grown to an unbearable drudgery which should never be inflicted on one who could read and write.

She stood with her hands idle, looking up at him, shy and curious.

'I wanted to talk to you before I went home.'

She still waited.

'That letter you wrote, because of that I wanted to see you.'

'Why?'

'Well — it changed things. It seemed queer, in a way, that you wrote it and so I came all this distance.'

'Teez Nantai Bigé says you didn't want to come. Perhaps you're sorry, he says.'

'No, I'm glad I came.' He hesitated, then asked in English, 'Are you a Christian?'

'I guess so. I dunno.'

'You oughta be. All of us who want to help the Inyans, we oughta be Christians.' He said it earnestly, then added, thinking of his uncle, 'We oughta know de odder side too, I guess. But we gotta be modern — dat's Christian.'

'Jack says you're bright. Is he bright?'

'He's all right.'

'But is he bright?'

'Well — sorta middlin.'

There was a pause, each thinking.

'You're goin to Keams Canyon?' he asked.

'Yess.'

'You're about old enough to go to a big school. You oughta transfer to Yellow Earth.'

'Maybe. Next year maybe.'

'Yeah. You'll learn more there.'

She returned to Navajo. 'It's hard on my parents when I'm gone. They have the sheep to herd and all. I missed school last year, when we came here, and they needed me.'

'Yet they want you to go, they say.'

'Yes.' She looked right at him and her eyes showed fire. 'After what happened to us, I want to go. Teez Nantai Bigé says you learn everything fast. Perhaps you'll be a leader like Tall Man some day. I want to learn like that.'

Myron flushed with pleasure. This girl had a special power, young as she was. In his mind it was she, not her parents, he associated with the decisions the older people had made.

'Perhaps you will,' he told her. 'Why not? White women are leaders, and Navajos ——' he laughed. 'The men lead because the women are pushing them.'

She laughed, too. He'd meant to say something about the old-fashioned clothes she wore, but now it would sound prim.

'I must start for home, I've a long ride ahead of me.'

'All right. I'll see you sometime.'

'Yes.'

He went off trotting, and feeling relieved. Seeing the girl alone, talking about those things with her, tied up a loose end in his mind. Jack wants to marry her. He frowned. Jack was so likely to backslide, and she was meant for something else. He began to think of all the things he'd meant to say and forgotten.

CHAPTER TEN

E HAD tried to go back to the hogahn where he stopped at noon, but the arroyo had risen in an impassable flood behind him. The steady rain had soaked him until even his hat leaked and his shoes squelched soggily as he pushed along, dragging the lame sorrel. The world was silver grey, he was chilled to the bone, and hereabouts was nothing to get under. With the way rivulets poured over the ground, he couldn't be sure if he was on the right trail, or any trail at all. Raising his head again to look forward, he saw a dark clump of trees — piñón probably — a partial shelter. He shivered and jerked at the reins. This was misery. And what a rain! Why did it have to happen just at this time?

There were four trees in the clump, and now he saw the mud-plastered dome of a solid winter hogahn beyond them. Shelter in any case, perhaps warmth and people and food.

The earth roundabout the structure was bare, no signs of inhabitants. Yes — hoofprints, already all but washed out, faint half moons full of water. They might mean something. No blanket or door covered the entrance. He stooped to enter it and called in, immediately aware of warmth and a fire inside, the mere conception of which sent a shudder through him.

A girl came to the doorway. 'You can't come in,' she said, 'the men are away.' She seemed nervous.

Even while his heart sank, he could see that she was attractive, noting her long hair neatly pulled back, her deep green bodice with its silver buttons. She looked like a person from whom to expect comfort and reception.

'My horse is lame,' he said, 'and I'm wet.'

'You mustn't come in.'

'When will your men be back?'

'Pretty soon.' She was uneasy, her eyes dodging his for a moment.

He knew the code, and knew, too, that he was Myron Begay, a Christian who didn't do wrong things. But how could he make her know that? Returned schoolboys had a reputation for rape. As he stood, bending to the height of the entrance, rain sluiced down the back of his neck. She stayed just inside, watching him, and behind her was the red glow of warmth and dryness. He straightened suddenly and turned to his saddle, untying the .22 rifle that lay across his bundle behind. He pushed it towards her, stock foremost.

'Here. Do you know what this is for? Take it, and let me in.'

Her eyes danced with amusement, the strained expression left her face as she received the gun.

'Bring in your saddle.' She withdrew to one side of the fire.

He unsaddled quickly and entered, dragging his gear, which he threw down near the door, then he squatted by the handful of coals and stingy flame which fed on a few small sticks thrust in star fashion, and looked at the girl. She was his age. He got the impression of a formed, a notable person, and of something puzzling. She was watching him closely. Amusement and nervousness were latent in her. He looked around, his eyes growing used to the half light.

There was a double handful of moderate-sized sticks, still damp, near the fire. Her saddle and bridle lay by the door on the north, the women's side, she had her blanket over her shoulders, an odd-shaped bundle in a flour sack lay beside her. Otherwise the place was entirely bare. Looking up towards the smoke-hole, through which rain fell as an irregular mist, he saw the fire-stick wedged between two logs.

He looked straight at her, grinning. 'So the men are away.'

He saw her hand take firmer hold of the gunstock.

'Don't be afraid,' he said gravely. 'I'm not like that.'

She studied him carefully with wise eyes, satisfying herself, and then relaxed. She glanced down at the rifle and her mouth twitched.

'I was going home,' she said, 'and the wash was up. So I came in here. When a strange man comes along ——'

'Of course. Is that all the wood you have?'

'Just what I could break off. There's a dead tree on that side, but the branches are heavy.'

'Well, I'm still wet.' Myron rose. He pointed towards his saddle. 'There's food in my pack.'

She gave him a look of keen amusement, then took on a meek expression as she reached towards it. Myron blushed to the roots of his hair. He'd spoken as if — well — as if they belonged ——

'I'll get some wood,' he said, and dove out.

It wasn't easy, smashing branches by jumping on them and heaving a rock down on them, and the rain was an actual obstacle, but he felt that he had to bring in more than plenty. It took him two trips to carry all he'd got, and she exclaimed with pleasure. By then, with the masking rain, daylight had almost disappeared.

His blanket had been laid between the fire and the south wall, arranged for him, an invitation to recline.

'You're carrying lots of supplies,' she said, putting his little coffee-pot by the replenished fire.

'I have a long way to go, and thought I might need to camp out.'

She spitted mutton on sticks, and set a couple of tortillas to warm.

'Where from?'

'From Ha'anoichí.'

'Where to?'

'To Nanjoshi.'

'Eh! You're going far.'

'I thought I could pick up a truck at Tohatchi.'

'Perhaps. They don't frighten you to ride in, those cars?'

'No. I'm used to them.'

The coffee boiled and she pulled it off the coals. He wondered how she'd filled the pot; some run-off of rainwater. Her movements were skilful, competent, there was smooth economy in the way she reached for things. He was sure she was only just his age, yet she seemed to have gone far beyond.

'Nanjoshi,' she said thoughtfully. 'Why there? People go there to get drunk, they say.'

It irritated him to have such a thing suggested.

'I'm just passing through there on my way to Shash Bit'o. To the school, you know.'

'You go to school there?'

'No, to Tlinj Tletsoi. There's someone I want to see there.'

Politeness could not pry further. She examined the mutton and found it ready. She gave him a thick sandwich of broiled meat and tortilla, then turned to the coffee.

'Have you a cup?'

'No.'

'We'll have to take turns with the pot, as soon as it cools enough.'

He had an impulse to tell her all about why he was going to Fort Wingate, to show her his reality and purpose. The food was all his, he noticed, wondering what was in her lumpy bundle. The rain had stopped, and one could faintly hear the rumble of flooded arroyos.

'The water'll be down soon,' he said.

'I hope so. Was it flooding the way you came?'

'Yes. I tried to go back, and I couldn't.'

'Just as I did. So we met here, in the halfway place.'

Now that he was warm and partly dry, and the food had made his middle snug, he had to be aware that she was a woman alone with him by the one fire. He remembered Ethel and was ashamed of himself. He was too inexperienced to note her breasts, to visualize a body, but he saw the charm and character of her oval face, and her supple slenderness. There was the puzzlement again of the blanket Indian not seeming inferior, and the foolish, proud voice saying I'm a man, I do what a man does, and a deep wish to be respected, not to offend.

'That's an odd bundle you have,' he said. 'Did you bring any food?'

'No. I was just going from my uncle's to my father's.' She unknotted the end of the sack. 'He sent him these.'

She dumped out a lard pail converted into a drum by tying a piece of inner tube over the mouth, a small drumstick, and a silver belt which she held up.

'Last night we were playing,' she said. 'A boy came by, a great singer and gambler, and in the end he lost everything except his horse. He wanted to bet that, but my uncle wouldn't let him. So I was taking the belt home in payment for a horse my uncle bought, and he threw in the drum for a joke.'

'A black-and-white pinto with a black head?'

'Yes, that's the one.'

'Singing Gambler.'

'You know him?'

'Yes. He and I were together a month or so ago.'

'Playing?'

'No. I don't do it. It's just a way of giving away things that it took trouble to get. You can have a good time without laying money on a blanket.'

She started to answer him and checked herself, one hand raised and her lips slightly parted. There was a sound nearer than the rushing arroyos, but like them and growing louder.

'A cloudburst, I think,' she said.

'Yes.'

It was coming fast, and its quality was frightening. They looked at each other. She laughed.

'We may get wet.'

Myron smiled in answer. Pending discomfort seemed somehow diverting.

The downpour marched roaring. Advance drops, then hard rain struck the hogahn, then a river flowed downwards from the sky. They snatched the fire from under the smoke-hole, hissing logs already wet, filling the place with smoke. The zone of ashes became a grey puddle, water spreading out from it met more coming in the doorway, until more than half the floor was turned to mud and only the western quarter, the host's place behind the fire circle, was really dry. The force of the water upon the logs above them seemed to press directly on their shoulders, they were surrounded by night and grey coldness and hostile rain as they crouched together near the back wall. Myron worked with chips and bits of bark, using his hat as a fan, till flame leaping up caught the smoking logs and light spread out again. They sat with their blankets round them, knees drawn up, united in wondering if their space of safety would fail. The river ebbed, became shafts, then drops, then began to die away. Myron rose and went to the door, standing in water and mud as he looked out. Little enough to be seen in the blackness; a tree vaguely outlined indicated an undestroyed world. He wondered just how long it had been.

The girl smiled as he returned. 'Is it still there?'

'It seems to be, as far as one can tell.'

He set to rearranging the fire, moving it as near as possible to its proper place, then wrapped himself in his blanket again.

'Do you think?' she said, and he caught the nervousness in her voice, 'this place — is it — has anyone — this storm coming right on us, you know.'

He looked around. He knew very little about what they did when a hogahn was abandoned after someone died, but the right answer was obvious.

'No.' He felt protective. 'There's no hole in the north wall, and that fire-stick, that means they plan to come back, I think.' He spoke firmly, as though he knew all about it.

She looked at him over the blanket she had pulled half across her face.

'You're going to school, you know writing and all those things.'

He waited.

'I wanted to go. I wanted to learn, but my uncle Returning Wisely wouldn't let me. His first wife had been to school, and they had a bad time.'

'I know.' Myron had heard of Returning Wisely from his uncle; a powerful medicine man, master of the Mountain Chant.

'I think he's changed his mind since, but it was too late. I was married.'

'You were married?'

'Three years ago, but not now.' She made a diving gesture with her hand. 'He was not young, even then.'

The little girls paired off with old men, the thing that made one feel all wrong. The picture of Ethel rose in his mind, but even more he felt and thought of this one, the sense of her maturity and also the even comradeship between them now, equal youngness violated by entrenched old men.

'Why did you want to go to school?'

'Everyone talks about the white men, perhaps if one understood them one could do something. That way I thought about it. But you boys who have been to school, you don't want to do anything. It's the women who hold everything together. Perhaps a woman can do it, I thought.'

Myron stared at the fire. The occasional spattering reminders of rain made their narrow space of dryness seem snug. They had been through something together, they were in a special world of their own. He was warm, comfortable. Piñón wood gives off a smoke which is a perfume, delightful to the nostrils, not stinging to the eyes. Between their fire and the wall the girl and he sat, meeting each other. This warm and living girl.

'You get mixed up and it's easiest to run away from it,

I think.' He heard his own voice and saw her listening.
'Lots of people just forget about what they learned, they
just sit down.'

He began really talking, easing himself to her, the two
things that would not come together and which, separated,
left the world broken in half, the certainties that faded, the
snags and resistances, Snyder, his uncle who wanted him to
stay now that it was autumn and time to talk of the gods —
you can't disbelieve what you never heard of — and Mr. Butler
to whom he was going for advice. Just the act of talking and
being so well attended brought many things into order.

'So I don't know,' he said, 'but I'm a Navajo. Too many
things are true, but they must fit some way. I want to get it
all straight. My uncle gave me the answer to some things,
but it has to be straight.'

As he talked, he had roused himself to a full sitting position,
looking at her from time to time and always finding the dark
eyes with him; he had talked to her and to himself, feeling
inadequate and having no idea how completely, between
word and voice and gesture and the changes of his face, he
told it.

When he finished he felt at once relieved and rather nervous.
What he had said — how odd would it seem to this girl?
In the narrow dry space between the wall and the fire, her
arm touched his from time to time, when he made a gesture,
shifted his position. She was intensely present. The wall at
their shoulder blades continued unbroken into the curve of
the low roof to the central smoke-hole, enclosing them in an
arch of firelight. Sensations, perceptions, came to him
heightened, and the long climb to the mountain shoulder
where the storm had caught him, the nightmare walk in the
rain, took away the sense of a specific place attached to
other places.

'I never knew a Christian before,' she said. 'At least, not
more than to know who he was. Are they usually like you?'

'I don't know. Most of the children go to church and

sing the songs, but they aren't Christian. As soon as they come home they forget all that, along with the rest. They just put their heads under a blanket.'

He didn't think of her as being the same age as girls who sat in the classroom with him. The effect of maturity that came from her marriage, her manner, the quality of this place, gave her a special character. She was impressed by him, she had caught fire.

'I'm trying to be something,' he said, words of his uncle's and of Mr. Butler's rising in his mind. 'I'm going to school. I'm learning all those things. In the end I'm going to do something for the Navajos.'

She saw his intense face. 'You will. The old men I have known' — she hesitated almost imperceptibly, and he thought of that husband, and the parents who gave her to him — 'the old people, they won't do for us. And the young ones, they go around like Singing Gambler, or they put their heads under a blanket, the way you say. But you will do something. I know it. Only you've got to understand the Navajo part, too. Now that you're here, you ought to stay the way your uncle wants, I think.'

'That's why I'm going to Shash Bit'o.'

She laid her hand on his arm. 'You're trying to get your uncle and that man — that Hasteen Bucla — to make up your mind for you, I think. You have to do it for yourself.'

He felt her hand, its live weight and the shape of her fingers, it went up through his arm and into him. When he turned slightly to answer her better, he faced the eyes, long and deep, and the sensitive, firm lips. She had warmth surrounding her like a visible quality, and his thoughts stopped, drowned out in the vivid sense of the person. Her lids half lowered over her eyes, and he heard her breath hesitate. Then she looked frightened. The swift leap of physical sensation shamed him. Immorality. He thought, if she knew she'd despise me. He drew back.

'I think I'm going to stay,' he said, his voice coming out uncertain, jerky.

He remembered Ethel. Not a blanket Indian, the sheep camp and fire. The disturbance in himself continued. The union between them was broken and he ached for it. A multitude of thoughts and sensations swirled in his mind, the broad talk of young Indians, moral principles, one is a man and does what a man does, and woman can despise one for holding back, they say. Something had been pent up for a long time. This girl's contempt would be unendurable. He reached out and took hold of her shoulder.

'No,' she said. 'Oh no.'

There was none of the mere flame of desire he had known so often in his thoughts and in dreams. Too many ideas and conflicts confused it within him, driving him against himself. Strength. Prove yourself. He said, 'In this place ——' his voice was harsh and broke, he couldn't finish and was unsure of the thought, but he pulled her towards him. He felt clumsy, young, uncertain, and that he must be none of those things.

She pulled back, looking at him with her eyes wide open, searching him. From his hand on her shoulder he could feel the tautness of her entire body. He was thinking that he had destroyed everything now. Himself saying don't be afraid, I'm not like that. He let go of her.

'I'm sorry.' It sounded miserable and inadequate.

He rose, put more wood on the fire, then came back and sat, not reclining but well up, his arms around his knees.

'I'm sorry.' He didn't know how to say what he was thinking. In her were delights at which instinct guessed and imagination quailed. He looked to see her angry face, and saw her calm.

'It's all right,' she said. 'It's natural to men, I think. Only for a woman, it's not just so simple.'

He didn't want her to think of him like that. 'I — I never — up to now, only now, with you ——'

She showed her frank surprise. 'You never?'

'No. Only, you see, since we talked together ——' The need to explain himself was lost in the need to tell her what with astonishment he saw that he felt about her, there was something big and she had to know it. 'You don't seem like girls, schoolgirls ——' This was a strange land in which he was trying to find his way. His words came out hard as he stared at her, trying to grasp what he saw so that he could tell about it. He started again. 'You said I wasn't like the young men you knew. Well, you too. I feel with you — something else.' He stopped.

She said softly, 'Oh, so. Not just girls?'

'No!'

She raised herself on her left elbow, studying him again. He saw a change that he could not name, his arm went around her and she came to him. Not taut now, not rigid, the sense of her body unbelievably soft as he slid down beside her. Clumsy, ignorant, with the flame blazing, wanting to go on in a harmony of motion, the confusion of clothes, fumbling, and self-conscious. But she knew. She moved and somehow led him, her touch was quaking ecstasy. Now far beyond what dream or instinct had ever prepared him for, now into the reaches of infinity, and this woman moved against him divinely terrible, and his capacity was divine. Sensation swept them swirling, it was she, she blinded him and he was master of her.

What have I done what have I done dirtiness lain with a woman sin what have I done her arms around him and her trusting body close against his rumpled clothes and grotesque attitude sin what have I done. Responsible, I did it to her have to marry perhaps did it wrong wrong, the things said, the trap of his own urging words to be lived up to. He resisted his desperate longing to push her away. A man. Disgust. A man. Even now he feared her contempt. But he had to move, to be separate. He made himself pull away gently, and saw her half smile and eyes that were content upon him, still seeing her beautiful and wanting none of her. He didn't look at her as he straightened his clothes and went to tend the fire. I've got to be decent, got to be decent. Loves me. A weight upon him. Loves me. Done enough wrong. Tales of cruel seducers, claptrap of white folklore moved in his mind. Show myself a man. Loves me. And she is fine, a fine person. He heard her move behind him. The lard pail drum reflected the fire; the sight of it suggested occupation, a bridge towards control. He picked up the drum and stick, then turned back to her.

She was sitting up, orderly save that her hair was loosened, pulling her blanket over her shoulders. He was astonished how normal she looked, and he managed to return her smile.

He sat in his place again, holding on to himself, and when she moved close to him was unable to keep from flinching away. She gave him a sharp, startled glance and there was a flash of pain in her eyes. He felt unutterably cheap, and knew that if she touched him he would flinch again. He stared at the fire.

'I'll make some coffee,' she said, rising.

She was gone for some time, getting water. In the blessing of being alone, the first force of reaction ebbed. Now there was no question of going to Mr. Butler. Maybe he couldn't even be a Christian any longer. Just a Navajo like any other Navajo. Was she bad, was she loose? What is a bad woman like? He didn't think she was. Just ignorant, and perhaps she loved him. The sooner he could get out of here the better, but meantime he had to behave well. His fingers tapped a rhythm on the drum, a hymn came to mind — My heart lifts up to Thee, Thou Lamb of Calvary — blasphemous now.

She came back in and busied herself at the fire, the type of her picture agelessly familiar. When she came over to sit by him, she put her hand to her loosened hair and smiled ruefully. She's not bad. What is she going to expect from me?

She arranged herself in her blanket, lying with shoulders and head against the bank of earth at the wall.

'I don't even know your name,' she said. 'We are where we are, and I don't know what to call you in my mind.'

'Big Salt's Son, I am called.' He hesitated, and knew he wanted to tell her. 'Seeing Warrior, that is I.'

Her expression became a little less guarded. Her eyes and lashes were shadowed as she lay, her face in shadow with the dark hair around it like smoke, and her half-smiling mouth between the straight nose and the round definite chin. She repeated the name, savouring it.

'And you?'

'War Encircling. I'm called Juniper.'

War Encircling. It suited. He thought vaguely, sinking into a tired silence within his mind, his fingers tapping idly on the drum. Juniper.

'Are you going to sing?'

He roused himself. Sleep and solitude existed in the real world, not in this one. One must do well, and talk was dead. An Anaji song came to his mind, but the gay lift was impossible. He took up the chants his uncle taught him as they came down from the mountain, sober, strong prayers; at the beginning his voice fell down, then he started again and got going. It was a sequence of four, and singing them relieved him, their meditative quality and the rhythm which could be marked on the drum, although drumming did not rightly belong with them. He came into greater possession of himself, less trespassed upon by her near presence, and with this, desire to show himself well began to balance determination to behave well. He ended the fourth chant.

'You can sing,' she said.

The Lazy Cousins song went back into childhood, he started it almost unconsciously, letting the drumstick go full force. Its own lift and tempo caught him up, he was drawn upwards in its rise. Anaji songs, young men's songs. A man is a man. He communed with himself, was alone within the house of song, and his blood began to circulate again. He followed it with another and then two for gambling, restoring his shattered sphere. One does what a man does. The coffee came to a boil.

She rose swiftly in one long line to step to the fire and tend it. As he looked at her, his many thoughts and feelings were coloured by a sense of triumph in regard to her.

'Truly, you have a voice,' she told him. She set the pot handy on the ground. 'Sing some more.'

That effort was over, he couldn't rouse himself again.

'No. I'm too tired. I couldn't keep on lifting it up.'

They fell silent, both watching the coffee-pot, impatient for it to cool enough to give them an occupation. They made no attempt at small talk.

She tried the lip with her fingers. 'It's ready, I think,' she put sugar in and stirred with a stick. 'Here.' She handed it to him.

It broke a tension, the metal container passing from her enclosing fingers to his, the still scalding, sweetened drink. He lay upon one elbow, sipping, then passed it to her. He knew her, there was intimacy. He didn't want to think at all, his tired mind let go its conflicts, everything in him slackened. He laid it all aside for tomorrow.

He became aware that something had ceased, there was an increased stillness in the night. He puzzled over it for a moment.

'The arroyos have gone down.'

She listened. 'Yes. All that water running away when we need it so much. First we have none, then too much, then none again.'

'Do you suppose one could make a lake? At school we studied about dams.'

They talked driftingly. The coffee could not arouse them, presently they began to nod, caught each other at it, and laughed. He looked out the door, then heaped up the fire.

'It's midnight at least, and clearing. It'll be cold towards dawn.'

They rolled themselves up side by side. In the last drowsiness before sleep he desired her, without questioning. It was a new shape of desire which knew itself and stated what it knew. He was far too near sleep to move, the wish rose and faded, blurred away as the ground under him softened and sensation dissolved.

He came awake slowly, conscious first of the sound of a match striking and the smell of smoke, then noticing that there were no sheepskins under him and remembering. He wanted to postpone moving, but felt that his being awake must proclaim itself somehow, and sat up. It was full day outside. The surrounding foothills still shadowed the hogahn, but through the smoke-hole he could see a fresh, brilliant sky. The storm-mood of isolation was ended, the world pressed upon his mind. Guilt. The girl by the fire smiled at him with a friendliness that made his heart sink.

'I'll go catch the horses,' he said, putting on his shoes. 'What does yours look like?'

'A grey, rather small, with a white mane.'

He went out with rope and bridle. Now he had to test what he'd learned these past months about horses and tracking. It was important not to turn out incompetent. His shoes had dried stiff. The morning was sharp, tingling, cold; the sunlight on a bit of the main mountain showing over the hills to the south looked delightfully golden. The world was fresh and washed and the colours all clear. He was pleased with himself when he found the tracks, and his spirits rose in spite of all. He succeeded in getting his rope over his own horse, bridling him, and then roping the grey when he tracked it down, so that he rode to the hogahn in fine spirits, until, as he came near, everything it signified rushed at him again. He'd have to eat breakfast, in fact he was hungry, but the sooner that was over the better.

She didn't speak to him when he came in. They were both constrained, and sharing the coffee-pot was awkward. She looked younger, more of a girl and less the completed woman, and had lost the liveness he'd felt so when first she'd blocked the doorway. He decided that she, too, felt badly about it after all. There was something he ought to do or say, but he didn't know what. Offer to marry her? He shrank from the thought.

They were brief with their eating. When he went towards his saddle, she said, 'Don't forget this,' and handed him the gun. He stared at it a moment, then laid it on his bundle.

'I'm sorry,' he said.

It didn't sound adequate or entirely fitting, but it was all he could think of. She wasn't looking at him.

'I may have a baby, you know.'

There it was. It seemed that he'd been getting ready for it for a long time.

'Then I'll marry you.'

'No.' Surprisingly clear and definite. 'I don't want to marry you. You're hardly ready.'

He felt annoyed. Marrying her was the last thing in the world he wanted to do, but he didn't expect to be scorned. For a time last night he'd had her admiration, now she brushed him aside.

'All right. But I'd be glad to. We — after all ——' The words wouldn't come.

'Don't worry about it.' Her voice was slightly sharp.

She went out, dragging her saddle, and he followed. He couldn't let her go on just that note.

'You're going home? Where do you live?'

'Up there, where you see those red cliffs — a little above that, on the edge of the timber. You're going on to Shash Bit'o?'

That was over with. He couldn't go to Mr. Butler now, but neither could he tell her that. 'I don't know. I'll think about it while I ride today.'

She looked at him curiously, then glanced at the sorrel. 'Is your horse still lame?'

'It's only stiffness, I think. I'll lead him till he warms up. He'll be all right when the sun gets on him.'

She mounted. 'I hope you have a good trip.'

'I may not go far. Perhaps I'll see you this autumn.'

'Perhaps.' Her tone was distant. 'I've got to get along.'

She quirted her pony and started quickly into a lope, while he stared after. But I said I'd marry her. Why, then —? Juniper. He started along the back trail, leading the limping pony. Vividly the good things came back to him, confidence, intimacy, passion. All lost now. Guilt. Sin. Blanket Indians are too ignorant to know how dreadful it is to have a baby like that; a girl just has to get married. But she wouldn't marry him. Not really a man. You're hardly ready. Impossible now to go to Mr. Butler, or back to Yellow Earth. He believed that what he had done was stamped on him for anybody to read, he even feared his uncle's gaze. Many unlike feelings at the same time contended within him, and those long, shadowed eyes and the fine mouth ... War Encircling.

CHAPTER ELEVEN

ÉANANIYÉ,
    Now a holy one paints himself,
        Kola nina,
    Now Wind Boy, holy one, paints himself...
With dark cloud he paints himself,
With misty rain he paints himself...

The sonorous chanting of the men behind him filled the hogahn. He stood up, in breech-clout and moccasins, facing the figures of Talking God and Female God, the two featureless, symbolic masks. Talking God changed the yucca whips in his hands. The boy's hesitation over being initiated, his fear of finding it only grotesque and barbarous, had centred in advance around this rite of being whipped by some man in a mask. He stiffened. The yucca touched him firmly, but not as a blow. There was no pain, no reality of whipping. He felt foolish, and suddenly it seemed as if the god knew and had known, the white mask with the cornstalk painted on it assumed expression; it was only something over a man's head, an ordinary man with the white buckskin hanging from his shoulder, but Talking God was there with his true face hidden and sunbeams around his head, Hasché Yahlti, the Grandfather. Now Myron was afraid his wrong thinking would be seen and he would be rejected, but the yucca was laid on four times. Female God began to put the sacred corn meal on him.

> With rain bubbles he paints himself,
>   *Kola nina*...

He heard the song, and turned sunwise for his back to be sanctified with corn. It was done. He sat down and covered his head again with his blanket while the next boy rose in turn and the song continued.

> To the plume on his head he paints himself,
>   *Kola nina.*
>   *É ananiyé.*
> Now a holy one paints himself,
>   *Kola nina.*

Under the blanket he crossed his arms on his knees and rested his head on them; the chanting came to him through the ground and his skin as well as through his ears, and he heard Talking God's call.

For two months it had flowed in a steady stream towards this: for two months the full activities of daylight life, the interruptions and normalities, had become thin, secondary, peripheral things strung on the one, continuing reality of Shooting Singer's face in the firelight, his quiet voice and the gestures, behind which marched brilliantly the scenes and divine characters of the great legends. He had asked for it perversely, as if he wanted to wrong himself; he hadn't known the stories were like that, as strong as the Bible and with a quality that struck more directly into the depths of his being than anything he had ever heard before.

Not preaching or doctrine, but stories which made all one story, and the people came up out of an older earth, and the gods lived and moved; the vivid images glowed in his mind, the words recurred during the active days intervening between night and night. They made the moon of crystal, bordered with white shells, and covered its face with a sheet of lightning and all kinds of water. They made Cholihi Mountain fast to earth with a cord of rain, and decorated it with pollen, dark mist, and she-rain. They put a yellow bird on its peak, and sent the Boy and Girl who Produce Jewels to live in it. The Divine Twins were born, the two boys travelled through danger after danger in search of Sun Bearer, they became men and Slayer of Enemy Gods stood forth, mature and ever young.

Within the great cycle of tale on tale he lived. Narrative forced no argument, once interest was captured and the characters came to life. Parts of the Bible made him tingle, and King Arthur was read to pieces at Yellow Earth, but voice, emphasis, pause, and gesture transcended the written word, and the characters were all Indians. It was a single stream, flowing up to this moment.

They uncovered their heads again, and the two men stood before them, masks in hand. The other neophytes were much younger than Seeing Warrior, but none of them young enough to be surprised when the gods were revealed as friendly neighbours, and yet it was a great moment. Now, carefully, the masks were put upon them. He looked out through the eyes of Talking God; it was rather smelly, and while the contraption was over his head divinity was present with him.

> It thunders above;
> He thinks towards you,
> He rises towards you...

The masks stood on the buffalo robe, and the first neophyte rose to give them pollen. The positive act of worship — Christianity tugged at Myron, but holding back was impossible now. He watched the youngster with the utterly intent, awestruck face.

> Now to your house
> He approaches for you.
> Now he arrives for you.
> Now at the door,
> He enters to you...

It was his turn; he had to walk carefully in the crowded hogahn, around with the sun. This was the act which would cut him off entirely, and he would belong to the Navajo gods. The name of Slayer of Enemy Gods flashed in his mind, the meaning of 'Enemy Gods.' He must be careful how he thought at this moment. The white and the blue objects standing on the buffalo skin were powerful, he was afraid of what they might know. He didn't frame any prayer as he put the pollen on, with the man who had been Talking God intently instructing him, but he was in intense communication with the symbols.

> He comes within
> He takes his offering.
> 'Your body is strong,
> 'Your body is holy.
> 'Now, I say.'

He took his place again, listening. Stripped as he was, with the air moving against his skin, the last words of the song were full of meaning. Your body is holy. They started the next chant. His uncle was conducting this, right now he knew the old man was happy. That caused him an extra gladness. With the others, he breathed the smoke of sacred herbs, heard the rest of the sequence of hymns, and went out. He really knew he was a Navajo. He had seen something great.

That was only the fifth day of the ceremony. People were coming in, but the main gathering would not be until the final, ninth night. It wasn't like a church service at all, it had nothing in common with Sunday. It went on and on from a slow beginning, parts were dull and parts were silly, and other parts stopped his breath with excitement. It built up with remorseless completeness, like the myths which each act and prayer and sand-painting evoked, its force grew and a whole existed. The sixth night, the seventh night, the eighth night, the ninth day. The trail of beauty. These men thinking and living one thing, the single effort and emotion covering the hogahn and the surrounding camps.

The spirit of the ceremony travelled with him when he went out to look after his uncle's team and his sorrel on the ninth afternoon. Even with the sun still high, it was cold, so that he walked briskly, whistling songs from the chant. The animals had drifted far. Tracking them, catching the sorrel, and bringing them all to a nearer grazing place, his mind ran free and idly over thoughts and perceptions most of which left behind only the pleasant sense of having been occupied. The higher parts of the mountains were white with snow, he wondered when they'd get it down here. Moccasins were queer to walk in. Parts of the ceremony kept coming to mind, the gods, incidents and scenes of the myths, and with them a sense of devotion, a will to be consecrated.

Before he left Tsaili, under Mr. Butler's teaching religion had begun to change from a formula of power into an emotion, but he'd lost that at Yellow Earth. The services of his sect were bare. Things that were coming to life in him responded to parts of the Bible, to some hymns, and to the mystery of the Round Table that all the boys liked so much. Mr. Snyder disparaged the Holy Grail, calling it popish and superstitious, but even he approved of an admiration for Sir Galahad. These were scraps, parts, of what came forth whole to meet the riches of the Navajo religion.

A boy could follow Galahad with hero-worship, but the Twins were like himself, Indian faces of young determination facing danger after danger, becoming men, Slayer of Enemy Gods and Child of the Waters. Pure as Galahad and much more useful. The Younger Brother's loyal support of Nayein-ezgani, the great deeds against the monsters, freeing the world. Slayer of Enemy Gods shone in his mind, a warrior, a hero, and an Indian.

He hummed a Nayeinezgani song as he walked towards the encampment. Many people would be arriving now, soon the last night would begin. He steps from mountain summit to mountain summit, and in the valleys between, the pines are slashed with white where his lightning has struck. Myron looked up to the mountains, half expecting —— He thought how odd it was; Jack had gone back to school, and he was here. School seemed unreal, the thousand thousand white men were far from the sufficiency of the Navajo country. Save for two trips to the trading post, he hadn't even seen a Bellacana in four months. He missed Jack, he ought to be initiated, too. Jack and Ethel bothered him, they might think he'd quit on them. But the answer was here. Afterward, he'd go back to school — he told himself that, but the thought pushed itself over the horizon of time, a saving grace comfortably remote. He wished they were here.

The top of the rise was marked by a flat, broken ledge of rock in corners of which cedars grew. From it one looked down a gentle slope, a quarter of a mile to the hogahns. Myron was surprised. Knowing that this was the last night, seeing people begin to arrive this morning, had not prepared him for the gathering that changed the character of the encampment. The white, prairie-schooner covers of the outspanned wagons spread in wide, irregular lines north and south of the medicine lodge, smoke of many small fires drifted in the moving air, in places forming a bluish haze close to the ground, mingled with the yellow haze of dust from hobbled horses lurching out to graze and riders coming in or visiting about. Along the two main trails more wagons moved, not many, a couple in sight, a few indicated by approaching dust, one showing its white top briefly against the horizon before it dipped below the level of nearer ground. Here and there rode men and women on horseback. The noise of heavy wheels and chains rumbled to where he stood, and a man's voice shouting at his team. He'd forgotten how long he'd been seeing people in twos and threes. He stepped forward, an initiated man who belonged, and remembered that Juniper might be there.

Her uncle, Returning Wisely, was expected, so her parents and herself were likely. Myron wanted to see her, wanted her to know that he was more of a man than he had shown himself to be. As he drew nearer the gathering, his eyes drifted over the groups.

He wondered what her parents were like, having a slight feeling of hostility towards them because of that early marriage, though he knew it was just ignorance. Shooting Singer thought his daughter ready for marriage.

This becoming a man wasn't simple. You thought you knew yourself, knew all about it, then something would open a whole new country, and when you'd gone into that, the old was changed, too. I've been an awful kid, he thought. It had happened again with the initiation: he believed he understood the religion, and then right at the part he thought would be a letdown, where he feared that ridiculousness would break through the will to faith, it happened, when Hasché Yahlti's whip was not intended to hurt — from there on. Without explanation he knew now how the ordinary man with the snowy white buckskin hanging from his shoulder, his head masked by the crude buckskin symbol with its feathers and paint, could contain the god. It was big. It was tremendous and he wanted to tell about it. Other people knew it, of course, but still it was his personal experience.

Consubstantiation — he saw the word in his own handwriting on ruled paper, recalling the close smell of sunlight through glass falling on pine desks, the sharp, cedar-and-rubber taste of the chewed end of the pencil. Con- and trans-, con- was right and trans- was popish. And this was it again. Blasphemous to say the word about these Navajo things — he didn't care, here where the lightning rustled in Nayein-ezgani's quiver. He thought defiantly of Mr. Snyder. Consubstantiation.

He was changed, and he wanted her to see it. He wanted to see her again.

His nostrils were assailed by smoke, dust, and the smell of cooking. Following Warriors had gone off on an errand, but his cousin was waiting by his uncle's wagon.

'I'm going to wander around a little,' he told her as he dropped his bridle and rope. 'I'll eat somewhere.' He pulled a blanket out of the wagon.

She said, 'All right.'

On impulse, he asked, 'Is Skinny Boy around?'

Her expression changed very slightly, 'I don't know.'

He grinned and she looked down. He sauntered off, knowing that he was hungry and food would be plentiful. There
were lots of people, many strangers, acquaintances to stop and
chat with, items of news.

Deer Woman, his aunt, stood in her wagon passing things
down to her husband. She greeted him with a gay *Hallah
hotsan!* and handed him the Dutch oven. Her husband took
his hand with a smile. He helped them make camp, giving
the news of Ha'anoichí.

'Why don't you let your hair grow?' she asked him.

'I haven't any wife to do it up for me.'

'There are lots of them here.'

'I'm look around.' He turned away, then stopped and
looked back. 'If I find one, it will cost you sheep and horses.'

She laughed. 'Get one to suit me, and I'll help pay for her.'

Yellow Man, her husband, said, 'Come back here and eat.'

'Good. I will.'

He drifted on. Many people, many kinds of people, faces
of unlike character, old men, children, and the seasoning of
grown girls scattered through it.

Skinny Boy hailed him. 'Where to, horse-tamer?'

They put hands on each other's shoulders. 'Just walking
around. When did you get here?'

'A little while ago. Come over to our camp.'

'No, I'm looking around. My uncle's working and my
aunt's gone off somewhere. There's no one at our wagon but
Willow Girl.' He pointed towards where it stood, near the
medicine lodge. 'So I thought I'd drift.'

Skinny Boy gave him a grateful look. 'I think I'll drift,
too. I'll see you later.'

It was getting truly cold as Sun Bearer rested on the edge
of the west before he went under. Myron pulled his blanket
well around his shoulders. Then he saw her. She was stand-

ing, surveying the crowd, at midpoint between the fire and where she had picked up the frying-pan. Her mother, a pleasant, firm-looking, solid woman, knelt by the Dutch oven, greasing it, and her father had his back turned, swinging an axe down on a knotty chunk of fuel. Myron stood just outside the edge of their zone, his heart beating. That was Juniper, it was she. She saw him, her eyes alert, speaking, then she looked away.

He realized that she could not account to her parents for knowing him. What sort of people were they? He could have made the acquaintance of any unknown family in the gathering, easily and naturally, but not hers. She knelt to the fire, setting the pan to get hot while she moulded a tortilla. He drifted on, feeling empty.

Working his way out of the crowd, at the outer edge he found himself facing a small fire in front of a car. He was thinking as he approached it that it must have taken some driving to get here, then he saw that the people at the fire were white, a man and a woman, accompanied by some kind of Indian who wore his hair in two long braids, bound with red-and-green tape. The Indian was speaking English. He was young, and wore a wide, black hat. Some kind of Pueblo, Myron decided. It upset him to see white people here, as if this inner country wasn't as safe as he had thought it to be. The car had a New Mexico licence.

The white man looked up and said, 'Hello.'

Myron just stared, his face blank.

'Can you tell me when the dance comes out?' he asked politely.

With slow stupidity the boy answered, '*Shi do pehozn da.*'

The Indian said, '*Amigo, cuando sale el baile?*'

'*Shi do pehozn da.*'

The woman laughed. Myron yielded to the temptation to smile; he didn't feel disagreeable towards these people, just wanted no traffic with them. He walked off.

That was a lot of trouble, driving all the way here from

New Mexico. Indians with braided hair lived around Santa
Fé, far beyond Gallup. That man had been to school, he
shouldn't be wearing long hair. None of them would be able
to understand what they'd come to see.

Two trucks stood parked together. Tall Man sat on the
running-board of one of them, looking smart and modern
in big hat, silk scarf, bright lumberjack, and beaded gaunt-
lets. Two young men, short-haired, lounged in the other.
There were half a dozen cases in the bottom of it. Myron
thought he'd like to get to know Tall Man, there was someone really smart. He wondered if he'd been initiated.

One of the young men said in English, 'Want some pop?'

He considered the question briefly. 'I guess not. It's too
cold.'

'We ain't got no white mule dis trip.'

They both laughed and Tall Man smiled.

'I'm headin for coffee,' Myron told them.

Tall Man said, 'This is bad weather for pop.'

'Yeah. But we'll sell some.'

'You're sure it isn't spiked?'

'Sure.'

Myron thought of a lot of things he'd like to say to the
delegate, but you couldn't shift right from kidding into serious
talk. He got to Deer Woman's fire just as the goat's ribs were
sizzling on the coals. Following Warriors and Willow Girl
were there, so was Skinny Boy. Other people dropped in.
He could eat and not pay attention to the occasional talk.
It was dark by the time eating was over.

Eight bonfires enclosed the rectangular dancing-space in
front of the medicine hogahn. Around them formed the
wider rectangle of people, with small fires here and there.
Shooting Singer and the patient came out of the hogahn and
stood facing east. The four First Dancers, the Atsa Tlei in
their masks, with Talking God, came quietly into the space.
Myron didn't notice them until the watcher called, 'Come on
the trail of beauty!' He left his family and moved to the front,

where the heat of the big blazes reached his face and winter night swirled round his ankles.

The medicine man began a long prayer, each line repeated by the patient as a litany.

> In the house made of dawn,
> *In the house made of dawn,*
> In the house made of evening,
> *In the house made of evening...*

Myron listened intently to the great words.

> In the house made of dark cloud,
> *In the house made of dark cloud,*
> In the house made of he-rain...

Could this really make a sick man well? Surely it was possible. It would be great if that haggard-looking man there was really cured tomorrow.

> With the dark thunder above you,
> Come to us soaring,
> With the shapen cloud at your feet,
> Come to us soaring,
> With the far darkness of he-rain over your head,
> Come to us soaring...

His uncle's deep voice, his certain, devoted face, his uncle's power. The patient repeated the lines with equal feeling. *He* had no doubts.

> With zigzag lightning high outflung over your head,
> Come to us soaring,
> With the rainbow hanging high over your head,
> Come to us soaring,
> With the far darkness of dark clouds on the ends of your wings,
> Come to us soaring...

Each image stated twice, driving the words home until standing there he saw it all in full colour, the piled-up attributes and circumstances which between them compassed the nature of a god's approach.

> With darkness on the earth, come to us.
> And I wish the foam floating in the flowing
>   water at the roots of the great corn.
> I have made your sacrifice.
> I have prepared your smoke.
> My feet restore for me.
> My legs restore for me...

It swept him up in conviction. This must surely work. But that wasn't all of it. He knew from his uncle that it wasn't just the sick man, in a way he was the excuse. They came to the end of the declaration —

> In beauty I walk,
> Free of pain I walk,
> Feeling light within I walk,
> With lively feelings I walk,

and began asking good things for all men, abundant clouds, passing showers, abundant growing things, fair white corn to the ends of the earth, yellow corn, blue corn, all kinds of corn, jewels of all kinds —

> With these all around you, may they come in beauty...
> In beauty old men will see you,
> In beauty old women will see you,
> In beauty young men will see you...
> In beauty the children will see you,
> In beauty the chiefs will see you.
> In beauty they will see you as they scatter,
> In beauty they will see you as they come home.
> May their roads home be beautiful on the trail of pollen.
> May they all reach home in beauty...

That was himself, his relatives, everyone, the creaking wagons and small horses moving in all directions tomorrow, the ordinary people going to their own places, and the blessing over them, spreading out.

> It is done in beauty,
> It is done in beauty!

They scattered pollen on the waiting dancers and sat down in the doorway of the lodge. Myron came to himself as Talking God's cry signalled the First Dancers to begin. He found a place to sit down where he could see well and be comfortable, and would not be talked to, near the east end of the northern line.

After the First Dancers were through, the Naakai came out, six gods and six goddesses with Talking God again, and Water Sprinkler. He listened to their thunderous, exciting song, familiar to him because people had been whistling it ever since the first frost. A man sitting next him borrowed a match, and made an inconsequential joke when he refused tobacco. Forty-eight times between now and dawn the dance would be performed, the teams alternating with all but identical songs. You didn't need to pay attention. Watching the first performance, he was disappointed, too inexperienced to notice niceties of footwork, but even so the music, carried on the syllables of a meaningless song, reached to him. It was harsh, it was surprisingly deep in pitch, resonant behind the masks, and it was powerful.

He lay back, letting the shifting dazzle of the fires clear from his eyes, and there were the stars, remote and clear and manifold, and the night air on his face. After a pause, the second team of Naakai came out. The word savage came to his mind as he responded to the disharmonies and at the same time was bothered by them.

> *Ohoho ho howé heya heya*
> *Ohoho ho hehehé heya heya*
> *Habi niyé habi niyé . . .*

People talked and moved about. The cold came up through the ground, it flowed in a shallow river just over the skin of the earth, and turned his blanket to cotton. He sat up. Getting close to the bonfires was no good, they scorched your face while your back froze, but people were kindling smaller blazes where you could draw near. Behind the hats and heads

and standing figures wagon tops loomed ghostly. He stood
up and began picking his way among the people, thinking
two things at once. He needn't have been so shy, and now
surely... At the first fire too many people were crowded.
A man called to him sharply; he held his foot, about to
descend on a sleeping child, and exclaimed. At the second
fire he joined the group which stood close around, facing
outwards. The warmth soaked into his legs, his seat, his
shoulders, while he still searched. Over there — no. He
watched that fire, and was sure, knowing he could always
spot the set of her head, but he held back, telling himself he
wasn't sure. It didn't matter anyhow, this was a good place.
The second team of dancers went out. The man next him
asked where he was from, they talked together, mentioning
the white people and the Indian with them. Another man
said the Indian was a Tewa from around Bead Water. They
all took time to consider the whites, and the two men agreed
it was a fine thing, *hojoni*, for aliens to come so far and lend
their interest, their help, to the Night Chant.

The first team returned. Water Sprinkler made everyone
laugh, as he was supposed to do, coming in late and getting
lost. Talking God gave his cry, and the music crashed again.
Myron went straight to the other fire. Perhaps because of
the women — Juniper and her mother and another matron
with a child in her lap — most of the people here were sitting.
Beside Bay Horse, her father, was a familiar youth; he tried
to remember that alert, handsome face — Singing Gambler.
Irritation was first, but realization of the opening given him
outstripped it.

He walked into the close circle and stood staring down at
his acquaintance. Singing Gambler raised his head slowly,
their eyes met, for a moment both were serious, and then as
recognition came to him, both smiled broadly and Myron
squatted.

'*Hallah hotsan!*'
'*Hallahani!*'

They took each other's hands and pulled at each other slightly. Myron didn't really feel as cordial as all that, but other factors made the performance genuine.

Singing Gambler said to Bay Horse, 'Now here's a man with a real voice.'

Juniper's father said, 'Sit down. Be warm.'

He seemed an agreeable man.

'You still have my bracelet,' Singing Gambler said.

'Yes. How's the pinto?'

'I traded him. Do you want a race tomorrow?'

'I don't know. I may be sleepy.'

'Where from?' Bay Horse asked.

'Ha'anoichí. My uncle is Shooting Singer.' That placed him, he knew. He felt himself to be wily when he asked, 'And you, where from?' He hadn't looked at Juniper yet.

'The Rim above T'o Tlakai. My brother is helping your uncle.'

Myron nodded.

'That's his wife.' Bay Horse indicated the woman with the infant, who smiled at him.

In making himself comfortable, he shifted his position, so that he could see Juniper. Her blanket drawn across the lower part of her face and over her head hid her well enough, but he guessed the amused look in her eyes.

'I thought you were going back to school,' Singing Gambler said.

'So did I, but here I am, using pollen.'

He thought he saw the edge of her blanket move, her eyes open slightly.

Ohoho ho hehehé heya. The song was a background.

Returning Wisely's Wife said, 'I've heard your uncle speak of you.'

'What have you been doing since we sang in the rain?' Singing Gambler asked.

'Harvesting, moving down to the winter range — all like that. And you?'

The boy grinned, the swift flash that made his face give light. 'Riding around, just riding around.'

He wore a new, fine blanket over the oldest, shabbiest clothes, a handsome turquoise ring, and brand-new silk headband. Myron envied him. Myron's clothes were of even quality, with nothing showy.

Bay Horse drew a laugh, saying, 'He's eaten out of every pot in this part of the country, and still he's thin.'

Singing Gambler asked, 'Have you learnt to smoke yet, schoolboy?'

With a purpose, Myron answered, 'I'm learning. Have you tobacco?'

He hadn't, but Bay Horse handed him a sack and a package of brown papers.

Myron said, 'This may cost you a lot of tobacco,' as he started rolling. His clumsiness diverted them all. The two women and the girl, a man standing by the fire sideways to them, a man sitting behind, were drawn together in amusement. Myron began to giggle. They were all laughing, and Juniper let the blanket fall away from her face.

Juniper's mother — her name was Red Woman — said, 'Here, give it to me.'

She made a cigarette deftly and passed it over. 'Can you smoke it, or shall I blow on it for you?'

The man sitting behind said, 'Pull in, brother, don't blow out.'

He heard Juniper's laugh, distinct among the rest. He knew her voice only in seriousness; this sound rounded out her humanity in a surprising way. He was blushing. Well, they'd think it was for other reasons.

Red Woman made a cigarette for herself and passed the makings along, but Myron had the whole audience as he started smoking, and his best act yet to come. He puffed gingerly. They were all united now, as if they were inside someone's hogahn, and everyone was looking right at everybody else. The singing had stopped again, he'd forgotten he was hearing it. When he thought the time was ripe, he drew in a deep puff, and the bursts of coughing that followed were so genuine he couldn't entirely appreciate his success.

The coughing shifted the run of his own feelings. As he lay catching his breath, he knew that he could have no direct talk with her here. He looked sidelong at Singing Gambler, then reminded himself that he wasn't interested that way, but only because she was special. There were things he needed to say to her, but it was out of the question. He was getting turned aside from the *hojoni*, the happy beauty which validated the ceremony.

He threw the rest of his cigarette into the fire.

'I must wander along,' he said, rising.

'Let us know if you come over the mountain,' Bay Horse told him.

Juniper's eyes met his, quick, complete. He kept his face plain with an effort. Had she told him, or he her? He walked straight back, north, until he left the crowd and the encircling wagons, and squatted, his blanket pulled close about him, in solitude. *O hoho ho hehehé heya, Eo lado eo lado eo lado eo lado nashé* ... The song pursued him. One did not have to listen to it, it continued of itself inside one; it was not a thing to be watched, but in which one lived. The complete change from the mass to loneliness swept down upon him. He looked up at the stars, the music might be coming from them. Behind the silent wagons the qualities of firelight showed and shifted. He waited long. At last he saw her coming and rose. He hoped she didn't think — expect ——

Two blanketed figures, boy and girl, facing each other in the darkness through a long silence; he'd seen it before, at the Anaji, on other occasions of gatherings, but it seemed odd to be part of that himself. In the starlight her eyes and mouth were shadows, as he remembered them before. They stood a long time without speaking. It was all right, it did not conflict with *hojoni*, the path of beauty. He had feared that desire would leap up in him, alien to the ceremony of which they were partaking, but instead he felt rather blank and dry inside. The vivid contact-sense of details of her body which he recalled sometimes, was missing; he saw her in her heavy blanket, and her face, and he wanted communication with her and no speech came out of him.

Finally he said, 'I wanted to see you.' It sounded ridiculous. Then with an effort, 'I've been thinking about you.'

She was as shy as he. 'So you stayed here, after all?'

'Yes. I handled the pollen the other day.'

He meant to tell her more than that, but how could one talk, standing here where people might come, where her parents might look for her?

'Your Hasteen Bucla, what did he say?'

'I didn't go to him. I made up my mind, after I left that place.'

He could see her well enough to think she looked pleased.

'I'll stay here till next fall, I think, then perhaps I'll go back to school.'

'Then you'll be at school a long time, when you go?'

'I don't know. Perhaps.' He dredged into himself for words. The unending music caught at a corner of his attention, he was alert for anyone coming. 'Things are different.'

Her right hand moved and came out from under a fold of her blanket. He could see it, held laxly near her left side. He could lock fingers with it and stand so, but that was courtship. He didn't intend that, he only wanted her to understand ——

'I wanted to talk with you,' he said. 'We can't talk like this.'

She didn't help him. Her hand went back under the blanket.

'I shall be travelling around,' he went on. 'I think I'll be coming by your place.'

'You can eat there,' she said. The answer was hospitable, but her tone indifferent.

He knew he'd failed again. If only he could tell her. Now

he wanted her fingers, and reached out, but she made no move, and when he touched her arm under the blanket it was entirely unresponsive. This was all wrong, he'd foreseen meeting her again so warmly, understanding, communication.

'That boy, Singing Gambler, do you see him often?'

'He came by once this fall, and turned up tonight,' she said carelessly. 'You know how he drifts around.'

Myron knew that, and his gaiety and charm and self-assurance. But what to say? How to say anything? Where had this gone so wrong? He had to go back to school yet, to be away from the Navajos. He couldn't do or be anything permanent now.

'My mother will be wondering about me,' she said, and with that she left him.

He watched her go. When she was at the nearer wagons, he wanted to call her back, but he didn't. He sat down on a wagon tongue. What's the matter with me? Now he knew what he should have said. Too late now, only it mustn't just end like this. A man was coming towards him, so he rose and wandered again. How long had the music been going on, how many re-entrances? He didn't know. He felt tired, and guilty at letting himself go into scattered, unhappy thoughts. His being turned towards the ceremony for relief.

After getting another blanket from their wagon, he found his aunts and his cousins, and Skinny Boy and his parents, and lay down among them. One could talk a little, watch, lie back and see the sky, stare into a fire, doze, watch again. The performance wove itself through sleeping and waking and coloured every posture of the night. Talking God's neat stepping took him along the lines and back, the rattles sounded like rain beginning as the dancers swung about, their voices rose again, their feet moved together. In drowsiness it blurred until it permeated the whole world. During the pauses between dances, he could hear faintly the quieter chants inside the lodge and the dull thudding of the basket drum. It went on until it had become a lifetime.

The dancers filed off again, but it was different, a change ran among the people; he sat up, blinking, and heard the first Finishing Song come from the medicine lodge. The east was turning white. He got up and went over there, but the place was crowded, so he sat down outside. The four short songs ended. He recognized his uncle's voice praying. Then it was over. Men were leaving the hogahn. Tall Man came out — so he had been initiated. He went to the door, where he could see his uncle and Returning Wisely and the patient. From where he sat rolling a cigarette, Bay Horse looked up and smiled.

Myron turned to the east, thinking the dawn prayers as he walked. Some of the people were beginning to move, some slept. Under the wagons many were rolled up in their blankets. People were going for water, down to the thin flow of the creek below the encampment. He walked out to where he could see the line. He felt light and alert, the short wakefulness brought by daybreak, with colour beginning to show and people and horses looking flat. He saw Red Woman going down, carrying a pail. He turned back. Returning Wisely's Wife was alone at the wagon. He scouted again, looking through the crowd, then to the country roundabout.

Juniper was dragging a long, dead branch. He went out to meet her. She stopped where she was, looking at the ground.

'Listen to me,' he said. 'Understand me. I know you're angry with me, but understand. I — I'm mixed up. I'm just finding out. Do you see? I have to know — to know what I am. Then I'm coming to see you.'

She raised her eyes. 'All right.' Then she smiled and her eyes danced. 'Don't wait too long, Mixed-up Boy. I might not wait.'

His spirits rose with the relief.

'I'm worth something, too,' he said. 'I'm worth waiting for a while.'

'Perhaps.' She drawled the word, looking at him sidelong, and laughed, and then she went on, dragging the stick of fuel.

2

Where the sheep were grazing in the box canyon it was safe enough to leave them during lunch. He'd ridden out with Willow Girl to help her get them across the wash, and then stayed for the morning, helping a little, talking idly, loafing there where the walls reflected warmth and it was pleasant enough in the sun. He took his cousin up behind his saddle, and as they rode down the main canyon, began teasing her about Skinny Boy. They hadn't seen him since they moved to their winter camp, save at the Night Chant.

'Don't be silly,' she said. 'I like him all right, but he's too young, and so am I. I'm not thinking about those things yet.'

She was fifteen. 'That's right,' Myron told her. 'But does your mother know that?'

'I don't know. The work's easier since you're here, but with the sheep and all, she'd like someone else camping with her, I think. But she wants a high price; anyhow, I'm not ready.'

'Even Skinny Boy?'

'Even Skinny Boy.'

'You're right, I think. We don't like those ways any more. I'll help you if it comes along.' His cousin had surprised him, she always seemed so old-fashioned. 'Fifteen is too young. I'm sixteen, and I'm too young.'

He fell silent, staring between his horse's ears. Sixteen is too young. I told Juniper — not too young for that, the hot, sweet touch. I think of her so much. Love, perhaps, I mustn't love an ignorant, I want — Juniper, War Encircling. I've got to find out soon and then go see her, straighten this out, have her understand, special she's special. The horse turned of its own accord into the road across the wash. In the end I go back to school ——

'Look, a car!'

Myron stared all around. 'Where?'

'Its tracks, on the road.'

Tire marks showed here and there in the half-frozen ground. Myron's heart turned over. What was a car doing over this way? Had they come after him?

Willow Girl said, 'What do you suppose it is?'

'I don't know.'

'What's the matter?'

'I'm thinking — if it's a Washington car come after me.'

'What will you do? We don't want you to go back now. I don't.'

Her last words pleased him. He'd never been sure just what she did think of him.

'I'll hide. You'll tell them — tell them someone like Singing Gambler came along and we rode off together. We — we were on our way to a Night Chant at — at, oh, somewhere way over west.'

'Dennihatso.'

'Good.'

'All right. But if you waited I could sneak out to you with some lunch.'

Myron snorted. 'This country's full of places to eat lunch.'

He knew now. He'd chosen back there when Talking God touched him, when he fed the masks, although it was Nayeinezgani he followed. You have to be one or the other, you can't be both. Why have I waited so long? He felt light, the world was clear. I've taken this side.

'Where will you really go?' Willow Girl was thrilled.

'I don't know. Just go around for a couple of days.' This afternoon, tomorrow morning. The sorrel's in good shape. Juniper. By noon tomorrow. 'Listen. Graze up around that same place, and farther up. I won't come back to the hogahn, I'll come to you first, and you can tell me if it's all clear.'

'All right.'

They rounded the butte by the drop into the arroyo, and saw the car, black and solid, standing beside the road just where it went down. Myron reined in sharply, they both gasped and sat watching.

'No one in it,' he said, and then, 'it isn't a Washington car.'

'How do you know?'

'That piece of metal they put on; Washington cars have it with white tracks on blue. This one is red and yellow.' He puzzled. 'Whose do you think it is?'

'I don't know. Could it be those white people who came to the dance?'

'No. They had a big, blue car.'

They were alongside it now, eyeing the short-snouted Ford.

'It's Tall Man, perhaps,' Willow Girl said.

'No. The painted plate is wrong for him. That yellow plate comes from east of the mountains. But it must be Indians. Down towards Nanjoshi lots of them have cars.'

They studied the road and the loose sand by the creek-bed.

'Two men went across,' Myron said. 'One of them walks like an Indian.'

'Yes.'

'I guess I'll go see. Hold on.' He quirted his pony up the farther bank and made for the hogahn at a good trot. Nothing seemed unusual. Smoke rose from the centre of the earth-and-log dome, no one stood outside. He went in behind his cousin.

Nobody spoke as he entered. He had straightened up and was still staring when Mr. Butler said, 'Hello, Myron. I'm glad to see you, my boy.'

Myron knew he said 'Hello,' but didn't hear himself. He was shaking hands. It was Mr. Butler. Even to this far place, to the winter camp, Mr. Butler had come. He sat down. It could not have been more monstrously significant if the academic building at Yellow Earth had come walking down the canyon after him. It reached, even to here it reached.

Myron supposed the strange Indian was an interpreter, like John at Tsaili.

'It's been a long time,' Mr. Butler said. 'And I had trouble finding this place.'

Myron didn't answer. Everyone was waiting. Willow Girl was expecting him to do something, but he couldn't. It was Mr. Butler. Food was set forth, and they ate, without heartiness. Mr. Butler ate out of the pot like an Indian. He seemed comfortable in the hogahn, he was the only person really at ease. He made a few remarks in his mispronounced yet competent Navajo, to which Shooting Singer responded briefly.

When they had eaten, the missionary said: 'I've told your uncle that you must finish your schooling. I told him how well you had been doing. You've missed two months now, Myron; it's time you came back.'

Myron stared at the fire. He had expected a flood of reproaches.

'I expect you'd rather not go to Yellow Earth. Is that right?'

Myron nodded.

'I've made other arrangements. I want you to come back with me.'

Myron told his uncle, 'He wants me to go to school again.'

'When we wrote those letters,' Shooting Singer said slowly, 'we promised to return you. But I was happy. Good things were happening. You have to go, I think.'

Myron said in English, 'All right.'

Myron sat beside Mr. Butler, while the interpreter lounged with jolted somnolence in the back seat. The road improved after it climbed out of the canyon, and shortly joined a better one, which allowed the driver to relax and talk.

'I couldn't come before,' he said. 'I was afraid I wouldn't be able to get away before snowfall.' Then, after a pause, 'I was truly sorry when Paul Snyder wrote me that you hadn't come back. What happened?'

Juniper, Shooting Singer, Nayeinezgani. 'I dunno.'

'It's easy to stay where you are, just stay on. I think you'd been away from the reservation too long. I don't blame your uncle, he seems to be a fine man. But of course, he doesn't know, he can't really understand the importance of keeping up your schooling.'

The road was bad for a spell. They were climbing a southern, lower extension of Chiz Lan Hojoni Mountain, a long, slow grade that made the engine pull. The two red tracks of the road went on and on, broken in places by dips, twisting a little, with grey-green low vegetation between them and grey-green bushes on either side.

'He said you were initiated in the Yeibichai Dance. Why did you do that?'

'I dunno.'

Mr. Butler's eyes were on the road. He looked disappointed. He wasn't acting the way Mr. Snyder would. Myron made an effort.

'I guess I wanted to know. You — you can't not believe someting you've never heard about. My uncle said dat. I just — kinda — went along.'

'That means you offered pollen to the masks.'

'Yessir.' How did he know?

'That's worship, you know. You're a Christian, you know, Myron, and you worshipped false gods. Surely you don't believe there's anything sacred about a painted buckskin bag pulled over a man's head.'

Buckskin bag.

'No, sir. I guess not.'

'You must not bear false witness against your God. "Thou shalt have none other gods before Me." In the end you know, God will find you out.'

Myron stared at the road ahead. God could reach over the mountains, to the remotest canyon. He overstepped all boundaries.

'I want you to stay in touch with your people. Perhaps ——'
Mr. Butler hesitated, then said, 'Perhaps Snyder was not quite the man for you. I've arranged for you to go to Santa

Fé; it's a more advanced school, and I know you will like the Reverend Charles Rensselaer there. You have a career to make; I'd be sorry to see you let go and sink back.'

At the top of the long climb, the divide, the road turned southward for a hundred yards. On his right hand Myron could see all the majestic, wild country he was leaving, mesa and butte and hill and canyon, and looking over his shoulder made out where jumbled red rock piled like whirling water. A black volcanic dike was a knife-like line of shadow across part of it; near that was T'o Tlakai, and Juniper's winter hogahn. War Encircling. So that was over, and he never straightened it out. God reached out — the kingdom, the power, and the glory — the power — Navajo is nothing, civilized is strength is Christian Slayer of Enemy Gods but God turns back the arrow.

Sometimes Mr. Butler spoke, sometimes he was silent for long periods. He did not press hard, did not try to drag out of Myron anything that had happened. No search for the shameful. Towards sunset they had supper at a trading post, and shortly thereafter swung onto the long highway to Gallup. The sun was gone to the west side of the mountains. Night closed down. The car made a steady, roaring sound over the graded road, its lights spreading an area of brightness into the night. That was what Myron remembered afterward; being tired in the front seat, the road turned to a river under the lights, and Mr. Butler talking, understandable, clear, wise, talking. The power.

PART THREE

CHAPTER ONE

MYRON glanced at the restaurant door out of the corner of his eye as he went past. There was a short, pockmarked Mexican leaning against the wall beside it. He went on down San Francisco Street, stood and rubbered in the window of a curio store, then came slowly back. He was going in this time, he had to go in.

Half the door stood open. He could look through to the dark, long counter at the end with mirrors behind it, and the tables along either side. A couple of men were sitting at one, there was the bartender at the back, otherwise the place was empty. The man by the door winked and spoke to him in Spanish. Myron started, felt guilty, settled his face, and answered, '*No sabe.*'

'*No sabe*, eh?' The man said. 'You from de school?'

'Yeah.'

'Lookin for a leetle home-brew?'

Myron started to exclaim 'No!' but checked himself. 'Maybe. I'm lookin for a friend of mine. He said he'd be in here.'

'Eendian boy?'

'Yeah. A big feller wit a black shirt and light yeller necktie. You seen him?'

'Yeah. I know heem. Go on een, he's eenside.'

Myron went in. That's a bar. This is where they sell beer and whiskey. Only pop bottles were visible behind the counter, but Don said that if they knew you... So this is what it's like. It didn't look so wicked.

The man behind the bar said, 'Hello, John. What is it?'

Myron made himself speak. 'I'm lookin for Don White Elk. He told me to meet him here.'

'That big boy with the hook nose?'

'Yeah. Dat's him.'

'He's in back, go on in.' The man jerked his head towards a door.

Myron turned the knob and went through to a second, smaller room, holding half a dozen uncovered tables and some plain chairs. The place was utterly free of decoration. Don sat at one of the tables, staring at a glass of beer. He wore white flannel trousers, full-cut, a black shirt with white buttons, pale yellow tie, and a citified, small felt hat on the back of his head. He looked up and stared in surprise.

'Well — what the hell are *you* doin here?' he asked.

He stopped in front of the table, looking down. White Elk smiled feebly.

'Aw, what's the matter? Don't be like that, big boy. Sit down.'

Myron understood that it took a lot of beer to make a person drunk. He guessed the Arapaho had only just started.

'I was lookin for you,' he said.

'Say, we ain't startin practice today, are we?'

'No. It's not dat. But gee, Don, Mr. Rensselaer, and Mr. Cowring, and all of dem are huntin for you.'

Don's expression changed, tightened. 'What for? Serafina, hunh?'

'Yess.'

'And you bein their pet dog, you told 'em I was likely here, and they sent you a-runnin after me, hunh?'

Myron flushed. 'I don't tell tales.'

Don stared at him. 'Maybe not.' With a slightly swaggering gesture he took a drink of the home-brew. 'But you're a hell of a Christer.'

Myron was determined not to lose his temper. He'd taken it on himself to do this thing, the beginning of his calling; he'd do it right. He drew a deep breath.

'I came after you, Don, so's to help you. Gee, you can get into a lot of trouble if you aren't careful.'

'Looks like I was in plenty trouble now, or Serafina is.' He laughed shortly. 'Has she had her baby?'

'Yeah. She had it about two weeks ago, but her folks only just learned it was you.'

'What do they want me to do?'

'Dey want to take you out dere.'

'And marry me to that Pueblo squaw? Nothin doin.'

Myron stared down at him, checking fresh anger at the word 'squaw.' The Oklahoma Indians were always sneering at the Southwestern people. And this was sin, just what you heard about.

'Look, Don, you're in trouble eider way. Dey're huntin for you. When dey catch you dey'll take you out dere anyhow. Or dey might stick you in jail. It's a lot better if you come of your own accord.'

'Jail me for knockin her up?'

'Dat's how Mr. Rensselaer was talkin.'

'He would!'

'Maybe. But what do you care about it?'

'Gee, Don —— ' Myron made a helpless gesture. 'Well, Serafina's a nice girl. And den, we been roomin togedder, and dere's de team, and all —— '

Don nodded. 'You're a funny guy. Sittin on the bed preachin sermons when I start to tell the boys about the fun I been havin. And pourin my whiskey out o' the winder. And then comin after me like this.' He grinned. 'I bet you had kittens, comin in here.' He stared at his glass, and drank down to the yeasty sediment. 'Well, I reckon she don't want to marry me no more than I do her. I guess you're right. Let's get it over with.'

Myron's heart leaped. Don was wrong, of course. Serafina was a good girl. He'd marry her, and then he'd straighten out and be all right.

'You aren't drunk, are you?' he asked.

'Hell, no. Not on one glass.' White Elk rose. 'Say, you come with me, hunh?'

Myron hesitated. The busses from the reservations would be coming in today, and he wanted to be there if Jack had got his transfer, but he couldn't quit on Don now, since he'd started this.

'All right. Better get someting to take de smell off you.'

'How come you know so much?'

'Listenin to you.'

Don bought Sen-Sen at the bar. As they walked towards school in the bright sunshine, he meditated.

'Say, Myron,' he said, 'if I just go in there, old Rensselaer's sure goin to crawl all over me. You go tell him I'm willin to act nice, and get him to lay offa me, will ya?'

'All right.'

'Trainin starts tomorrow,' Don said. 'But you're always in trainin. You don't know what it means. I was a fool to come back here.'

Myron didn't answer. Even though you knew they were wrong, the Eastern Indians at the school, from Oklahoma and Dakota and those places, made you feel like a rube. Don was one of the worst, but you couldn't beat him on the football field.

They recognized Mr. Rensselaer's car among others in front of the administration building.

'I guess I'll wait here,' Don said, sitting on the running-board.

'You aren't goin to run off?'

'Nope. I plant my stick here.'

Myron went up the steps and into the office. Mr. Cowring the Superintendent, Mr. James the Principal, Mr. Rensselaer, and Father Adolph were there. They looked at him in surprise.

'What is it, Myron?' Mr. Cowring asked.

'Don — Don's outside. He says — I mean — I guess he feels like he kinda wants to do whatever you say.'

Astonishment spread on their faces, then Mr. Rensselaer began to smile, looking approvingly at Myron.

'You're sure you want to take him out there?' Cowring said.

'Of course,' Rensselaer told him. 'Ready, Father?'

The Superintendent said, 'I've got a couple of things to finish up. Then I'll be along if you want me.'

'We expect your help,' Rensselaer answered.

'Certainly.'

At the door, Myron tugged at the clergyman's arm. 'Mr. Rensselaer.'

'Yes, my boy?'

'Don't — don't scold him, please. He's goin to be all right.'

Rensselaer stared a moment, then smiled. 'All right, Myron.' He patted his shoulder.

'And — he wants me to come along.'

'That's fine.'

He followed them to the car where Don stood sullenly waiting. He felt triumphant and acclaimed. Soldier of Christ.

The clergyman and priest occupied the front seat, a little stiffly. The complications of marriage between a Protestant and a Catholic had not been settled between them, and they were watchful of each other.

After they had gone several miles, Don asked, without looking at Myron, 'Is it a boy or a girl?'

'I tink it's a girl.'

Don grunted.

Myron glanced at him from time to time. Don was going to marry Serafina and then he'd straighten out. He'd see the light. You couldn't let a guy go to jail. He was such a swell athlete. Next hat I get, Myron decided, I'll get a little one like that. Big hats — rubes — those clothes cost money.

'Say, Don,' he said.

The Arapaho looked towards him.

'You didn't buy dem clothes in Santa Fé?'

Don was glad of something to talk about. His sullen look decreased.

'I got the tie here, but the rest I bought in St. Louis.'

'St. Louis!'

'Sure. We got up a team this summer, eight of us boys, and went on the road.'

'Team? Oh — dancin.'

'Yeah, any kinda dance you want, only don't forget to say it's a war dance. We went to Hot Springs and Pipin Rock and all them places. Boy, we had fun.' He grinned. 'Plenty tail. White girls.'

Myron wished he hadn't spoken. Don was bad. Don and Serafina — well, there'd been Juniper. It could just kind of happen. Of course he knew Don was loose, but bragging on it now when he ought to be sorry... He wondered where Juniper was now. Married probably. Last year — two years. Two whole years ago. It made him uncomfortable to remember the reservation and the way he backslid. But Mr. Rensselaer said that since he'd really repented and gotten over it, he should think of it as a valuable experience. He said it would be an inoculation. I've tried to make up for it.

They had left the highway and were jouncing over the dirt road to the Pueblo. Myron had been there once before. It seemed deserted, just one woman came to a door and looked at them, and a dog drifted across the plaza. They held their dances out here, right in front of the church. It didn't make sense.

Father Adolph led the way to a house. Don, stiff with resistance, tagged close behind Myron.

The family had been waiting for them. There were Serafina and her baby, her father and mother, her elder brother and sisters. The others greeted Mr. Rensselaer and Father Adolph politely — they all spoke English — treating the priest with marked respect, but she stayed in a corner, and hung her head when Father Adolph went over to her.

Her father — his name was Agapito Batista — told them all to sit down. Myron took a chair in a corner, where he was out of the way. He thought perhaps he ought to have stayed outside, but he wanted to see what happened, and what a Pueblo house was like.

The big, whitewashed room was neat. At one end was a double bed with a very clean counterpane, there were an oil-cloth-covered table on which a lamp stood, and plenty of chairs. A pole hung parallel to the long back wall, with ceremonial garments folded over it, the heavy shawls embroidered with symbols of rain and the returning seasons, blankets, buckskin leggings, strips of beadwork. Two war bonnets hung on pegs, and on another peg were a bunch of shell and turquoise necklaces and a rosary. There were several photographs on the walls, two pictures of saints, and a brilliant calendar carrying greetings in English and Spanish from a store in Española. Myron looked at the people. Agapito and his son wore their hair in two braids, otherwise they were dressed like hard-working whites.

One minute you thought how civilized they all were, the next you decided they were just ignorant Indians.

Agapito asked if the road had dried out. It rained a little yesterday. Then there was a space of silence, and just as Mr. Rensselaer cleared his throat another car drove up and Mr. Cowring came in with Miss Liter, the Girls' Advisor. There were more greetings, and the Advisor talked to Serafina a moment, examining the baby. Serafina smiled faintly. Then again the silence hung. Myron looked at Don. You could get nothing out of his face. Serafina's family seemed calm.

Mr. Rensselaer turned to the Superintendent. 'I was just about to say — ah — that I understand that Donald here is willing to do the right thing.'

Don stared at the floor. Serafina lowered her head so you couldn't see her face.

The missionary continued, 'This is a most unfortunate occurrence, but I am happy to think that now he is ready to make amends.' He spoke slowly, to make sure that the Indians understood him. 'I think the thing to do is to get a licence and have them married right off.'

Father Adolph said, 'At the same time I can baptize the baby. You won't have to wait for my regular visit.'

Rensselaer said, 'Perhaps Donald would prefer to have it baptized in his own church. What do you say, Don?'

Don made no answer.

Father Adolph leaned forward. 'This is a Catholic family, the child is a Pueblo child. A Catholic wedding and baptism are inevitable.'

Rensselaer cleared his throat and looked grim. He was about to speak when the Superintendent interrupted him.

'Suppose we hear from these folks. What do you say, Agapito?'

The Indian turned and spoke to his daughter in Tewa. She answered briefly. He spoke again. His son said something, his wife made a remark, he spoke at some length, then he turned to Don.

'Where you from, boy?'

Don answered in a low voice, 'Oklahoma. I'm an Arapaho.'

Agapito said something else in Tewa and his wife seemed to agree.

'She don't want to marry heem,' he announced.

Myron stared. Don looked once, swiftly, at the girl, and let out a slow breath.

Father Adolph said, 'Do you realize what you're saying, Agapito?'

Rensselaer exclaimed, 'But she must marry him! She can't have an illegitimate child, you know.'

Agapito said: 'He's no good. We don't want heem. She'll feeneesh school, and by-m-by she'll marry a Tewa boy.'

'But the child ——' the priest said.

'De child's all right. She's got her folks. She don't need no Oklahoma husband.'

Rensselaer said: 'Let the girl speak for herself. Her ideas may be different. Serafina, my dear.' Serafina barely moved her head. 'You must decide this for yourself. We want you to do the right thing, and we'll all stand by you. We respect your father and mother, but — but surely you want to marry Don? Don't you?'

In a very small voice she said, 'No, sir.'

Miss Liter rose and went over to her, and knelt beside her chair, laying her hand over the girl's. 'Are you sure, my dear?'

'Yes'm.'

The young woman remained there, looking at the baby.

Father Adolph sighed. 'I rather feared this would happen.'

Rensselaer jerked his head towards the Superintendent. 'Can't you do something about this, Walter? It's monstrous.'

Cowring shook his head. 'I've been through all this before. I can see their side of it. What could I do?'

'Order them to marry.'

'I've no authority for that.'

'But you've got to do something!'

'Don has to be expelled, I'm afraid. That's all I can do.'

'And the girl?'

'What is there to do about her?'

'You won't let her back in the school!'

'She's one of our best students. How old are you, Serafina?'

In a low voice she answered, 'Seventeen.'

'She's aiming to be a trained nurse. No, I won't cut short her education.'

Rensselaer's face had become quite red. 'I shall communicate with Washington at once. What about it, Father Adolph?'

'In the past, they've always been sent home. It didn't seem to stop the others. I don't know.'

'If the Office instructs me to expel her,' Cowring said, 'of course I shall do so. I've been among different kinds of Indians for a good many years. Generally, in my experience, this doesn't mean that the girl is bad. It doesn't justify cutting short a promising career.'

Rensselaer muttered, 'Monstrous!' Myron knew what he was thinking. Washington had been crazy these last few years. 'But the baby, you can't have that in the dormitory.'

Cowring said, 'What about the baby, Miss Liter?'

Miss Liter pondered for a moment. 'Couldn't we board it in the hospital? Then Serafina could learn how to take care of it. And I think it would be a great help in teaching the girls infant care this year.'

Both the priest and the clergyman looked startled, and were about to speak.

Cowring cut them off. 'Gentlemen, I think we can continue this discussion better somewhere else. Let's go back.' He glanced at the quiet, attentive Indians.

The others took the point and rose. Myron and Don followed them out, climbing into the car behind the two silent men who occupied the front seat.

Out of a long silence Don said, 'I don't want to get fired.'

Myron couldn't think of any answer. They needed him in the backfield, but of course he had to be fired.

'I want to finish here and then go to Haskell. I don't want to go home and work on a farm.' He thought again and added, 'They ain't a-goin to fire her. Well, the hell with it.'

It wasn't fair punishing Don and not her. Everything was haywire. Miss Liter sitting next to her patting her arm. Girls' Advisor — Boys' Advisor. The Matrons and Disciplinarians had never stood for that stuff. The Boys' Advisor was nothing but a Disciplinarian with a new name and no power, anyhow; he was lazy, that's how Don had been able to sneak whiskey in. But the Girls' Advisor was supposed to be something extra special. Miss Liter'd been to college.

There's the good side, and the bad side, and there they are. Plenty of bad white men, like the ones who sold liquor. This summer, staying with Jerome McCarty, he'd seen how the trader gave the Indians flour and sheep to help them hold an Anaji — a squaw dance. But Washington used to be on the good side, and now it kept changing around. The Christians were the only ones who stayed right. You had to be a real Christian. Then you could have a clear conscience and amount to something. Clear conscience — Juniper. Was

Juniper bad? No. You couldn't put that word on a person like her. Ignorant, heathen — good people on the bad side. Ethel would know better. Was he bad? He'd never told Mr. Rensselaer about that. He'd repented, but now he was remembering it, he understood a little more about Don and Serafina.

As they were driving through town, Don said, 'Well, I won't be seein this much longer.'

Myron felt sorry for him. It was an awful thing to be fired.

'I'm sorry you're goin, Don,' he said. 'It's tough.'

'Thanks.'

As it was now well into the afternoon, Mr. Rensselaer fed the boys at his own house after dropping Father Adolph. Little was said during the meal, but one could tell that his attitude towards Don was friendly. The boy had been willing to do the right thing; it was the girl who refused her duty. It was nearly four o'clock when the boys walked onto the school grounds.

Two busses and a truck stood on the driveway, and there was another in front of Merritt Lodge. Many boys and girls were drifting about the campus, stopping here and there for greetings, forming groups, or just roving.

'They're comin in,' White Elk said.

'Yeah.'

'Well, I guess I'll go to the office and get my orders.'

'You'll be comin up to de room?'

'Oh, I guess he won't kick me out till tomorrow. So long.'

'So long.'

Myron was glad to be alone. He drifted across the campus, stopping now and then to speak to friends, searching. He saw Jack almost as soon as Jack saw him. They walked up to each other shyly, their eyes shining. Their hands stayed together.

'How are you, big boy?' Jack said.

'Pretty good. When did you get here?'

'Just now, in de bus. Ethel and me bot got transferred.'

'Ethel? Is she here?'

'Yeah. I ain't seen her since lunch. She's around some-wheres.'

'Gee!'

This was right. This was just the best of luck. Ethel and Jack were here.

'Say,' Myron asked, 'where'd dey put you?'

'In dat dormitory over dere.'

'I'm in Merritt Lodge. We got rooms, you know Four fellas in a room. Say — one of dem's just been kicked out. He's leavin tomorrow. Maybe I can get you in dere.'

'Dat'd be great.'

'Let's go sit down somewheres.'

They made themselves comfortable on some steps.

'What was he fired for?' Jack asked.

'Makin a baby. He's one of dese Eastern Inyans. Dey're sure tough. And dis place ——' Myron looked around. 'It's a good school, but it's crazy. You can talk Inyan all you want to. And de boys and girls go round togedder. Like dat.' He nodded towards a sauntering couple. 'So dis girl, a Tewa — *Ana Shashi*, you know — she had a baby.'

'Dey loosened up at Yellow Earth, too,' Jack said. 'Only you got to be careful. And de grub sure got good. A lot of tings changed since you left. We got advisors and all like dat.'

'Same here. De grub is swell. Only — de girls — dey oughtn't to let dat happen.'

'Keepin dem apart never did no good. You remember? Dere was two at Yellow Earth while you were dere.'

Myron said 'Yeah' doubtfully. 'But dis is a funny place. Dey'll give you lessons on how to be an Inyan. Weavin and silversmittin, and paintin kinda Inyan-style pictures instead o' copyin regular white ones de way we used to do.'

'Sounds goofy,' Jack said. 'Can dey sell de stuff?'

'Yeah, dey sell some of it.'

'Den it ain't so goofy. And dem pictures in de dinin-room, dey're keen!'

Myron frowned. The dining-room walls had been covered by Indian painters with heroic-sized murals out of their tribal life and ceremonies, Hopi, Keres, Tewa, Taos, Navajo, Kiowa ... There was even a sand-painting from the Night Chant there. Mr. Rensselaer said it just encouraged them to backslide.

'You still got your medicine bag?' he asked.

'Yeah. You bet.'

No use trying to explain, then. Jack was Jack.

'Where were you dis summer?' Jack asked. 'Last time you wrote to me — last spring — you said you might be comin home.'

'I went to stay wit Jerome McCarty — Hasteen Tlipai. You know, de Inyan preacher.'

Jack grunted.

'I learned a lot. I'm goin to be a preacher, and den I'm goin to get on de Council.'

'You'll never get onto de Council if you're a Christian.'

'Didn't you ever hear of Jake Morgan?'

'What's his Inyan name?'

'I dunno. He runs a mission near Shiprock. He's on de Council. He's one of de strongest men dey've got. He's educated, and de white men can't fool him.'

'Maybe so. But when de white men wanta do someting, dey'll just go ahead and do it.'

Myron was startled. 'I tought you were goin to school, like Ethel and me, just so's to be able to stand up to dem.'

'Yeah. I'm goin to learn what I can. But sometimes I tink de best ting is just to live on Black Mesa and be Navajo.'

'Maybe. Did you see my uncle?'

Jack had seen him once. They discussed reservation news for a while, then Myron rose, saying, 'Let's see if we can find Ethel.'

They located her finally, standing with some other girls newly transferred from Keams Canyon. She was bashful and her handshake was limp, but Myron thought she was glad to see him. He wanted to stare at her, but prevented himself. She was changed. It wasn't just the American dress, but her face had changed, her breasts were high under the cotton print, she had ceased to be a little girl. She looked neat and smart and bright.

He and Jack drifted on, and he began to tell about the football team. He felt excitement in the middle of himself. Something exactly right was coming true.

After supper he found Ethel again. She was nervous, and kept glancing around while they talked.

'Are you scared of someting?' he asked. 'You don't have to be scared. You ain't used to a big school like dis. I'll take care o' you.'

She blushed slightly. 'Yeah, it's big. And — and so many different kinds of Inyans. And den — I never talked to a boy before, not at school. Are you sure dey won't do someting to us?'

'Sure. Didn't dey change tings at Keams Canyon?'

'No. I heard dem talkin about de new orders. Dey said it wouldn't last, it was just dis Commissioner we got now. So dey didn't do nuttin about it.'

'Maybe dey're right.' Myron pondered. 'Yeah, I guess dat's right. It won't last. Seems like he ain't Christian. Dey'll have you studyin weavin.'

'Dey said — Miss Allenby, I heard her say — he's some funny religion — Commonest, I tink she said.'

'Communist. Dat ain't a religion, it's a — a Russian idea to — to kinda turn everyting upside down. The Communists want to take down de flag and make us into Russians. I don't see how one of dem could get to be Commissioner. He's gotta be a Republican.'

'Well, dat's just what I heard Miss Allenby say. She don't know so much; she's de intermediate grade teacher and she's kinda dumb.' She looked at Myron admiringly. 'I guess you know about dem tings.'

'Yeah. I'm studyin up on dem. It's part of what you

gotta know if you want to be a real, useful citizen.' The way she listened to him was warming. 'Gee, I'm glad you're here.'

'I'm glad to be here, I guess. I feel — I feel kinda strange. It's sure different. All dese buildins and trees. Dey're sure pretty. It's a good school, I guess.'

'Sure it's a good school. Dere's some funny tings go on here, you gotta watch your step, but it's a good school. It's about de best.'

There seemed to be nothing else to say. After a while Myron remarked, 'Well, I'll be seein you,' and left her.

He felt actively happy as he walked through the cool twilight to Merritt Lodge. The next thing was to get Jack moved into his room. Don would leave tomorrow.

Don was sitting on his bed, humming an Arapaho song and tapping a pencil on a book in time to it.

'Hello, big boy!' he said, 'I ain't goin to be fired!'

'Hunh?'

'I went and saw Mr. Cowring, and Mr. Rensselaer stood up for me. They're goin to give me another chance. Boy!'

Myron said, 'Good. Dat's fine.' He supposed it was right.

'Yeah. I'm goin to behave myself. It ain't so hard; we start trainin tomorrer and after that comes basketball, and then pole vaultin. When I go back to Oklahoma, I'll have me some fun.'

Myron nodded.

'You sure did me a good turn, big boy. It was me comin along voluntary that done it. Yeah, you did me a favour.'

Myron nodded again. Now Jack couldn't room with him. Suddenly it struck him that the net result of so much effort was just about nothing. His own emotion seemed a little ridiculous. He remembered how Miss Liter's eyes bugged out, and Mr. Rensselaer's expression, when Agapito dissolved the whole thing. At the time it hadn't occurred to him that they were funny. Himself too, probably. Well, if Don stayed here and behaved himself, he might straighten out altogether, and that was the main thing.

CHAPTER TWO

J ACK handled the file delicately. The beauty of cast
silver is its smooth, flowing look, which file-marks can
spoil. Occasionally he glanced at the photograph of
the old buckle he was copying. Four other boys stood
at the long bench. Their hammers pounded a lively noise, now
and then someone made a remark. It was fun to work with a
bunch like this.

Woodrow Wilson, the Navajo shop instructor, came and
examined Jack's work. 'Dat's all right,' he said, 'only you
gotta smood dem edges a little more.'

'I don't wanta get it all scratched up.'

'Use de stone and take your time. My fadder always said
take lots o' time. "*Hajogo, hajogo*," he always said. A good
job is fulla time. You can put it up for sale when you finish it.'

'I guess I'll keep it myself.'

'All right. You got credit comin to you. Dat's a dollar
and four bits wort o' silver.'

'Okay.'

He polished carefully and steadily with the soft stone.
Sure this was good. It was meant to be good and he'd taken
care all the way along. Figuring out new designs was no use;
no matter how hard he figured, he always ended by making
the same old bracelet, but this picture, it was keen. *American
Indian Welfare Association* was printed across the top. They
were a smart bunch, he guessed. They seemed to take a lot
of trouble over the Indians, he wondered what they got out
of it. He compared buckle and picture again. Ethel ought
to be tickled.

Once again he went through the emotion of deciding to stay over the summer. He'd promised, but from time to time he just plain wanted to go home, and then saw that staying was right. That's Myron. He can talk you into just about anything. He thinks of so many things, and he knows just how to say them. Next spring we graduate, and there's a lot to learn during the summer. Just this once, and then no more school, ever. Marry Ethel, the cattle country and the big cornfield, his father and mother and uncle, and Buckskin Man and Singing Beads all seeing it the same way, and Ethel, Abinah Bitsí. She looks so well in Navajo clothes. If I make enough money, next year I'll fix her up a silver necklace, like that one Philip's making. Her people aren't so poor as they used to be, but not much jewelry. Abinah Bitsí. Teez Nantai Bigé. She'll have to come back another year or two after I'm through. Myron's going to stay on. Myron — he wouldn't do that — but he does pay a lot of attention to her. The buckle was about finished. He tested the set of the turquoise in its centre — firm enough. He looked at the picture of the antique original. A good job. He held it out towards Woodrow.

The instructor turned it over carefully, felt it, hefted it. 'Okay. It's a good job. Dat's a real Navajo buckle. *Yahtí lan.*'

Jack felt glad. He could make a thing like this and give it to Ethel, even if he couldn't talk or stand out in the school the way Myron did.

He caught up with her as they were leaving the dining-hall.

'Let's take a walk,' he said. 'I got sometin for you.'

'All right.'

Spring had been absorbed into summer. The level sunlight came between the buildings and splashed on the big trees. Shade was pleasant. They went past the Senior Girls' Dormitory to where chamisa and greasewood grew tall along the ditch. Standing among the bushes, one felt private.

Ethel pinched off a leaf and looked at it. 'It's pretty here, but I'd be glad to smell — what you call it — *ts'ah* again.'

'I'm stayin here dis summer,' Jack said.

'You're stayin?'

'Yeah. I told Myron.'

'You kinda like to do what Myron says.'

'When he's right. He tinks harder dan we do. When I graduate, I ain't comin back. I'll know what I got to know, and dere's plenty to do back home. So I guess I'll learn some more dis summer, and make a lotta jewelry and sell it, and get some more money.'

'Your folks — what'll dey say?'

'Dey can get on all right. I'm sendin dem a letter. I tought you could take it and read it to dem.'

'I ain't goin home '

'You ain't?'

'No. A girl can't bum her way like a boy can. You know how it is. A coupla years ago dey took you all pretty close to home, now dey've kinda forgotten about it again. Most of de Hopi girls and us are stayin here, unless deir folks can meet dem at Winslow.'

'Yeah. Dat's right.'

'Well,' she said, 'maybe I can finish a year earlier dat way. You ain't goin on after you graduate?'

'No. Dat's all right for Myron. He's only kinda half Inyan ——' Jack hesitated. 'He's all right, you know, only he's different. He's smart. Like de debatin prize and de way he talks English. I ain't goin to mix up wit white men and Washington and all dat. Only we want to know enough so dat if any white men mix up wit us, dey can't fool us. Tlichisenili's safe; dey can't do it dere like dey done out where you folks used to be.'

'Yeah. Only you won't always stay at Tlichisenili.'

He understood her. When he married he'd go to his wife's place.

'I got dis for you. I made it.' He pulled out the silver and turquoise buckle. 'It's good. It's a copy of an old-time one. You can fix it on some kind of a belt.'

'Tanks.' She turned it over in her fingers. 'It's pretty.'

She slipped it in the pocket of her skirt. Her hand remained just above the pocket. Jack linked fingers through it. She didn't move.

English was inadequate, he dropped into their own tongue. 'If I do well this summer and next winter, I'll make you a belt to go with it, the big placques.'

They stood for several minutes, looking at their joined hands through which so much was passing. The sun had gone behind the Jémez Mountains.

'Then when you do go home and put on your own clothes, you can wear it and it will be handsome.'

'Yes.'

Another pause, crowded full, smooth-flowing.

'It's so good in that valley,' he said. 'Our parents have thought about us, I think.'

There was a light in her face, curious, the set of her features and her eyelids sleepy, and yet her face luminous. Their fingers were strong upon each other, they moved together. His other arm went around her and they were kissing. He felt as if he had turned to weightless fluid, he felt sanctified. She was trembling.

Two people, white men, spoke on the path beyond the bushes. They separated and stood still until the men had passed.

'We'd better go in now, I think,' she said.

'Yes.'

They walked hand in hand until they were close to where other students idled and talked before the building.

'Tanks for de buckle, I'll wear it,' Ethel said.

'All right. I wish we was bot goin home. Only — well I promised him. And — I dunno.'

'He's right. You're plenty smart, and we want to do just right. Listen — don't talk to him about us.'

Jack asked sharply, 'Why not? You ain't ——'

'No. Only he has funny ideas. You know.'

'Yeah. All right.'

He left her at the Junior Girls' Dormitory. Too bad those men came along, he thought, they broke into it. I'd like — well, I don't want to make a baby on her. The teachers would fuss and holler, and Myron — Jack almost giggled. They say it's bad for a girl, having a baby at sixteen. I dunno. If she had a baby we'd get married right off and stop all this bother School's a lot of work. Fun, too. He heard the slap of hands catching a football, and looked to see White Elk holding it. The thought of fall reaching into the end of spring. Myron stood with his back to him.

Stepping forward lightly on his toes, he was in time to intercept the return pass with a whoop, and began to run. White Elk tackled him.

'Come on,' he said as he got up. 'Let's play touch-tackle before it gets too dark.'

'Okay.'

Myron said, 'What's hit you?'

'Nuttin. I just feel good.'

CHAPTER THREE

J UNIPER walked in a wide, slow circle around her flock. The animals grazed in a scattered formation, requiring little attention, the two dogs lazed under bushes. The whole country, the rocks, the trees, lay under the sleepiness of late afternoon, but she was restless. It was entirely reasonable for her father and mother to decide to bring a second wife into the hogahn, but the idea upset her. It brought things to a head, somehow. Her cousin, Red Woman's niece, was her own age. She liked the girl. Her mother was through with having children and all that, there was a lot of work to be done, her brothers had married and moved away, and she herself had brought no son-in-law to replace them. But she did not want to live in the same enclosure with her cousin on those terms.

She looked up the canyon. No sign of a rider in its wide stretch. He would be coming along soon, and when he saw the sheep he'd turn aside for a word with her away from her parents, not pressing, not indecorous, but letting her know. Singing Gambler. He said he was changing his name, he said he had grown out of the childish stage of eternal playing. She knew in advance how his voice would sound as he rode towards her, how he would smile, and how he would turn in the saddle, looking down at her. What held her back? Ever since she first saw him in Returning Wisely's hogahn she had liked him, but then the storm brought Big Salt's Son and she lost the trail. Big Salt's Son; he had become unreal, but she could remember the shame of his shame, and the long ache of waiting. Singing Gambler knew himself. A remainder of disbelief, a fear of finality, a waiting for her inmost voice to say yes.

Just as she had foreseen it, his song reached her and he came loping. Just so the song ended and he smiled, looking down at her. She wished she were wearing a blanket, to pull it across her face.

'How hot it is,' he said. 'But now I am refreshed.'

No one else said things like that.

'I'm glad you came.'

He was a man who had had pleasure with many girls, a man who could pick and choose if he wished. Yet her simple remark made his face light up.

'You know,' he said, 'I keep coming and coming here. I think sometimes, perhaps you see too much of me. But I know that what I really want is here.'

He was grave now. How clear his face was. The strength of his feeling and its sweetness reached her fully. Yes, oh surely yes.

'I don't see too much of you.'

'Why pretend?' he said. 'I want to speak to your parents about it, if you are willing. I want to be with you always.'

'Yes.'

Her voice sounded faint. She wished she had a blanket to pull over her face, and she wanted him to come down off that horse and touch her. He dismounted in one quick flash of movement, and now she was completely sure.

2

Bay Horse's Son-in-Law stopped and mopped his brow. The old man at the other end of the field hoed steadily, slowly, pausing seldom. He got a lot done in a day. Corn is hard work. At least, you don't have to keep at it all the time, but the hoe gets heavy. Sometimes the Son-in-Law worked furiously, sometimes he dawdled, at other times he was steady. It was comical, Bay Horse's new wife and Juniper had their babies almost together, and that mite was his son's uncle. The thought of his baby, Warrior Comes Forth, encouraged him with the hoe. The old man — not so awfully old, but still, about fifty — went right on making progress along his row. Hoeing corn and having babies.

He chuckled. I hope I'll last like that. And with Juniper. I don't see how you could want anyone else when you have Juniper. Will she grow old? He thought of girls he'd had before his name was changed, the wide travel and the fun without tomorrows. I made some babies, but now I've got Warrior Comes Forth. Eh! I'm not that wanderer any more. No gambling all summer. Next fall we'll have some fun, when the hiding-stick games start again. The hoe stays heavy. He began to think of a song about how heavy a hoe is, he kept working on it until it came out. He hummed it to himself and grinned.

When their work brought them together, Bay Horse paused with a sigh. 'What's that song you're humming?' he asked.

'I just made it.' His son-in-law straightened up and stretched.

'Sing it.'

> *A-a-a-a ai-ya ai-na*
> *a-a-a-a ai-na,*
> When my son is grown,
> *ai-ya-ho,*
> The hoe won't be heavy
> Any more for me.
> *a-a-a-a ai-na.*

Bay Horse laughed. 'Better pray for a daughter. Your son will marry and move away. One needs a son-in-law.'

'Give me time.'

They worked their way to the opposite ends of the field. Bay Horse's Son-in-Law saw a man coming up the valley. He was riding a black horse, loping, and singing a song about 'The white man plants potatoes, Then he plants old clothes to guard them.' The young farmer sighed. A year ago that was himself, loping along the canyon. He watched the rider draw near, and recognized Travels Around.

Travels Around turned aside and came to the cornfield, calling a greeting and holding his horse back from trying to eat the green shoots. Bay Horse's Son-in-Law came out to him.

'What are you doing?' Travels Around asked.

'Ripening. All sorts of ripening.'

Travels Around looked puzzled.

'That's what the Winter People call us,' he explained. 'The Ripeners, because we plant corn.'

Travels Around grinned. 'I heard you had a crop.'

'Yes. About fifteen days ago.'

'How do you like this life, settled down and hoeing corn?'

'It's good. It's very good.'

'If *you* like it, it must be good. The Ripeners — have you been to the Winter People?'

'Yes. Years ago. I was there about three months.'

'What are they like? I've been to a lot of places, but I never went there.'

'You ought to go. You can have a lot of fun. They have fine horses, and they'll pay you twenty dollars a month and feed you, to herd their sheep for them. It's easy herding, too, the grass is good all over. They gamble a lot. They have a game with four white bones that you hide, you can play it in summer, they have our games, and they have cards. They like singing, but they aren't good at it, and any Navajo who can sing is welcome among them. You know, none of the Apaches can lift their voices the way we do.'

'Yes. The Chishi sing heavily. I've been down there.'

'Yes, it's the same thing.'

'But — one hears that they're dangerous.'

'No. They're good people, except when they get drunk. When they're drunk, one wants to step aside.'

Bay Horse had come up and was listening. 'Is it true they talk like us?' he asked.

'Almost the same, only they twist it a little. They say *doya* for *dota*, and *nijoni* when they really mean *yahté*, and things like that. But you understand them all right.'

'Do they drink much?' Travels Around asked.

'Whenever they feel like it. They make *t'o tlipai*, you know, like the Chishi, and they live near towns where they buy whiskey. Sometimes they all get drunk.'

'All of them!' Bay Horse exclaimed.

'Yes. They get together for something, and the Mexicans come with whiskey, and the men and the women all get drunk. Then they mix up with each other's wives, and they fight, and that's when you want to step aside. If they knock you down, they jump on you.'

'They sound like people to stay away from altogether. They were always warlike.'

'They're good people. They treat you well. You can make money there, both working and playing.'

'Do they like Navajos?'

'Pretty well. Only they think we're thieves. Whenever something is stolen, they go after the Navajos.'

'Do they catch them?' Travels Around asked.

Bay Horse's Son-in-Law grinned. 'Generally not.'

They talked a little longer about the Apache tribes, Bay Horse recalling the tradition of how the Navajos broke off from the Winter People, and the old wars with the Chishi. Then Travels Around left them.

As they walked home, Bay Horse said, 'You talked as if you had a good time when you went over there.'

'Yes. I — you know, I'd forgotten about it. Then when I was talking it all came back to me. It was fun.'

He went on alone to his own hogahn. Yes, that had been fun, wandering about. The round handle of the hoe pressed on his shoulder. Suddenly he felt shut in, but at the sight of Juniper by the fire, the baby on her lap, the feeling vanished. She smiled when she saw him. He held the baby while she finished cooking. His own child, how wonderful! He played with it, marvelling at its unco-ordinated, futile motions and the perfection of its almond-shaped, black eyes. He sang his new song and told her of Bay Horse's answer. She laughed at him.

'A daughter next, let us hope,' she said. 'You're only one son-in-law replacing three sons. Daughters are better.'

'That's right.'

After he had eaten he spoke about seeing Travels Around. She put the child in its cradleboard when she had fed it, and then lay close by him, listening and watching the play of his expressions. He got going on the Winter People, telling about the country of grass and tall trees and lakes, about their tipis and their horses, about the great autumn assembly when all the tribe camped together and Indians came visiting from everywhere, Navajos, Utes, Jémez, Zías, Tewas, Keres, Taos — the great gathering, singing all night, feasting and playing all day.

She commented as she might on any interesting subject, but she didn't like it. She wondered if there had been Apache women — but that wasn't the main thing. It was the memory of his past existence shining in his eyes. The wanderer. Would it pull too hard one day?

She said, 'I'd like to go there with you sometime.'

He beamed. 'Eh! We could have fun. Next fall, perhaps, for the gathering.' He told her more about it. 'Going there with you — that would be different. Like putting salt on something. It would be good.'

He laid a hand on her shoulder, and leaning his head back against his rolled blanket, sang a love song. It was all part of the same man, it all put together to make him. The rest was up to her. So far, it was all right.

CHAPTER FOUR

WHEN the coach called to Jack and he started running back and forth, warming up, Ethel felt her heart pound. Now they would both be in there. She felt that something was going to happen, she felt important. At times, recently, she had wished that the three of them could be united as they had been, with Jack still loyally enjoying Myron's prominence, but if she had had the chance now to end the competition between them, she would probably not have chosen to do so.

Jack went in at left halfback in place of Ambrose Sinemptiwa, who had turned his ankle. It was the beginning of the second half, and he was the first substitute in the backfield; the game was too hot to use second-string men unless absolutely necessary. Albuquerque hadn't scored yet, but had kept the ball in Santa Fé's territory right along, and on the last few plays their big Apache fullback had been running wild through the line.

Margarito Hernández, the quarterback and captain, slapped him between the shoulder blades. 'Come on, break 'em up.'

Mindful of the referee, Jack made no answer. He, Margarito, and Myron took their places behind the line, with White Elk farther back. Albuquerque was using straight plunges and so centre played close behind the guards.

They sent the play at Jack's side, of course, with Santa Fé's left tackle sprawling helpless, but he was right in there and spilled the interference with a driving dive. Myron came over the pile — Margarito wondered how he got there so fast — and hit the runner with a smack you could hear all over the field.

Albuquerque lost six inches. They disentangled themselves, players patting the two halfbacks on their shoulders, but Myron and Jack didn't look at each other. The stands were yelling.

On the next play Albuquerque gained one yard, fourth down and four to go on Santa Fé's twenty-yard line. The Santa Fé line went into formation with a new snap.

Margarito called, 'Thirty-two, eight.' He expected a drop-kick.

Out of the side of his mouth, Myron said to Jack, 'All right. Break it up.'

Jack didn't answer.

The two Navajos broke through simultaneously. Two men took Jack out, but on Myron's side the quarterback was busy with right end. He saw the kicker just letting the ball fall, and went through the air in two long bounds. Hurried, the kick went wild over the line, and it was Santa Fé's ball.

Margarito sent Myron between guard and tackle from kick formation with White Elk standing back and holding out his hands. He didn't really expect to gain much, but it wasn't what Albuquerque was looking for. Jack's drive ahead of Myron partly did it, that and the way Myron span and fought when Jack was down. Three men stopped him for a five-yard gain.

The quarterback saw that something was indeed happening. Tease had never played like this before. The two Navajos were on fire. They seemed to ignore each other, but they were playing together. He tried the same play again and Albuquerque's mountainous Havasupai guard stopped it dead. As they rose, Myron and Jack looked at each other without a word, their eyes seeming to snarl.

They needed to be farther from their own goal line. Margarito called for a kick from the same formation. Don White Elk got it off fast. The ends became tangled with the Albuquerque defence, and Jack and Myron were racing down under a high, slow, straight, end-over-end punt. The safety man saw them coming, he got a look at their faces and signalled for a fair catch. They just stopped themselves in time not to foul and waited, arms outspread and faces tense, in case he should drop the ball or take too many steps. He didn't.

Each of them had been going to hit that Apache so hard they'd jar his teeth loose. They'd been going to make a fumble. They looked at each other while the team came up, the snarling momentarily forgotten.

'Next time,' Myron said, half to Jack, half to the fullback. Jack grunted.

The Apache said, 'Nuts.'

Albuquerque couldn't gain ground. The Apache made an earnest attempt to break Jack's ankle in a scrimmage, but Myron stepped on his face. They were always working together, they didn't seem to pay any attention to each other, didn't speak, but where one was the other turned up and joined in. Albuquerque kicked and Santa Fé started down the field with steady rushes. Margarito didn't know what had got into Jack and Myron, and he didn't take time to speculate. He was a practical-minded little Tewa and a noble scrapper himself. If the two Wan Sabis were inspired to win the final game for him, that suited him. He watched them, to see if their fire burned out or they began to go haywire.

On Albuquerque's thirty-eight-yard line they were momentarily stopped. Fourth down and two to go. Margarito hated to lose the ball, the way they were driving, yet two line plunges in succession had gained only half a yard. Well, it was safe territory for the trick pass, and that would bring in the Begay-Tease combination again. He looked at the two of them as he called the play. They'd do.

Don pretended to be going around the short end with the ball, Margarito's and Jack's drive at the other end looked like part of the fake. Then Jack wriggled through to an open place behind the opposing line. It all had to be quick as shooting.

Everyone had expected a kick or another plunge. The

stands held their breath. Myron standing by himself with the ball, looking around as if unsure what to do with it, unutterably calm save for the clamped line of his mouth, seemed to tower above the field. Two men were closing in on him. His arm moved swiftly, suddenly, a perfect pass, straight and hard, but not too hard, high to avoid interception, but possible for a top-notch player to catch handily, placed exactly over Jack's left shoulder. Jack rose in the air, caught the ball, and came down running to gain another two yards for a total of six, before he was downed. The stands went wild.

He'd handled the same play before with Sinemptiwa, but differently. He usually lobbed the pass, slower, easier to intercept, putting less strain on the catcher, but this time he had given it vicious perfection.

He and Jack were impassive as their team-mates slapped their backs. The two sides jumped back into line, the march continued.

Fourteen to nothing. The field between the stands was dusky, the west a red glow of sunset. The students shuffled, joking, laughing, boastful, towards the buildings. The Albuquerque boys and girls climbed into their busses. The tension, the excitement broke up, and it was Saturday evening again.

Walking towards his room, Myron felt washed, bruised, and unhappy. Jack had been *good*. Jack — if one could make peace, but there was Ethel. He dragged up the stairs and sat on his bed, staring at the wall in a black, profound depression. Finally he decided to go and eat supper.

After supper he went back up to his room, having no heart for the sociable in the community building.

Half an hour later, Don came in, with a newspaper under his arm. 'Hyah, big boy!' he said.

His cheerfulness was grating. Myron grunted.

The Arapaho sat down beside him. 'What'sa matter? Gettin the letdown, hunh?' Receiving no answer he went on:

'Cheer up. Boy, you were *good*, and I don't mean maybe. God dammit, you were great. You're the school hero.'

'Jack's de hero,' Myron said.

'He was good, too, but you were the works. Don't let it get you down.'

'I feel sorta funny. I don't feel right.'

'Here, take a look at this newspaper.' Don handed it to him, open at the sports page.

His name was in the headlines, in the opening lead, and he had a paragraph to himself. Jack was mentioned, so was Don, but he was featured.

'You better go to college, feller,' Don said. 'Lots of schools would give you scholarships.'

Myron said, 'Well, it was luck. Margie gave me de ball to go over de line.' He looked at the paper again. 'Jack — you know what he did. Dey oughta have ——'

'What do you keep worryin about him for? I know you used to be buddies, but he's just a hick. Forget him.'

'He ain't a hick. He's a good Navajo.' Myron fell silent. He didn't know how to explain. Finally he said 'Aw, nuts.' He was sick of this. He grabbed his hat and went out.

He felt a little better in the dark. Music came across the campus from the community building. He drifted towards it. Ethel was in there, she would be expecting him, wondering why he didn't turn up. He stood just outside the door, with his hands in his pockets. Through the window he caught glimpses of couples turning. It seemed as if somehow he'd forgotten about her since the game, and he'd been thinking only about Jack. That had been settled, ended, more than a month ago; they both understood, as if they'd explained it to each other. It came over him that he really had been the star of the big game, and Ethel was inside there, and he thought she was waiting for him, that perhaps tonight, at last, she would be his girl and stop hanging in between.

He walked up the steps and turned in at the door of the big room, stopping a moment at the threshold. Some couples turned on the floor while the Victor played, boys and girls stood or sat about, a few read magazines. The Girls' Advisor and two teachers chatted in the corner. There was Ethel in a group, and Jack standing on the outside of it, watching her. He looked at her for a minute, as if he saw her more clearly while she didn't know he was there, feeling the sense of her presence, then he crossed the room.

She was pleased and faintly flustered when he came up, her colour mounted. Jack looked sullen. The others in the group showed a flattering awareness of him, the big man, the top man of that day. Across the room, a boy raised his two hands, joined, and shook them towards him; one of the teachers, looking up, said, 'That was great work, Myron.' Assurance mounted in him.

He said to Ethel, 'Hello. Let's dance.'

'All right.'

His right hand felt her back, his left hand locked her right; as they stepped, their bodies touched lightly. He was dancing with Ethel, she was the girl for him, meant for him, ever since that early time. Beside her no one else was important. Jack had sat down in a corner and was reading a magazine.

'I want to talk to you,' Myron said. 'Let's slip out.'

'We — dey might notice.'

'Come on. We can just step out de door.'

'All right.'

It was cold outside, but helpfully dark. When he took her hand, he felt a tremble run through her. He made two false starts at speaking, then his words came easily.

'I've been watchin you ever since I first knew you. You — it was dat letter first, you know. You aren't like all de odders. You're like me, you're goin somewhere. I been watchin and watchin you. Gee, Ethel, all dis summer, all dis past year, I been wantin to get to you. You're my girl, see? I want you to be my girl, and stick wit me. I'm goin to take care of you and help you, and when we bot get t'rough we'll live civilized.'

'I — I dunno. My folks ——'

'You don't have to bodder about your folks when I'm around. You aren't goin to need sheep or any of dem tings wit me.'

It was Myron talking and she believed him. Jack seemed commonplace. Myron was adventure, conquest, he surrounded her entirely and cut off anything else. She held to his hand, waiting.

He kissed her, first on the forehead, then on the cheek. She put her head down against his neck, and he held her tight, feeling her body against him, her warmth. He wanted to shout. She was inactive in his arms, not like that other one. She was a good girl.

He wanted everything to be the very best. There would be no wrong, and in the end a marriage. Marriage. He put his face down and found the corner of her lips. Then her arms really took hold of him.

It was cold, they both began to be chilled. They went in together and danced back to the centre of the room. When the record ended, they joined a talking group by the fireplace, making a point of moving slightly away from each other.

Jack put down his magazine and went straight to Ethel. Almost at the same moment, the Girls' Advisor said it was bedtime. Myron left immediately. He didn't want to talk to Jack. If he had to fight him he would, but he hoped he wouldn't have to do that. He was entering Merritt Lodge before he fully realized that he had kissed Ethel, that she was his. She had a silver buckle Jack had made her. He'd give her Singing Gambler's bracelet. Gee, it was fixed! She was his girl, she loved him. He'd kissed her. Gee! Now if he could straighten it out with Jack, but anyhow —— Oh, Gee!

CHAPTER FIVE

HE WAS tired of Santa Fé just then, tired of having a career and a calling. He'd flunked algebra again, and he still had a long way to go before he could take the College Boards in French and European History. He thought he'd like to go right out on the reservation, clear to Ha'anoichí, and forget about it all for a summer. People expected so much of him. Another year of Santa Fé, tutoring with Mr. Rensselaer and all that, and no one his own age left in school. If only you didn't have to know so many subjects to get a scholarship.

He'd told Mr. Rensselaer he wanted to go home, but the clergyman talked him out of it. Now he felt angry, he had half a mind to go home anyhow. With Ethel leaving — would she wait for him? At least she wasn't going to Tlichisenili, that was some comfort. He'd get to see her later this summer, when he went to stay with Mr. Butler. But from Ha'anoichí he could ride over there any time, it was only about two days. Drifting along on horseback, watching the country and worrying about nothing. How would he be on horseback now? Could he still ride? Jack told him, before he left last spring, that he wasn't an Indian any longer.

But I am an Indian. I'm going to go to college and be ordained, and I'm an Indian. I'm going to be the first regular Navajo clergyman. And bring it to my people. The Navajos can be anything in the world, we can be everything white men are, just like white men. So long as that which stands up in you is strong. His thoughts hesitated over Shooting Singer's phrase. He nodded. With that, we can be anything.

If he could talk to Jack, now that a year had gone by, could he make him understand? Ethel was Christian. Right from the start, from that letter, she'd been meant for him. Would Jack see? He'd give a lot to get past the stony face that Jack had given him.

Mr. Rensselaer and Mr. Butler wanted him to keep on working until he got his scholarship. He was old now for entering college, they said. Well, it isn't just fun being a Christian. It's something big; you've got to put it first and lose other things for it. He who loses his life shall find it. That's right. One way or another, he'd have had to break with a heathen like Jack some time. But he wished ——

He turned into the school grounds. It isn't what you want to do, but what you have to do. When you've been chosen. She'll wait for me. My duty is to stay here. It's a long climb, but even Jerome McCarty hasn't been ordained.

She was loitering behind the fine arts building. When he saw her looking at him, he knew what she hoped for, and felt defeated for a moment. But this was the way it had to be. For her, too, to be worthy of her.

'Mr. Rensselaer tinks I ought to stay here, on account of tutorin,' he said.

'Oh. Dat's too bad.'

'Well, I guess he's right. I'll be twenty-two next year, and dat's old for goin to college. I can't lose any more time. But I'm sorry.'

'It's goin to be kinda lonely at dat mission.'

'Dey're good people. I went out to Gideon last year.'

'Yeah. But I don't know dem.' She looked around the campus and then at him.

'I'll get out dere sometime dis summer, while I'm stayin wit Mr. Butler. I'll see you den, sure.'

'Dat's good,' she said. 'Let's walk.'

They strolled side by side.

'You see,' he explained, 'Mr. Rensselaer, he's givin me a kinda junior college course. While I'm makin up for dese exams, I'm goin ahead, too, so I can graduate soon. Den dey'll ordain me.'

'It seems funny,' she said, 'an Inyan bein a regular preacher.'

'Why not? Odder tribes have done it. Den dey'll give us a mission, like I told you. We'll have a regular house wit a kitchen and books, and — and a lamp on de table, and everytin.'

'Yeah. Dat beats a hogahn. I've been sleepin in beds too long.'

They walked several steps before Myron answered. 'Sleepin on de ground's all right. It can be good, really good. It's not just de house, de comforts. It's de work we've got to do. De work — you and me, we *know*. We can show our people. Like de speech Doctor Entwistle made yesterday, you young people who are graduatin are goin back to make de futures of your tribes. Only most of dem — you know — eider dey go back to de blanket, or all dey figure on is how to buy a car and drive around in it. But we *know*. We were picked out, way back.'

'Gideon's awful far from home,' she said. 'I'd like to see my folks.'

'Aren't you goin to visit dem first?'

'I'm goin to de mission, and den on to Tlichisenili for a week, dat's all. I'd like to be where dey could kinda come around when dey felt like it.'

Myron started to speak, paused, then said, 'Well, dere isn't any mission for you to work at, near Tlichisenili.'

They had reached the sheltering bushes along the ditch, and now stood facing each other.

'Why don't you come out to Gideon and study wit Mr. Boyle dis summer? Why can't you do dat?'

'Dat's a good idea! Say ——' His face clouded. 'Gee — Mr. Rensselaer would want to know why. He wouldn't see it. And den — Mr. Boyle never went to college. I don't know if he's got de education.' He felt as if he were pumping uphill. 'But it's a good idea. I'll try it. I'll be out dere for some of de time, anyhow.'

He took her hand. The afternoon sun was strong, it was hot even there in the shade. Their fingers felt sticky and slippery against each other. She was wearing the bracelet he'd given her.

'I wish we could do de way we like,' he said. 'I wish we could just stay togedder, and go on picnics like we did last summer. But I got to get into college. Dat's de real, main ting. So it's got to be dis way, I guess.'

'Yeah. I guess so.'

He longed for some different response from her, this last afternoon. Something to lift him up.

'Dey were nice, dose picnics, weren't dey?'

'Yeah.'

'When we're married, we can go on dem any time we want to.'

'You can't sing no Inyan songs when you're a preacher, nor no jazz. Only hymns.'

Myron frowned. 'Sure I'll sing dem. I don't care what dey say, if you like dem, I'll sing dem.'

The quality of her touch changed slightly. 'You ain't scared to say dat?'

'No. I mean it.'

She looked pleased. He kissed her, several times on her cheek, her forehead, then her mouth. It was extraordinary how doing that changed the way he felt. He lost the nagging sense of failing, and knew that she was his.

'I'd like to marry you right now,' he said. 'We're old enough. Only den dey wouldn't let me into college. But I'd like to.' Their warmths penetrated their summer clothing, against each other. Now her arm was really tight against his side and back. 'Oh Ethel. *Aiyanoshné. Aigisi aiyanoshné. Je aime vous.* Dat's de French for it. Dere aren't enough languages to say it in.'

She turned her face up to his again and they really kissed. The big bell ringing startled them.

'Supper,' he said. 'Too soon. I'll see you again afterward?'

'Yess.'

They kissed again, then started back to school.

'When you go home, you — you'll be seein Jack?'

'Him? I guess he's married by now.'

2

On account of Circling Bull, they wouldn't let him play that fall. Albuquerque and St. Francis both protested against keeping the two grown men on the team. The genuineness of Myron's continued study could be easily proven, but the Sioux was taking the same art course for the fourth time, although his paintings already sold well, and he was always free to keep commercial dancing engagements. Football and basketball seemed to be his only real school activities. As a result, Myron was barred, too.

Circling Bull departed for home, wearing a natty, double-breasted suit for which he had not finished paying, and carrying two big suitcases which contained among other things artist's supplies, a quart of rye whiskey, two dance costumes, two silver cups, ten silver and bronze medals, a package of red paint consecrated in Taos kiva, and four eagle breast-feathers from Acoma.

Myron helped coach. He hated sitting on the sidelines during games, and used to feel blue afterward. All his old friends were gone, the students were beginning to look like a lot of kids to him. He dove into his studies, burying himself in them, and wrote long, carefully evolved letters to Ethel, treasuring her brief answers. College — graduation — and then the house with many rooms, and Ethel. Going forward together, the great work to be done. Nearer and brighter, next summer with examinations passed and scholarship assured, free to see all he wanted of her, and with that first achievement to show her.

She'd been glad to see him last August, though he'd been able to manage only three weeks. The Boyles made much of him. They were suspicious of letting him go out alone with her, but after he'd talked to Mr. Boyle about his hopes and plans, the missionary had trusted him. And it had been all right, although sometimes it had been hard not to go too far. She was a good girl, that made it easier. She wasn't very happy at the mission. Mrs. Boyle was cross, she said. She didn't see where she needed her education to wash dishes and sweep, this wasn't getting her anywhere. Myron told her to be patient and stick it out, she was bound to learn a lot by living with people like the Boyles. But it made him angry that Mrs. Boyle should snap at Ethel, it wasn't Christian of her. When he next saw Mr. Butler he'd talk to him about it; it was too hard to write about a thing like that.

Often and often he thought of what it would be like to be married to her, remembering details of her voice and gesture, sometimes thinking in terms that made him ashamed. In prayer, he thanked God earnestly for enabling him to win her, asking for her protection and that Mrs. Boyle should be kind to her.

In November she wrote that she was going to Tlichisenili. Her mother was sick, and there were her father and younger sister to be taken care of. It was a hasty letter. Buckskin Man had come to Gideon and was waiting. 'He has a horse for me. I don't know how he thinks I'm going to ride all that way. And I have not got no clothes for it.' He wrote to her, rather hopelessly, in care of Tloh Chin Trading Post. Heaven knew when a letter would get there, or when or how it would be passed on to her. And even if she wrote to him, it might be any length of time coming. It might get lost. He prayed for her comfort in that hogahn, for her fortitude, and for those letters. December, Christmas, and January. If only just one letter would come, please God. Just one letter to say that she's all right, and she isn't looking at Jack.

Jack was heathen. He was backward. He had turned away from the light. But he was Jack. Any girl could like him —

remembered clearly, more than remembered, felt. A man to be afraid of. Maybe he's married. Oh Lord, I hope he's married. Make Ethel strong.

A letter came in February. It had been a month getting to him. He stuck it into his pocket as though he was afraid someone would see it, and went straight up to his room. By good luck, his roommates were not in. He opened it slowly, feeling his heart striking heavy blows against his ribs. The first wild surge of joy had settled into painful excitement. Written in pencil on two small sheets of ruled paper, her hand.

> Mr. Myron Begay
> U. S. Indian School
> Santa Fe, New Mex.
>
> Dear Friend —
>
> I meant to write to you sooner, but it is hard to write here and I am very busy. My mother was sure sick. She is better now. I wanted them to take her to the hospittal but they had a sing instead. A Fire dance. It cost sixty sheep and two horses and a silver belt. So she got better anyhow. I have to stay a little longer, helping her. We got a big flock of sheeps now. I got one letter from you. It took a long time coming. I tell people to ask when they goe to the Traders. I am well. I hope you are well. It is cold hear.
>
> Yours sincerely
>
> ETHEL

She hadn't mentioned Jack. She didn't even mention him. He's married. He's married and moved off. They had a sing. That's what that religion does, when a person ought to go to the hospital, but it hadn't fooled her. Paying all that for heathen medicine that couldn't cure anyone. Ethel's all right. She's all right. She isn't thinking about Jack. He knelt down and prayed.

God had been good to him. God reaches in, to Shooting Singer's winter camp, to the grazing lands below Tlichisenili. It was up to him to be worthy. He drove at his work with different vigour. The relief of that letter eased his studies for long afterward.

He hardly realized how much time had passed since that word from her. Spring arrived by surprise, the apricots blossoming, the cottonwoods washed over with new green. He hadn't noticed. And now there was the panic of approaching examinations, the utter necessity of doing well, of getting all those different subjects exactly straight and pat in his head. Only at times, like Sunday afternoons, when he tried to relax, did he really know how much he wanted news of her again. He didn't even have the solace of writing to her; it was impossible to go on sending letters into the void. Sometimes his learning buzzed in his brain. He was uneasy at work and frightened when he let up.

Sometimes when he was studying, a girl's voice or laughter outside sounded like Ethel, and he would start and then remember. The boys were kids, but the older girls seemed women. He avoided them.

Only a short time now, a few weeks to the exams and then I can go out there, go out there. If Jack's hanging around, I'll know what to do. If I pass — that blocked the run of feeling towards reunion to come. Flunking would destroy it. He turned back to his book and his notes. A boy and girl walked by outside, her stockingless legs were smooth and brown, her face a mystery. I've got to pass. And then I'll go right out there. I will pass.

CHAPTER SIX

H E LAY on his shoulder blades with his head propped on his saddle and his crossed knees the loftiest part of his anatomy, tapping a stick against the bottom of a frying-pan, trying to recall a song a visiting Taos had sung. *Wé-ya-hé-ya wé-ya hé-yo-o* . . . It was a lovely, light song, and it went well with thinking about girls. As he lay, the long, white slope of the tipi rose within his vision, the lower part contrasting with dark green pines, the upper part with blue sky. More in front of him he saw Painted Girl doing something about lunch. She wore a light-blue dress with a square, orange yoke, and orange near the hem, and a wide belt studded with brass, after the manner of the Winter People. The two braids of her hair were tied with blue ribbon.

Wé-ya-hé-ya hai-ya. No, he couldn't get it. Those Taos had a voice of their own, a sweet, far-carrying voice. They couldn't sing Navajo and he couldn't sing Taos. He remembered some of the words, and wondered what they meant. Something pleasant for a girl to hear, he thought.

Painted Girl said suddenly: 'You can't do it. You have to live in an adobe house to sing that.'

He grinned at her. She was good fun. In many ways she was good fun. She was peeling potatoes. He sang, 'The white man plants potatoes.' The Winter People live well. He went on to the Magpie Song, the Hello John Song, knowing how she listened to him behind the shyness of those braids half hiding her face, the caution of her mother inside the tipi. He'd started 'The hoe is heavy' before he realized it, and stopped himself abruptly, still tapping on the pan.

You went to a gambling and then you heard of another, and then of a Mountain Chant and you went on to that, and then you were so near the Winter People that it was silly not to go see them. I must start for home pretty soon, he thought. Yes, very soon. She'll be angry.

Through the wide-spaced, tall pines before him he saw three men riding. The one in front was a blond white man; it was Lean Face, who told the Indians what to do about their sheep. Lean Face was good fun, he could talk the Apache dialect pretty well, and he knew lots of songs. If he was inspecting around here, he might come back to Many Fights' tipi this evening. In that case, they'd play and sing. He was remarkably nice for a white man, almost like an Indian.

Left Hand, the policeman, rode behind him. Left Hand was all right; not an interesting person, but all right. Lean Face looked glum, perhaps he'd found some scabby sheep.

The third man focussed his attention. It was Brave Man, the policeman from Tees Napornss. Yes, it was. What was he doing way over here, a long week's ride from his district? Singing Gambler stopped drumming on the frying-pan. Here's where I go home, he thought.

Lean Face said, '*Tanjoh.*'

He answered, '*Tanjoh,*' as though he'd been born among the Winter People.

Broad Woman came out of the tipi, saying, '*Tanjoh, tanjoh,* come in, sit down.'

Lean Face said, 'We want to talk to this Ripener.'

Brave Man pushed his horse up front. 'You have corn to hoe, grandfather,' he said. 'Your wife is tired of waiting for you.'

Painted Girl dropped a potato on the ground. She picked it up, wiped it on her skirt, and let it fall into the pan. Then she rose and walked into the tipi.

Singing Gambler had risen to his feet. 'All right,' he said.

His hard goods, his winnings, were in the tipi. All along he'd counted on bringing them back to her. Now Painted Girl was in there. Lean Face said something in English.

'We can lunch here, he says,' Brave Man interpreted.

Many Fights would be coming back. 'If we're going, let's go,' Singing Gambler said. 'My horse is right over there'; he made a decision. Those things were for Juniper. 'Just wait till I get my goods.'

She stood in the middle of the tipi, her hands hanging by her sides, still holding her knife. He knew these people, she might go for him; he wasn't afraid of that, but of her eyes, full of heavy fire. He was sorry, he didn't want her to feel like that. He scooped up his compact little bundle.

'Ripener!' She said it as if it were an insult. 'Just a thief like the others.'

He stood straight and smiled at her. 'No. Can I help it if I am sent for?' This required an effort, Juniper had always been first, but the poor girl —— 'When the police come, what can I do then?' He reached into the bundle and took out a string of turquoise. It was worth half of all the rest, but it was the first thing he touched that would come loose. 'Keep this for me, blue-painted girl.'

She took it, watching his face, 'You'll come back?'

'I said, "Keep this for me."'

Warm colour ran up in her face and she began to cry. He left the tipi, feeling his hands sweat and wondering if she were going to have a baby.

On the afternoon of the third day, in answer to a remark of Brave Man's, he sang the song, 'Blame not me but the gods. How can I help it, If women love me?'

He sang it in his old way, his head thrown back, his voice high-reaching, his teeth showing in his smile, but he didn't feel just like that. He'd meant to return of his own accord, with his winnings in his hand, and the police had come for him. There were many girls, but the thought of losing Juniper darkened the sun and made one's middle heavy.

2

There are many girls, but only the one Juniper. And that was Warrior Comes Forth who looked at him and then went on plucking the warp strands of the loom. What a nice little yellow shirt she'd made for him, and the edge of the weaving that he could see looked handsome. He noticed many things, but he had to pay attention to Juniper sitting there. It was the same face he had always known, the familiar face, the oval and the long eyes, the fine nostrils, the delicate mouth, the definite chin, and the wings of dark hair sweeping back, the calm face of the woman with whom he was one, to whom he belonged, who could become ... The voice he knew so well and never forgot, greeting him quietly. But behind the face, under the voice, it was different.

He said, 'I've brought you some things,' and dumped out his winnings, jewelry and hard, round dollars.

She said, 'You went to the Winter People?'

'Yes. There was another game at Tsé Tlichi, and then a Mountain Chant at T'o Dotosoni, and then I heard of a game at Hatso Ntyel. Then I thought I might as well go on over and get some of those people's goods while I was at it, for us to have. I was just finishing when Brave Man came.'

She studied his face. There were many girls, but she was one of those women who have a key to life. She was looking at him. Those long eyes.

'You can take it with you,' she said, pointing to the bundle. 'Don't bother to unsaddle.'

He stepped back and leaned one hand on his saddlehorn. She became far away, the world filled with an empty silence. He moved his jaws twice while his mind raced, seeking, over a smooth surface affording no hold.

At length he said: 'When Brave Man came, I was thinking about coming back. Right at that time I was deciding on it. I have never let you out of my mind. I have sung your songs only to myself. I have been for you, always. You and my son.'

She put out one hand and touched a post of the loom, then returned it to her lap. He had never seen a face so completely calm and blank.

'You don't expect me to sleep with you whenever you happen to come home?'

A man has to stay whole. With the loveliest girl in the world, even with Juniper, he has to stay whole. Just looking at her, he knew that if he said anything it would be wasted. The best thing to do was not to say it. Then a man still had something to take away.

'Keep the hard goods,' he told her, hearing his voice from a distance.

'If you leave them here, I'll throw them away.'

'Let them belong to my son. There's more than a hundred dollars there.'

'All right.'

He swung to his saddle as a man should, in one smooth motion. Without letting himself pause, he started off at a walk, a trot, a lope, into a strange, drab world. How odd that the bushes and trees looked the same, the sand was still bright, the rocks still painted. He realized that he was done with hoeing corn. He knew that the fullness of losing Juniper had not yet torn at his heart. A man cannot be owned by a woman. He decided to go west and see what the Mokis were like.

CHAPTER SEVEN

JEROME McCARTY came into the room smiling and
making a humorous demonstration of shame.

Dr. Butler said, 'Come in, Jerome. We'd almost
given you up.'

'I was stuck in the mud near Leupp. We had a heavy rain
over there. I had to wait until some Hopis came along in a
truck and pulled me out.'

He pointed to his mud-heavy trousers and shoes, and smiled
again. He took a seat at the table, nodding to the others.
Butler tapped a pencil on his memorandum pad.

'I guess you know what this meeting's about,' he said.

McCarty nodded.

'I have another communication from the Board. They want
us to take definite action against this administration. Or the
way they put it ——' He referred to a letter lying open before
him. '"An interdenominational delegation is going to
Washington to ask the Commissioner for a definite answer,
yes or no, as to whether he is an Atheist. Whatever his
answer may be, his new circular order number D26L41 leaves
us no doubt as to the dangerous nature of his policies. We
feel the situation to be particularly acute among the Navajos,
with the new day-school program there. This, the largest
tribe of Indians in the United States, must be saved from
blindly following a professed advocate of paganism."'

Larrimer said, 'The Navajos never followed anyone
blindly, but I know what they mean.'

Boyle said, 'The Navajos are news. They've been publi-
cized. If they oppose this man, attention will be paid to them.
This New Deal!'

Butler raised his hand. 'We do the Indians no favour if we mix them into general politics. Let us confine ourselves to the Office of Indian Affairs. Are you all familiar with that order?' He looked around the table, then said thoughtfully, 'It seems correct according to the Constitution.'

Rensselaer cleared his throat. 'It *looks* constitutional, yes, but if you go deeper — gentlemen, this is a Christian country. The founders of the Republic never intended that the Bill of Rights should operate to prevent the teaching of God's word. Let us grant for a moment that it may be incorrect for religious instruction to be compulsory in a school supported by federal funds.'

Boyle snorted.

'Just grant that for a moment. The new order allows co-operation and a limited use of school facilities. It's a practical matter, Mr. Boyle; that's a poor point of attack. But when the order also allows the child to have religious instruction *by a medicine man* if he asks for it, why, then the thing becomes ridiculous. The matter reverses itself; it becomes a ruling to discourage Christian missionary efforts and encourage heathenism. It's indefensible.'

Butler nodded. 'Well put, Charles.'

Larrimer said quietly: 'Most of the Indian Service employees know that. This administration can't last forever. Does anyone know of a school where this order is being put into full effect?'

'That's only half an answer, Ned,' Boyle said. 'It's the tendency, the whole tendency that must be checked.'

Larrimer said, 'Of course.'

'Trubee was bad enough,' Boyle went on, 'but Farraday tops them all. He's a sentimentalist. Wants to preserve the tribes, worships Indian culture. Filling the Indian Service with young radicals. This business of organizing the tribes — Soviets, that's what he wants to set up. He's a Communist.'

Butler said: 'At any rate, his religious policies are seriously bad. These day schools completely frustrate mission work.'

'Yes,' McCarty remarked. 'The children go right home. Back to the medicine men.'

'The key points of attack are two,' Larrimer said. 'They depend on each other. We must prevent the tribe from organizing under the Connell-Thomson Act. Are we agreed on that?'

The men looked towards McCarty.

The Navajo nodded. 'We have our Council, that's enough. These permanent tribal organizations under the new law — they're a move to send us back to the blanket, to cut us off from the rest of the nation, instead of helping us to merge into the great body of the citizenry. The so-called self-government is a trap. It's segregation.'

Smedley, who sat at the end of the table opposite Butler, asked, 'How did that law ever get passed?'

'That Indian Welfare bunch,' Boyle snapped. 'Them and the women's clubs, and a flock of radicals, and a lot of high pressure from Farraday.'

Larrimer continued. His quiet, dignified way of talking went well with his white hair. 'The way to get at that, and our main line of attack with the Indians in any case, is the stock reduction. This so-called self-government is just what Jerome said it is; it's also a device to shift the onus of further reducing the sheep, and the purpose of that, I do believe, is to render the Navajos dependent upon Washington's bounty.'

Butler said: 'I've been in the Navajo country some thirty-six years. From my own observation, from the accounts of old-timers, and all the expert studies, I have come to believe that the reservation is overstocked and really is in danger of becoming a true desert.'

'The experts!' Boyle growled.

Smedley asked, 'How about it, Jerome?'

'With the tribe increasing the way it is, of course we have to have more farming and less grazing. The range *is* overstocked. But see how the Government is going about it! Why don't they develop more water first, more irrigated land? Then the demonstration areas — large tracts of our land put under fence, and when poor Indians want to graze their hungry sheep there, seeing the good grass, they have to get permission from an absolute autocrat, usually one of these experts with no sympathy or knowledge of the people.'

'These controlled areas are producing good grass?' asked Butler.

'They pick out favoured spots,' Larrimer said contemptuously.

Butler saw Boyle cycing him. Either Boyle or Smedley would be glad to tell the Board — 'I just want to get it all straight,' he said. 'Being stationed at Wingate, I don't get on the reservation as I used to.' He began drawing angular diagrams on his memorandum pad.

Rensselaer asked, 'These areas were fenced without consent of the Indians?'

McCarty hesitated. 'I wouldn't quite say that. Of course high pressure was used, and local Indians were tempted by the pay for doing the fencing. The fact remains that they are there. And in some quarters there's a rumour — a suspicion that when the Commissioner has enough land fenced and covered with good grass, he's going to sell it off to white men.'

'That's absurd,' Butler said. He caught Boyle's eye, and returned to his diagrams.

'Perhaps it is,' Rensselaer said, 'but it indicates tribal distrust of their self-styled benefactor. Don't you gentlemen see how all Mr. McCarty's points hang together? Here's an overpopulated, overstocked desert reservation; the Government asks the Indians to make incredible sacrifices, by means of which they *claim* that in the indefinite future they can make the place a garden.'

Boyle interrupted with 'They say that if the sheep are reduced by half, they can make the survivors twice as large and covered with twice as much wool. There's an absurdity for you!'

'Quite so. Meantime, instead of encouraging the Navajos to solve their problem by going out into the world and living as white men, what are they doing? Protecting the old religion, encouraging so-called Indian arts with all their emotional tie-in with ancient times and ways, building day schools, whooping it up for tribal self-government, for holding the Navajos together, for holding them back. Gentlemen, this program must be stopped.'

Butler nodded, and Boyle exclaimed, 'That's it!'

'Two things we must be careful to speak well of,' McCarty said. 'The attempt they're making to get the old Navajo country east of the reservation added to it. That's going to be a hard fight, and we must actively help. The other is the water development; only on that score, we want twice, four times as much as is being done.'

'That's all clear, then,' Larrimer said. 'How do we go about it? Jerome, you and other Christian leaders are agreed on this? You can work together in the tribe?'

'I believe so. Most of us.'

'In that connection,' Rensselaer put in, 'I'd like to mention young Begay. I think he could be useful.'

Larrimer looked at him enquiringly.

'Allan and Mr. McCarty and Mr. Boyle, I believe, can vouch for him. The boy has just passed his examinations for Zwinglian with flying colours and has received a scholarship. I've promised him a summer on the reservation.'

'I know him,' McCarty said. 'An excellent young man and a good speaker. He comes from a backward part of the reservation, and he might, he *might* have some influence in his own clan there. Otherwise, young and unknown as he is, no one would listen to him.'

Butler cleared his throat, then hesitated. 'Local white opinion near the reservation is important. Myron is a likeable and sincere young man. If he could speak to mission societies and other such groups, he would make a strong impression. And remember, he knows the religion, he was initiated. That's invaluable to his testimony.'

Rensselaer nodded. 'Good. His recent success has given him confidence, which he badly needed. But he's overtired and longs for a vacation, we must allow him his well-earned rest. He's waited at Santa Fé this long only so as to hear about his examinations.'

Smedley said: 'I've a mission meeting at Flagstaff next week — July fifth. It falls very pat after the pagan dances and art exhibition the chamber of commerce and the museum there put on in connection with the Fourth. If he could come and speak at that, it would be a relief to me. They have heard me all too often. Then he could go on into the reservation from there.'

'Excellent,' Butler said. 'It will try him out. Then perhaps in early September ——' He looked enquiringly at Rensselaer.

'Certainly. He'll be delighted to do it.'

Larrimer said, 'Let's get back to the main campaign. Now, I've been contacting some of the other denominations...'

PART FOUR

CHAPTER ONE

SLAYER OF ENEMY GODS let out a breath in the faintest of sighs. At the same moment, Child of the Waters turned towards him, his right hand resting on his knife of dark flint. They looked into each other's eyes. They had encompassed it, from the sacred mountain of the centre to the ends of the world between the two oceans, the little parts, the smallest things, and the great whole.

Child of the Waters said, 'Now.'

His elder brother said: 'A way is about to be opened to us. One of our People is going to do something which will let us act. We can bring something about.'

Standing at the end of the Rainbow Trail they took in their country again, without effort and in an instant, loving it and its people.

'We are their helpers,' Child of the Waters said. 'That is what we are for.'

They continued, looking down upon the country they had cleared of monsters, the people they had guarded, while their thoughts communicated.

The gods cannot help a man until he opens the way for them. They could not give corn and other planted foods to mankind until Natinesthani was ready to receive the idea of going to the end of Old Age River. They could not help him to go there until he had done his utmost for himself. When the People are bewildered, when their leaders disagree and tug in all directions, the gods cannot merely step in. They must look for men who can be guided towards the truth. They may plant a little act which takes years to ripen. One way or another, men have to draw the gods to them, and the gods must work through men. Only the gods have patience enough to do that.

They became covered with their armour of dark flint, dark flint moccasins, dark flint leggings, dark flint shirts, dark flint head-dresses. Sheet lightning rustled softly through the overlapping pieces of gleaming stone, so that they quivered like leaves in a faint breeze. Zizgag lightning came out of Nayeinezgani's quiver, flashing and returning. They stood on a short rainbow, under a blue beam from their father Sun Bearer, with their mother's white shell hanging high above them.

CHAPTER TWO

important

MYRON went out by himself, to think and to gather his forces. He was excited and nervous, and those ladies kept fussing over him. They were very nice, but they made him feel choked and even with all the excitement, the fatigue that kept buzzing in his head made it hard to talk to them. He carried the mask in a paper bag under his arm. From the house where he was to speak, a dirt road led to big pine trees near at hand. Widely spaced, the sun poured down between them, and the air was heavy with balsam. Beyond their tops he saw part of the peak of San Francisco Mountain with flecks of snow on it. Dokoslid, the sacred mountain of the west. He was going to begin with a remark about that; Mr. Smedley said it was a colourful literary allusion.

He sat in the shadow of a big tree. At moments he felt sure that he would make a mess of his speech, but he told himself that that was just because he was tired. First about being on the slope of Dokoslid, and from that to Navajo country and pride in being a Navajo, and so to what a young, modern Navajo wanted, his aspirations, a Christian, progressive people going forth into the white world. The chains of ignorance and superstition that held his people back, that isolated the drop in the barrel. From there he made a transition to the Government's program to hold the Indians back by keeping them tribal. The truth about this self-government trap. Communism. So on and so on. He checked it over; he knew it all right. He decided he wouldn't say much about stock reduction. He'd heard his uncle and other older

men tell how the country was drying up, and Tall Man —
Trumbull — had voted for it. Trumbull was smart. He
wasn't sure stock reduction was so wrong; Mr. Smedley
didn't raise sheep.

All that led up to the dramatic part, where he told them
what some of the old superstitions were like. The initiation,
being whipped. Mr. McCarty said sometimes they really
whipped hard. Well, just say, 'whipped.' Boys practically
nude, in just moccasins and tiny little — what was that word?
— yes, 'totally inadequate' breech-clouts, standing up in
front of young girls. The girls didn't undress, but exhibiting
the boys was bad enough.

Then, Mr. Smedley said, 'Tell them what it's like to have
the mask put on. Tell them how smelly it is.'

Well, yes, it had been sort of smelly. And of course it was
unsanitary. Spread germs. Dirty masks. Yes. Then the
climax, taking the mask out and showing them the ridiculous
object before which my people bow down in superstitious awe.

He touched the bag with one hand. He didn't want to
uncover it out here. First place, it was the wrong mask,
Nayeinezgani, all black with four lightnings going down one
side. Mr. Smedley said it didn't make any difference, but it
did in a way. Nayeinezgani was kind of admirable, and then,
he was a lot more dangerous than Hasché Yahlti, now in the
months when lightning can strike. That's superstition;
there aren't any such gods. It was pretty close to the Navajos'
own country, here on the slope of Dokoslid.

They made the mountain of the west fast to earth with a
sunbeam. They adorned it with yellow shell, with black
clouds, he-rain, yellow corn, and all sorts of wild animals.
They placed a shell dish on top, with two eggs of the yellow
warbler in it, covered with sacred buckskins, so now there
are many yellow warblers on Dokoslid. Over all they spread
a yellow cloud, and they sent White Corn Boy and Yellow
Corn Girl to dwell there.

I won't quote any of that stuff at the beginning, he decided.

It would sound funny when I'm talking against the religion. It's all just fairy stories, anyhow. A Christian has no fear.

He looked at his watch; twenty to five, time to start back. He felt tired all through, but after this he would be able to rest at last, to let go, and to see Ethel.

Myron told Mr. Smedley not to worry, he had his talk well memorized. The missionary remembered that the young man had been a prize debater. He went to a mirror and checked over his costume. Dark suit, dark tie, stiff collar. It was hot, but it looked dignified. The Hopi native missionary he met last night wore glasses, they gave an added touch. He wished he had a pair.

He and Mr. Smedley and one of the ladies went into the big room together, where about twenty people sat on rows of chairs. The lady talked first, and she went on and on. A welcome breeze from a mountain rainstorm eased the stifling heat. At last she finished, and it was Mr. Smedley's turn. He prayed first. Then he said he'd be very brief, but he wasn't. He made some jokes at which the people laughed, although Myron thought they sounded too much like school-teachers trying to be funny. Then he introduced Myron, saying a lot of very nice things which made one feel at once uncomfortable, surprised, and elated.

Once he got going, Myron was all right. A thunderclap threw him off his stride near the beginning, but he mastered that. He made his points and transitions in good order, and saw that his audience was with him. When he got to the initiation he hesitated, but the eager response to his mention of the whipping and the all-but-nude boys carried him forward to his climax.

'Dis belongs to Nayeinezgani,' he said, drawing forth the mask, 'de so-called Slayer of Enemy Gods.'

Through the window he saw a brilliant, angular streak of lightning. It flashed four times in the same place. He remained with his mouth open, frozen, through the following crash. The audience had their backs to the window so did not see the flash, but some of them commented on the noise. He swallowed, coughed, and after a few stammering words went smoothly to the end.

They applauded him heartily. He felt weak and rather ill. It had been different from making a speech at school, and then he'd been frightened, not for any real reason, but just scared and all sorts of pictures of the god running in his mind when it came right at that moment. He wanted to go off by himself, but there was grapejuice and cakes, and everyone wanted to talk to him and ask him questions. Many of them asked if there weren't other indecent rites that he hadn't mentioned, they seemed to want them. He told them, truly, that as far as ceremonies he had seen, the only other thing was that couples did go off together into the bushes sometimes, during the squaw dances, but the Navajos disapproved of it. The questioners irritated him. The Navajos might be ignorant, but they were not dirty.

At last the meeting broke up. He told Mr. Smedley, who was enormously pleased with him, that he thought he'd go for a walk. It had been a big day, his first real public appearance, he felt that it was the true beginning of being a preacher, told himself how successful he'd been, but nothing would banish the bottomless, black mood into which he'd fallen. He guessed it was because he was tired, but that didn't seem to be the main thing. He felt all wrong. He hadn't got over that fright entirely; he'd certainly been scared. Coincidence, you could see how ignorant people came to believe such things. He looked up, over his shoulder, to see the peak against sky which was taking on the evening quality. All clear now. It was hotter in the main part of town while the sun lingered, but he wanted the walls on either hand and the many people. The street was still lively with visitors to the celebrations, which lasted several days, white men, both Anglo and Spanish, generally tricked out in more or less cowboy style, Indians of many kinds. He heard Navajo spoken all about him, and avoided the speakers. He felt guilty and ashamed, and kept on reasoning with himself. It was like that time after the football game, only different and ever so much worse.

Then I kissed Ethel, it was then I won her. Jack and I had stopped being friends before that. Jack was heathen and it had to happen sometime. Jack's face with its determined look, the new little boy at Yellow Earth standing up to that big Chishi. Two children making their way together, determined together... An old association brought up the young Twin Gods in his mind. Not that he'd ever thought of himself and Jack as being like gods, but there had been something you understood about those two Boys playing and setting forth for adventure together. You had to turn your face against Jack, against the Twins, you had to give your testimony against them. They were almost as vivid to him as the memory of his friend. I can't ever enjoy thinking of them again, they're false gods. Desolation swept over him. He shook himself. What's wrong with me? I'm through now, and I'm going to see Ethel and have a vacation. I'd better eat.

He couldn't face going into a bright, crowded place. The streets were growing cool now, at the restaurant doors thick heat and clamour came forth. There were the lights of a movie, that looked better. 'Air-Cooled.' Dark, quiet, and cool. Happily, with my interior feeling cool, may I walk. He shook his head. Stop that. A Western and a romance, he hoped the Western was on. The lady in the ticket window hardly looked at him, she was used to Indians. She didn't know that he was the one who defied Nayeinezgani and all the people clapped hard.

He was just in time for the Western; there were cowboys and horses, and fast riding, and that was fine. Then there were some Indians whom the movie people took for Apaches, but anyone could see they were Sioux, and they were all villains and cruel and treacherous. The picture made them seem pretty bad, and at the same time made fun of them. He got up and left. People ought to know that Indians weren't like that.

It was much cooler outside now. His feet felt heavy and his legs ached, but he kept on wandering, sometimes in the bright blocks, sometimes in the dark side streets, not wanting to go back to the house where he and Mr. Smedley were staying. Tomorrow Mr. Smedley would find a car going towards Gideon and get him a ride. Then Ethel. Then the whole rest of the summer, at ease, and the long horseback days alone. Picnics with Ethel; something dragged at him, discolouring his pleasure. The mission, Ethel, they were all right, but there was something wrong with going among the Navajos. He saw the dark faces, the poor clothes, the old men and the boys his age, and he didn't want to come before them. Why did I say that about standing up in a breech-clout, and about the whipping? False testimony. But how could you explain to them that even if the Navajos are wrong, still it's not — it's not... He stood still on a dark street corner, wrestling, with a sense of physical effort.

He turned sharply and walked down the street. Everywhere he turned, every way he looked, things seemed wrong. What was the matter? Tired, that's it, I'm tired. I wish my head would stop humming. Is Ethel really Christian? Why does she love me? If I could go out there, right now, right now. Maybe she's still at Tlichisenili. Oh. Maybe there's a letter for me at Santa Fé. Ethel, her trust and admiration, comfort, peace. There is no such god, those gods don't even exist. Thou shalt have none other gods... He crossed the railroad track, and was vaguely aware that most of the people he passed were speaking Spanish, now a few bars and eating-places were scattered along the street, from some of which came music. Promising Ethel to sing jazz, Navajo songs, too. He imagined a tune in silence, and the very thought of even the most meaningless gambling song was intensely painful. I'll never sing them again.

He turned up a side street leading back across the track. It was dark here. He could hear the blurred voices of two men walking towards him, talking Spanish, and when they were near him, saw them with their arms across each other's shoulder. He caught the smell of their drinking, and stepped aside to let them by.

One of them half turned, peered at him with out-thrust face, and said something. Myron stepped farther aside. The man laid a hand on his arm and spoke again. He jerked away and walked on rapidly. The man shouted, 'Whatsa matter, you Eendian son of a beetch?'

Both of them broke into catcalls, and then threw unintelligible Spanish after him. You didn't have to understand it. When Mexicans turn insulting, they use a mocking, high-pitched voice which is inescapable. Myron clenched his fists, thinking Nakai, dirty, smelly Nakai.

'Son of a beetch!'

The other man yelled, '*O-ho-ho-ho*,' in a recognizable parody of the final Night Chant tune.

Myron's mind was a whirl of quick thoughts and feelings, the ever-villainous Indians of the movies, the ladies prying for dirty ceremonies, the contempt ready to jump forth . . .

'God damn Eendian!' The screech seemed to hit him.

He felt light on his feet. *What's the matter with you, half-back?* Jack said. He swung around. Nakai, just a couple of smelly Nakai. He was alive. He didn't even notice that fatigue was gone as he charged for his tribe. He didn't hear himself raise the wolf-bark. He was vaguely aware that there was no referee to prevent slugging. His coat was a nuisance. It happened fast. Something hit his shin painfully and there was a blow on the side of his head. He hit a face twice, was grabbed, and pounded a stomach. He crouched, and made a quick, lifting tackle, sending one man staggering back, then turned to give full attention to the other. He used his hands, his shoulders, his knees, and his feet, and suddenly the second man broke and ran, staggering a little, but hesitating not at all in his intention to get well away.

As the first man came back, Myron saw the knife. He didn't have time to be frightened as he punted, his up-swinging leg taking his enemy at the knee. The Mexican cried out, and slashed as he fell. Myron felt the knife tear his coat. He sprang for the man's hand, grabbed, twisted. The knife dropped and he threw it far. Then he jumped. He jumped four times, and when the man stopped trying to rise, he knelt and began battering. He saw nothing, he thought nothing. The red film misted over what he was doing, and he battered. Suddenly he thought of the knife and searched for it. He'd heard it fall, but now he couldn't find it. When Yei Tso, first of the Enemy Gods, was dead, the Younger Brother took his scalp. A flint knife. A flint knife. He searched. He felt calm, very much in hand, but he had to hunt fast. *My headdress of dark flint. The flint youth am I. E-na. My heart of clear flint. The flint youth am I. E-na.* No sign of it. He returned to his enemy.

The man lay still. It was dark in the street, and quiet. The man lay still. Between two lightless houses he and this man's spirit stood in an enclosure. He wanted to stoop and make sure that the man was dead, but the second part of an ancestral, inescapable pattern had set in full tide. He turned and ran.

He stopped running on the edge of the bright centre of town. How did he come to have his hat in his hand? His coat was cut in a long gash down the left side, his face battered, his knuckles bloody. He felt his throat. One wing of his collar rose up sideways and his tie was way out of place. He retreated to a darker section.

Where sidewalks gave way to dirt road, he straightened himself as best he could. But I can't go back to Mr. Smedley. Murder. That other man will say — Indian — murder. I can't go to him. Or Mr. Butler. Or anyone. Ethel. Oh Lord! Oh Lord God, help me. Ethel. Leave here, leave here, get away from here. The dead, the blood-guilt hastened up to him so that he cringed. Get away from here. Killed a man. Go home. Ethel.

Over the pass, through the gap to the northwest, lay the

road to the Navajo country. Heavily he started walking, skirting the heart of town, out past the filling-stations. By and by one would come to where there were no houses and he could rest. Tired; he thought he knew about being tired, but now he was emptied until his leg bones bent, and his sinews gave so that at each step he had to take up slack. He tried to pray as he tramped, but after what he'd done he wasn't sure about God. No more college. An end to ministry, service. Must get away. He plodded on. Mr. Butler, Mr. Smedley, Mr. Rensselaer, Mr. Boyle, Mr. McCarty, Mr. murder angry guilty horrible end of work an angry god. God. God. God. Looking for the knife. *Flint youth am I.* God, the gods, at war with lightnings. Ethel, oh Ethel. Murder guilty Mr. Butler Mr. Smedley Mr. Butler Mr. Snyder.

He had no idea how far he'd walked. The paved road turned aside, and under his feet was dirt. Tall pines came to the edge of the ditch. Thinking of sheriffs and law, he dragged himself yet another half mile, then left the road. The springy mat of grass and needles eased his ruined legs and called to his body. He went up over a rise, into a hollow, and found a rock which made an enclosure with three saplings. Into that he crept.

He felt a little more protected, as if here the dead man, the *Chindi,* could not follow close, as if he'd put him off the track. The woods were lonely and silent, in their vast darkness all manner of things could be. Shooting Singer said, with perfect assurance, 'I have attended to all that.' Kneeling, he started the Lord's Prayer, was horrified by the sound of his own whisper, and said it through intensely, in silence. Christ's prayer, Who had lived on earth, been a boy, grown up, suffered. Did He war against the other gods? The power and the glory — am a jealous God — that was God not Jesus reaching over mountains, overthrowing the Divine Ones, wise untiring Nayeinezgani. Offended all offended murder the wrath the power murder guilt, his stomach sick at the memory of jumping pounding the unresistant prostrate horror not dead perhaps not entirely killed. Oh God, don't let him be dead. Caught between the gods, the great enemies fierce angry against each other.

From kneeling he sank to a huddled crouch. Black, dark woods, dark horror seeping in from under the great trees to his centre. That which stands up in me lies down. The guilt, the following guilt, Chindi. He looked over his shoulder, trembling. Shooting Singer coming serenely from the woods. *Maid who becomes a bear Sought the gods and found them, On the mountain tops Sought the gods and found them.* The recitation was mechanical, he was hardly aware of the words. *Truly with my sacrifice Sought the gods and found them. Somebody doubts it, so I have heard.* Dimly as he continued he heard his own voice in the hypnotic, heavy rhythm. The cold reached through his clothes and slid over his skin. His clothes were weightless. He heard a voice chanting. He crouched in breech-clout and moccasins, still carrying the blood upon him, uncleansed, alone in enemy territory, praying. *I wander among their weapons.* His own loud voice startled him back to himself. He pulled the torn jacket closer. Too tired. His mind blurred, the darkness tended to become a grey haze, then when he opened his eyes it was darkness again. He saw stars through the treetops. He dug a hole for himself in the deep pine needles against the rock, and curled into it, shuddering. Greyness closed in on him.

CHAPTER THREE

NEITHER Indian nor white, neither Christian nor Navajo, nothing at all, a cypher, zero, he plodded slowly under the pressing heat. A hard, pebbly soil, grassless, spotted here and there with low-growing cactus and small, pale shrubs, stretched out before him. Quivering heat glanced upward from the surface, the light made him squint continuously. Far ahead a jumble of painted country fiercely open to the sun shouted of trials yet to come. His hat, a smallish, green felt, became heavy and the headband was slippery, but he needed the slight shade of its brim. His once white shirt, splotched with brown dust, let the sun directly through; his trousers of dark serge clung to his legs, flopping and soft. The heat underfoot came through his shoes.

His mouth was sticky with thirst and his stomach was empty. The whole mass of Dokoslid rose clear and following behind him, brown foothills, the green mountain, and the rocky peak piebald with snow; he avoided looking back at it. Somewhere here he would cross the reservation line, and then in some favoured place he would find Indians, food and drink, shade in which to lie down.

Raising his eyes, he saw a fence stretching out of sight to east and west. That was the line. There was no gate in sight. When he got close, he saw the fence was six-strand, high and tight, to keep in the strongest bull and the smallest lamb. He could go west to the highroad, but that was a mile or more. There might be a gate on some trail near here, or one might waste hours of strength searching. He squatted despondently. Climb it in a minute.

For a moment it was a relief to be still, then the heat closed down in a different way, the air dead around his face. Not really hard to climb, but an extra effort, and the menacing barbs. It gave him a sense of being unwelcome. He stared at a post with its nails and the 'Property of the United States' sign at the top. It seemed right, a hostile face turned towards a man who gave false testimony against his tribe. How could you make those mission people understand that it could be superstitious and ignorant and false gods, and still be beautiful? They wouldn't let you say that. God wouldn't let you. If you were for God, you hated all those things. Enemy Gods. Then God threw me out. Murder.

Then would Ethel cast him off too? First thing was to see Ethel, tell her straight out about it. She loves me, does she, will she still? Why love me? I thought I was pretty bright, but I guess — against his hip he could feel the warmth of the envelope which contained the notice of his scholarship for 1935–36. He rose with a sigh. Well, here goes.

The strands were too close for crawling through, so he climbed over, tearing his trousers in two places and scratching his forearm. When he was down on the other side, he stood thinking for a minute, then stopped and scraped up a handful of the hot, cindery soil. Navajo soil. It didn't look very friendly, nor did the country. It's what I have. It's the one thing I can always have. He dropped the handful as he moved forward. An Indian can go up and down, one way or another, but the land is what always remains. He glanced around. This part doesn't look very valuable. He looked down at his trousers, their general effect now was thoroughly Navajo. It all goes together, we have to dress like our country. I'll clean up before I see Ethel. There was plenty of water around Gideon, he remembered, some Indians and Mr. Boyle had irrigated fields there. Well, that's far from here. When shall I find a hogahn?

He wondered how much longer he could keep going, feeling steadily more thirsty, and slightly giddy. Just got to keep on going. Over a rise and across a shallow dip and over another rise, no shade, no resting-place. A definite trail on which showed the clear, unshod hoofprints of Indian travel, encouraged him enormously. He followed it northwesterly.

That cheer died away and weakness returned as another hour's travel brought him nowhere in an unknown, empty, and unreadable country. At last he saw a man coming, pushing his pony at a good trot. He waited in the trail, thankfulness welling up in him. Would the man stop for him, speak to him? Or turn aside and hurry by? Tall, straight-shouldered, slender, long hair under a wide, battered hat, shell and turquoise necklace on a sun-faded, dusty, orange shirt, blue jeans, moccasins, a young man riding indolently, an utterly Navajo young man, a personification.

The rider looked at him with curiosity. Handsome, under a heavy coating of dust, a familiar, aquiline type, like a person one knew all about.

Acting carefully, Myron gave him a casual 'Where to, tell?'

'To Many Houses. And you tell, where to?'

'To Ha'anoichí.'

The rider bent forward, staring. Myron stared. The man's lips parted, drew wide, and the even teeth flashed in that light-giving, thorough smile.

'Eh, my brother!'

'Brother!' The flood of thankfulness broke through inside of him. He smiled, but he could not trust himself to speak while their hands lingered together. Singing Gambler said, 'Walking?' but he couldn't answer, only cough.

'I thought you were a white man at first, and it was you all the time. That funny hat, and your face is so pale.'

Myron said, 'I've been in a house all winter.'

Singing Gambler looked sympathetic. 'Did the police get you?'

Myron began to laugh. The police, police. Did the police, have they, are they — it was funny and it hurt. His laughter ran up high in the dancing sunlight, Dokoslid bowed over to listen. This man came riding and said ——

Singing Gambler slipped to earth and caught him. 'Easy, my brother. Gently. The sun is strong.' He looked Myron over with real attention. 'Sit here, in my horse's shadow.'

Slowly his breath came to rest. He was ashamed.

'I have walked all the way from Many Houses, last night and today.'

'Coyote!'

'I haven't eaten, and since I left the trees, there's been no water on the road.'

'You travel fast. You're worn out, I think. There's a hogahn back here not so far. Get on behind me, and I'll take you there.'

'All right. Thanks.'

Singing Gambler saw he was in trouble, he asked no questions but gave his help. He didn't see the guilt, the divine wrath. The dead man followed less close upon his heels. You may be exhausted and starved with thirst, but the horse does the walking for you. On a horse, you can get through.

'I'll take you there,' Singing Gambler said. 'It's late, anyhow. I'll start again for Many Houses tomorrow.'

'Why are you going there?'

'For the celebrations. The races and dancing and all that.'

'You're too late,' Myron said. His voice sounded harsh. He controlled it. 'There were three days of it, and it's all over.'

'Oh. Well, I'll go over west and look at the Wide Canyon and the Supais then, I think.'

'You're travelling far.'

'Yes.'

After they had ridden some distance, Singing Gambler said, 'Do you remember Juniper?' He twirled his quirt, watching him.

'Juniper? Why — yes.'

'I married her.'

Myron said nothing. He remembered her quality, some-how she didn't quite seem the wife for this man.

'It seems odd to you, perhaps. She is a great woman, a beautiful person. I thought I could change myself. For a short time I changed myself, but then it was too much for me, and then I was too much for her. So I'm travelling.'

Myron showed his understanding by a non-committal, friendly grunt.

'You knew her. When we were at that dance — do you remember — you looked at each other and she went out after you. I was afraid of you then. But you went back to school —— ' He paused, considering the idea of a man who could have had Juniper and left her. 'I can't mention her to strangers, but you saw her, so I tell it to you.'

Myron said, 'That's too bad. I'm sorry.' What had hap-pened to Singing Gambler squeezed his heart with the thought of Ethel. His was not the only trouble in the world.

'We have a son, a fine boy. But I did the wrong things and she just told me not to unsaddle. The boy, that keeps on reaching out and tugging.'

'You're going to go back in a while to ask her again?'

'No, I think. You know her. I'd have to turn into some-body else. What I am is not what she can live with.'

'But —— '

'Just don't ask me about it, my friend.'

Myron fell silent. It seemed too much to have other people suffering, too. He wished he could fix it for this man to be perfectly happy.

Where a trail ran off from the one they followed, Singing Gambler said, 'Here's where they get their water. You want some, don't you?'

'I do!'

They skirted the edge of a steep drop. Pointing into the depression, half canyon, half valley, his guide said, 'Way over there, under the bluffs — see — that's where I ate lunch. Then over that way, farther on, are two more hogahns.'

The sand turned to a purple-brown rock, the trail was a smooth-worn ribbon tumbling down into a cleft now entirely full of shadow, at the bottom of which grew some grass and scrub-oaks. The pony, stepping prettily with accurate placement of each small hoof in turn, took them down to the smell of water, a wide drip over wet stone slimy with water growths, a narrow pool, and reeds. Damp sand soaked up against Myron's stomach while he filled himself, wet his hands and face, made himself new. He dawdled in the luxury of wetness, and at last drew back, replenished.

They sat with their backs against the cool rock. Myron refused to smoke. Singing Gambler looked around the place of water with pleasure.

'Here with the rocks close about, voices should sound well. Let's sing.'

'I can't lift it up now,' Myron said. 'I ——' There was too much, one couldn't tell about it, didn't want to. 'I'm — well — in between.'

'You have some trouble, I think.'

'Yes. I may end in jail. Back there, I killed a man.'

'What!'

'A Mexican. I killed him with my hands and feet. He was ——'

Myron stopped, seeing Singing Gambler's face as he rose.

'When?'

'The night before last. So I came right on.' Was this man going to betray him? 'I covered my tracks pretty well, I think, I mixed up my trail.'

Singing Gambler relaxed slightly. 'Well, he may not have followed you.' He glanced upwards. 'The sun will set in a few minutes. My brother, I don't want to be near you after dark. You must find a singer quickly. You may have shaken him off, but ——'

Myron thought, Accursed.

Singing Gambler went on: 'A Mexican, you say? Well, it shows that even a schoolboy can be a warrior. Listen — do you remember, I showed you where the trail went off to those other hogahns?' The gambler looked him over. 'You need help. Perhaps you've got rid of it. Anyhow, you need help. Take my horse and go to that place. Don't turn off to the hogahn you can see, I'm going there. Hurry up, it's getting late.'

'But you ——'

'I'm in good shape. I can get a horse with my earrings or something.'

'I can walk.'

'You need a horse and saddle. Go along.'

'Well, here ——' Myron fished out some money. 'Here. I've nine dollars.'

'Did you take this off the Mexican?'

'No.'

'If you're going on, looking for help, you'll need something. Have you any more?'

Myron felt in his pocket. 'About a dollar.'

'All right, I'll take this, then. Now go along, before it gets dark down here. Those people are all Ashkaantsoni; just tell them you're in trouble with the police, and I sold you the horse. They'll never give you away to the white men.'

About to mount, Myron paused. 'But if you're afraid of me, why do you send me to those people?'

Singing Gambler smiled slowly. 'You covered up your tracks, perhaps you have got free of it. Only, knowing this, I feel uncomfortable with you. They can take care of themselves, I think.'

Myron laughed. He mounted, his long legs fitting comfortably to the stirrups, and quirted the horse into motion. 'I'll see you somewhere.'

'Yes.'

He was so much of a piece, warm-hearted and selfish. As the horse lurched and scrambled upward, Myron hoped that the man could find what he lacked and win back Juniper.

It was partly just wanting not to have any more suffering and loneliness in this world, and partly for himself, for Ethel, for a world in which things could work out that way.

The Ashkaantsoni clansmen received him pleasantly. Few strangers came that way, and during the summer months only three families, owning few sheep, remained in this section. They pastured in the crevasses and gorges leading down to the little Colorado River, and grew their corn in certain spots of pure sand where moisture lingered deep down. Their food was poor, some wild roots, meat of two prairie dogs, tortillas, and coffee very sparingly sugared. The children were two girls, a small boy, and a baby. The eldest girl had been back from school about a year. She looked frail, and coughed a good deal. They were all cheerful and took pleasure in the smallest item of news, any new subject for thought and discussion.

Myron said he had gone to Many Houses in a car with some friends, and there had got into trouble and had to run away. He bought his horse from a man who came by here yesterday. They recognized the animal. The father, noting his haggard face, said that young men got into a lot of trouble in towns, on account of the whiskey. Schoolboys were inclined to run wild when they first came home. He hoped the traveller was going to settle down now. Where was his home?

He said he lived near Tsaili, and when that meant nothing to them, explained that it was at the foot of the Lukachukais.

The man said that was far away, and questioned him about his country. He answered in detail, with pleasure, astonished to find how clearly he remembered it, the grazing, the water, the people, the mountains. Then they discussed this dry section. It was time the rains began.

'There have been clouds in the northwest,' his host said, 'but they break up again. Then we have seen fine, dark clouds around Dokoslid. Did any rain fall over there?'

'Yes, there was one. A he-rain, very short.'

'The men here in this canyon are going to the spring tomorrow, to pray, to help the rain coming. Perhaps you will stay over and help us.'

The mere invitation was like sudden good news. He knew the happy union of men building a prayer together. He stared into the fire. Perhaps he would not be struck down for attempting to pray, perhaps no such gods existed; it didn't matter, one way or the other it would be false. He loved these poor, friendly people. Belief or no belief, I want to respect what they are doing.

He said slowly: 'No, I think. I have been away at school a long time, away from all those things. I'm not able to help at that just now.'

'You have eaten the pollen?'

'Yes. But I am worrying about things. I am disturbed in my mind. I might hinder the work, I fear.'

'Yes. Perhaps you are right.'

'Tomorrow, as I go riding, I shall think well about rain. I shall look towards wherever clouds gather and remember you happily.'

'Good.' His host smiled slightly, pleased by right thinking in a sacred matter.

A little later Myron said he was tired, and borrowed a tattered blanket and a sheepskin. Lying on sand still faintly warm, with the air becoming cool around him, he sighed deeply. He missed a pillow, he was out of practice for this. Am I doing harm to these people, staying here when my guilt, the dead, the Chindi — I know there is no Chindi. I know I don't believe that. It's in me only, if I told them they'd be frightened, unhappy. I carry it, whatever it is. I have to work it out.

2

Dust, settling into the weave of his unsuitable trousers, had changed them to an irregular, dusty, dark grey. Even if he could have afforded to buy a pair of overalls, he was afraid to go near a trading post. A penniless and ragged drifter, the people received him as they would any other young man. When the sun had scorched him and his hair was long about his ears and around his neck, they ceased to identify him as a scholar. He was just a traveller with a little news of places farther west, rather taciturn, evidently very poor, though he had a good horse, a chestnut with a black mane and tail and black stockings. They were generous in providing him with meat to take with him, and at Tusjé a woman gave him an old blanket.

Many nights he slept out, but hunger, reinforcing loneliness, would send him to the hogahns again to eat and give news and tell an unreal log of his travels, and sit among the friendliness. If they knew they'd be afraid of him; worse than that, if they knew what he'd said, if they knew how he had let lying thoughts stand in the minds of those white people, and then turned to the ignorant, superstitious savages for help when he got into trouble. He was glad to go off by himself to sleep, glad to get away in the morning and be alone. He would urge his horse forward, farther from Many Houses and the thunders of Dokoslid.

The chestnut horse was the one constant in his changing scene, his means of life and his companion. After he left the extreme desert of the west, he took pains to care for it well, and troubled to make sure of its grazing when there was no food for himself. After he passed beyond the fertile valley of Tangled Waters the rains broke; looking to the southwest he saw massive clouds and pillars of falling water, and rejoiced for the Ashkaantsoni. As he crossed the Hopi country the grass began to thrust up pointed blades, his horse improved in condition, and when even in the worst of he-rains all he got was a soaking though the thunder rolled, he was heartily thankful for the storms. Sometimes he forgot about himself entirely in the newness of the country he traversed, sometimes in a fresh, early morning he sang, but that was impossible as soon as he thought. Often he wanted to push his horse on and on, through noon hours, past places of good grass, past nightfall, but he made himself pause. There was no reason why the animal should suffer for his fears and sins.

Though he could neither pray nor sing, he thought constantly about God and the gods, going round and round a series of old paths that became smooth and hateful, and restored pain each time at the same points. Camping alone at night, in the darkness he would be afraid, of no definable thing. He dreamed mainly when he had stopped at a hogahn, an old dream with new confusions. There was the house with the lamp on the table again, and a girl in civilized clothes whom now he could never quite see, but who was sometimes Ethel, and a woman knelt by a hogahn fire, and he couldn't get up the mountain to his uncle who had the Answer, a brilliant, precious stone, in his medicine bag. Sometimes Mr. Butler, or Jack, or other people got into it, but the worst was when the gods seemed to be near, or his uncle was coming and he knew that his uncle would perceive it all. They were unclear dreams of broken incident and with few known people who looked like themselves, dreams partly of hopeless seeking, and partly of fear and the struggle to escape.

He travelled on, thinking out no goal beyond Ethel. He would tell her all about it. As a Christian, she wouldn't fear the Chindi, and when he had talked it over with her, then perhaps he himself would understand. Perhaps she would show him.

The wide valley in the centre of which lay Gideon spread out at last before him. He saw the stone house, the barn, the chapel with its tiny spire, the green fields. Before he went down, he dug himself some yucca roots. Leaving the trail at the arroyo, he followed up its bed, wary for quicksand, until he was hidden. There he bathed himself in the thin trickle, scrubbing his hair and shirt and body with the soapy roots. It made him feel fresh. There were ceremonial ideas, too, attached to such washing, the idea of cleansing oneself. That was all right. That was fitting, now he was going to be helped.

His shirt dried quickly in the sun, and came out almost white. He hated putting on the gritty pants again. A comb would be a help, but he owned no such thing. Well, at least he was clean.

The irrigation ditch ran quiet beside the road, with rich grass along its edges. Eager though he was, he didn't have the heart to deny his horse a spell of cropping, then he pulled it away, telling it it would get more later. He passed a string of Indian fields, then came the taut fences around Mr. Boyle's. How brilliant the alfalfa looked, how lovely water was in this land! Why did a white man have these fields, here in our country? He wasn't running a boarding school or a hospital, he had only a few mouths to feed. About five acres of alfalfa, and he owned only two horses for the farming. The horses eat — three crops a year — he'll sell — at twenty dollars a ton — well, better than two hundred dollars a year. He'd never thought of that before. Irrigated land was priceless. Mrs. Boyle is cross to Ethel. The Ashkaantsoni family praying for rain on their spindly corn. Are preachers greedy?

When he reached the mission he tied the horse to the fence, where it could reach stray clumps of the rich, green crop. He doubted that the Boyles would recognize him if they happened to see him. He knocked on the back door.

A girl about seventeen years old came out. He noticed her long hair done in a bun on top of her head, her neat house-dress and sneakers. After the women he'd been seeing in the hogahns, her face seemed oddly dead. She looked him over as if sizing him up, then her expression livened a little.

'What is it?' she asked in Navajo. 'Come in.'

'I'm just looking for — for Abinah Bitsí.'

'For whom?'

'The girl who used to work here. Ethel Harding, her Bellacana name.'

'She went to Tlichisenili they say, when her mother was sick. She stayed there.'

Myron simply felt blank.

The girl said, 'Come in and rest. It's hot.'

He walked into the kitchen, which at this hour was faintly cooler than outside, and took a chair.

'Where from?' the girl asked.

She might tell things to Mr. Boyle; Myron thought fast. 'From Bakho Tletsoi, over west near Besh Nana-aj. I knew that girl at school, and just now I had nothing to do, so I came over here.'

'That's too bad. Have you had any lunch?'

'No.'

She brought him cold meat and bread.

'Will you stay around here a little while?'

It was ridiculous. Now this blow had fallen, and the girl was making up to him.

'I'll go back home, I think.'

'If you just come around to the church on Sundays, you can eat here right along. You went to school, you know how it is. I have to work here now, because my parents are poor. These people make me angry but they pay me.'

Myron simply wanted to finish the food and get out in the easiest possible way.

'I don't mind church,' he said. 'I'll look around.' He cleaned up the last crumbs. 'I have a horse out there, and one must know where to sleep.'

He didn't laugh, but it was a close call. Outside, he stood with his hand on his horse's neck, telling it about the absurdity. Then he dragged the animal away from its plunder, heading north, letting it walk while he faced the fact that Ethel had not come back to Gideon.

3

He was trying to straighten out his own feelings as he followed the chain of uplands which led to the heart of Black Mesa. It was mid-afternoon, and if he didn't reach a camp soon, he thought he'd stop anyhow, as the grass here was good.

He saw the hogahn as he rounded a point of rock. It was the kind of well-put-together shelter to which people return year after year. There was a loom under a pine tree. A man and woman and some children stood by the fire-circle, huddled together. Farther out was a saddled horse, sleeping on three legs. Making the third point of a triangle was another man sprawled limply on the ground, face down, and near him Myron saw the sun gleam on a rifle barrel.

He was slow in understanding what he saw, then he turned his horse about. He had had enough of violence and bad things, he had his belly full of it. Where the first trees cut him off from the sight of the hogahn, he stopped. Being nothing, being nothing at all, beneath harm, and the innocent, ignorant people who feed a wanderer. He knew what terror lay over that family. Perhaps this is what I'm for now, to do the dirtiest jobs. Not so much to do. What can I fear? Pay back a little of the kindness. He swung the reins against the chestnut's back and trotted slowly back.

As he came to a stop, the man said, 'Better keep going, grandchild. Something has happened here.'

He leaned forward over his saddlehorn. 'I can help you, perhaps, grandfather.'

'No. There is nothing to do, I think, only something for you to fear if you stay around here.'

'I have a charm, grandfather.' He dismounted. 'Let me look.'

The man watched him, puzzled and surprised. Myron made himself draw near. There had been a first-aid course. The dead man lay like another, the dead are terrible. I know better, and then, what difference to me? He knelt down, he touched. There was the bullet hole, one hardly needed to make sure. He was choked and unsteady with the wish to get free of this. He looked up at the grey-haired man, who watched him in wonder, and the woman and family behind him.

'How then, grandfather?' he asked.

'His gun there was stuck. We tried to work it loose, and then it spoke.'

'He lives here?'

'No, he was passing through. We have known each other many years.'

The young man stared at the older one, thinking. He knew the fear of the dead as well as they did, but at the same time he knew better.

'I'll put him away,' he said. 'I have a special charm. Just keep away, all of you. Keep clear of it.'

The man looked at him with infinite relief. 'You know how? You are a singer, perhaps?'

'I know how. I am not a singer, but I know a sacred thing.'

The man nodded. A long vigil, a great fear, the possible need of leaving this favoured place and this home, were being taken from him by a strange young man, short-haired and ragged and handsome, wearing a white man's hat and shoes.

'That's his horse over there,' he said.

'Hold it for me. And let that horse of mine graze, grandfather.'

'Yes.' The man frowned, and looked around. 'Beyond that corner, a cleft goes in and there are rocks.'

'Good.'

He got the body in a fireman's lift. It took all his shoulders and his wide back muscles as he staggered to his feet, then it was fairly easy. He remembered about mixing up the trail, smudging his footprints, resting four times. Even after he was out of sight, he made himself follow the requirements, as though not to do so would be to break faith with these people.

It was cooler in the shadow of the cleft. The corpse had changed character by then, becoming less fearful, very heavy, hostile. He was casual about lowering it to the long crevice he selected, and then as he began laying up stones, there again was a man, the housing of a man, being enclosed for all time. Some part of him must know what's happening. I must not go thinking wrong. He forcibly prevented himself from being hasty as he walled up the crevice, and noticed that his hands were trembling.

It was an enormous relief to be out of the cleft again. He picked up the rifle and took the horse by the reins. The family watched him from their hogahn. They were afraid of him now. He had to go back in.

There was a good blanket on the back of the saddle, wrapped around an armful of grass. Taking off the bridle, he let the horse eat, watching it after he'd examined the rifle. Whatever had made it stick, the gun was all right now. He threw out the empty shell and saw a new one slide in. A thirty-thirty costs a lot of money. The man's own family could profit by this and the horse, but because of the way people think, these useful things must be destroyed.

The horse had cleaned up the fodder. Well, cousin, they say you'll go with him. The animal's eyes daunted him, the superbly unsuspecting, clear expression to which no such idea could penetrate. He nerved himself and fired, true to the spot.

There were prayers to say, but he didn't know them. The horse lay there in front of the crude tomb. You looked like a good man, you had a friend who was fond of you, I am not treating you with disrespect, I am not laughing at you. I think that now you know better than some of these little ideas about doing things just so. I wish I knew what you know now, I wish I'd been born when you were, when things were clear, Navajo or alien. Finally he thought, this man is just another Indian, but he is just as good as people who know a lot more. He rose, hesitated, and touched the horse's flank before he went out. As soon as he turned his back on the tomb, he wanted to run, but he didn't. He was sweating violently by the time he came into the open.

The people watched him from a slight distance while he caught the chestnut. He smiled sourly; below or above, but not among. He mounted. A woman's voice called to him sharply, the mother of the hogahn walked towards him with her arms full. He rode a few steps towards her.

'I am not followed,' he said. 'I told your husband I knew something. That is true.'

'My husband has gone to tell his family,' she said. 'You have helped us all, us and them. Here is something for your travel; I noticed that your blanket isn't very good.'

She held out a fine blanket and a flour sack heavy with food. He took them silently.

'You have your charm, you know a sacred thing,' she said. 'But we are just people, we are frightened.'

'That's all right, grandmother. A boy like me can sleep anywhere when he has a blanket and food.'

He stirred his horse to a trot, without looking back.

CHAPTER FOUR

HE SAT slouching, with one foot out of the stirrup, looking down on the hogahns of Tlichisenili. Here was the first remembered place. Hundreds of miles now lay in his memory, scores of campfires. Beyond here his mind's possession leaped forward to the western mountains. As he looked at those hogahns down there, he felt the same impersonal pattern of people, food, the same exchange of news that he had known so long. Only not here; here there would be enquiry, explanations to make or avoid. Ethel. If he could just see her alone, before having to account for himself to any of the others. Ethel. What could she and he make for themselves now? There's a life to make, he thought. If she'll marry me, marry a murderer — if she'll do that, we can get work at the Agency, interpreter or something. We can run sheep and farm for a while if we have to. In the end we'll pull ourselves up out of this.

Work, a job, a house, position. Not just a poor young man drifting, running away. Murder — jail — did the man die? Was he recognized? He'd met a Navajo policeman at Binbito, and another at Iyakin; they weren't looking for anyone. There had been no word of a posse or a search of any kind. Still the memory of that savage thing rode after him. Not civilized, not Christian, and not Indian either. Nothing, riding a horse given by a man who was afraid to stay near him, fed by strangers as he travelled. Nothing. Zero. X equals zero. Myron — M equals zero. Ashin Tso-n Bigé equals zero.

He roused himself and descended into the valley. It looked the same, there was a new hogahn not far from Buckskin Man's. The corn was waist-high and even higher in places, showing how long it was since he stayed with the Ashkaantso people. Singing Beads was weaving, and there was someone else in the hogahn. He was surprised at his own calmness until he realized how his heart was pounding. He slowed his horse down, delaying arrival. Singing Beads was watching him, shading her eyes with one hand. She wouldn't recognize him.

He turned sideways in the saddle and sat staring, waiting. It was Ethel's face, her features, inside the hogahn there, and yet it didn't seem anyone he knew. Older — the native dress, perhaps. He looked at Singing Beads, and then directly at the girl again. Her eyes widened, her hands busy with the spindle ceased moving.

'Is it you?' she said.

'I think so.' He smiled uncheerfully.

Singing Beads said, 'Eh! The boy from Ha'anoichí. Dismount.'

She received him warmly, saying as they touched hands: 'You've changed. You look as if you'd been working, and you're growing your hair.'

He said, 'No one to cut it. I've been travelling, that's all.'

Then he had to step into the hogahn and touch hands with Ethel, as if it were just anyone. She avoided his eyes. She *was* different. The shape of her face was somehow changed. What was it? To get her alone, to speak with her. He must look pretty queer himself. It wasn't just her Navajo clothes with the wide silver belt and the silver buttons; for a moment they called up the half-formed girl he had first known, Buckskin's Daughter, but this woman was as far from that as she was from his Ethel. He had a quick, despondent sense, I've lost her, and fought it down. Not so easily. So many months, so many happenings to us both; knowing each other has to be remade.

He sat down in the shade. Singing Beads returned to her weaving, Ethel took up her spindle. Now, until Buckskin Man arrived and he was told to unsaddle, he must be just an idling visitor. A question about Jack came to his mind, but he did not want to mention him.

Singing Beads said, 'Where from?'

'From Many Houses.' The truth for the first time.

'Eh! So far! How many yesterdays?'

He counted. 'Thirty-two. In some places I remained two nights.'

If he told them all of it, roughly, to smash all this pretence and waiting, killed one man and buried another — with that suppressed, all communication became constrained.

'Where to?' The interested, polite questions.

'To see my friends, my country, my family.'

'How does it look to you, this country?'

'This is the first I have seen that I knew before. It is good.'

Singing Beads said, 'The travelling made you thin. It becomes you.'

He wondered what he did look like. 'It's a long time since I've seen my face,' he said. 'Have you a mirror?'

Ethel — Buckskin's Daughter — fumbled in a pile of goods. 'Here.' She reached the small circle of glass towards him. He took it, saying, 'Here's where I frighten myself.'

The remark was all too true. Even at arm's length the mirror wouldn't take in his whole head, but by sections he saw the stained and battered hat, the hair curling over his ears and along the sides of his neck, the dark, mahogany colour of his skin which lay close against the bony structure of his face, the sparse, wiry whiskers sprouting here and there. There was nothing left of the almost-white, sleek face for which he had wished a pair of glasses. Just plain Indian. Nothing. Let M equal zero. Zero to the nth still equals zero. They were watching him, it wouldn't do to look too long. He rubbed his chin and made himself smile.

'At least I might get rid of these weeds, if someone will

lend me' — he was going to say a razor, but switched it — 'a pair of tweezers'

Singing Beads laughed. 'My husband will, I think.'

Ethel asked, 'Are you going to that school? Did you get in?'

The certificate was still in his pocket, hard-won, meaningless. He remembered that he had a means of talking privately with Ethel even in her mother's presence.

After a moment's thought, he said in English, 'I passed all right. I got a scholarship.'

'Good.' She used Navajo, not taking his lead.

Her mother said, 'I've used up my black yarn.'

Ethel picked up a large hank lying beside her, and rose to take it to her mother. Perception and comprehension made his mind swing, and then he dropped below feeling into a sort of hopeless calm. She was very plainly pregnant. She met his eyes as she returned to her place, and looked away quickly. He stared blindly across the valley. The last thing, the last. Now truly nothing. I thought nothing before, but there had been this left. A punishment, a curse. Those angry gods. All promises, pledges, kisses, and arms tight holding, gone, faded, as gone as a light blown out. The girl he'd kissed was gone, changed completely. Now nothing.

When he had collected himself, he said, without looking at her, 'You fixin to get married?'

After a considerable pause she answered, 'I am married.'

Singing Beads shifted slightly, so that she could watch them without seeming to, while they talked in Bellacana.

'Who to?'

'Jack.'

He dug in the sand with a twig. 'Yeah. I kinda tought you were goin to wait for me.' He didn't sound really convincing to himself.

Another wait, then, 'I'm sorry. I — I guess — well, I'm kinda like Jack. I ain't got your brains. I want to live at home and be an Inyan. I can't keep bodderin about all dem tings, like you can.'

When he made no answer, she said, 'Don't be too mad at Jack. You know, him and me ——'

'Yeah, I know. I guess I know. Jack's all right.' He wrestled for a moment. 'I ain't too hot myself, eider.'

Unexpectedly she said, 'You sure look like just about anyone right now. But when you get set, I guess you'll be plenty.'

'Maybe.'

He dug some more in the sand, letting himself fall into a sort of coma, from which a question of Singing Beads' aroused him. He told them about the country he'd traversed, the rain, the crops, the grass and sheep, differences in the ways of the people, the alien Mokis islanded among the Navajos. Like all the others, they loved this talk of far places. What with this last ride and previous visits to missions, he realized, he knew the Navajo country as few of his people did.

A voice singing reached from across the valley. A rider moved along the rim, tiny with distance. Buckskin's Daughter rose.

Myron thought, perhaps at least I can have a friend again. If I can't, it's all right, I wouldn't blame him, but at least I can find out. He stood up.

'Perhaps your husband has a pair of tweezers,' he said. 'Do you want to ride over behind me?'

Singing Beads looked pleased, but said nothing. He realized how closely she had been watching him.

2

Puzzled, Jack watched them coming. It looked like Myron, but it couldn't be, not that scarecrow. Then he saw it was Myron, and he stood still beside his saddle, holding his bridle in his hands. For a long time he'd been ready for the coming of a prosperous, well-dressed young man, a danger, and here was something else. Navajos often go ragged, but this one was exceptional. Lean as leather, burned brown, his mouth changed, seeming more of a man, more dangerous. Bringing his wife on an underfed horse. He waited.

Buckskin's Daughter slid down and went into the hogahn, where she started doing things about supper.

Jack said, 'Where from?'

'From Many Houses.'

'Where to?'

'I don't know. Just riding around.' Myron turned the ends of his reins between his fingers.

'To this place, perhaps.'

'I came here.' He twisted the leather. It's over, why hang on to what doesn't exist? If I can bury dead men, I can do this, too. 'I wanted to know. Well, now I know. This is how it had to be, I think.'

Jack's face lightened slightly, but he was still on guard. Between them and the hogahn, Ethel was reviving the fire.

'Dismount. There'll be food soon.'

'Good.'

Standing on the ground, Myron ran his hand over his chin and grinned. 'Look at my whiskers! Have you a pair of tweezers?'

'You do look hairy. Come inside.'

Jack dug the instrument out of a bundle. 'Keep them. I have another pair. Here's a mirror.'

'Good. Till now, I've always used a razor, but this is better in a dry country, I think.'

Myron examined his face, felt around with the bent steel, plucked, and grimaced. Jack smiled.

'You'll get used to it, and it lasts a long time.'

'I suppose so.'

Jack washed while a couple more hairs came out, then said, 'You'd better bring in your saddle. Your horse will find good grass around here.'

Myron went out without speaking. When he came back in with his gear, he felt talkative, remarks of no importance surged up in him.

'I thought that if I saw you again, you'd be dressed like a white man,' Jack said.

'Well, I'm not wearing moccasins.' Myron glanced down at his rags. 'I do look like the end of the big drought, don't I? These trousers were never made for riding. Well, that's how I am now. I have nothing.'

'What happened?'

'Something. I don't want to talk about it.'

After supper, when the sun no longer roasted the valley, they lounged about the small fire.

Staring at it, Myron said: 'The other night I camped out where there was almost no fuel. I had a hard time getting a fire to burn. So I began to think what life would be like if we had no fire. I'd have no knife then, I thought, no cooked food, no iron rings on my saddle. One could make a saddle in the old way, with wood and rawhide, I thought, and one could use a flint knife. But as soon as one shaped the flint, he would have fire again, it came right back. So I gave up.'

Jack threw his head back and laughed. 'So you're still there, inside, after all! Do you remember when you wanted to find out what it was like to be blind, and you walked right into the Matron!'

'I tried just keeping my eyes shut first, but I always got scared and looked. So I blindfolded myself, and I ran smack into her. How that woman could slap!'

Ethel giggled. 'One of these days you'll try sitting on a cactus to see what it's like.'

He answered slowly, 'That's about all that's left.'

3

At Cottonwood Leader's request, he stayed over the next day for a meeting they were holding to discuss the things Washington wanted the Navajos to do. The request was flattering, he was glad of the rest, and his horse would profit by the day's grazing. In the late afternoon about a score of men gathered outside Cottonwood Leader's hogahn, among them half a dozen young Indians from the Conservation Camp a few miles away. A smaller number of women sat outside the main circle. Myron took an inconspicuous place. He felt better with his whiskers removed, and wearing a fairly new pair of blue jeans Jack had given him.

Only a few men spoke. The mass of the meeting would listen, unless something unusual developed, and finally out of reflection and long silences a common agreement would emerge. One old man objected on religious grounds to the mere idea that the sheep could harm the land, citing the old legend about them. The others pointed to the evidence of common observation; they said it would be a hardship to cut down their flocks, but if the grass kept on being destroyed, in the end there could be no flocks at all. As to reorganizing the tribal council and making it stronger, anyone could see that that was needed, they said.

Myron grew excited as he listened, feeling the old speech-making call of debating days. The long waits between speeches made him nervous, the naïve concepts of some of the speakers filled his mind with illuminating things to say. Perhaps here was his chance, his beginning of being something. The man who was nothing could inform, arouse, and lead these people, if he didn't merely agree, following along with them.

His excitement mounted. One had an instinct not to debate with the old men, but now some of the younger ones were adding their opinions. He remembered well enough what Smedley and Rensselaer and McCarty had taught him. He was a stranger here, one of the youngest, a guilty man. He kept quiet.

Pointing to him, Cottonwood Leader said, 'Here is some-one who can tell us something, I think. What is your opinion, grandchild?'

'Who is he?' an old man asked.

'Shooting Singer's nephew from Ha'anoichí. He has been a long time at school, going far beyond the others. He has been all over the Navajo country, he says. Just now he has ridden all the way from Many Houses, he says, seeing things.'

Myron stood up. A moment's doubt as to what kind of speech he could make in Navajo faded as he heard his own voice. This was a familiar use of power. The arguments were in order, familiar, ready.

'It is true, as my grandfather said, that I have gone far ahead in studying the white man's knowledge. Also, at different times, I have travelled this Navajo country from Tsé Bitai in the northeast to Besh Nana-aj in the southwest. But I am young, I have been mostly away from this country, I am ignorant in many ways.

'One thing — I have talked much with white men, with people friendly with the Navajos, I have heard what they think about Washington, about this Washington Chief we have now. Perhaps my eyes have been opened. Perhaps I have seen something.'

Speaking in Navajo was indeed different; in English his thoughts had to come around a corner, now thought and word sprang up together. Swinging into the matter of stock reduction, he repeated McCarty's demand for more water, repeated the whole line of argument that had been given him.

'Washington has just been surprised to learn that if no animal grazes on a piece of land, the grass grows taller than if something eats it. That is the great wisdom they are handing out to us. If we have no sheep at all, in many places the grass will grow waist-high, they say. How beautiful the land will be then! And we, of course, we can crawl around on all fours and eat the grass.

'You all know how they are fencing everything, putting fences around pieces of land all over our country. You can look in and see the grass where no sheep go. Why are they doing this? Why are they spending so much money to build fences for us? Why did they buy seventy thousand head of goats from us and then come around, as they are doing now, and ask us to sell them a hundred thousand head of sheep?'

He looked around. All the faces were turned towards him. They were following him.

'Why do they want us to have a bigger council, and this government they talk of?

'Listen. You all know how Washington is. Do you think Washington would spend all this money, give jobs to so many men, just out of love for the Navajos? Do the traders give you free flour and coffee? Does Washington Chief send you presents?'

Somebody laughed shortly. He paused and looked around again.

'It is a trap, I think. They give us a big council, a government, so that they can run it and yet make us take the blame for what happens, I think. By and by we shall have few sheep, we shall be poor, we shall be hungry. We'll be glad, then, to get jobs building even more fences, I think. Then one day they can say, "See, the Navajos have few sheep, and much land they are not using." Thus they will say, pointing to the many measures of land covered with grass and flowers. So then they can sell that land to white stockmen, even inside the reservation. And we, we can go down to the railroad and sit by the stations, holding out our hands for nickels. That is where all this leads, I think.'

He sat down. The following silence was far longer than any before, he didn't think he could stand it. He kept thinking of convincing things he might have said. A lanky, middle-aged man began to speak, slowly and thoughtfully, without rising.

'The government men picked four of my sheep, and four from each of my neighbours over yonder, until they had forty ewes. They did not choose the best, just any sheep, the first four they came to in each flock. They put them inside one of those fenced places, and each thing they did with them, they sent for us and explained it. Instead of letting the bucks run with them all year, as we do, they kept them separate until Little Winds month. That way all the lambs were born in the spring, at one time. And so on, many good ways of doing, they showed to us.

'Now you all know that with forty ewes, we are doing well if we get twenty lambs that survive, and even some of those we can't sell. But from this forty they got forty-four, and they were all fat. The wool was heavier and no ewes died. Those forty sheep made more money than a hundred running outside, the way we run them, and all the time the grass stayed good. It even got better.

'They have shown us how we can restore the land and make more money with half as many sheep. In each thing they did, they took great pains to teach it to us. I do not think that men who do that are planning to rob us. Our sheep are starving each other, I think.'

An old man stood up. 'Long ago, when we were only a few thousand people, the whole tribe gathered together to settle things, and the leaders spoke for each band. Now we are too many to do that, so Old Chief from Washington gave us a council, and in that he did well, I think. But there is more to be done. I live near Dennihatso, so if I want to vote for a delegate I have to go to Natahni Nez, five long days' ride. Who of us in my section knows our delegates? None, I think. Those Indians who live near Natahni Nez pick them for us. So when the council decides something, we people pay no attention. It's time we strengthened ourselves, it's time we had our own delegate, and you people up this way yours, and so for each part of the country. And I do not think we are likely to pick men who would take orders from Washington. That is how I am thinking.'

A stocky, short-haired, youngish man rose. 'For two years I have been working around here, building dams and ponds and sinking wells. When the work started we knew nothing, and we had white men over us. They taught us; as fast as we learned, we took their places, so now the leaders are

Indians and only a few white men come around to oversee what we are doing. I am a leader in the place of the man who taught me.

'Now we have Indians using scrapers, running tractors, bulldozers, and graders, pouring concrete, doing all those things. We are learning how to take care of ourselves. That doesn't look as if we were going to be made into beggars, I think.

'Another thing. It's all right to talk about bringing water up everywhere, but it can't be done. In some places if you sink a well you'll get water, in other places nothing but a hole.' He glanced briefly at Myron. 'I went to school, and I have travelled a little, but by and by I got over it.'

Myron stared at the ground between his feet, resting his elbows on his knees and his chin on his hands. He lacked the courage to rise and depart. Somebody asked the lanky man a question about the sheep demonstration, there was a little general talk, then the meeting broke up.

He walked to Jack's by himself. Zero to the nth equals zero. He approached their fire reluctantly, sitting down near his friend.

'My father says it may rain tomorrow,' Jack said.

'That's good.'

'Are you going to Ha'anoichí now?'

'I don't know.'

Jack rolled and lit a cigarette. Ethel put bread into the Dutch oven.

Jack said: 'I think I'll catch a steer and kill it tomorrow. We've been having too much mutton. Do you want to come along?'

'I have to travel again.'

'Your horse needs another day's rest. I'll lend you one for the day.'

'I can't stay on here. I'm ashamed.'

'You think one way, we another. That's all right.'

'No. I was showing off. I was trying to be big. I'm nothing and I tried to blow myself up into something. So I'm ashamed.'

Ethel said, 'Your horse won't understand about that. You'd better stay.'

'All right.' It occurred to Myron that he had never really known Ethel.

CHAPTER FIVE

MORE or less mechanically, he followed the trail from Tlichisenili past Tsaili. He avoided hogahns as much as he could, missing many meals and sleeping out. The guilt caught up with him at Tlichisenili, it came leaping out of his mouth. The following day, riding with Jack, got him over some of the worst of his feelings, but still he was ashamed. He felt himself to be swamped in lies, there was no certainty anywhere. As he drifted across the desert, he listened to himself as if he had been a Navajo in the audience, criticizing his speech with the mind of the men who had answered it, until he squirmed in the saddle.

Mr. Smedley, Mr. McCarty — were they liars? Mr. Boyle — the irrigated fields and Mrs. Boyle mean to her help. What did Mr. Butler think? Mr. Rensselaer. Encourage the Indians to go out into the white world, abandoning tribal ways. Work in somebody's kitchen. Mr. Snyder — a bad man. Mr. Boyle. I don't like Mr. Boyle. That opened a surprising train of thought, from which he drew back, shocked, and constantly returned. At the end of three days he knew that he definitely disliked Boyle, Smedley, and McCarty, and really liked only Mr. Butler. Indians laden down with superstition, ignorant of the great world outside, could be right when all those men were wrong.

God was against the Navajos because they followed Nayeinezgani and the rest. So the Christians were against the Navajos; that was why they wanted them to stop being Indians, to break up. Then they'd get them under God. So the old war continued. God would probably win in the long run, He had the power, the thousand thousand white men.

On the fourth day he looked down from a canyon's rim upon familiar hogahns, a settlement of friends of Shooting Singer's. He turned back, circling northward. His uncle must come, in the end. Yes, sometime he would have to face him and, as in his dreams, the medicine man would detect all the lies and betrayals. Not yet, though. Cheez Lan Hojoni Mountain rose as a blue-green shoulder in the northeast, and he headed for that. He would be complete. There was one more person to see. There was no point to it, no reason, but he would go there. Holy Young Woman Sought the gods and found them ... I am seeking for something, somewhere I'm going to get an answer. It looks like a long ride. Truly with my sacrifice, Sought the gods and found them. What sacrifice? I haven't even pollen. What gods? Somebody doubts it, so I have heard. Why did they put that on the end of a prayer? He imagined a medicine man of long ago, in the old costume, making and chanting that prayer. The old, assured face out of antiquity looked straight at him. Somebody doubts it, so I have heard.

As far as the rim-rock above T'o Tlakai he asked his way; thereafter he would have had to name a person, so he hunted for himself. On a mid-morning, he came to a cornfield where a woman was hoeing. She looked up, stared, then came to the edge of the field, carrying her hoe.

It was Juniper. Her face was thinner, she looked mature, formed, but it was still Juniper. He told Singing Gambler that he remembered her, but he had forgotten, long ago he had forgotten. Wherever I go, I run into my own foolishness. She was always greater than I. She was still eyeing him and his horse, and her voice as she asked 'Where to?' was cold, rather wary.

He was ready to believe that she knew all about him on sight. He stammered in answering, 'Just riding around.'

'Where from?'

'From Many Houses.'

'Where's that?'

He pointed southwest. 'Down there. Beyond the Moki country.'

'Where did you get that horse?'

He'd forgotten about it. Of course, that explained her tone.

'Your husband sold it to me.'

'Sold it or lost it?'

'Sold it. Out of kindness he let me have it cheap.'

'Oh. He was at Many Houses, then?'

'Near there. I was lucky to find him. I needed help and he gave it to me.'

'Did he tell you to come here?'

'No. I wanted to.' Myron looked at her in surprise. 'Don't you know me?'

She frowned, thinking. 'You look familiar. No, I don't remember you.' She cocked her head in a remembered manner, then surprise showed in her face, and after it a disturbed look. 'Oh. It's you.' After another pause she explained, 'It's been so long, and you look older.'

He smiled. 'So do you.' He turned sideways in the saddle, making himself easy. 'It's been — well — six years. I am older. About a hundred years older, I think.'

'You kept on going to school?'

'Yes. They came after me, you know.'

'I heard.'

'I was planning to visit you, but it — they reached in after me.'

'Well, that's how things happen. Are you through with school?'

'Yes. That's all over now. So you sent Singing Gambler away?'

'Yes. His idea of a home is somewhere to rest when there's nowhere else to go.'

'I'm sorry.'

'There's nothing to be sorry about. One makes mistakes, and when one goes to straighten them out, there are good things to give up too. It's painful, but there it is.'

'Where's your baby?'

'The little boy? Over at my mother's hogahn. I can't watch him while I do this.'

'Why are you doing it?'

'My father had to go away. Men seem to be scarce hereabouts.'

'Here's one.'

She smiled. The old, amused Juniper. 'You want to hoe my corn?'

'Why not? I have nowhere to go.'

'Do you know how?'

'I did once.'

'Delightful! Dismount.'

He set to work soberly, without display, at the slow, steady rate of work he had learned from his uncle. He felt useful. The field had been neglected too long. Although the corn was fairly high and ears already forming, it needed a complete weeding. The small piece Juniper had done was thoroughly worked, but it's too hard labour for a woman. At school they'd used modern, small-bladed hoes. The Indians stuck to the old Spanish type with a head half as big as a spade and a short handle. You had to put a lot of back into it. It would take three or four days to put this field in order; sunflowers grew almost as high as the corn, along with guaco and some thistles. Where the corn was still low in one corner, the depressions around the clumps should be cleaned out, and brush set up to shelter it. The rains were not over yet, the water could be made to settle there.

He continued in this way, enjoying his remembered knowledge and demonstrating to himself his union with an important thing. His back and arms tired soon, but he kept on for a while out of stubbornness. Then he straightened and rested.

'There's a lot of work here,' he said, 'and I'm out of practice.'

'Haven't you farmed since then?'

'Just a little, at school.'

'I know how you feel, I've been finding out myself, this last little while. My father has another field down the canyon, you see. It's too much for one man.'

'Well, if you will feed me, and if there's grass for my horse, I'll stay here awhile and clean this up.'

She looked at him doubtfully. 'I can do it. You don't have to take it all on.'

He laughed at her. 'It's the steady eating I want.'

'Oh.' Puzzled, she studied him again. 'Well, we'll see.'

He set to work on another row. When he came back near where she sat, she said: 'It's almost noon. I'm going to help with lunch. The hogahn's just around that point of rock. Food will be ready by the time you get to the end again.'

'Good. Take my horse. Will you unsaddle and hobble it when you get there?'

'All right. It knows where to find grass around here.'

He was glad to stop, tired, and furiously hungry, when he finished the row. He felt his muscles as he walked to the hogahn. There he found Juniper, Red Woman, and a third, younger woman, whose child played with Juniper's. After the meal, while he lay sleepily relaxed in the shade, Red Woman questioned him. She stayed within the bounds of good breeding, but it was plain that she wanted to learn all about him. He understood it; here he was, hungry and penniless, within a few days' ride of his home, willing to work for his food when his uncle, also, had cornfields. And her daughter would be in her mind, of course.

He was minded to let it go and drift along. Rejection was ordained for him. There was Juniper, her face softened in repose, looking younger now that she had rested. He didn't want to run away with her watching. He propped himself on one elbow to a half-sitting position.

'I have not been to Ha'anoichí since the last time I was out here, when you all saw me. I shall not go there for some time yet, I think. I am looking for something. Do not ask me what it is; there is something I have to find out. I have come from beyond Dokoslid to here, not in a straight line. Perhaps I am about to arrive where I must go, perhaps I shall stay long in one place or hurry through many, perhaps I shall go clear to the Ute country, or south, or east, or anywhere. I go where I am taken, where my thought takes me. That is all.

'Now I see a cornfield that needs working, grass for my horse, and food in the hogahn of my friends. When a man keeps travelling, he misses a lot of meals, and his horse grows thin. So I am thinking, here is something I can do in return for what I want.'

Red Woman considered his words. 'My husband will be back tomorrow. Tonight you must sleep away from here.'

'All right.'

He was disappointed when Juniper made no move to accompany him back to work, then he realized it would have been unreasonable for her to do so. His afternoon's labour was lessened by a hard shower, during which he rested under a rock, watching the field become soaked, recalling parts of songs about the corn and the rain. When the thunder rolled he quoted to himself, 'The voice that beautifies the land,' remembering with the lightning flash his fear that Nayein-ezgani might aim an arrow at him, but not actively fearing it.

The remainder of the afternoon was pleasant. He rested, thinking it was near time to stop, smelling the wet earth and looking over the part he had done and the fresh-washed plants.

> I walk among
> The great corn plants.
> I speak to my corn,
> It holds out its hands to me.

The changing light of the end of the cloudy afternoon made him feel lonely. He hoed mechanically, chopping along.

Juniper's voice telling him to come and eat startled him with a quick rush of pleasure. He came out smiling.

'You've done a lot,' she said. 'You're strong.'

'It was cool after the rain, although it made the sand heavy. I used to be strong, but for the last year, until I began travelling, I sat indoors all the time.'

He felt the same relaxing of his muscles and enjoyable fatigue and hunger as coming off the football field after a hard day's practice. His mind occupied itself with the simplicities of food and rest, and there was the sense of work well done, and of tomorrow taken care of without worry. He ate heartily, and when he was laughed at for beginning to drowse, gathered up his blanket and went out to a sheltered place he had noted, out of sight of the hogahn.

Bay Horse returned the next day, and worked with Myron during the afternoon. He planted this field in addition to his own, on account of his son-in-law, he said. That young man had been very pleasant, he came of a good clan, he seemed willing to work, but the hoe was too heavy for him. He was glad of Big Salt's Son's help. Now Juniper could attend to her weaving and alternate with his second wife in herding the sheep, making things easier and more profitable all around.

Myron was interested in the matter of the second wife, Fire Maker, who was Red Woman's niece. He thought he ought to be shocked, but she seemed quite happy, and she and Red Woman united could dominate Bay Horse when they wished to. Christian law said only one wife, but these people weren't Christians. It seemed sensible on the whole, so long as it didn't mean selling off a young girl, the way it happened to Juniper long ago. The same thing could be good or bad for different people at different times. In this case, it worked. He carried his thoughts no farther. For four days of steady labour he ate tremendously, slept profoundly, and rested his mind.

Bay Horse had his own field to tend to, so after that one afternoon Myron worked alone. He was glad of that. It was

Juniper's field, and he wanted to be the one who put it in order for her. He considered her while he hoed, not so much thinking as evoking her presence. So much had changed, and so completely, but she was still the person he had known; fully grown up, but still the special person forgotten and now keenly remembered. She came twice to see how he was getting on. Each time her approval lifted him up, and when she was gone the place seemed empty and the colours duller.

In the evenings he spread out the tale of his wandering, which had now become almost a recitation, making an effort to talk well, thinking of new, interesting things, or incidents that made them all laugh, to maintain her interest, her attention upon him.

On the third night he went to bed thinking, not of any past thing, but of Juniper and the green corn, and that about her was peace and a resting-place.

She came out to see him on the fourth afternoon. He thought she liked talking to him. She didn't hurry away. He felt excited and slightly short of breath while he faced her.

'Do you miss that man?' he asked abruptly.

'Sometimes. One misses delightful things, although they cost too much.'

It was a hopeful answer. He wanted to ask something about himself, but saw no way to.

A first puff of rain-bringing wind brushed by them, then there was a driving swirl of wind and sand. It flattened Juniper's skirts against her thighs, moulded her bodice. She had thrown her hand up over her eyes, for the moment it was as if he watched her in secret. Having one child had not spoiled her breasts.

'I must run,' she said.

She went lightly, vaulting the brush fence without effort. The first, fat drops splashed on Myron's shoulders and he made for cover.

That night he had to keep himself from looking at her too

much. She gave light, he thought. It was what she was and what her body was combined; the two gleamed together. Her small motions and gestures were delightfully packed with her own quality, everything she did belonged to her. When he rolled up in his blanket, he remembered with new vividness what he had once known with her, and immediately the thought of Singing Gambler came forth. His mind edged towards, and backed away from, and returned towards visualizing. That man, too, with her — he writhed, and his mind drew back again.

When he started work the next morning, he knew he'd be through before the day was out. As he swung his hoe, going step by step down the rows, he meditated intensely. He wanted to be sure, he wanted to be right. Juniper. The end, the answer, the resting-place. The house with a table and a lamp had become hard to imagine and unimportant. Even a hogahn is not a necessity. At the end of a row he straightened, looking round him at the plants. It stretches out its hands to me. Sure, absolutely sure, but she, what will she — unimaginable that Juniper would want — he fell to hoeing. Through the hours it formed in him. I may not like what I'll get, but I'll try.

He finished in the middle of the afternoon. He superperfected the last little piece, looked around for places in need of further treatment, uprooted some insignificant young weeds, then suddenly shouldered his hoe, telling himself, 'Come on!'

He scouted Red Woman's hogahn from behind a rock; only the old woman was there. So far so good. He made a wide circuit to pass it unseen, to where he could see Juniper's loom by her own place. She was there, with her child. This far the signs were for him. He walked over to her and laid down his hoe.

'It's finished.'

She had dropped her hands from the loom.

'You'll be going on, then? Looking for yourself?'

Her last words made him pause, then he passed over them. 'I've found what I was looking for, I think.'

'What did you find?'

'The answer. Peace. I found it here.'

She didn't ask him more, but went on watching him. He thought she was disturbed, moved by something, and guarded. He spoke slowly, finding his words and bringing them out one by one.

'You remember, once I — I ran away from you. I was all mixed up by the white men, I was foolish. I wanted a lamp on a table.'

'You wanted what?'

'Never mind. Things didn't matter, silly things, kinds of clothes and a kind of house, and things like that.'

'You wanted to lead your people.'

'Oh — yes. I wanted to be important. Until just a little while ago I wanted to stand out, I kept adding to myself. Then something happened and I became nothing, nothing at all. Finally I began to think. Now I know. I learned it in the cornfield, I learned it looking at you.'

He swung his hand, indicating the hogahn and loom. 'This is what I want. This, and you, and work to do for you. I'm a Navajo again. I always was one, only it was hidden from me. My relatives will give me sheep and horses. All I want in the world is to live here with you and be at peace.'

She glanced towards the child, which sat chewing on a piece of stick. 'With this, and all?'

'Why not? I know I'm not like him. I can't charm as he does, I'm not handsome —— '

'You're handsome enough. Too much so, since you grew up.'

His mouth quivered towards a smile. 'Well, that's something to the good. Anyhow, I can hoe corn, I can do the work and stay by you. I want to make you my life, you can count on me. I didn't know it, but you've been in me ever since that time. Now I know. You're all there is for me.'

'You want to live with me, and farm, and attend to the ceremonies? Just that?'

'Just what every man does. Only with you, for you.'

She studied her hands in her lap. He dropped to a position sitting on one knee, so that he could see her face. Yes, she was moved. He had seen her like this before and it made him quake. How beautiful. She turned her head to face him.

'And all your schooling? The leadership? The things that had to be put together?'

He pushed aside with one hand. 'Just ideas. What's going to happen will happen. The gods are fighting it out. Nothing will touch us here, in our time. What's the use of pretending I can make the river change its bed?'

She said: 'It won't do. You say you are nothing. Perhaps you are right. You were something once, even though it was mixed up, but you leaned on those white men, and then you leaned on your uncle, and then, I suppose, on the white men again. You have always leaned on someone, I think. Now you want to lean on me. Perhaps one day someone will give you a new idea, and you'll do what you did before with me. Perhaps not. But do not ask me to carry you. I have had three failures, three pains. I don't intend to have a fourth.'

She seemed to become distant and then to come near again.

'There were three of us,' he said, 'as I told you that time. We set out together. The other two learned what they needed to learn and then they stopped. Now they are happy. I have seen them. I kept on going, I kept on trying to stretch myself. The Jesus writing says, "Can a man add a measure to his height by thinking?" That's what I tried to do. I worked and worked. All I got in the end was ruin. So I am through with that, I have tried it out and I know. Now I've found out what I really want, what I can keep on with for my whole lifetime.'

'What was this ruin?'

'I killed a man.'

'What?'

'In Many Houses, there I killed a man, a Mexican. He was drunk, and he and his friend were yelling at me, making fun of me for being an Indian. I had been telling lies, or part lies that were worse than whole ones, about the people and about the gods. So I turned back and began to fight. There were all the lies and then those men...' He described it, the fighting and what came after.

She listened with her eyes fixed on him and her lips slightly parted. Before he was through, she reached out and pulled her child to her. He ended.

'You haven't been cleansed?' she asked. 'You haven't been to a singer?'

A heavy feeling came over him. Here was the mere superstition, even here.

'No. Whatever I may be wrong about, there are some things I know. One is that the *chindi* of a dead man does not come walking after us. Those are things the people think up at night when they know no better.'

She studied his remark, looked at him, looked at her child. 'Perhaps so, perhaps not. Who knows what these things mean? When a man puts a mask on, anyone who has heard the stories knows the gods don't look like that, I think. It's all a mask. Perhaps that Mexican is right behind you now, perhaps there is nothing. But you've ridden forty days to get away from something. You say you're looking for something, but I say you're running away. Perhaps it's just inside yourself, but there it is. Now you think you've found a refuge. You think I can roll it away, but you would only forget for a little, and then remember it again.'

Again as he sat staring at her she seemed to recede to a great distance. Twice he opened his mouth to speak, but had only silence in his throat and mind. He pulled himself together.

'You saw me cultivate that field. That was work, it was good. I was happy doing it. That's not just running away. It's something I had forgotten and found again.'

He held out his hands and turned them. Hands and wrists were powerful, burned to the deep colour of well-worn leather.

'I can work, I can do things for you. I have the will to keep right on for you.' He thought for a moment. 'Oh, of course I know, you have to remember that man. I don't expect you to feel things for me you don't feel. But I can be what he cannot, and here we can make a life together.'

Juniper, he thought, Juniper slipping away. Almost under his hand, and as he reached out for her she slipped away. Unreachable.

She said: 'You see. Every time you speak, you show yourself again, seeing only yourself, your thought wandering on crooked trails. Whatever you may know about things that are and things that people just imagine, I am afraid of you now. Whether it's a *chindi*, or whether it's fears and bad thoughts, you are not a person one wants always staying in the settlement.'

He sat for a long time, unmoving. The sense of loss, yet one more loss, beat upon him, too much, piling up beyond support, but he was not surprised. Of course it happened like this. How could he have anything?

'I expected this, I think,' he told her. 'I look back as far as I could see, and it all points this way. Only — this last little while — oh, well.'

She said, 'I'm sorry,' then, with stronger feeling, 'You're a real man underneath there, somewhere; every now and then you come forth. I hope you can find it.'

'I thought that here ——'

'No, not here.'

After another wait he rose. 'All right.'

He saddled up and left without having too many questions asked of him by the others. He said it was time he went to Ha'anoichí. His horse was brisk after its rest. He rode at an easy pace till sundown, then unsaddled where he found grass and fuel. For most of the night he sat gazing into the fire, emerging from the mere negative of hopelessness occasionally when the sense of Juniper, the visualization of her, tore at him and sent him wandering again along the sterile canyons of regret.

CHAPTER SIX

H IS course was directed by two factors, a vague desire to go higher up the mountain and a strong wish to be entirely alone. He followed trails going generally upward, avoiding all hogahns for two days until hunger drove him to visit for a noon meal. The people there thought him queer, and were relieved when he went on.

The following day he came into the tall timber, the loneliness of aspen groves, the sadness and hush under the great pines. He rode at a walk, reins hanging slack, not trying to arrive anywhere.

Nothing, just nothing. Worse than that, it follows me around. The track of an evil thought is crooked and endless — his uncle's words. I carry it with me. It shows upon me. Worse than nothing. Juniper, the interlude of serene days, forgetfulness and hope, recurring in memory, and he could sink into it a moment, recapturing, and then swing full face onto the end again. Juniper. Ethel and he were two shadows meeting; the two who were promised to each other had ceased to exist. Juniper lived and he made a hope for himself, and was left with ache and longing and emptiness.

Not Navajo, not Christian. In between with an evil thought. You can be like a white man, but can you be a white man? No. Navajo or nothing, so nothing. What a world of lies. The days and years stretched ahead without purpose or flavour, grey and interminable. Go to Ha'anoichí, herd sheep, farm, live with Shooting Singer. Impossible. The medicine man praying. I told Juniper I would attend to the ceremonies, like any other man. To sit among the prayers divided between disbelief and fear, wrong-thinking, blasphemy. Looking over my shoulder for God. No. I don't like it, it bears me down, but let me at least face what I am. Carry it myself, don't go injuring other people with it.

Whatever I am, that I must be. Be what? I don't know. There is some use for me. He told himself that, but he imagined nothing. The answer, the shining thing. I look for it. I move myself from place to place looking for something in myself. Moving helps. Seek for it. On the mountain-tops Sought the gods and found them. Will any god help me? Natinesthani was a broken gambler, Reared in a Mountain was running away from the Utes. Somebody doubts it, so I have heard. Foreseeing me. Shut out. Juniper, oh Juniper.

He came to a spring by a rock, with good grass near-by. It was nearly evening, so he made camp. His horse rolled luxuriously and then grazed. Show it food and its worries end. He gathered firewood, knowing the night would be cold, and fearing the spaces under the trees.

He ate all the currants off a small bush he found, easing his hunger. Then he wrapped his blanket close around him and sat propped against the rock, facing his fire, wishing he could stop thinking.

After dark, he thought he'd like to pray. If the gods want to destroy me, let's get it over with; perhaps I can find them, perhaps I can get in line with something good. He started, reasonably enough, with his uncle's bear songs, and stumbled in the middle of the first one. He didn't remember all of it, try as he would he couldn't get it all straight. Then he was frightened, a mutilated prayer, rejection again. He thought of Christian prayers, and put them aside, afraid to call God in here, to place himself again between the warring powers. What appeal could he use? The trail of beauty — how far from his trail! I want to find out what I am for. I want to be for something, to belong to something, to have it stand up in me again. The old age trail, the path of beauty. So far from me, but it's all right to ask for it. With beauty before me may I wander, With beauty behind me may I wander, With beauty above me may I wander, With beauty below me may I wander, With beauty all around me may I go wandering. Now on the old age trail, now on the path of beauty may I travel. In beauty.

It helped a little. He was afraid to go farther, to name a god. Thought persecuted him. He dozed in snatches and had bad dreams. Some of the currants had not been ripe. The night wore through, and daylight found him weary and stiff. He idled by the water until the sun was high, then caught and saddled his horse with heavy motions.

The forest oppressed him now, he was glad when the trail, instead of continuing to climb, swung around the mountain on a level. Towards the end of that day he came out onto a series of wide, rolling meadows, and from time to time he saw sheep in the distance. He was painfully hungry, and felt that he would like to speak to people.

A group of three hogahns came in sight, in front of one of which a wide, brush sunshade had been erected. He saw a couple of wagons and a number of horses, and men and women moving about. A gathering, probably some kind of ceremony. He could eat and then sneak off. He headed for it.

There were about thirty people there, men, women, and children, mostly around the cooking fires under the open-sided enclosure. As he dismounted, he saw that one of the hogahns had been renewed and enlarged with fresh evergreen boughs. From it he heard faintly a man's voice praying. The sound first made his scalp prickle, then he found his throat choked and had to blink his eyes. He longed for it.

He exchanged the usual questions and answers, exercising restraint to keep from simply grabbing at the food. His home was at Ha'anoichí, he said. Speaking around a mouthful of mutton, he told the man next to him that he'd been to the rim above T'o Tlakai on a visit. The man finished his coffee and passed the cup to Myron. He filled it. Since he was in the foothills, he'd decided to come up this way and see what was on top of Cheez Lan Hojoni, he said. He had finished cultivating his corn, and decided to wander a little. They exchanged notes on rain, corn, and crops.

He had been well guided, the man said. Here they were working at something good, he was in time to help and share. Myron reached for another tortilla, with which he scooped gravy and small chunks of meat out of the bottom of a pot. The sun was setting. The man was eager to tell about what was going on, he felt happy about it, and went into the story at great length. Myron felt shy and unused to so many people, he had to keep on noticing everyone, their manifest happiness tugged at him. He got the main points of the story.

A girl had been frightened and had fallen into a twitching sickness. She had wasted away very fast. It was so serious that they held the Mountain Chant for her, even though it was summer, a 'closed' Mountain Chant without any gathering, or public show on the last night. In four days thereafter she recovered entirely, now she was perfectly well, he said. Since then the rains had been generous, and everyone was pleased. So now they were having the Hojonji, the Towards Beauty ceremony, to complete it. Thus her cure would be made perfect and everyone would be blessed. Tonight was the last night, and the traveller was just in time to help.

'Here's something you don't always get,' he said, holding out a package of ready-made cigarettes.

Myron took one. The man was middle-aged, with regular features and an agreeable mouth. Under a dark blue headband his hair was brushed back neatly, tight over his head, with a queue behind; he wore a faded khaki work-shirt against which hung a necklace of four strands of wampum with occasional turquoise beads, blue jeans, and red moccasins with silver buttons. He was an ordinary man, and Myron wanted to be completely ordinary with him. In the darkness now, his awkwardness with the cigarette was partly concealed.

From the medicine lodge a voice called, 'Come on the Trail of Beauty!'

People drifted in, not hurrying, casual. Myron went on sipping coffee.

'I can't help you, I think,' he said. 'I have been away at school a long time. I don't know the songs.'

'Have you ever taken the pollen?'

'Oh yes, long ago. I've done all that.'

The man smiled broadly. 'This is just right for you, I think. You have been away, but one can see that now you are living as the people do. You just had an impulse to come here, you say. So you arrived right at this good time, to pick up these things again. It is good for you, and good for us, I think. These things are not always chance.'

'Perhaps.'

He found the cigarette useful, providing occupation for hand and mouth, delay when he wanted to think. It would seem strange indeed if he went away without helping. He didn't want to rebuff the friendliness. If just for a little while he could unite. I have said I would carry it myself, whatever is wrong with me is mine, I can still wish these people well, I can desire good things for all of them.

Delaying, stringing it out, he finished the cigarette.

'Let us go in,' he said.

He found a place against the wall on the men's side, next to the door. They were singing strongly when he came in, and the sound confused him at first, as though it affected his vision. He adjusted himself to a comfortable position, drawing his knees up to let a boy sit in front of him, and when his forces had been gathered, looked around.

The girl sat in the central place, against the west wall of the hogahn, facing the fire and the door. Under her were spread bright new calicoes, blue, dull orange, yellow, and a snowy buckskin. She wore new moccasins and a new, green skirt. Her hair fell loose over her shoulders. A bunch of eagle plumes, tied to the top of her head, hung down one side.

She looked solemn and remote. Her face-painting struck Myron as grotesque, the black on the lower part, the white above, and he was disturbed at first by her torso with the half-formed breasts. An echo of true words telling a lie came to him. There was no evil here.

The women, ranged along the north side, wore their usual dress, velveteen bodices and strong-coloured, wide skirts. Jewelry glowed in the firelight. The medicine man, sitting by the girl, was dressed in old style, velveteen tunic and calico leggings. Of the other men, packed together, most, but not all, had long hair; many wore moccasins, a few had jewelry. Three or four wore headbands, the others had come with hats on. For the rest, they were dressed in ordinary, cheap work-clothes, rather ragged, faded, not too clean, the costume of people across whose palms but little money passed, who rode many miles in the course of ordinary work, who wrestled with the sheep at the dipping vats, and wielded the heavy-bladed hoes. To a person used to the formality of Sunday clothes in church, this shabby dressing was disturbing.

The chanting seemed tuneless when one was not used to it, heavy, and narrow in range. The rather slow beats were strongly marked, both by the music itself and the rattles in the hands of four men. That rhythm did have a certain calling force. Myron moved uneasily. The whole thing was faintly ridiculous.

Their casualness would have been truly shocking in church. When one of the men with a rattle got tired, he passed it to some other qualified person, usually with a jest. People spoke to each other occasionally, now and again someone left the hogahn, not everyone joined every song. No one minded that Myron, gorged with food and short of sleep, lay silent against the wall, sinking deeper into drowsiness.

He wondered how many songs they had sung now. Extraordinary for people to remember such a lot, many of them were very long. Raising his head, he blinked his eyes wide open. The paint on the girl disturbed him no longer, it had

ceased to disguise her face and served only to set her apart.
Dawn Girl, Pollen Girl, perhaps. Over her face they had
drawn morning light, evening light, and soft darkness.
Her hair hung down like rain, with the eagle plumes beside
it. Beautiful, her young presence there as she sat on the
bright calico. The medicine man's assistant handed her a
sacred bundle to hold. He made motions of brushing evil
out through the smoke-hole. Myron drowsed again. The
heavily marked rhythm was hypnotic, joined with the quality
of the music to which he was now attuned, the swinging,
choral refrains. He didn't know these songs, but he could
follow them in a general way. They dealt with the coming-
up of people onto this earth, and the formation of the sacred
mountains. A long song about the mountain of the east
was repeated, almost unchanged, for the mountain of the
south. Becoming familiar with the refrain, he sat straighter,
singing softly. The man he had talked with looked across to
him, smiling. How happy everyone was. It was good to be
here. Now they were singing about Dokoslid in the west.
He hesitated, then joined in. I'll help all I can, I'll put the
rest aside, keep it inside myself.

The next sequence was more complex, hard to pick up. He
reclined again. A young man next him offered tobacco, and
he made a passable cigarette. He looked out from behind it,
his eyelids sagging down. The faces were what one saw, the
clothing ceased to matter. As they had done in ancient times,
the people in buckskin, and cloth of their own weaving, the
half-naked people before them, back to the beginning, the
strong, dark faces smiling and singing, recounting good things.
He saw the ancient people who knew nothing of white men,
the unbeaten warriors. How good it must have been then,
when there was just one trail...

A general stir and talk aroused him. Women came in with
food. It was well after midnight. The medicine man was
cheerful and untired, though there had been no resting and
taking turns for him. Myron ate a little and drank two cups

of coffee. He woke up. They idled for half an hour, talking about small things, laughing readily, as one should. Then they took up the songs that lead towards dawn.

He was open to the music now, it stirred and excited him, along with the images of the words, the things named. Hour by hour these people were filling the hogahn with *hojoni*, with harmony and happiness and beauty, drawn from the eternal reservoir, the ultimate God. From the days when there was only one trail, single-hearted men and women brought up an ancient strength. They sang of the first hogahn that the gods built, of the earth, the earth and sky together, the mountains paired together, the four colours of corn. They blessed the land with the eternal, enduring things, and with the strength of the living people.

Whenever he could, he sang with them. To help, to give himself some of this quality. Against the certainty of their faces he had to know the outside, enormous world pressing in, the numbers and the doubts. What can be done to preserve this good thing, he wondered, aching while he sang.

A song ended, the eighth of a sequence. The place was charged with restful, beneficent power. The medicine man looked towards Big Salt's Son where he sat by the door.

'Grandchild, how is it outside?' he asked.

The wanderer stared. In a desperate whirl of thought he remembered something Shooting Singer had told him. He went out. The night was intensely quiet, ghosts of light hovered over the cooking fires, a faint air moved. In the distance he heard a horse pull off a mouthful of grass, crunching and contented. Along the east there lay a narrow band of grey which turned to silver in a fine line at the very horizon. Perfect timing, Day Bearer was just beginning to flutter his eyelids. He took a deep breath and went back in.

He said, 'Daybreak.'

Smiling, the medicine man said, 'Good.'

As he resumed his place, his heart was beating as if he had performed a major rite. They lifted up the last song, a chief of songs. The words were not so much unless you felt what they called up. The white mountain brings it, the blue mountain brings it, so around the four corner mountains and the centre, and the meaningless refrain crashing in after each line, and then the corn — not so much the words, but now everyone sang intensely and no one idled. His blood had been caught in the dominant rhythmic theme. The voices, the music of this, were pure excitement, this was unity. Song is a thing, it can rise up brilliant and lift you off the ground, it can spread out, shining, to unite many with a listening earth, with gods not compelled, but caught in one harmony. The rhythm switched and broke against itself, rattles and voices shifted a fraction of a beat and for six syllables his heart was held up and his breath stopped, then it returned again to the main beat, leaving a sensation as if his very blood, released, was singing.

Immediately on the heels of this the song reached its end. They did not shout, they sang, but their voices were a proclamation —

> E-ya, Hologani!
> In beauty he brings beauty,
> E-ya kéya!

People cried out, '*Hojo! Hojo!*' Myron said, '*Hojo!*' He had forgotten himself.

The girl rose. Accompanied by the assistant and a woman, she went sunwise around the fire and then out of the hogahn. They moved in silence. Truly, she seemed divine. Painted with the meeting of dawn and darkness, she went out to it.

The medicine man took out his little bag of pollen and sent it around, the women passing it from hand to hand until it reached the boy sitting in front of Myron. There, in the east, the sacrament should begin. The boy partook gravely and simply, as once Myron had knelt in church. What it would be like to be where he was!

He passed the pouch to the wanderer, a little, buckskin

bag a palm's breadth long. In it was corn pollen mixed with sacred objects. There would be white shell, turquoise, red stone, dark stone, crystal. He knew the gestures. Slowly his fingers entered, took a pinch. The golden dust was at once sweet and sharp on his lips. He touched a little to his forehead, his chest, let a few grains fall to the white east, the blue south, the yellow west, the dark north, then sprinkled the last of it in a line in front of him. The old age trail, now on the path of beauty may I walk. He had drawn it before him. He passed the bag to the next man, slowly it went around.

That was the end of it. They went outside. He felt drained and his head was ringing. Some were rolling up in their blankets, some gathering at the cooking fires, a few rode away. He didn't want to talk to anyone. He couldn't bear the perfect acceptance with which they would regard him now. The cool, vast morning stretched out before him. He caught and saddled his horse.

CHAPTER SEVEN

SLOUCHING in the saddle with his eyes half closed, he would hear the music as if someone was singing softly just behind him, and he could see the faces. As soon as he began to pay attention, it all went away and his head became silent again. Then he would straighten and look around. He dismounted once and lay down under a tree, but immediately he became wakeful. There was the thought that he'd been close to blasphemy, coming unpurified to the medicine lodge. Although he knew for sure that the prayers had been good, still the sense of guilt and divided belief remained. It was the thing that had made Juniper reject him. As he sat there he went through the original offence again, the lying speech, and saw the lightning.

I have to settle this, he thought. The time has come. I have to find myself and choose my side. He mounted again and rode on. To think, to meditate, but how could one do that with the doubts and fears and emotions swirling in one's heart and mind? Despite himself, memory followed the course of his fight with the drunken men, and he relived again the horror of that final fury. Then he became a broken man. College and fame and the well-fed, well-clothed life. A new suit and a stiff collar. The music hummed in his ears again. Phrases of beauty tormented him, the unattainable harmony, *hojoni*.

A place to think, a place to pray. Foolish to continue afraid of praying. If it is forbidden, if I am to be destroyed for it, all right. Let us settle it. I can't go on like this.

At a water-hole he got down and drank deeply, then he looked around. He was on a high, open shoulder of the mountain. At a little distance above him rose a small butte, on the rocky top of which grew a few piñóns. That will do, he thought. He unsaddled his horse and turned him loose. He drank again, washed his face, and walked to the place. It took rather a scramble to get to the top of it, so that he arrived short of breath and glad to sit down in comfort against a tree. It was well past noon. He was tired, but not sleepy.

To pray Prayer of all kinds, the Lord's Prayer. He hesitated. If you have to tell lies to be on that side ... He stared at a new thought, wrestled with it, put it down and took it up again. The faces of the men who instructed him, a parade — but Mr. Butler is a good man. A good man, but he doesn't understand. Then — it formed in his mind, it became large. Then really and really I'm not Christian. I'm against that God. Then — then — I'm glad it happened to me, to make me break away. Pretending — no, I believed — but all wrong. I'm truer now than I ever was then. Just in time. It was a tremendous thought, and he studied it for a long time. Shooting Singer said, 'One thing I know, our gods do not make war on each other.' But he didn't really know, or else the missionaries were wrong. Sometimes they didn't seem to agree with their own teachings about God and Jesus. Love, forgiveness ... But this stayed clear: what those men wanted, what the teachers, the disciplinarians of old times had wanted, was wrong. They were enemies of the Navajo. He felt as if he'd been let out of a narrow enclosure. He continued contemplating the matter, getting used to it.

So then, the Navajo gods — could he approach them? He couldn't believe a lot of little things that the ordinary, uneducated Indian accepted. The Navajos had lots of foolish ideas. The Chindi, for instance. Yet if the ghost didn't exist, his internal strife and guilt did, the horror still lingered behind his shoulder. You kept running across things like that in any religion, like the way they explained the Creation in the

Bible, and so many other things. You can't get around the trail of beauty, *hojoni*, the divine harmony. Can I find the gods? What is behind the masks of the very gods themselves? Sought the gods and found them. I'm ready to pray now.

The sun was setting, the wide outlook he had from his high point was filling with areas of blue shadow, the Lukachukai Mountains to south of him were turning to a purple mirage. He took off his hat. He had no breech-clout, no moccasins, no pollen — well, those things were just the dressing of ideas, they weren't important.

> Maid Who Becomes a Bear
>   Sought the gods and found them,
> On the summits of the mountains
>   Sought the gods and found them,
> Truly with my sacrifice
>   Sought the gods and found them,
> Somebody doubts it, so I have heard.

That last line, foreseeing him. He got into the swing of the song.

> On the summits of the clouds
>   Sought the gods and found them...

Another doubting song came to mind. A wise old man, long ago, at the beginning, a learned man with cedar bark headband, shell necklace, and buckskin kilt, looking down the ages straight at the boy who became Myron Begay.

> From the pond in the white valley —
> A young man doubts it...

Darkness flooding up from the lowlands encompassed him. Refreshed by coolness, his voice rose stronger, his hand unconsciously beat time as if it held a rattle. He remembered one of the Visionary's Songs. It suited.

> I walk on high with them,
> Beside Hasché Ayuhi there am I.
> One walks before,
> One walks behind,
> In the middle, there am I.

He was taken up in the beat of his own singing, his hand moving steadily. He was oblivious of his body and hardly heard himself.

> I walk below with them,
> Beside Hasché Yahlti there am I...

Before he finished one prayer the next one came to him following an unplanned logic.

'In the middle there am I,' he sang, and without hesitating,

> He thinks towards me,
> He rises towards me,
> He comes towards me...

Shooting Singer the teacher sang them to him, the kindly face and voice of his uncle, the face of a wise man long ago, at the very beginning. He sang on.

Something was wrong. In the solitary darkness the evil hovered close behind him and he was frightened. It took him some moments to get hold of himself. Then he realized that he had been silent a long time. He had been trying to remember a prayer, and not able to, and so he had fallen into a dark blank. He wondered what part of the night it was.

I shall do what I came for, now, he thought. I shall name the ones I fear most. Perhaps they will destroy me, perhaps not. I shall come to the middle of it. He hesitated, opened and shut his mouth twice, and then sang —

> Now with Slayer of Enemy Gods I come,
> From the house made of dark knives I come,
> Where the dark knives dangle on high I come,
> With a sacred tool I come, fearful to you.

> Now with Child of the Waters I come,
> From the house of serrated knives I come,
> Where serrated knives dangle on high I come,
> With a sacred tool I come, holy to you.

Finishing that, he went on immediately, urged by fear and excitement not to pause, with the song that had the same words save that each verse ended, 'You have the treasures, holy one, not I.' After that, one more —

> Now Nayeinezgani, alone I hear him,
> Through the sky I hear him,
> His voice sounds all about,
> His voice sounds, divine.
> Now Tobadzischini, alone I hear him...

He remained in darkness. When he had finished, he was still there alone with his heart beating violently, but he knew something was preparing to happen. It was time to announce his name, for whatever power it might have, or however it might lay him defenceless.

'I am Seeing Warrior,' he said. 'Here am I alone, Seeing Warrior. I am seeking the truth with my name, Seeing Warrior. I have been calling for a long time. Now for the fourth time, I am Seeing Warrior waiting here.'

He sat, listening, staring, in the profound silence. The darkness became infinite. He lost all sense of time or place, he was no longer aware of his body, of fatigue, or of any fleshly sensation.

From his high place the world stretched away to the four sacred mountains. The four corners of the world enclosed him, white in the east, blue in the south, yellow in the west, dark in the north, and the centre was of all colours. Above arched the turquoise sky. On the four mountains the Four Singers stood, raising their voices in a harmony too clear for human ears, but the silence of the attuned spirit could receive it. Fear and the expectation of a great happening welled in him.

It was an intolerable brightness at first, decreasing in fury as it spread out. Now it was coming.

They stood high and far off, on a bent rainbow, just as the stories told. Slowly they descended towards him, and at the same time he was lifted up, until the two gods were near and only slightly above him. They appeared as what men who portray them try to show. Nayeinezgani was painted black, with the bow-symbols on his body. He carried his bow in his hand. On his black mask the four zigzag lightnings were real, the jewels of brightness were beside his eye-holes, sunbeams floated over the top of the mask. Tobadzischini was painted red, with the scalp-symbols. He held his flint knife in his hand; over his mask, too, the sunbeams glowed, and the jewels of brightness shone beside his eye-holes. Lightning was all around their weapons. *With a sacred tool I come, fearful to you.*

They were both of them looking at Seeing Warrior, their heads slightly inclined. He felt their unseen eyes, and shrank back, struggling with his terror. Let it be settled. Let it be the truth, whatever it is. Here is truth. He straightened his back, looking up at them.

They ceased to be masked or painted, the very gods showed themselves, smiling. All his life he would be remembering and trying to comprehend the strength, beauty, love, and understanding of those two faces. *With a sacred tool I come, holy to you.* He stretched out his hands. Tell me, his mind said. Use me. Their eyes were on his, communicating, drawing it up out of himself.

They seemed to be rather like mirages. Two were there, yet only one, who was neither. There was a person there, not brown, not white, not describable. There were many, yet only one, who comprised them all. The divine harmony of the four directions filled the world. Through the weaknesses of men the Enemy Gods crept back upon the earth. Frail men disguised them with names and words of goodness, so that people mistook them for the Holy Ones they sought to destroy. Seeing Warrior understood; words, actions, teachings of his own lifetime lay spread before him, each in its true colour.

Consciousness stirred faintly. A sense of deep happiness was disturbed by physical discomfort. Slowly he realized that he was lying awkwardly on hard rock. His left arm was asleep, and a small stone pressed into his side. He moved, opened his eyes. Dawn was in full colour along the east. He sat up. Now he remembered; some of what had flooded him was too strong for his mind to deal with, he would be taking it up through his life, and perhaps never have all of it, but his spirit responded to it even now. He remembered, he knew what he knew.

Facing the east he made the dawn prayer with a free heart. Then he watched the full daylight come, recalling his vision, digesting it, while canyons and mesas and valleys became brilliant below him, and the sunlight washed over the mountains. Then he went down to the spring. He felt at once weak and refreshed. The first thing to do was find a hogahn and eat, then he would go to Shooting Singer and pick up the life which was meant for him. He stirred his pony to a lope. The morning air was fresh, the horse went willingly. He thought of his uncle, of Juniper, of the good things of his world and its people, without distraction. He lifted his voice and sang till the rocks echoed.

2

He felt shy at the first hogahn where he ate, doubly so because the people there had seen him at the Hojonji and received him so happily. It was not the old sense of shame and separateness, it didn't make him feel badly at all; he was delightfully glad that these people liked him, he felt diffident, and was quiet, enjoying them. As he rode on he considered the sense of effort that had been removed. It was not only the ending of bewilderment, it was something that he had been always trying for and now had let go of. Importance — I always tried to make a splash; by being too much or being nothing, always separate, always different. I pushed. Showing off. He squirmed inwardly. There are thousands of clever young men among the Navajos, and most of them know something I don't. I know something, too. The very size of what he knew made him feel little. It will be a long time before I grow up to that. What's the hurry? Hurrying like a white man. He smiled. What time is it? You're ten minutes late. No longer necessary to hurry, to startle people, nor yet to try to run away and hide, pretending he wanted to be nothing at all. I am I, and that's that.

Life stretched ahead of him to the unknown and hardly imaginable territory of old age; work, and time, and growth, inviting exploration. When he thought of living, he thought of Juniper. Now more than ever he knew how much she mattered, she was part and parcel of the new harmony. No use pretending it would be pleasant if she could not be won. He could hardly blame her. How blind I was then! Will she believe that I have changed? And even if she does — she was moved last time. It seemed silly to think that she could possibly want him.

The sun warmed his sinews and pressed along his limbs, the loping of his horse quickened his heart, calling for song, and as he sang, feeling himself alive, his vision shifted and possibility defied reason. He had never before known what one could feel about a woman, he had never let himself know. It was all one part with really living, it had nothing to do with any argument or logic, it was not a question of hope or probability. Of course he was going to do his best to marry her. It might take a long time, and it might fail entirely, but that was the trail for him. Juniper, War Encircling.

All his perceptions and sensations were quickened, the colours of the rocks and sand, the wind on his face, affection and admiration for Shooting Singer freed to run full course, that woman, that lovely person, not far from here. Of necessity he would have to pass near her settlement. Then, why not? He wasn't riding to deliver hasty news, but taking up the course of a lifetime. If he saw Shooting Singer in four or in six days made no difference. And besides — he smiled at himself. The point is that I want to see her as soon as I can. His pony loped with a steady, lifting rhythm, his body soaked up the sun, he raised his voice till his song re-echoed through the wide canyons.

On the third afternoon he reached the fork where the trail ran off to Juniper's, and turned in, stirring up his horse with a quirt stroke so that it leaped, shaking him in the saddle and making him laugh. His heart felt big inside him, his excitement was not all pleasure. He rode fast, singing.

Off to one side he saw Bay Horse's second wife with the sheep — a good sign, probably Juniper was still working on that blanket, perhaps he could see her alone right now. A good beginning.

She was sitting by her loom, but there was someone with her, a man, and a horse stood to its reins near-by. They had turned to see who was riding behind that song as he came into view. He fell silent and stopped pushing his horse. The animal dropped to a slack lope, to a trot that shambled into a walk, and came to rest of its own accord a few feet from them.

That man was always appearing differently dressed, Myron thought, but one could recognize him anywhere; he must have prospered among the Supais. He was wearing a new white sombrero, a necklace of turquoise and coral, and a white woolen vest of Mexican weave with a striking red design, over a sky-blue shirt torn at one elbow. His son stood between his knees, and his hands were around the child's waist as he smiled at Myron.

'Eh, grandfather! The little horse carried you far.'

Myron glanced at Juniper. She was waiting, with a look of surprise, almost of wonder.

'Dismount,' she told him.

He still stayed with his feet in the stirrups, thinking. Too late. I might have known. Too late. This was what I wished for him, back there. I wished it for him. One couldn't just ride away, he couldn't just let go . . . He swung his leg slowly, dismounted, and went over to touch hands with them. He made himself comfortable in the shade of the hogahn doorway. The horizontal warp-strands of her loom, like white rain, and the short piece of blanket at the bottom with its bright design made a framing background for her, behind and over it the shadow-dappling tree. Beautiful. He saved my life. So fine-looking, the two of them. I might have known.

Singing Gambler asked, 'Where to?' The child tugged at his necklace.

One must answer, a man does not break down. 'My uncle's house. Did you go to the Supais?'

'Yes, but I didn't stay long.' His face clouded. 'And you — did you get rid of your — your trouble?'

Myron answered gravely, with words that were remembered as he said them, 'I have attended to all that.'

Singing Gambler accepted the statement with equal gravity. The wonder showed again behind Juniper's watching.

The memory of what he had seen was a well of strength. I pick it up here, I prove that I can do it. He forced himself out of the daze of feelings.

'You prospered on your travels,' he said.

Singing Gambler grinned. 'Up and down. Yes, in the end I did some collecting. And you?'

'Not so badly, counting from where I met you. A horse and saddle, a pair of pants, a new blanket, and — and some other things.'

'A new blanket?' Singing Gambler looked at Myron's saddle.

He contemplated the roll behind his cantle. 'Eh-yeh! All this time I've been thinking of it as new, and it doesn't seem to be so any longer.' They all laughed. 'It's been a long ride. I was remade.'

'How?'

'Those first days in the saddle! I found out all about how my legs were put on.'

Singing Gambler told the child, 'Gently with my necklace, strong-hand,' then said in a puzzled tone, 'Why? How do you mean?'

Myron thought that over and laughed. It was curious, he heard himself laugh, his exterior reacting mechanically. 'Ever since you were a child, you have gone on riding, you never stopped. One might as well expect you to have a stiff face after eating a big meal. But there must be something active that you've stopped doing and started again, and all your muscles told you about it.'

Juniper said: 'That makes one think. That one little thing makes one see much about going to school. I never knew riding could tire one that way.'

Singing Gambler said, 'Yes, there have been things.' With a slight change of voice, he said, 'Hoeing corn, for instance. Eh! How the hoe can pull across your shoulders.' His smile had a twist to it. 'But what's the use of school, then, if it makes everything so hard for you?'

Myron hesitated before he answered. It was Juniper that he wanted to make understand. 'During those years, I learned some useful things, some very useful things. Well, while I was doing that, that was all I could do. It was worth while, I think. Then, to get the other things, I had to begin at the beginning again. You saw me, shortly after I tore my pants on the fence.'

'Eh! I saw you. You looked more like an end than a beginning.'

'I must have. Well, after enough aches and pains I'll catch up with all of you who never went away. I'm catching up, I think. And when I do, I'll be ahead.' I'll be ahead, but without, without...

Juniper was watching them both. 'And can you tie the two things up together?' she asked.

'Perhaps. If I can be sure what's first and what's second. One can have too much in his mind at once. There was a story they taught us at school ――― ' He told them the fable of the fox and the cat, and they both laughed.

As he talked, he was thinking that now he would get out of here. This was enough. He did not want it to get so late that they invited him to eat, he could not possibly spend the night here. That would be unendurable. He wanted to be alone, to look his loss in the face and to stop covering up, holding off what he felt.

Just then Singing Gambler rose. He cradled the child against his shoulder a moment, before passing it over to Juniper.

'I must go,' he said. 'I must get to Coyote Killer's before dark, and he lives beyond those red rocks.'

Myron realized that his mouth was open. He shut it and stopped staring. He must not show, he must not let it show —— Singing Gambler came over to him and their hands met; for a moment the gambler's hand held his in a firm clasp.

'How curious it is, the way you and I have been tied together,' he said. 'Who would have thought it when we met on Black Mesa?'

'Yes, that's right. I hope we can sing together some more. Do you know where my uncle lives?'

'At Ha'anoichí? I can find it.'

'Good.'

They watched him go, heard him lift up his voice, and did not speak until man and voice were gone. It seemed impossible, he could hardly believe it was true. He felt his heart beating.

'That man and I are like east and west,' he said finally, 'yet how I like him.'

'Yes.'

'But — but why — ? I thought, seeing him here —— '

'He came to make sure, and to see the little warrior here. We've been together all day. What one needs, what makes it possible, is lacking between us. It's all over.'

'I'm sorry.'

After a pause, Juniper said, 'You've changed again.'

'Yes. I found it.'

'Yourself?'

'Oh yes, that. But I'm not worrying about myself any more. I'm through with trying to astonish people so as to make myself important. There's lots of time to grow in, if I have it in me to grow. If not, all right.'

'Then you've still given up trying? You no longer wish to lead?'

'I don't care who leads, so long as the people go in the right direction. I'm not going to tell you what I saw up yonder, it's not something one uses in an argument. After I've been at Ha'anoichí awhile, I shall tell it to my uncle, I think. We are going to disagree on some things, perhaps, but the main things we can discuss together. Perhaps I have hold of the truth; perhaps, when I have lived long enough among my own people and really know their life, I shall have the ability to show it to them. In that case, in the end I shall be followed. But I'm not standing up in front pointing myself out when I'm only a young man beginning to learn.'

'If you stay with your uncle like that, will you become a medicine man? That was what he wanted.'

'No. In the old days, if the same things had happened to me, that would have been the thing for me to do.'

It was Juniper he was talking to, Juniper watching him and listening. He leaned forward, his eyes on hers, making short, emphatic gestures with one hand as he picked words that would tell her what he knew.

'Our world is changed; that is no longer the way for me. Just following the old Navajo way won't save us, and we can't walk in the white man's trail. We have to give up a lot of little ideas, that we have held because they were the best we knew. If we want to save ourselves, we have to learn to use the white man's knowledge, his weapons, his machines — and — still be Navajos.'

He watched her earnestly, to see if she understood. If he couldn't tell it to her, he hardly cared who else might believe him. Her face there, alive with listening, her deep eyes, as beautiful as truth itself.

'We can do it. Our life, our prayers, are full of truth. *I know*. And I know all about trying to be a white man, and I know about trying to be a kind of Navajo whose world has ceased to be, I think. That is where I have reached. Now I want to get to know my relatives and my neighbours, to learn the country and the life, and find my place, and as time comes and things happen and I grow wiser, to use what I have learned.'

The child on her lap squirmed. She put it on its feet and let it wander.

'Now I see you,' she said. 'You have come out.'

He studied his own hand, nerving himself to say what might bring a hopeless answer.

'Long ago I ran away from you. A little while ago I wanted to hide behind you. Now I simply want to marry you. It's not a sudden thing, it's woven into me along with the rest. I don't expect you to take me now, when he has just ridden away. I can't think of any reason why you should take me at all, and I can think of lots why you should not. But just thinking of you when I'm alone makes my blood sing.' He made a helpless gesture. 'There's nothing I can say that will tell it.' He searched for some way to express the longing certainty of beauty which filled him, and gave up.

'And this child would not disturb you?' she said.

'I answered that before. Why should it? Its father and I are good friends.'

She said slowly, 'I have to think, you know.'

'Of course. And you need to really know me.'

There seemed to be a light behind her face, and she looked frightened. For the first time he felt that a man might also protect her.

'I put you out of my mind long ago,' she said, 'but I never did forget you, I think.'

'I, too. I closed my eyes and just ran. I must go first to

my uncle, I think. I have to get it all completely clear inside myself. Then I want to come and visit in this canyon.' He smiled. 'You'll need help with the harvest soon.'

'You will be welcome.'

He did not move or speak. He saw her face against the white rain of the loom, the colours of her dress, the green tree splashed with yellow sun, and the bright sky behind, and he remembered the smiling faces of the gods.

THE END